TOO LITTLE, TOO LATE

Praise for *Too Little, Too Late*
'A winning combination of food and romance ...
Caddle will have readers laughing and crying along
with the heroine every step of the way'

Irish Times

Praise for *Shaken and Stirred*
'An engaging warm slice of life with which all women
will be able to identify'

Books Magazine

'A warm and engaging read about five colleagues in a
Dublin marketing company'

Heat

'A warm and funny novel perfect for that sunny beach
or a rainy day read'

ri-rá

Also by Colette Caddle

Shaken and Stirred

About the author

Available for the first time in the UK and British Commonwealth, *Too Little, Too Late* was a No. 1 bestseller in Ireland.

Colette Caddle's highly-acclaimed second novel *Shaken and Stirred* was an international success.

She lives in Dublin with her husband and son.

TOO LITTLE, TOO LATE

Colette Caddle

CORONET BOOKS

Hodder & Stoughton

Copyright © 2001 by Colette Caddle

First published in Ireland in 1999 by Poolbeg Press Ltd
First published in Great Britain in 2001 by Hodder and Stoughton
A division of Hodder Headline

The right of Colette Caddle to be identified as the Author
of the Work has been asserted by her in accordance with
the Copyright, Designs and Patents Act 1988.

A Coronet Paperback

2 4 6 8 10 9 7 5 3 1

All rights reserved. No part of this publication may be
reproduced, stored in a retrieval system, or transmitted,
in any form or by any means without the prior written
permission of the publisher, nor be otherwise circulated
in any form of binding or cover other than that in which
it is published and without a similar condition being
imposed on the subsequent purchaser.

All characters in this publication are fictitious
and any resemblance to real persons, living or dead,
is purely coincidental.

A CIP catalogue record for this title is available
from the British Library

ISBN 0 340 79442 9

Typeset in New Baskerville by
Palimpsest Book Production Limited,
Polmont, Stirlingshire

Printed and bound in Great Britain by Clays Ltd, St Ives plc

Hodder and Stoughton
A division of Hodder Headline
338 Euston Road
London NW1 3BH

Dedicated, with love, to the memory of my dad,
Stephen Lynott

Chapter One

'And the barman turned to the drunk and said, "You can't leave that lyin' there!" And the drunk said, "Thas not a lion, thas a ghiraffe!"'

Annie looked blankly at Stephanie. 'Your jokes are getting worse. Don't give up the day job.'

'Oh, but I want to!' Stephanie groaned. 'Want another coffee?' She stood up and started for the counter of the deserted café.

'I thought you had to be back in the restaurant by twelve?'

'A few minutes won't make any difference.'

Annie blinked. Things must be bad if her annoyingly punctual sister-in-law was considering playing hooky. 'So what's up? Tell Auntie Annie,' she ordered when Steph returned with two steaming mugs.

Steph flopped into her chair and looked at Annie, her vivid blue eyes large and mournful. 'My boss is being his usual self – an overbearing, incompetent prat!'

Annie nodded wisely. 'Ah, just the usual then. If you're so miserable, why don't you leave? You'd walk into another restaurant, no problem.'

'Think so?'

'Of course. You'd be snapped up.'

Stephanie looked doubtful. 'By another Michelin Star restaurant in the centre of Dublin? I don't think so. Anyway what other restaurant would give the manager's job to an ex-bank clerk?'

'Liz gave you the job because she knew you would be good at it,' Annie reminded her. 'And you are.'

Steph sighed. She wasn't so sure any more. 'The thing is, Annie, I don't want to leave Chez Nous. I love my job. It's just him. I can deal with the others, even George.'

Annie shivered. 'That man gives me the creeps.'

Steph chuckled. 'George is a bit of a lecher but he's a good chef. No, I can handle him, and the other lads are great. Well, Sam's an asshole, but you get them in every walk of life. It's just . . .'

'It's just Chris,' Annie surmised. 'So what are you going to do?'

Steph lit a cigarette and considered the question. 'Probably kill him. I'd do it really slowly.' She licked her lips in anticipation. 'With a great big kitchen knife and first I'd stick it right into his—'

'Spare me the details.' Annie took a cigarette from Steph's pack. 'Don't tell your brother.'

Steph rolled her eyes. 'Joe knows you sneak the odd ciggie. He's not stupid.'

Annie made a face. 'Now where were we? Oh, yes, you were planning Chris's murder. Things weren't always this bad though, were they?'

'No, of course not. But lately I can't seem to say or do anything right. He's difficult with everyone but I seem to get the worst of it. Probably because I'm a woman.'

'I'd say it's because you stand up to him. And if you do it in front of the others . . .' Annie shrugged.

Steph chuckled. 'Yeah, you're right, that really gets him going. Maybe if we got Liz to come back it would put him on the straight and narrow.'

Annie frowned. 'I love Liz dearly but she's the last person who could sort out Chris.'

'Do you think he's any nicer at home?' Steph asked doubtfully.

'Well, she's still married to him. Maybe he has hidden talents.'

Steph snorted. 'They must be buried. Imagine, he's the father of such a beautiful little girl.'

'The gods were kind and Lucy got all of Liz's genes,' Annie said with a giggle.

Steph laughed too. 'Oh, if Liz heard us she'd be disgusted.'

'It's rough when you can't stand your best friend's husband, isn't it?'

'It's even worse when you have to work for the pig!' Steph retorted. 'If Liz had come back to work after Lucy was born things would be very different.'

'Do you think so?'

'Absolutely! Chris wouldn't be able to slink off whenever he wanted for a start.'

'It is a shame she didn't go back. She was such a great chef.'

'I'm sure she still is if we could only convince her to re-enter the workforce.'

Annie shook her head. 'I doubt that will ever happen now. From what you tell me Chris wouldn't be too keen on sharing the limelight again.'

Steph sighed. 'You're right. A bit of a cheek really

considering that she was the driving force in the old days. He'd have never even thought of starting his own restaurant if it wasn't for Liz. He'd still be a sous-chef in that bistro in Temple Bar if it wasn't for her.'

Annie smiled. 'Maybe that's a slight exaggeration but she was certainly the brains behind Chez Nous.'

Steph nodded furiously. 'And it was her idea to go after a Michelin Star. Chris thought she was nuts.'

'*And* she was the one who gave you a job.'

Steph's expression softened. 'She was so good to give me a chance like that.'

Annie grinned. 'Liz knew you were bossy enough to make a great manager.'

Steph flicked the wet spoon at her sister-in-law. 'Thanks a lot!'

Annie calmly wiped coffee off her chin. 'Does Liz know what's going on between you and Chris?'

'I don't think so. I certainly haven't said anything and I don't think Chris tells her anything about the business any more.'

'He'd be afraid to say anything bad about you. Liz would never believe him.'

Steph made a face at her. 'Well, it's nice to know I've got at least *one* friend.'

Annie ignored her. 'So she hasn't got a clue that you're unhappy?'

'No. I try to behave myself when she's around. On a good day I can even manage to smile at him.'

Annie's green eyes twinkled mischievously. 'Good, that will stand in your defence when you top him!'

'Oh, Annie, what am I going to do?'

'Stop moaning for a start. Now let's look at the options. Killing him is one. Any others?'

Steph tilted her head to one side. 'I could buy him out.'

'Okay. Do you think he'd be interested in selling?'

'That was a joke, Annie.'

'Why?' Annie replied equably. 'You've got the money your Uncle Jack left you. I'm sure you could get a loan for the rest.'

Stephanie blinked. 'Me, own Chez Nous? That's mad! Oh, look, I've got to get back.'

'Okay,' Annie smiled calmly.

Steph eyed Annie warily as she put on her jacket and picked up her bag. 'I'll give you a ring.'

'You do that.'

'Yes, yes I will.' Steph hurried off, pausing briefly in the doorway to stare back at her friend.

Annie chuckled as she stubbed out her cigarette. Joe would kill her for putting such wild ideas in his little sister's head. Though the more Annie thought about it the less wild it seemed. In fact owning her own business could be the making of Stephanie. It would bring some badly needed stability to her life and it might even encourage her to settle down and get married. Annie finished her coffee, gathered her bags and stood up. If only her problems were as interesting as Steph's, she thought as she made her way over to the supermarket. Now what would she buy for dinner tonight?

'Where the hell were you?' Chris barked as a blonde head flashed past the kitchen door.

'Is there a problem, Chef?' Steph poked her head around the door and flashed him a cheeky smile. She was damned if she was going to make excuses for being less than five minutes late, in front of all the kitchen staff.

'You've to sort out the wine order and I told you I want Reilly's to take back those rotten potatoes.' Chris glared at her before going back to the fish he was preparing.

'I've sent in the wine order,' she replied calmly, 'and Reilly's are sending over a van to pick up the potatoes and drop off replacements. They've also agreed to give us a discount on the next order.'

Chris snorted and continued filleting.

'Anything else I can do for anybody?' Steph caught Conor's eye and winked.

'There's an offer.' George sidled up and slipped an arm around her slim waist.

'Don't hold your breath, George.' Steph slipped easily out of his grasp and into the hallway.

'Stephanie?'

Steph turned and smiled at Marc, one of their newest and nicest recruits. He was very quiet and worked hard – now there was an unusual combination in a chef, she thought wryly. 'Yes, Marc? What can I do for you?'

'I was hoping to take some time off. *Maman* – she is not well. Chef said I should get you to check the roster. He was not . . . eh . . . happy.' Marc faltered, his cheeks red.

'I can imagine. Come on up to the office and we'll see what we can do. Is your mother back in hospital?'

'*Oui*, yes, and *Papa* he wants to be with her, but it's such a busy time.' He shook his head worriedly. Michel Le Brun ran a small vineyard near Bordeaux and lived in constant fear of his grapes being rejected by the local co-operative.

'I understand. How much time do you need?'

'A week?' he suggested hopefully.

Stephanie took out the work roster and checked it carefully. This should really be Chris or Conor's job but it had somehow become her responsibility. If she got the balance wrong and they were understaffed, she got bawled out not only by Chris but the other chefs too. Thankfully there was no problem this time. No one was on holidays, no one was off sick and two trainees had just started. 'Pat has Saturday off. You can go on Sunday but could you be back for dinner the following Saturday?'

'*Bien sûr*, certainly. Thank you, Stephanie.' He smiled broadly and ran back down to the kitchen.

Stephanie threw the jacket of her black wool suit carelessly over the back of a chair and turned her attention to the post. Lots of brown envelopes. Great! She was still wading through them an hour later when Chris came in.

'I've got to go out. Any problems, talk to Conor.'

Stephanie looked pointedly at her watch. The lazy bugger! It was the second time this week he'd done a runner at lunchtime.

He scowled at her. 'Everything's in hand and it's unlikely there'll be any more customers arriving at this stage. Good experience for young Conor anyway,' he added gruffly.

Stephanie didn't bother to reply. When Chris had left she put on her jacket and took out her compact to check her hair and make-up. She touched up her foundation, renewed the coral lipstick and after flicking a comb through her short bob, she went down to the restaurant.

She stood for a moment in the doorway and drank in the atmosphere. She always got a buzz when she saw it so full. The large room hummed with muted conversation and staff moved quietly and efficiently between the tables. The stark white table linen made a dramatic contrast to the dark green of the walls and carpet. And the cheerful fire crackling in the grate of the large fireplace softened the formal scene.

'Hi, Steph.' Liam, one of the waiters, smiled shyly at her.

'How's it going, Liam?'

'Busy,' he replied and hurried past.

The restaurant was full and five tables were on starters, while three waited for their main course. 'A great time for the head chef to walk out,' Steph thought grimly. She headed out to the kitchen to see how Conor was coping. A rush of heat hit her as she pushed open the door. The noise was deafening between the sound of chopping, beating and chefs yelling at the junior staff. They were a motley crew of different personalities from a wide variety of backgrounds but they all shared this one passion. Steph had seen Pat throw out a whole pan of sauce if he wasn't happy with the texture or seasoning. George cursed anyone and everyone near him when something went wrong but would break into song minutes later. Conor would refuse to cook beef if the meat hadn't been hung for long enough and argued vociferously with Chris over the menu if the necessary herbs weren't available. In stark contrast, the pastry chef, John Quigly, talked to no one and no one bothered him. He was first in each morning and the first to leave. He worked quietly, efficiently and merely blinked when Chris screamed or raged at him. Steph sometimes wondered if he was a bit deaf – not necessarily a bad thing when you worked for Chris. Being the manager in such an environment was no easy job. Some days Steph had to play referee, sometimes psychotherapist and occasionally she even had to roll up her sleeves and muck in! It was totally mad. It was great.

She went over to Conor, but when she saw the look of fixed concentration on his face, she moved on to Pat who was preparing a sauce to accompany the confit of duck.

She sniffed appreciatively. 'That smells good.'

He flashed her a grin. 'Taste.' He held a spoon to her lips.

She tasted and nodded her head, rolling her eyes in ecstasy.

That wasn't enough for Pat. 'Is it too bland? Maybe a little more seasoning?'

'It's perfect,' she assured him firmly. Pat was one of the few chefs in Chez Nous who invited comment. Most of them were dismissive of opinions from anyone front of house. Steph was no exception.

She moved on to watch Marc tie small bunches of string beans together with incredibly narrow strips of red and yellow peppers. She shook her head, amazed at his patience. Jim was at his side painstakingly piping the Chez Nous version of creamed potatoes into a perfect cone. He looked up at Marc expectantly.

Marc inspected the creation. '*Bon*,' he said simply.

Jim grinned happily.

Steph walked to the door, pausing to look back at her colleagues, oblivious to her and engrossed in their work. Maybe Annie was right and she would be able to get another job but she didn't want to. For all of the problems and hassle with Chris, this was where she belonged.

Chapter Two

'Yes, Paddy, I understand that but . . . well, yes, I see your point and I do agree . . . I'm sure Chris didn't mean that quite the way it sounded . . .' Steph looked up to see Conor in the doorway. She waved him in. 'Yes, Paddy, I'm sorry about all this and I'm sure that Chris really does appreciate your point . . . yes, yes, of course, right, sure, thanks . . . bye now, thanks again.' She put down the phone and banged her head on the desk. 'Oh, God, I'm definitely going to kill the man!'

Conor laughed. 'That sounded like fun. Was it Paddy Brennan?'

Steph nodded. 'Chris told him where to shove his fish and that his bill could go the same way.'

'Our boss, the diplomat. You can always rely on him.'

'It's not funny, Conor! He can't treat people like this. We won't have any suppliers left. And what if he starts on the customers?'

She offered Conor a cigarette and he lit up and stretched his long, lanky frame in the chair in front of her.

'The suppliers are well used to him, Steph. You worry

too much. Paddy will call him a few names, but he won't want to lose the business. The two of them will be back drinking together in a couple of weeks and it will all be forgotten.'

'You're right,' she agreed. 'And I know I should lighten up. It's just that—'

'He drives you around the bend? I know. Sure he's as bad with me. But you can't have everything. I'm bloody lucky to be a sous-chef at twenty-four. And the more Chef skives off, the more experience I get. If it weren't for George . . .' He grimaced.

Steph nodded sympathetically. George was as big a thorn in Conor's side as Chris was in hers. 'George isn't good at taking orders at the best of times. Taking them from a young fella like you can't be easy for him.'

'He doesn't take orders from me,' Conor protested. 'That's the bloody problem. He goes over my head to Chris all the time.'

'They're old mates.'

'I don't give a damn—'

'Got a minute, Stephanie?' Sam cut in on Conor without even looking at him.

Steph sighed. Sam was always trying to stir things up with Conor. 'Can't you see I'm busy, Sam?'

'Don't worry about it, Steph.' Conor stood up and pushed past him. 'I'll catch you later.'

Steph wished she could go too. Sam was a reasonably good head waiter but he was like a creaking door, constantly whingeing about something. Unless Chris was around. Then it was 'Yes Chef, no Chef, anything you say, Chef.' She forced a pleasant smile on to her face. 'So what is it, Sam? What's so important?'

'We're very low on napkins.'

Steph blinked. 'Yes?'

'Well, it's your job to order them,' Sam pointed out peevishly.

'So it is. Thanks for reminding me. Have we a full house tonight?'

The head waiter gave her a long-suffering look over the rim of his book. 'No, we don't. We could fit in two tables for two or one for six. The new play's opening at Andrew's Lane tonight, that may bring in some punters. We really should think about doing some kind of promotion or advertising.'

Steph said nothing. It was unlikely the new play would bring in customers. Chez Nous wasn't the kind of restaurant you dropped into on the off chance – unless you were a tourist and didn't know any better. They needed to do something to improve business. It was the third time in as many weeks that they'd had empty tables on a Thursday.

'Lavinia Reynolds's review may be hurting us,' she said at last.

Sam frowned. 'The review wasn't that bad.'

Steph's eyes widened. 'Are you kidding? "Prices are up and standards are down at Chez Nous." That's as bad as it gets. Lavinia's out for blood.'

'Why not invite her back?' Sam suggested. 'You could point out that everyone has a bad night.'

'It might work,' Steph admitted grudgingly, 'but the invitation would have to come from Chris. Lavinia wouldn't stand for less and there's no hope of Chris agreeing to grovel to her.'

'Pride is cold comfort when you go out of business.' Sam turned on his heel and walked out of the room.

Steph stuck her tongue out at his receding back.

Still, he was right. She'd have to have a word with Chris.

Several hours later she was driving too fast across the East Link Bridge, tapping her finger on the wheel in time to the song on the radio. She glowered at the little old lady who attempted to cut her off on the bend.

'Not on your life, missus,' she growled. 'I'm late. Again!' Sean would murder her. It was the second time she'd kept him waiting this week.

Stephanie had first met Sean Adams at a party in Ruth's flat over fourteen years ago. Within a month they were inseparable. And then Ruth died. And that was that. Sean left to work for Apple in Cork and Steph plodded off to the bank every day. It never occurred to Sean to ask Stephanie to go with him and Steph probably wouldn't have even heard him if he had.

He'd been back in Dublin two years now. Ten years, a failed marriage and one son later. Stephanie had bumped into him in Doheny and Nesbitt's and before she knew it they'd slipped back into the same easy relationship. They rarely discussed Karen, Sean's soon-to-be-ex-wife, or his son, Billy. Sean didn't offer any information and she didn't ask. She was just happy he was back in her life. The only fly in the ointment was his insistence that they should marry as soon as he was free. Stephanie loved him but marriage? She shivered. Not that there was anything wrong with him. No questionable underwear in the middle of the bathroom floor. No funny habits – that she knew of. And it was nice to wake up beside him in the morning. Just not every morning. Sometimes she liked being alone.

She changed gear and turned up through Clontarf heading towards Malahide and her little apartment right on the coast. She glanced again at the clock. She was almost thirty minutes late now but at least they were eating locally. It had been a while since she'd been in Bon Appétit and she was looking forward to a relaxing evening and great food.

As she drove, her thoughts returned to the crazy conversation she'd had with Annie. Lord, the woman was completely insane! Imagine suggesting that she buy Chris out? Steph laughed out loud. It was a totally ludicrous idea. Wait till she told Sean. As if she could possibly do it. It would be great if she could, of course. But she couldn't. It was completely out of the question.

The traffic lights in Malahide village were red and she quickly tilted the rear-view mirror to inspect her make-up. Mother of God, she looked like she hadn't slept for a week. They weren't bags under her eyes they were suitcases! She really needed to get a few early nights. And cut out the booze for a while. And she'd definitely join the gym and start working out every morning. 'Maybe I'll start a new regime tomorrow,' she murmured as the lights changed. 'I could go for a jog before breakfast – oh – maybe not.' After all it would be another late night tonight and Sean would probably stay over. She grinned. She could always have a horizontal workout instead!

Sean Adams drummed his fingers against the side of his glass as Stephanie continued to study the menu. He knew she wasn't choosing her meal. She was sizing up prices, studying combinations and storing them away to relay to Conor tomorrow. It was his own fault for suggesting they eat at Bon Appétit. When she was in a decent restaurant she wanted to experience as many dishes as possible. She often charmed the head waiter into giving her half portions of two main courses.

'Are you ready to order yet, or should I send out for a McDonald's to keep me going?'

She flashed him a dazzling smile. 'Oh, don't be such a grouch. What are you going to have?'

Sean didn't have to look at the menu. He'd made his selection fifteen minutes ago. 'The bisque followed by the Sole McGuirk. Is that okay with you?'

Steph looked indignant. 'Of course! Though I thought you might like to try the Clonakilty black pudding to start.'

'I suppose I would,' he agreed grudgingly.

'And I'll have the scallops,' she continued happily. 'I suppose you *could* have the sole but then there's the duck – okay, okay, sole it is,' she said hurriedly when she saw his expression. 'I'll have the duck. Now what about the wine?'

Sean scanned the list. 'How about a half bottle of white Hermitage to start and then the Côte de Beaune?'

Steph licked her lips contentedly. 'Perfect.'

They gave their order and settled back with their drinks, enjoying the warmth of the fire in the cosy lounge. 'How was your day?'

Steph grimaced. 'Crap. Yours?' She listened with half an ear admiring the way his dark wavy hair stopped half an inch short of his shirt collar. The way his eyes sparkled as he talked about his business. The way his lips curled in a lopsided smile. He looked particularly gorgeous tonight in a grey suit, shirt a pale blue and a silk tie that was a blaze of colour, showing the more rebellious side of his nature.

'So it looks like I won.'

'Sorry?' Steph smiled apologetically, realising she hadn't heard a word.

'The Senfield contract that I told you about?'

She nodded enthusiastically. 'The American plastics company.'

'That's right,' Sean nodded, pleased that she'd remembered. Karen had never shown much interest in his work. 'I got the contract.'

'But that's fantastic!' she squealed. 'Congratulations!'

Sean laughed as a couple of people jumped in alarm. 'Thanks, but there's no need to tell everyone.'

'Of course there is. They should all drink to Dublin's newest entrepreneur. My God, Sean! You're only in business two years, and look at what you've accomplished.' She lifted her glass. 'I'm so proud of you. Well done!'

'Thanks, I must say I am pretty chuffed with myself. It was a fairly close race at the end between me and an American company. I was sure they'd get it on the grounds of location. But Barry Green – that's Senfield's IT director – liked the presentation I put together and I got the job.'

Steph shook her head in wonder. 'That's brilliant. So where are they based?'

'Phoenix, Arizona. I'll be going over there quite soon to take a look at the operation.'

'How long will that take?'

He shrugged. 'Probably a couple of months.'

Her face fell. 'Two months! What am I going to do without you for two months?'

'You could always come with me,' he said lightly.

She laughed. 'Oh yeah, right. And Chris would give me some spending money too!'

He leaned forward and took her hand. 'I'm serious. Come to Phoenix with me. You may as well. After all, you're completely miserable at work. It would be good for you, for both of us.'

She stared at him. 'You want me to leave?'

'Why not?' he asked. 'I left my job and made a new life, why shouldn't you? There comes a time when you just have to move on.'

'But you're not talking about me making a fresh start,' she said sadly. 'You're saying I should throw in the towel and go on holiday. I mean it's not as if I could even work in the States.'

'You could get a job when we got back. You'd walk into another restaurant.'

Steph smiled faintly. That's what Annie had said. No problem. But how could she walk away from this job without feeling a loser? Her dad had always said that there was no point in running away from your problems. No matter what you did for a living, you were bound to come up against difficult people or situations. You just had to knuckle down and learn how to cope with them. So why couldn't she? She'd wanted to tell Sean about her conversation with Annie but now it all seemed a bit silly.

'So will you come?' he asked.

'Oh, Sean, I—'

'Your table is ready, if you'd like to follow me.'

Steph stood up, grateful for the interruption, and followed the waiter.

'You never answered me,' Sean commented as they wandered back to the apartment, hand in hand.

Steph sighed. She'd managed to avoid resuming the conversation all night but she couldn't put him off any longer. 'I can't go with you, Sean. I'm going through a rough patch at the moment but I'd feel a failure if I gave up now.'

'You're a good restaurant manager, Steph. That doesn't mean you have to stay in Chez Nous. Your skills could be put to better use somewhere else. Where you had a boss that appreciated you. Meanwhile you and I could have some quiet time together in sunny Arizona. Wouldn't you like that?'

'Of course, but I don't want to leave Chez Nous. Please don't ask me to.'

Sean sighed in frustration. 'So I have to go alone?'

Steph smiled at his sulky expression. He looked like a spoilt little boy. 'It's not for long, you silly sod and I'll still be here when you get back.'

'Are you sure about that?' He paused and turned her face up to his.

She reached up to kiss him. 'I'm very sure. Let me prove it to you.' Her eyes twinkled mischievously in the darkness as she led him up the steps to her apartment.

Chapter Three

'What time is your flight?' Steph fiddled with the frills on the sofa cushion.

'Ten.' Sean took her hands in his and held them tightly. 'Look, Steph, don't come to the airport. Let's just say goodbye now. I'll call you as soon as I get there.'

Steph swallowed her protest. She knew how Sean hated emotional farewells. 'Oh, good, I wanted to do my nails anyway,' she said airily. 'Now, you behave yourself over there, do you hear? Don't you go falling for anyone else. None of those leggy blondes.'

'There's only one leggy blonde I'm interested in,' he murmured pulling her to him. 'Oh, it's going to be so weird going to restaurants and eating what I want to eat.'

Steph punched him. 'You make me sound like a bossy old cow!'

Sean grinned. 'You're not that old.'

'Miserable sod. You're supposed to be nice to me,' she complained. 'You'll be leaving soon.'

Sean's eyes grew serious. 'And you should be coming with me.'

Steph pulled away. 'Let's not go over all that again,'

she begged. She was beginning to think she was nuts to be staying behind. What if Senfield's wanted him to move there permanently? What if he really did meet someone else?

Sean looked at his watch and stood up. 'Right. Time to go.'

Steph returned his kiss and stood at the door long after Sean's car disappeared around the corner. Eventually she went back inside, curled up on the sofa and hugged the cushion to her. If she closed her eyes she could still smell his aftershave and almost believe that he was still here. But that scent wasn't going to last two months. She'd have to keep busy and that way the time would go faster. And of course he'd come back. Of course he would. She hugged the cushion tighter to her.

It had been much easier when he'd left her to move to Cork. But they'd only been a couple of kids then. And all she could ever think about was Ruth then. There had been no room for Sean or anyone else. But that was a long time ago. They were adults now. She was different now. That was all in the past.

'Ask me another question, Steffi,' Ruth implored, pulling distractedly at the mass of brown curls framing her small face.

Stephanie took a drag of her cigarette and blew the air out the window. 'Okay, okay,' she agreed, scanning the book in front of her. 'Why is transpiration useful to plants?'

Ruth paced the room, chewing on her pen. 'Eh, I know this one . . .'

'You know every one,' Stephanie replied.

'Eh, because it supplies water and minerals to the leaves and cools them down in hot weather.'

'Correct. See, I told you, Ruth. You know it all.'

'And do you know it all?' Catherine West said from the doorway, a tray of tea and biscuits in her hands.

'Oh Mam, you're the best.' Stephanie tried frantically to stub out her cigarette behind her back. When she finally succeeded, she hopped off the bed and cleared books off the corner of her dressing-table. Her mother set down the tray. 'Of course I know it all, Mam. Oh ye of little faith!'

'Of course you do, dear. Take a break now, Ruth love. A cup of tea will do you good.'

'Thanks, Mrs West. You're very good to let me study here. I wouldn't get a minute's peace at home.'

Ruth was the eldest of six children and it was hard to find a quiet corner in the three-bedroom semi-detached house. Steffi was lucky. With only one brother, she had a bedroom all to herself. Ruth couldn't wait to leave home. She'd miss her mam but it was the only way if she was ever to get a bit of privacy.

'Now don't stay up too late, girls. A good night's sleep is more important at this stage. Best of luck tomorrow, Ruth. You'll be fine.' Catherine paused halfway out the door. 'Make sure you put that cigarette out properly, Stephanie.'

Ruth burst out laughing when the door closed. 'There's no fooling your mam, Steffi.'

Stephanie shook her head in wonder. 'I swear she's eyes in the back of her head. Either that or she's got the place bugged. Ah, one of these days I'll have my own place. I'll get a brilliant job, buy a car and a nice little flat in Ranelagh. What about you, Ruth?'

Ruth didn't believe in daydreaming. She had very definite plans for the future. Once she got into Trinity it would be plain sailing. She'd work like the devil himself to get the best *possible marks. She'd get her degree in computer science and then she'd join one of the big companies. Maybe IBM. 'A flat would be nice,' she said finally. 'But it's all very well talking, Steph. What are you going to actually do?'*

This was a conversation the two girls had regularly. Ruth was amazed at Steph's casual attitude towards getting a job and Steph couldn't begin to understand Ruth's driving ambition. For all their differences though, they were best friends and while Ruth helped Stephanie with her maths homework, Stephanie helped Ruth with Shakespeare and Yeats.

'I'll apply to the banks and the insurance companies and the Civil Service. You know, the usual. I'm not like you, Ruth. I'm not sure what I want to do yet. I need some time to figure out what I'm good at.'

Ruth nibbled on a digestive biscuit. 'I can't believe the Leaving Certificate actually begins tomorrow.'

Steph twirled around the bed. 'Imagine. In two weeks' time we'll be finished with school for ever. No more uniforms, no more homework! Oh, it's going to be a great summer.'

'I'll have to get a job,' Ruth pointed out. 'I need to save up some pocket money for college. Dad's paying all my fees, I can't expect him to fork out any more.'

'Yeah, he'd give you his last penny if he had to,' Steph agreed. 'His darling daughter, brainy and beautiful.'

'And modest,' Ruth added. She threw her maths book to Steph. 'Ask me something.'

Steph groaned. 'Do I have to? I'm actually beginning to look forward to tomorrow. At least I won't have to spend the day swatting with you.'

Ruth was unperturbed. 'Don't forget I'm coming over tomorrow night. We need to cram for the Irish exam.'

22

'So will you call her?'

'Who?' Chris looked blank.

Steph sighed in frustration. 'Lavinia Reynolds,' she repeated. 'Will you call her?'

'Stupid oul cow. She wouldn't know good food if it jumped up and bit her.'

'Maybe not, but she's still the most respected restaurant critic in Dublin. It's better to have her with you than against you. Look at Jean-Jacques. She's done him a lot of good.' Reverse psychology, she thought smugly, as his face went purple.

'That bastard!' Chris spluttered. 'He doesn't cook. Everything comes out of a freezer and into a microwave.'

'Allegedly,' Stephanie replied, straight-faced.

'Okay, I'll talk to her.'

'Good. Here's the number.' She handed him a card and waited.

'Now?' he asked uncomfortably.

'No time like the present,' she said cheerfully.

He dialled the number. 'Lavinia, my love, how are you?'

Stephanie stood up, smiling. Sometimes, just sometimes, she got her own way.

'Hello, Steph?'

'Annie! How are you?' Steph leaned back in her chair, glad of the interruption. 'How are things?'

'Fine. I was wondering if you fancied a night out. We could get Liz to come along. Just the three of us like in the bad old days.'

'Sounds good to me. I could do with a few laughs.

Just promise me it's not going to be your place with a bottle of Bull's Blood.'

Annie laughed. 'God forbid! Why did we ever drink that stuff?'

'Because we were impoverished little bank clerks, that's why!'

'No, I was thinking of something a bit more up-market. When's your day off?'

'Tomorrow, but I've got an awful lot to do. How about Monday?' Steph suggested instead. The restaurant was closed on Mondays.

'Yeah, that's fine. Why don't you come over early? We could go and have a sauna and a beauty session.' Annie and Joe were members of an élite health club in Clontarf that also housed an excellent beauty salon and hairdresser's.

Steph smiled. 'That sounds like just what the doctor ordered. Liz probably won't go for it though. You know what she's like.'

'Oh, you'll be able to talk her into it,' Annie said confidently. 'Tell her to bring Lucy. Danielle would love it and she can stay over.'

'That's a good idea. You're not just a pretty face. I'll give her a call and ring you back.'

'Steph!' Liz grinned as she recognised her friend's voice. 'How are things? I haven't talked to you in ages. I hope Chris isn't working you too hard.'

'Of course he is.' Steph's laugh was just a little too hearty. She quickly changed the subject. 'How are things? How's that beautiful goddaughter of mine?'

Liz settled herself at the foot of the stairs and cradled

the phone in her lap. 'She's great. I seem to spend my life chauffeuring her from ballet class to parties to swimming. Her social life is better than mine, but then that wouldn't be hard.'

Stephanie didn't miss the sad note in her friend's voice. 'Then, as usual, my timing is perfect because we're going out on the town. You, me and Annie. We'll get the glad rags on, have a few drinks, a bite to eat and then on to one of those trendy clubs for a bop. How about it?'

'Oh, I don't know, Steph! I'd have to get a baby-sitter and I've nothing to wear since I put on all this damn weight and then, well, Chris doesn't really like me to go to clubs without him.' She caught sight of her reflection in the hall mirror. Her mane of dark hair was dishevelled and badly in need of a good cut. She wore no make-up and there was a smudge of flour on her nose. She wiped it away with floury hands and succeeded only in spreading the damage across her cheek. She looked at herself in despair. The large brown eyes mocked her for the dowdy mum she'd become.

'Stop making excuses,' Stephanie broke in on her thoughts. 'It's all arranged. You take Lucy over to Annie's and she'll organise a baby-sitter for the three of them. She can even stay the night. Come on, Lizzie, you know Lucy would love that.'

Liz wavered. 'When were you thinking of?'

'Monday? We could make a real day of it. First we'll go to the beauty salon in Annie's club. Then back to my place for a little drinky while we get into something black, slinky and sexy – it'll be just like the old days.'

Liz laughed. 'No Bull's Blood, okay?'

'No, I promise I'll spend at least three quid on the

wine! Lord, the airs and graces of you. In the good old days you'd have drunk cider and liked it! Anyway, then we'll go on to a club and bop till we drop.'

'That should take all of ten minutes,' said Liz drily.

'Oh, shut up,' Steph said briskly. 'You're thirty-five not ninety-five.'

Liz glanced back at her reflection. The sloppy jumper and leggings didn't do much to hide her bulging stomach and flabby thighs. 'I don't feel it.'

'Oh come on, Liz, it will be fun. Lucy will have a ball.' Steph was alarmed at her friend's tone. She sounded so depressed.

'I'm not sure what Chris will say.'

Who gives a shit? Steph thought, but said, 'I'm sure he'll be delighted. He's always saying you should get out more.'

'He is?'

Steph crossed her fingers. 'He is. So, now that we've dealt with all your excuses, madam, what's it going to be?'

'Let's do it,' Liz said simply.

'That's my girl! I'll pick you up about two? Seeya then.' Steph rang off before Liz could have a change of heart.

'We're all set,' Steph said when Annie answered the phone.

'Great stuff? What time?'

'I'm picking them up at two, so we should be with you by half past.'

'Grand. Seeya then.'

When Liz put down the phone she was still smiling. It would be nice to have a night out. It was ages since she'd got dressed up and gone out without Chris in tow. She frowned as she thought of how her husband was likely to react. She found it hard to believe he'd told Steph she should get out more. He hardly ever took her out these days but didn't like it when she went out without him either. Maybe he was jealous. She chuckled softly. That was a nice thought! If he still got jealous, surely that meant that he still cared? Maybe there was hope for them yet. If she could just get him to spend a bit more time at home. She looked at her figure critically in the mirror. It was no wonder he was losing interest in her. She'd let herself go. She couldn't really blame him if he strayed – she wasn't doing a whole lot to hold his interest. She'd never been beautiful, not like Steph. She thought of her gorgeous, confident friend. She had it all, Liz thought enviously and wandered back to the kitchen and her pastry.

She caught sight of Lucy through the kitchen window scampering around the garden with a jamjar, chasing after unsuspecting bees. She smiled fondly at her antics. Oh, well. Maybe Steph didn't really have it all.

Steph sat frowning at the phone. It looked as if she wasn't the only one having problems with Chris. Liz didn't sound very happy. She wondered if Chris was playing around. George had hinted as much on more than one occasion, and he would know. They were great boozing buddies and Chris was the type who'd boast about his conquests. The question was what would any intelligent woman see in him? And what would her guide dog think?

She put Chris to the back of her mind and forced her attention back to the books in front of her. Her brother would be here in an hour to go over the accounts. It wasn't going to be a pleasant afternoon.

Chapter Four

Stephanie parked her blue Toyota Corolla outside the imposing detached house in the quiet cul-de-sac off the Stillorgan Road. She blew the horn a few times and was greeted with shrieks and giggles as a little body raced down the driveway, teddy bear in one hand, pencil-case in the other.

'Hiya, Auntie Steph,' Lucy said breathlessly as she tugged on the back door.

Steph reached back and swung it open for her. 'Hello, princess! All set?'

Lucy nodded enthusiastically. 'Mummy said not to bring any paper. She said Auntie Annie would have some. Do you think she will?' Lucy looked worriedly at Stephanie.

'I know she will,' Steph promised solemnly, 'and I happen to know she has colouring books. And there are lots of other surprises too.'

'What are they?' demanded Lucy excitedly, hauling herself up by Steph's headrest.

'You'll find out soon enough, young lady,' Liz said as she pulled open the door and flung a couple of bags in beside Lucy. She strapped the wriggling child into her seat before climbing into the passenger seat.

'Hi, Steph, sorry to keep you waiting, but this one takes so much time deciding what she's going to bring.'

'Well, Mummy, I had to show Danielle my new pencils and Ted would have been lonely if I left him at home.'

'Quite right, Lucy.' Steph started the engine and slipped into first gear. 'Let's go, folks!' She turned northward onto the Stillorgan Road heading for Joe and Annie's house. It was a beautiful sunny day, though still cold, and Steph took the coast road so that they could enjoy the view across to Howth Head.

Liz settled back in her seat and sighed contentedly. 'I feel very guilty. I have a mountain of ironing to do, the kitchen floor needs to be washed and there are a hundred and one other things I should be doing, but I'm not.' She grinned wickedly. 'I'm having a day off!'

Twenty minutes later the three women sat at Annie's kitchen table sipping coffee and chatting while the children played outside in the garden.

'Don't take off your coat, Lucy,' Liz called out warningly. She turned back to Annie who had been talking. 'Sorry, Annie, but as soon as she sees the sun, she wants to put on her shorts and T-shirt!'

'They're all the same.' Annie glanced fondly out at the three children who were unsuccessfully trying to persuade Oscar, their twenty-year-old Labrador, to perform tricks. Danielle was making a big deal of looking after her little friend and Shane was trying to act indifferent and cool but failing miserably.

'I love this kitchen. It's so big and bright. You really did a great job with the redecoration. I must do something about my place.' Stephanie groaned as she thought of all the work that needed doing in her apartment.

Liz winked at Annie. 'I didn't think you'd be staying there for much longer. Isn't it time you moved into Sean's pad?'

'Yeah,' chimed in Annie. 'When are you two going to give us a day out?'

'Oh leave me alone, will you? You know I'm not the sort to settle down.'

'I think Sean is. Is everything okay with you two?' Annie added when she saw the faraway look in Steph's eyes.

Steph sighed. 'Sean's gone to the States.'

'He's emigrated?' Liz looked at her in shock.

'No, of course not, you pillock! He'll just be gone for a couple of months.'

'You never mentioned this before.' Liz looked at her curiously.

'No, you didn't.' Annie eyed her indignantly. 'What on earth is he doing in the States for two months?'

'He won this huge contract with an American firm.'

Annie's eyes widened. 'Wow, that's great. He must be thrilled.'

'He is about the job. He's just not too impressed with me.'

Liz looked confused. 'But why? What's his contract got to do with you?'

'He wanted me to go with him.'

'And you said no,' Liz said flatly.

'Of course I said no!'

Annie nodded enthusiastically. 'Well, I'm not surprised! How dare he ask you to go on holiday with him, what a cad!'

Steph stuck her tongue out at her sister-in-law. 'It wasn't like that. He wanted me to pack in my job.' She lit a cigarette and took a long, deep drag.

'Well, would that be such a bad idea? I mean, you are thirty-two,' Liz said, missing Annie's warning glance. 'Isn't it time to forget the job and start thinking about a husband and family?'

Annie gave up on subtlety. 'Shut up, Liz, and have a scone before you say something that really gets you into trouble.'

Liz looked puzzled. It made perfect sense to her. Sean was lovely. Good-looking too. A bit like Tom Hanks – or was it Tim Robbins? And there was no doubt that he was crazy about Stephanie.

'So how did you leave it?' Annie asked.

Steph shrugged. 'I told him I wouldn't give up the job, he went off into the sunset and that was that.'

'Well I'm sure Chris will be glad that you decided to stay, don't you think, Liz?'

'I doubt if he'll care,' Liz replied without thinking. 'He's thinking of selling up.'

Stephanie almost dropped her mug and Annie's mouth fell open in astonishment.

Stephanie was the first to recover. 'He's selling up? It's the first I've heard of it. When, exactly, was Chris planning to tell me?'

Liz fidgeted uncomfortably in her seat. 'Well, it's not definite. I'm sure he'll talk to you as soon as it's settled, but well . . .' She wasn't sure how much to say. Chris had warned her to keep quiet but Stephanie was her friend. 'He hasn't done anything about selling up, honestly, Steph. But he's been offered a job. A new restaurant in Galway wants him and, frankly, I want him to accept it. If he does, we might actually manage to get our marriage back on track.'

The other two women tried to look surprised.

Liz shook her head and smiled sadly. 'Oh, come on. I'm not a total fool. I think Chris might be messing about. I suppose I thought if I stuck my head in the sand it would all go away. Maybe it's just a mid-life crisis, a temporary thing. Anyway, if I could get him away from Dublin, we'd have a better chance of starting over. I'm sorry, Steph. I don't want to see you left high and dry, but my marriage and Lucy come first.'

Stephanie squeezed Liz's hand. 'It's okay. I'll survive.' She met Annie's questioning gaze and laughed.

Liz looked from one to the other. 'What is it? What's so funny?'

'Annie thinks I should buy Chris out, don't you, Annie?'

Annie shrugged. 'Seems like a plan.'

Liz gaped at Stephanie. 'You?'

'Why not me?' Steph protested.

'But how?' Liz asked. 'You don't have that kind of money, do you? And how could you run it without Chris? Or were you thinking of turning it into a little coffee shop?'

Steph stared at her. 'No. I'd keep it exactly as it is. Well, not *exactly* the same. I'd probably give the place a face-lift, a more modern and up-beat image. And the menu definitely needs updating.' She looked at Liz's crestfallen expression and immediately felt guilty. 'As for money,' she looked heavenward, 'God bless Uncle Jack.'

'I'd forgotten he'd left you that money. You must have

been thinking about this for ages.' Stephanie looked at Annie who burst out laughing again.

'Oh yes, she's been planning it for ages,' Annie said, wiping a tear from her eye.

'Ages,' Stephanie agreed solemnly.

Liz looked at them, bemused.

'Enough of all this.' Annie cleared the dishes from the table. 'Time we were making tracks.'

As they drove away from the house, with the children running after the car waving and shouting, Annie stretched across the back seat and sighed contentedly. 'This is the life! I can't remember the last time I was out without the kids. I feel as if I'm playing truant from school or something. It's great, isn't it Liz?'

'Oh yeah,' Liz replied vaguely, still shell-shocked by what Stephanie had said.

Stephanie glanced over at her. 'Honestly, Liz, I haven't given any thought at all to buying Chris out. Please don't say anything to him. It's just one of Annie's mad ideas.'

Liz sighed loudly. 'Oh, I should have known! You've been pulling my leg. God, I'm so gullible. I actually believed you.'

Steph looked at Annie in the rear-view mirror. Annie winked back at her cheerfully.

Stephanie leant forward and threw more water on the coals. The three women were enveloped in a cloud of steam.

Liz groaned. 'Oh, for God's sake Steph! Will you stop

that? I won't have the energy to tap my foot tonight, never mind dance!'

Annie mopped the sweat from her brow with a fluffy lemon towel. 'Rubbish, once you've had a nice cold shower you'll be ready for anything.'

Liz looked horrified. 'Well, you enjoy your shower, I'll wait and have a nice bath at Steph's. Yes. A hot bath, a glass of wine and a magazine, thank you very much!'

'It didn't take you long to get used to the good life, did it?' Steph teased. 'Half an hour ago it was, "I wonder what Lucy's doing now? I wonder if Chris will miss me?"'

'Oh, shut up and leave me alone,' Liz threw her towel at Stephanie. 'It's all ahead of you. I know you don't think so now,' she insisted as Stephanie shook her head, 'but your time will come and when it does, Ms West, I'll be the first to say "I told you so".'

Steph's laugh was forced. It seemed unlikely Liz would get her wish. Annie was right. Sean wouldn't hang around for ever. As soon as his divorce came through he'd want the ceremony, the ring, the whole ball of wax. And if she didn't agree . . . She sighed.

'Sean's a lovely man,' her mother had said more than once, 'and he thinks the world of you. You could trust Sean.'

Annie prodded her with her toe. 'Hey, sleepy head, we're going to be late for Jeanette if we don't get a move on.'

'Yeah and we don't want to make her angry.' Liz rolled her eyes dramatically. 'We might come out bald!'

Laughing, the three women headed back to the changing rooms, donned their robes and set off to the beauty salon.

∽∾∽

The hairdresser grabbed handfuls of Liz's dark locks in her hand and then dropped them in disgust. 'Split ends.' She eyed Liz accusingly in the mirror as if she'd committed a heinous crime.

She turned away for a quick consultation and Liz looked at Steph in horror.

'I feel like I'm back in school,' she hissed. 'I thought I was supposed to be here to relax and enjoy myself.'

Stephanie flicked through a copy of *Cosmopolitan.* 'Haven't you ever heard the saying, "suffer to be beautiful"?'

Jeanette swung back to Liz with a bright smile. 'Never mind, we can work wonders for you. First, I think you need a complete new look.'

'No, I don't think so. Just a trim for me,' Liz said primly.

'No, Liz, really, Jeanette's right,' Annie insisted. She glanced at Jeanette. 'And maybe some lowlights too?'

Jeanette nodded approvingly while Liz looked around in panic.

'Oh, I really don't think . . .'

'You relax and let me do the thinking.' Jeanette signalled to one of her girls.

'Shampoo for Mrs Connolly, with conditioner.' Liz was led away, like a lamb to the slaughter.

Chapter Five

'Chris is going to kill me,' Liz said for the tenth time as she studied her new look in Stephanie's bathroom mirror.

Steph came up behind her with a glass of wine in one hand and a magazine in the other. 'He's going to love it. You look stunning! The haircut takes years off you and it makes your eyes look huge and so brown! Now hop in that tub, drink some wine and get in the party mood. We're going to paint the town red!'

After Steph had left Liz turned back to study the stranger in the mirror. It was true, she admitted, the style suited her. Jeanette hadn't taken too much off the length, but she'd given it more shape. It looked a lot more sophisticated. The eyebrow-shape emphasised her large wide-set eyes and the facial had left her skin glowing and healthy. She slipped into the tub, took a sip of her wine and settled back contentedly. She hadn't felt this good in a long time. Maybe this change of image would make Chris sit up and take notice. She thought of how sulky he'd been this morning when she'd kissed him goodbye. He didn't like her going out with the girls. She opened her eyes wide and smiled, maybe that was the answer. Maybe she was just too available. After all, men liked a little mystery, didn't they? She'd discuss it with Steph and Annie later. She slipped further down into the bubbles, reached for the magazine and was soon lost in the wonders of collagen implants . . .

Stephanie stretched out on her bed and watched Annie apply her make-up. 'Liz looks great, doesn't she?'

'Sensational. Pity it'll be wasted on that scumbag.'

Steph groaned. 'Oh, don't mention him. You'll spoil my appetite.'

'Where are we going?' Annie asked.

'L'Écrivain.'

'Oh, very posh! I'd better not tell Joe. He'd have a heart attack.'

'My brother's not mean,' Steph protested.

'Keep your hair on. I was only kidding! God, blood really is thicker than water. So tell me. What are you going to do about Chez Nous?'

'I don't know, Annie. It would be such an enormous responsibility. Huge. And what about a head chef? Conor's very young but the thought of hiring someone . . .' She stared at the ceiling, her mind racing. The idea excited and terrified her. She knew that she was a good restaurant manager. And she firmly believed that not only could she maintain Chez Nous at its present level, but in time, she could improve it. There were plenty of successful restaurants in Dublin where the owner wasn't the head chef. So what was stopping her?

Annie smiled at her in the mirror. 'You really like the idea, don't you? Did you tell Sean?'

Steph shook her head. 'I was going to, but then he

told me about Arizona. Once he started talking about me leaving Chez Nous for good there didn't seem to be much point after that.'

'Oh, Steph, that's not the same thing at all. Sean would be delighted for you if you were your own boss.'

'I'm not so sure. I think he'd prefer me to do nothing at all.'

Annie sighed impatiently. 'That's crap and you know it. The only reason he suggested you leave is because he knows how miserable you are in Chez Nous. For God's sake you've told everyone except Liz how fed up you are.'

'But I can't just let Chris drive me out.'

Annie reached over and patted her hand. 'No you can't. But you can't let this come between you and Sean either.'

Steph hung her head. 'I know.'

'So be nice to him next time he phones?'

Steph nodded with a reluctant smile. 'Yes, boss.'

Annie turned back to the mirror. 'I really think you should give some serious thought to buying Chez Nous though. Why don't you come over at the weekend and thrash it out with Joe. If it's a crazy idea he'll soon tell you!'

Steph chuckled. 'Yeah, he would, wouldn't he? And he knows the state the books are in.'

'That bad?'

'They could be better. Something needs to be done, and quickly.' Stephanie broke off guiltily as Liz arrived in, wrapped in a towel and singing 'I Could Have Danced All Night'.

Annie groaned. 'I can feel my hangover starting already.'

Stephanie insisted on applying Liz's make-up, while Annie looked on and gave advice. Annie and Liz puffed happily on Steph's cigarettes as they chatted. If their husbands could see them now, Steph thought. It was just like old times. All they needed was a bottle of Bull's Blood!

With Liz's make-up complete, Steph went off to rummage in the wardrobe for something to wear. She grinned ruefully at the amount of blue in her wardrobe. Sean always said that blue was her colour. She leant her head against the door. She missed him more than she'd expected—

'Hey, Steph? Can I take some of your perfume?' Liz called.

'Why not?' Steph laughed as she grabbed a red dress she rarely wore from the back of the wardrobe. It was a little risqué with a plunging neckline and a side slit which showed a fair amount of thigh. It would turn heads but that was exactly what she needed right now. Some dancing and flirting with no strings attached. Yup, she decided, this was the dress to do it.

Annie was coolly sophisticated in a black satin trouser suit. The beautifully cut jacket revealed an ample cleavage. The emerald earrings and pendant Joe had given her for her birthday complemented her startling green eyes and completed the chic image. Jeanette had trimmed her hair and soft auburn tendrils framed her heart-shaped face.

'Oh, you look lovely, Annie.' Steph looked at her friend in open admiration. 'We'll have to do this more often.'

'We certainly will. Have you fallen down, Liz?' Annie rapped on the door of the loo.

'Coming.' Liz slipped the dress over her head and smoothed it down over her hips. She turned to the mirror and was taken aback at the pretty woman looking back at her. Steph's little black dress covered a multitude. She almost looked slim! She took a deep breath and opened the door. 'Not bad for an oul one, eh?' she said.

'Wow, girl, you look hot!' Steph twirled her around while Annie attempted a wolf whistle.

'You don't look so bad yourself,' Liz replied eyeing the dramatic red dress. She'd never have the guts to wear something like that. It emphasised Stephanie's fair skin, slender frame and golden hair. Gold earrings and strappy golden sandals completed the outfit.

Annie clapped her hands. 'Okay, enough of this mutual admiration society. Finish your wine and let's get this show on the road. The taxi should be here any minute.'

Liz knocked back the remains of her drink, and was slipping on her coat when the intercom buzzed.

Stephanie threw open the door with a flourish. 'Come on, Cinderellas. Let's go to the ball!'

'Oh, that crème brûlée was delicious.' Liz licked her lips with relish. 'Why is it that everything that tastes good is bad for you?' She looked mournfully down at her stomach.

Stephanie laughed. 'Forget about your weight for tonight. You can dance all the calories off later.'

'I could quite happily sit here all evening.' Annie sipped her port and watched the bevy of efficient waiters swarming around the tables.

'Isn't that Lavinia Reynolds over there?' Liz whispered

excitedly. 'She looks great for her age. Didn't she write something recently about Chez Nous?'

'She did,' Stephanie replied grimly. 'None of it good.'

Liz's eyes narrowed. 'The miserable cow.'

Annie laughed. 'Oops, watch out, she's coming over.'

'Stephanie darling.'

Stephanie rose and the two women kissed air.

'Enjoying how the other half live this evening? How's that wonderful boss of yours?'

Stephanie glanced at Liz uncomfortably. 'He's fine, Lavinia. Have you met Liz – Chris's wife? And this is Annie West, my sister-in-law.'

Lavinia eyed Liz curiously with a twisted little smile. 'How nice to meet you both. Isn't this the most wonderful restaurant? Next to Chez Nous, of course.' She gave a hard tinkling laugh. 'Well, I must get back to my party. See you quite soon, Stephanie. Ciao.' She moved on, leaving a cloud of heavy scent in her wake.

Steph's fake smile equalled Lavinia's. 'Ciao, bitch.'

'She's obnoxious, isn't she?' Annie said amiably.

Liz frowned and said nothing. There was something about the way that woman had looked at her . . .

'Annie! How are you? Where's Joe? Don't tell me he let you out on your own? Stupid man.'

Annie stood up to hug an extremely attractive man. 'Edward! How are you? Joe's at home. This is strictly a ladies' night out.'

'And what lovely ladies,' he replied, glancing admiringly from Liz to Stephanie.

'Oh, sorry, let me introduce you.' She smiled at her friends. 'This is Edward McDermott. Edward, this is Liz Connolly and surely you've met Joe's sister, Stephanie before?'

Edward shook hands. 'I can assure you I would have remembered,' he said gravely.

Stephanie felt her face flush but he'd already turned to Liz. 'Not the chef from Chez Nous?'

Liz was taken aback. Not many people associated her with the restaurant these days.

'Ex-chef,' she corrected. 'My husband runs the business now. I'm just a housewife.'

Annie could have cheerfully kicked her for the apology in her voice.

'That's a pity,' Edward replied, 'I used to have offices around the corner from your restaurant, oh, it must be five years ago now. Your desserts were the main reason I used to go there.'

Liz's face lit up. 'Really? How nice that you remember.'

'Well, I hope you plan to rejoin the culinary world at some stage. It's a shame to hide away that kind of talent.'

'Why don't you join us for a drink, Edward?' Annie said, enjoying the effect he was having on her friends.

'Oh, I can't, I'm with someone.' He nodded towards a table at the back of the room. 'Good to see you though, Annie. Tell your lug of a husband to give me a call. I owe him a thrashing on the squash court. Lovely to meet you, Stephanie, Liz.'

With a wave he was gone.

'Wow,' breathed Liz.

Annie smiled. 'Nice, isn't he? If it weren't for Joe . . .'

Stephanie looked at her in mock horror.

Annie was unperturbed. 'There's nothing wrong with looking at the menu.'

'He's so nice. Imagine him remembering my desserts,' Liz said dreamily.

'Very romantic.' Steph grinned at her friend's lovesick expression. 'I hate to remind you two, but I'm the only single woman at this table. So what does he do, Annie?' She tried to sound off-hand.

'He's a lawyer. Joe's known him years. They met at Trinity. I'm surprised you haven't met before.'

'Is he married?' Liz asked suspiciously.

Annie shook her head. 'No and I can't image why not. He's a partner in some large firm, rolling in money, drives a beautiful car and he's great with Dani and Shane.'

'A positive paragon but he seems to be spoken for.' Stephanie nodded towards Edward's table. A very attractive redhead was leaning towards him, smiling into his eyes.

'Hardly surprising. He's gorgeous and nice.' Liz was definitely smitten.

'Enough drooling, ladies,' Annie admonished. 'Drink up. It's time to hit the clubs.'

They went out to the waiting taxi and gave the driver directions to the trendiest nightclub in Dublin.

'Lord, I'm getting old.' Liz pushed her way back through the swaying bodies to their table and took a long gulp from her glass.

Stephanie flopped down beside her. 'Oh, I don't know. I think we can hold our own against that mob.' She nodded towards the dance floor. 'Would you look at Annie flirting with that fella? He doesn't look old enough to vote! What's she like? If my brother could see her now . . .' Steph's voice faltered as she saw the look on Liz's face. 'Liz, what is it? What's the matter?'

She followed Liz's gaze and saw Chris standing at the bar. A beautiful girl, about twenty, with long blonde hair stood at his side laughing at something he was saying. As they watched, he slipped an arm around her.

'What's up?' Annie arrived back, out of breath from her efforts on the dance floor. Stephanie nodded towards Chris.

Annie blinked. 'Oh my God, oh Liz, Liz? What are you going to . . . Liz?'

Steph ran after Liz as she headed determinedly across the room. 'Liz, you don't know what the story is, there could be a very simple explanation.'

Liz gave her a withering look without breaking stride. When she reached the bar, she tapped Chris on the shoulder.

'Liz!' Chris flushed and paled. His expression said it all. 'What are you doing here? Just dropped in for one with George. He insisted. I was just leaving . . .'

Liz threw her drink in his face and then turned an icy glare on the bemused girl.

'You silly little bitch. Do you make a habit of chatting up married men?' She gave a harsh laugh, but her eyes were bright with tears. 'He's pathetic,' she continued, 'but you must be desperate.' She stared at Chris in disgust and stormed out of the club with Annie hot on her heels.

Chris made to follow her, but Stephanie planted herself firmly in his path.

'I think you've done more than enough for one night, don't you?' she said, before following Annie and Liz out of the club.

Chapter Six

'How is she?'

'I don't know, Annie,' Steph whispered into the phone. 'She hardly said a word last night, and I haven't seen her this morning. I'll take her in a cup of tea in a minute. What have you told Lucy?'

'Just that Liz was spending the night with you. She wasn't too bothered. She's having too much fun with Dani.'

The bedroom door opened and Liz emerged, looking pale, her eye-sockets black with smudged mascara. 'Is that Annie?'

Steph nodded and Liz took the receiver.

'Hi, Annie. Would you do me a favour? Could you keep Lucy until tomorrow?'

'Sure,' Annie said, surprised at the composure in her friend's voice.

'Can I talk to her?'

'Sure,' Annie said again and put her hand over the mouthpiece. 'Luceeeee,' she yelled, 'your mum's on the phone!'

Lucy came running down the stairs and grabbed the phone. 'Mummy? You'll never guess. Dani has pencils just like mine and I drew a picture for you and one for Daddy.'

Liz rested her head on her arm and let her daughter prattle on for a while. Finally she cut in. 'Well, it sounds like you're having a great time. Would you like to stay another day?'

Lucy squealed with delight. 'Oh, that would be great, Mummy.'

'Okay, love. I'll pick you up tomorrow afternoon. Be a good girl for Auntie Annie now, won't you?'

After a few more moments of blowing kisses, Liz handed the phone back to Stephanie and went back into the bedroom.

'Liz? Liz, are you there?'

'No, Annie, it's me. She's gone back to bed.'

'She seems all right. What do you think?'

Steph sighed. 'Oh, I don't know. She's too bloody quiet. I'd be a lot happier if she cried or screamed or something.'

'Did *he* call?' Annie couldn't even bring herself to use the man's name. God, if she got her hands on him . . .

'He hasn't stopped calling. Look, I'd better go and see how she is. I'll call you back later.' Steph rang off. After a tentative knock, she put her head around Liz's door. 'Can I come in?'

Liz nodded mutely.

'Are you okay?' Steph asked inadequately.

Liz smiled grimly. 'Nope, but I'll survive.'

'What are you going to do?'

'Kick him out, of course,' she replied, pulling on her jeans. 'He should have left for work by now. Do me a favour. Grab the Yellow Pages and find me a locksmith in the Stillorgan area. Ask him to meet me at the house in two hours.'

Steph stared at her. 'That's a bit drastic, isn't it?

47

Would you not talk to Chris first? He may not have actually *done* anything.' Steph couldn't believe she was defending the bastard.

'No, Steph. I saw something last night that confirmed my suspicions. He's playing around, has been for years. If I don't act now, I never will. Please help me,' she pleaded, her voice trembling slightly.

Stephanie nodded silently, went back into the living-room and began to thumb through the phone book.

Liz let herself into the hall and fell back against the door. It hadn't been easy getting rid of Stephanie. She'd wanted to come in and stay with her.

'You'll be late for work,' Liz pointed out, 'and the boss isn't exactly understanding.'

Stephanie had finally left and Liz was halfway up the stairs when the doorbell went. The locksmith.

'Hello, love. You called about changing some locks? Had a break-in then? Bloody disgraceful the thugs running around these days. Don't you worry, love, I'll sort you out. Point me towards the damage.'

Liz sighed wearily. This was all she needed: a chatty, cheerful tradesman. 'I just want the front-door lock changed and a safety chain added.'

The man frowned, examining the lock. 'Looks fine,' he remarked.

Liz bit her lip. 'It is, but I lost my bag, and the keys were in it. I don't want to take any chances.'

The man nodded wisely. 'Oh, you're right there, love. You can't be too careful—'

'You're right, I can't,' Liz interrupted. 'I'll leave you to it. Call if you need anything.' She ran upstairs and pulled out the two new Samsonite cases from under the bed. 'No, fuck him,' she muttered and shoved them back. Instead, she got three plastic sacks and proceeded to crumple his clothes into balls and shove them roughly into the bags. She thought about cutting up his shirts and suits. She'd seen a woman on a talk show once who'd cut the right arm off all her husband's suits. It seemed funny at the time. Her eyes filled up. It didn't seem remotely funny now. No it would be a childish act and, more to the point, it wouldn't make her feel any better. Then there was the woman who'd raided her husband's very expensive wine cellar and left a bottle on all the local doorsteps, along with the morning milk. Well, Chris didn't have that much wine. He drank it as fast as he bought it. No. She'd keep what was left and drink it herself. She looked at her watch. Twelve noon. Was it too early to start now? She turned her attention to his tie rack. Chris was very proud of his ties. They were all of the very best silk. It was the one purchase he made himself. He didn't like her choices, they were usually too subtle for him. She looked at the variety of flamboyant and garish colours. She could cut them up, she thought idly. That would upset him. It didn't seem enough, though. What could she possibly do to him that would make him hurt the way she was hurting now? What would make him feel as if his heart was breaking in two? She slid to the floor and let the tears come. Once she started crying it was hard to stop. She sobbed uncontrollably, rocking back and forth like a child.

'Eh sorry, missus, I did shout. Eh, are you okay?' The workman stood in the doorway, shuffling from one foot to another and looking distinctly uncomfortable.

Liz scrambled to her feet, and wiped her eyes. 'I'm fine. What do I owe you?' She wrote a cheque and hurried the embarrassed man out of the house. Next she phoned for a taxi. She went back upstairs and started to snip the ties into neat little pieces. Oh well, so she wasn't imaginative. She found a large brown envelope and dropped the pieces into it. She sealed it and stuck it to the side of one of the bags. She tugged the bags downstairs, pausing to blow her nose and wipe her eyes. When the taxi arrived she gave the driver the address of Chez Nous and two twenty-pound notes. 'The bags are for Chris Connolly, the owner. He's waiting for them. They're very important. Make sure you deliver them to him personally.' The taxi-driver agreed readily, delighted with his fare.

Liz closed the door, slid the safety chain into place, went into the kitchen and opened a bottle of wine. 'Cheers, Chris.'

Stephanie tiptoed past the kitchen and climbed the stairs to the office. She wasn't looking forward to seeing Chris. She was afraid she'd kick him somewhere that would put paid to his antics and that wasn't a great idea. He was still her boss. She opened the office door and stopped short. Chris was in her seat looking pale and haggard.

He looked up at her from bloodshot eyes. 'Morning. Sorry if I gave you a start. I wanted to talk.'

Stephanie nodded mutely and took the seat opposite him.

'Is Liz okay?'

Steph's eyes narrowed. 'What do you think?'

'I do love her. I'd never do anything to hurt her. I was just having a bit of fun.'

Steph began to wish she had kicked him.

'It didn't mean anything. If I could just see Liz and explain. Nothing happened.'

Steph raised an eyebrow. She definitely should have kicked him. 'I must have imagined it all, so. It must have been someone else I saw in that club. Some other dirty old man who was chatting up a girl half his age.'

'I don't owe you an explanation,' he said angrily. 'Oh, look, Steph, help me out here. Talk to her. Tell her I'll take her away for a few days, she'd like that.'

Steph looked at him in disbelief. He really had no idea of the mess he was in. She almost pitied him. Almost. 'I'm afraid it's going to take more than a holiday, Chris. Liz is very upset.' She reached for her bag and pulled out her cigarettes. 'I really don't think—'

The phone rang and she paused to pick it up. 'Yes? Oh, right ... okay Sam, I'll tell him.' She put down the receiver and looked at Chris. 'There's a taxi-driver downstairs with a delivery for you. He says he has to give it to you personally.'

'What the hell does he want?' Chris said with an irritable sigh and went downstairs with Stephanie hot on his heels. Three black bags were stacked in the hallway. Chris peered into one and then looked at the taxi-man in confusion. 'What's all this?'

'Dunno,' he replied cheerfully. 'The lady said you'd understand. There's a note for you there.' He pointed at the envelope. 'Bye now.'

Chris tore open the envelope. 'Jesus Christ.' He dropped it and patches of silk drifted to the floor like confetti.

Stephanie suppressed a giggle. She watched Chris rummage through the bags. 'It's all my stuff,' he gasped. 'She's thrown me out. The bitch has thrown me out.' He turned to Stephanie, his face pale. 'You've got to do something.'

Steph nodded. 'You're right. I'll get started on tonight's menus.' She turned on her heel and ran back upstairs. 'Good girl, Liz. Good girl.'

Chapter Seven

A nnie shook her head in wonder. 'I wish I'd seen his face. I can't believe Liz cut up his ties.'

'Neither could he,' Steph replied drily.

'Do you really think she's finished with him for good?' Joe asked as he topped up their glasses.

Steph shrugged. 'Hard to say. She won't talk about it. She seems in reasonably good form, though.'

'She can't be. She was crazy about him. She must be just putting on a brave face. You don't get over twelve years of marriage, just like that. I bet she'll take him back.'

'I'm not so sure, Annie. It's been four weeks now. The real crunch comes when Chris moves to Galway. Which brings us back to the matter at hand. Do you still think I'm mad, Joe?'

When Steph had filled her brother in on her plan he had told her she was barking. But Annie and Steph had pointed out all the positive points and he'd finally agreed that it might just be possible but he'd need to have a very hard look at the books and talk to some people in the business.

'I'm in the business,' Steph had pointed out. Sometimes Joe treated her too much like his little sister.

'Let him check things out,' Annie had suggested gently. 'It's a good idea to get a few different viewpoints.' Steph had agreed but it hadn't stopped her doing a bit of digging herself. If she was going to become the owner of a business she couldn't rely on her brother all the time.

'Maybe, maybe not,' Joe was saying now, in his usual cautious, careful way.

'Bloody accountant.' Steph grinned at him.

Joe ignored her and continued, 'I think the restaurant's a good investment and you know it better than anyone, but you need to do a lot of research before you commit yourself. For example: what's involved in holding on to the Michelin Star?'

'Way ahead of you,' Steph said through a mouthful of bolognese. 'I was talking to Conor about that, in a casual sort of way of course. The Star belongs to the restaurant, not to Chris. Once the menu remains much the same, they'll let us hold on to it and then judge us as usual for next year. Their findings are announced in February. That would suit me just fine. I'd just have to maintain standards for the remainder of this year and I'd be able to concentrate on making plans for next year.'

Joe looked sceptical. 'What are the chances of Chris agreeing and you taking over so quickly? It might be wiser to think in terms of next year.'

Steph shook her head. 'I don't agree. Chris is desperate to do something to get Liz back. He's scared to death that she's dumped him for good. The other problem is his attitude. He's been slacking off lately and it's affected the restaurant's standards.'

'What about a chef?' Annie asked.

'Conor,' Steph replied without hesitation. 'I know

he's young but that works to my advantage, really. It's a wonderful opportunity for him and he'll jump at the chance. He's another reason to move quickly. If we're not going to make any immediate changes Conor will have plenty of time to develop his own ideas. He's also unknown. It's an opportunity to build the reputation of the restaurant and not the chef. That way, when he eventually moves, it won't cause too much of a stir.'

'But you've raised another point,' Joe said. 'Chez Nous is inexorably linked with Chris Connolly. Will people keep coming if he leaves?'

'We have to use the critics to make sure they do. PR is going to be very important. If Chris plays along, then he can endorse Chez Nous and its staff. It's no skin off his nose, he's leaving the city anyway. I'll need to hold on to Conor for about two years – if I lost him any earlier than that it could be a problem. I'll have to make his terms very attractive. What?' She stopped as she saw Annie and Joe exchange looks.

Annie laughed. 'When you started talking, it was "if" and now it's "when". It looks like you've made up your mind.'

Steph smiled slowly. 'Maybe I have.'

'What does Sean think?' Joe asked.

Steph stared at her plate. 'I haven't told him.'

Annie frowned. 'I thought you talked every day.'

'It's only for a few minutes and Sean seems to be rushed off his feet. I don't want to bother him with this now.'

'I'm sure he wouldn't mind,' Joe argued. 'This is a big decision to make alone.'

'But I'm not making it alone. I've got you two.' She smiled broadly.

Joe shrugged. 'Fair enough. Your next step is to talk to the bank manager. And my other advice is don't rush into this. There's plenty of time.'

Steph rolled her eyes at Annie. 'Okay, brother dear, I promise not to rush into anything. Now can I ask one more favour? Would you look over my business plan before I go to the bank?'

'No problem and I'll put together some notes for you on the current state of your finances. It's not too bad, but it could be better. Then again, I'm sure it's the same story for a lot of restaurants. I'll go with you to the bank manager if you like.'

'That's okay,' Steph said hurriedly. She was grateful for her brother's help, but she didn't want him to take over. This was her baby. 'I suppose my first job is to talk to Chris. I can't say I'm looking forward to that. I'm the last person he'll want to sell to.'

Annie started to clear the table, 'Has he talked to Liz yet?'

'He's tried, but she hangs up when he phones and she won't answer the door when he comes around. He nearly had a fit when he realised she'd changed the lock.'

'What about Lucy?' Joe asked.

Steph thought about her poor little godchild. 'I don't think Liz has told her anything yet, but Lucy's a clever little girl. Liz won't be able to keep her in the dark for much longer.'

'Poor kid,' Annie said sadly. Lucy was a lively, bright child and she and Dani were great friends. Sometimes Annie worried that Danielle was too quiet and shy, but when Lucy was around she came to life.

Annie finished loading the dishwasher and she and

Steph sat over their drinks while Joe went into the living-room to watch the match.

'So how is Sean?'

'Okay,' Steph replied glumly. 'I think he's fed up with me, though. Can't say I blame him. It's only when you think about rats like Chris, you realise how lucky you are.'

'Amen to that. Do I detect a softening in Ms West?'

Steph sighed. 'Maybe I've been a bit hard on Sean. I was thinking . . .'

'Yes?'

'Well, maybe when he gets back I'll suggest that we move in together.'

Annie nearly choked on her wine. 'Are you serious?'

Steph nodded gravely. 'Yes, I think it's time. He's been a bit odd lately. If I don't do something soon I'm afraid that I might drive him away.'

'I can't pretend the thought didn't cross my mind,' Annie said mildly. 'I don't know how he puts up with you.'

'Thanks very much!'

Annie smiled sweetly. 'Just being honest, pet. That's what friends are for.'

Sean wiped his hands nervously on his jeans, lifted the gun, aimed carefully and fired. He was shocked and disoriented by the noise, despite his earplugs.

Barry laughed. 'You were way off the mark, dude. Have another go.'

Sean took a deep breath and turned back to the row of cans in the distance. It was five in the evening but the Arizona sun beat down relentlessly on the stark, barren desert. He aimed and fired. Again, with no success.

Barry threw him a full can from the cooler. 'Have another drink, it might improve your aim.'

Sean leaned back against the four-by-four and took a long swig from the can. He watched, enviously, as Barry blew away the row of cans with the semi-automatic.

'Easy when you know how,' drawled Barry and he wandered off to set up a new target.

Sean sighed and looked up at the cloudless sky. He'd been away from home for over a month and was missing Stephanie like hell. He'd been out on the tiles most nights since he'd arrived, but he still couldn't banish her from his mind. He watched Barry approach. He was becoming very fond of this laid-back American. Nothing seemed to faze him.

'You should stop thinking and start shooting,' Barry observed shrewdly and shoved the semi-automatic into Sean's hand.

Sean sank under the weight of the gun. 'I can't lift it, never mind shoot it. What else have you got?' He walked around to the back of the truck and inspected the arsenal. Arizona amazed him. Everyone seemed to have guns – for sport, hunting and protection. Barry had more than thirty in his collection, but he'd chosen just four for today's sport.

'Here. Try this.' Barry handed him a 44 Magnum.

Sean looked in wonder at the weapon in his hand.

'Be careful. There'll be kickback,' Barry warned.

Sean aimed and fired the gun. The shot forced his arms up and he gasped as he felt the wrench in his shoulders. Barry grinned at the shocked look on his face.

Sean tried again. Finally he hit his first can and, with renewed confidence, whooped as two more hit the deck. 'Jeez, ten minutes with a Magnum and I feel like Dirty Harry! This is fun.' He aimed the gun again and thought of his accountant. He hit the can square and it flipped off the rock. He thought of his bank manager and another can bit the dust. He laughed. 'This is great therapy altogether!'

'Yup,' agreed Barry, 'and a lot cheaper than a shrink.'

Two hours and many dented cans later, Sean sat in the passenger seat watching the sun set over the desert as Barry guided the truck back to the main road. He'd never seen anything more beautiful. Steph would love it here. He sighed. Everything he saw, every restaurant he went in to, he wondered what she'd say, what she'd think. He raked his hand through his thick, curly hair. He wished, not for the first time, that she would make a commitment. But she wasn't interested, he thought bitterly. She cared more about that damn restaurant than she did about him. He knew that many of their dates happened purely because she wanted to check out the competition. He sighed again and Barry shot him a sidelong glance.

'Anything you want to talk about, Bud?'

Sean shook his head. 'I wouldn't know where to begin, Barry. Woman trouble.'

'Oh, okay. You just need another beer. And a little . . . distraction.' He swung the truck off the road and into the car park of a bar that he hadn't taken Sean to before.

'What's this?'

'This, Sean, is where you get to have a beer in the company of some lovely ladies. At a price of course.'

59

Sean stared at him. Oh, what the hell. He could do with another drink and it would be nice to be around women who were interested in what *he* wanted for a change. 'Sounds good, Barry. Lead on.'

Chapter Eight

Stephanie paced the office nervously. She'd asked Chris for a meeting two hours ago and he still hadn't surfaced. She knew better than to repeat the request. He'd only keep her waiting even longer.

Chris looked at his watch. Let the bitch wait another while. He wondered what she wanted to moan about this time. God, he'd love to fire her, but he couldn't if he wanted Liz back. She'd never forgive him for sacking her best friend. He slammed pots around as he thought about Stephanie. Bad enough that he had to put up with her in work, but her involvement in his personal life was really annoying. It was weeks now since Liz had thrown him out and she still wouldn't listen to reason. She'd never have had the guts to take such drastic action on her own. Stephanie had always been a bad influence. It made him sick that she was his daughter's godmother as well. Why had he ever agreed to that? But then that all happened years ago when Steph had been a friend. Before she'd turned into the bossy little shrew she was today always telling him how to run his own restaurant. Bloody cheek! And now she was encouraging his wife to behave disgracefully. Yes, Stephanie West had got above herself and was far too opinionated for his liking. He washed his hands, donned a clean apron and headed for the office. Time to go and see what was wrong with her this time.

Stephanie was stubbing out her fifth cigarette of the morning when Chris walked in. She immediately lit another. 'I want to talk to you about the restaurant,' she said without preamble, her voice trembling.

'What's your problem now?'

She swallowed hard. She mustn't let him rattle her. Not today. 'No problem, I just want to know if you're planning to sell up or not.'

Chris's head jerked up. 'What are you talking about?'

'Liz told me about the offer you got. Are you planning to take it?'

'What the hell has it got to do with you?'

'I think that's pretty obvious. Chez Nous is my livelihood.'

Chris said nothing.

'I think it's a good idea, Chris,' she said more gently. 'Liz seems pretty keen to move out of Dublin.'

Chris sighed and ran his fingers through thin, greying hair. 'I know and going to Galway might just clinch it, but it's easier said than done. Finding a buyer, sorting out all the legalities, selling the house . . .'

Stephanie sent up a silent prayer of thanks. He still didn't have a buyer. 'I'll buy it.'

Chris threw back his head and laughed. 'Oh, Stephanie, it's not quite that simple.'

She bristled at his tone, but said nothing.

'You can't decide to buy a restaurant, just like that,' he continued. 'It's a little bit more complicated than that.'

'I didn't,' she replied quietly.

'You didn't what?' He massaged his temples wearily.

She turned to face him. 'I didn't decide "just like that". I decided several weeks ago and I've most of the finance arranged.'

She got some satisfaction from the startled look on his face. Chris finally found his tongue. 'Jumping the gun a bit, aren't you? What makes you think I'd sell to you anyway?'

She looked him in the eye, for the first time. 'How many other offers have you had, Chris? Let's cut the bull. You want out and I have the cash. What do you say?'

'You've one major problem,' he said ignoring the question. 'What about a chef? George couldn't handle it and Conor's too young.'

'He'll be fine once he gets some more experience under his belt. Anyway, that's my problem, not yours.'

'What would you do in the meantime? Close the restaurant? That could be dangerous, and you'd lose the Star.' He looked at her triumphantly.

'I've no intention of closing. I want you to stay on and run it until he's ready.'

'Stay on and work for you! You're joking! Why should I—'

'Because if you think about it for a minute it would suit you very well indeed.'

'And how do you make that out?' His voice dripped with sarcasm.

'If you go to Galway now, Liz won't go with you. Even you must realise that.'

He looked at her sullenly, but said nothing.

'And if you go without her, you'll be completely tied up in the new job and you won't have any time to commute to Dublin and sort things out.'

Chris shook his head irritably. 'One minute you're telling me I should go and then that I shouldn't go. I don't know what you're on about.'

'Look at it this way,' Stephanie said patiently. He was weakening, she could feel it. Steady now, steady. 'If you took this job you'd have to find a buyer and go through all the legal hoops, so you wouldn't be in a position to move for a few months anyway. Presumably, whoever made you this offer realises that?'

'Well, yes,' he admitted reluctantly. 'They agreed to wait up to a year, provided I sign the contract immediately.'

'Well, there you go,' Steph said triumphantly. 'You could stay on here for a while, keep an eye on things. Conor could go off and get the experience he needs and you could channel all your energy into convincing Liz that she should take you back.'

A glint had returned to Chris's eye. She could almost hear his mind at work. Once he signed the restaurant over to her all of his financial worries would be over. And he wouldn't have to work too hard either. He'd have George, Pat and Marc doing all the dirty jobs.

'It might work,' he said finally.

Steph pretended surprise. 'Are you agreeing with me, Chris? Do we have a deal?'

Chris shrugged. 'I've had enough of this bloody place. You're welcome to it. But we still need to talk money. I'm not just selling bricks and mortar here, you know. I've built up an excellent reputation and an impressive client list.'

'Of course,' Steph agreed humbly.

'Good. I'm glad we understand each other.'

64

Steph wanted to dance around the room but decided to restrain herself.

'Do you think she'll take me back, Steph?' There was an ominous tremble in Chris's voice.

Steph gulped. 'I don't know,' she answered honestly. 'She hasn't said anything. If you like, I'll try to get her to talk to you, but I can't make any promises.'

'That night, Stephanie. I was only . . .'

'Please, Chris, I don't want to know.'

Chris nodded, his face grim, and stood up. 'Why don't you put your proposal in writing and I'll let my lawyer take a look at it?'

Chapter Nine

Steph and Liz sat in a corner of the large but slightly gloomy restaurant. Liz had taken care with her appearance, but the black wool dress just accentuated her pallor and her face seemed thinner.

'So he wants me back,' Liz said dully.

Steph smiled brightly. 'Yes, he does. He's very sorry and realises what a prat he's been. I told him I wanted to buy Chez Nous and he seems very interested. He's ready to do anything to get you back.'

Liz said nothing.

Steph watched the blank expression on her face. She tried again. 'I know how much he hurt you, Liz, but maybe it's time to forgive him. I think you're right to make him sweat for a while – he deserves it. But remember he may not have done anything more than chatted up that one girl. Anyway you won't know until you talk to him.' Stephanie almost choked on the words but she had to say them for her friend's sake. She knew how much Liz loved Chris and there was also Lucy to think of. She couldn't let Liz throw her marriage away without at least trying to help. She looked around irritably. 'We've been sitting here ten minutes and we haven't even got menus yet.'

Liz looked around the restaurant absently. 'Why did you want to meet here?'

'It's only been open a few weeks. I wanted to check it out. The chef was poached, excuse the pun, from The Food Factory. He was developing quite a reputation there and so there's a lot of interest in this place.' Steph paused as a harassed-looking waiter hurried towards them.

'Are you ready to order, ladies?'

Steph looked at him in disbelief. 'We haven't seen a menu yet,' she pointed out testily.

'Oh. Right.' He hurried off again and returned with the menus a few minutes later. 'Do you want something to drink?'

Steph glanced at Liz's pale, tense expression. 'Some wine, I think. Can I see your list?'

The waiter sighed loudly and hurried away again.

Liz sniffed. 'Helpful, isn't he?'

Steph laughed. 'I suppose I should be delighted. If this is the way they treat their customers, we've nothing to worry about.' She fell silent as the waiter returned with the wine list. It consisted of three pages and the variety of prices and regions was impressive. She ordered a white Bordeaux and turned her attention back to the menu. 'What do you think?' She asked, ignoring the fact that Liz hadn't so much as glanced at it.

Liz forced her attention to the menu in front of her. What did she think of it? Frankly she didn't give a damn. She didn't care. She didn't want to be here. She didn't want to eat. She just wanted to curl up in bed and see no one, talk to no one. She'd agreed to come out today because Steph had nagged and nagged. In the end it was easier to give in. She looked at the selection. 'It's

67

interesting,' she said. 'There's a good choice in both the starters and the main courses and they're quite light. That's important in a lunch menu. Most people have to put in an afternoon's work and if the meal's too heavy and there's wine involved then they're not going to get a whole lot done.'

'I agree with you. It's one of the things Chris and I argued about ... oh sorry, Liz. What a dumb thing to say.'

'It's okay, Steph. You say "one of the things" you argued about. Does that mean you argued a lot?'

Steph cursed herself for opening her big mouth. 'Well, lately we did. He thought I interfered too much. If I tried to discuss a menu, he'd tell me to concentrate on my job and leave the food to him.'

Liz winced. 'I can't believe he talked to you like that. Why didn't you tell me?'

'How could I talk to you of all people, Liz? You're his wife, for God's sake.'

'Was,' Liz corrected.

Steph opened her mouth to argue but shut up as she saw the waiter approach, pen poised.

'Ready to order, ladies?' he said with a thin, watery smile. They gave their order and as he turned to leave, Steph called him back.

'Yes?' he said abruptly.

'The wine?' Steph stared pointedly at the empty glasses

'Oh right. What did you want?'

Steph looked at him in frustration and repeated the order. Liz giggled at Steph's frustrated expression as he disappeared again. 'Maybe we should have just settled for a glass of the house wine.'

Steph grinned. 'The food better be good after all this.'

The waiter brought the wine. It was the wrong year but Steph decided to hold her tongue. They'd die of thirst if she sent him away again.

'Nice wine.' Liz emptied her glass.

Steph cringed. God, surely she wasn't going to take to the drink. 'Could be colder,' she replied, 'and it's overpriced. Anyway, what do you think of the place? I think the furniture is wrong.' She looked around the room. There were only two other parties in the restaurant. A table of four businessmen and a couple in a quiet corner who only had eyes for each other. She looked at the tableware. The glasses were good quality and a reasonable size but the cutlery was light and insubstantial – it wouldn't last long. Whoever had decked the place out was new to the business. It was put together on a budget and wasn't designed to last. But they'd got it right with the napkins and tablecloths. They were good quality linen.

Liz looked around her half-heartedly. 'I'd say it looks better at night. Anyway, forget about this place, tell me more about you and Chris.'

Steph fidgeted with her fork. Damn. She'd hoped Liz had forgotten that conversation. 'There's not much more to tell. He seemed to lose interest in the business. Profits have gone down in the last few months. That got me mad, then he got mad with me for pointing out his "inadequacies".'

Liz looked at her in dismay. 'The quality suffered? It was Chris's fault? But he seemed to be working so hard, he was never home – oh . . .' She trailed off, realising how Chris must have actually been spending his time. Her mouth set into a hard line.

COLETTE CADDLE

Steph rummaged for her cigarettes. She'd promised Chris she'd help and instead she was damning him.

'The quality suffered a bit,' she admitted, 'but there's been a lot more competition this year. Three new restaurants have opened in the last six months and they're hurting us. Anyway, I didn't help. I could have handled things better.' She hated herself for saying the words. She'd stopped blaming herself long ago for Chris's mistakes, but Liz didn't need to hear that.

She watched Liz as she fiddled nervously with her glass, lost in thought. She'd lost weight and looked drawn and tense. There was a fragile air about her. It reminded Steph of Ruth. She shivered.

Liz looked up absently as the waiter placed her salad of smoked chicken in front of her.

Steph leaned across to inspect. 'That looks good.' She'd opted for the soup.

Liz nodded, trying to appear interested. 'Yes. The colour's good and there isn't too much dressing. There's nothing worse than a soggy salad.' She popped a piece of chicken into her mouth. 'It's good. Very delicate and light.' She nodded appreciatively, though the food tasted like cardboard in her mouth. She chewed mechanically and pushed the plate towards Steph. 'Try some.'

Steph helped herself to a forkful of chicken and salad. 'That's great. You know, you almost sounded like a chef there. I can't remember the last time I heard you talk about food like that. Would you ever consider going back into the business?'

Liz shook her head dismissively. 'I never really thought about it.'

'You should,' Steph said firmly, sniffing the aroma

drifting up from her soup. 'You're a damn good chef and the challenge might do you good.'

'I don't know, Steph. I'm not ambitious like you. I only ever wanted to be happily married with a family.' She gave a harsh little laugh. 'I thought all women wanted what I wanted – husband, family, security. Security, that's a laugh. You must think I'm stupid.'

'Only sometimes,' Steph said with an affectionate smile. 'But you have a very interesting way of rewriting the past.'

'What do you mean?'

'You were always much more ambitious than me before Lucy came along. In fact if it wasn't for you, I'd probably be still in that bloody bank.'

'I suppose,' Liz agreed doubtfully. 'Will you ever marry Sean?' she asked abruptly. Personal tragedy allowed you to cut through the bull and ask all kinds of intimate questions.

Steph gulped, caught off-guard by the question. She laughed. 'I doubt it.'

'Don't you want children?' Liz persisted.

Steph froze. 'No, Liz, I don't.'

Liz cringed at the disgusted look on Steph's face. Annie was right. She really didn't know when to keep her mouth shut. 'How's the soup?' she asked for want of something better to say.

'Sorry?' Steph looked blank for a moment and then dutifully picked up her spoon. 'Oh, right, yes, it's very good actually. You know if they iron out the problems with the service, I think we could have some heavy competition on our hands.'

Liz looked at her sadly. Steph couldn't switch off long enough to discuss relationships, never mind have one. Maybe she should take Chris back. Life with him, whatever his behaviour, was infinitely better than the prospect of being alone.

'Who was that?' Tom West looked up from his newspaper as his wife came back in from the phone. He was a large, heavy-set man, with steel-grey hair, tanned skin and brown eyes. It was a year now since he'd handed over the reins of the business to Joe and his attention these days was focused on his garden and his golf.

'Stephanie. Good news.'

'She's marrying Sean?' he asked hopefully.

Catherine West rolled her eyes. 'Don't be silly, Tom.' She sat down gracefully in the chair opposite. She was a youthful sixty-four and it was obvious where Steph got her looks from. Catherine had the same incredible blue eyes, though hers had faded with the years. Her hair, once even blonder than her daughter's, was now darker and peppered with grey. She kept it in a neat bob, brushed back off her face. Her figure was slightly fuller these days, but she was still a very attractive woman.

Tom chuckled. 'Well, there's no harm hoping. So what is the news?'

'Chris has agreed to sell the restaurant to Stephanie.'

'I think she's mad. What does she want to take on a responsibility like that for? She should be saving Jack's money for a rainy day.'

'Don't you say that to her,' she warned. 'As long as she's happy, and she is.' For the moment, she added silently to herself.

'I won't, I won't. When's she coming down?'

'Probably not until Monday.'

'That Chris is a real slave driver. Though she'll be working even harder when she's her own boss.' He saw his wife's expression. 'Oh, Catherine, I'm proud of her, love, you know that, but I just wish she'd settle down a bit. She always seems to be on the go.'

Catherine nodded. She knew exactly how he felt. They'd always encouraged Steph in her ambitions but assumed that she'd marry one day and have a family as well. That was looking more and more unlikely. She sighed as she thought of her beautiful daughter. Not many people realised how insecure she really was. Ruth's death had had a terrible effect on her.

Catherine had been thrilled when Sean and Steph had got back together. No one understood Steph as well as he did. He knew her. He'd lived through that terrible time with her. Catherine had hoped that the years would have dimmed the memories, dealt with Steph's fears, that she'd be ready to settle down, but Stephanie seemed as determined as ever to remain single.

Tom looked at the sad expression on his wife's face. 'What's wrong?'

'Nothing. Would you like a cup of tea?' She stood up and headed for the kitchen.

'That would be nice, love.' He looked after her and shook his head. She could deny it all she wanted, but he knew she worried about Stephanie just as much as he did. Maybe Sean would convince her to marry him yet. He must call him when he got back from Arizona and organise a game of golf. Have a chat, man to man. He smiled, happy with the idea, and went back to his newspaper.

Steph walked briskly down Merrion Square towards Hennessy, McDermott & Wallace. Joe had suggested Edward as the man to sort out her legal affairs and Stephanie was more than happy to use her brother's friend. Especially when he was as good-looking and charming as Edward. She'd taken extra care with her appearance today, discarding several outfits before finally settling on a cherry-coloured suit with a tight fitting jacket and straight skirt that stopped just above the knee. She wanted to look smart, businesslike but feminine. It was obvious from Edward's dinner companion that night in L'Écrivain that he liked good-looking women.

'And what's that got to do with you?' said the small voice in her head. 'You want a lawyer, not a boyfriend.'

There's no harm in looking good though, she reasoned.

She ran up the steps of the imposing Georgian house and pressed the button on the intercom.

'Coffee?'

'Yes, please.' Steph smiled and looked around her with interest while Edward talked to his secretary. His office was more like a study, with a large mahogany desk that dominated the room and green leather chairs that were both large and comfortable. To contrast the heavy furniture, the curtains were cream with a green regency stripe and a cream rug lay in the centre of the polished wooden floor. The only decorations on the stark cream walls were Edward's framed qualifications and a large map of Dublin. Edward looked completely at home in his dark double-breasted suit, pale cream shirt and burgundy tie. His dark, wiry hair was short and Steph couldn't help wondering what he'd look like in a powdered wig and gown.

Edward's secretary arrived with a tray of delicate china and a steaming pot of coffee. Edward asked about Joe and Annie while he served her. When he settled back with his own cup, he turned the conversation to the business at hand.

'Our first priority is to set out the ground rules with Chris once you've taken over. I've drawn up a draft contract, based on what you've told me. You can take it away with you, see if it's okay. Have you hammered out the figures with Chris yet?'

Steph groaned. 'Yes, after a lot of bickering, smoking, moaning, more smoking . . .'

Steph told him the figure she'd agreed with Chris.

'Seems reasonable. And what about your loan?'

'Ah, well, that's not going so well. My esteemed bank manager is a little on the conservative side. He's not convinced that Conor will be up to the job. He's put off by his youth. I'm afraid his idea of a good restaurant is probably an all-you-can-eat steakhouse.'

Edward laughed. 'You're probably right. Bank managers are the last people to actually spend money. Have you thought of an alternative?'

Stephanie looked at him curiously. 'What do you mean?'

'Would you consider a silent partner?'

Steph laughed. 'I don't know anyone with that kind of money.'

'You do now,' Edward said quietly.

Steph's eyes widened. 'You?'

'Why not? I like to put my money into new enterprises.

It's a lot more satisfying than bonds or savings accounts. It would have nothing to do with Hennessy, McDermott & Wallace. It would be a personal investment. Why don't you think about it? Give me a call in a couple of days.'

Stephanie was lost for words. It would solve her problem and save her from grovelling to that small-minded bank manager. But what level of involvement would Edward want? She'd have to talk to Joe. 'I will, Edward,' she said finally. 'It's a very interesting proposition.'

An hour later she walked back across Merrion Square in a daze. It seemed she might have lost a lawyer but found a business partner. If it were possible, she'd prefer to run Chez Nous on her own, but there was no denying that a silent partner would make life a lot easier. And working with Edward McDermott – now there was a tantalising proposition!

Chapter Ten

L iz put down the receiver, exhausted. She seemed to spend her life on the phone lying to her mother, to Annie, to Steph. Yes, she was fine. No, she couldn't make lunch, she was visiting X.

X would be whoever she wasn't talking to. Her mother thought she'd spent yesterday with Steph. Annie thought she'd brought Lucy out for the day. Steph thought she was at a party in a neighbour's house tonight – that was a laugh! She hadn't mixed that much with her neighbours before but now that Chris was gone, she avoided them like the plague. She didn't need the third degree. She waved and smiled when she was coming or going, but she never stopped to talk.

Lucy peered over the banisters at her mother. Why had she told Granny that they were at Auntie Steph's yesterday? Lucy frowned. She'd better not ask or Mummy would shout at her. She missed her daddy, but the amount of time she spent in Auntie Annie's with Dani made up for it. She got to see her granny and granddad a lot more too. She loved going to Granny's house. There was always a special surprise for her. And Granddad showed her how to plant flowers in her very own little patch in the garden. It was strange how much she got to go out now that Daddy didn't live with them. And when she did see Daddy, he wasn't as grumpy as he used to be.

Everything would be fine if Mummy wasn't so sad. She hardly ever played games with her any more and she always smelled of cigarettes. She seemed to spend an awful lot of time sitting with the curtains drawn, watching TV and smoking. The television was always on and Mummy didn't seem to mind what Lucy watched as much as she used to.

'Lucy! Hurry up, we'll be late for school.' Liz pulled a jacket over her dirty jumper, and brushed her hair half-heartedly. She felt so tired. She'd go back to bed for a couple of hours after she'd dropped Lucy.

Liz cursed her luck. There was no parking outside the school. She wouldn't be able to drop Lucy. She'd have to park up the road and walk back with her. Please God, that nosy Miss Harvey wouldn't be at the gate. That's all she needed. She took Lucy's hand and walked briskly towards the school. At the gate, she gave her a quick peck, before turning and hurrying back towards the car.

'Liz?'

Liz froze and turned slowly, pinning a smile to her face. Edward McDermott was walking towards her, a wide smile on his handsome face.

'Edward, hi. I didn't know you had a child here.'

Edward laughed. 'Oh, I don't. It's my niece. I'm on a day off and my sister's not too well so I offered to do the school run.'

Liz looked from his immaculate beige chinos and

white polo shirt to the clothes she'd thrown on and cringed. Why the hell did she have to meet him looking like this? She forced a polite smile and turned back towards the car. 'Nice to see you again.'

He followed her. 'How about a quick coffee?'

She looked up in surprise. Why was this gorgeous man asking her out for coffee? God, she must look really pathetic. He felt sorry for her. He'd probably heard all about Chris. Her expression hardened. She didn't need pity. 'Maybe some other time.'

'I'll hold you to that.' He stood watching as she climbed hastily into her car.

She barely nodded before pulling the door shut and driving away much too fast. She was breathing very fast and was feeling almost tearful. What the hell was wrong with her? A man had asked her out for coffee and she'd panicked. She pulled into the driveway and ran for the door, her head down. Inside, she caught sight of herself in the hall mirror. God, she was a disgrace. Her hair was greasy and unkempt, her skin was grey and her eyes heavy. Damn it, she'd have to get rid of that bloody mirror. The phone rang and she walked past it up the stairs. When it stopped, she took it off the hook and rolled up in a ball on her bed. She wouldn't get in. She'd just lie down for half an hour. Then she'd have a shower and do the ironing.

Liz woke to the sound of the doorbell ringing persistently. Damn them, she thought. She looked at the alarm clock. Christ, it was one o'clock. Lucy! She scrambled out of bed and ran down the stairs. When she opened the door, Miss Harvey stood there with a tearful Lucy by the hand.

'Oh, Miss Harvey, I'm so sorry, you see I haven't been well and . . .'

Olive Harvey looked at the dishevelled Mrs Connolly, and the untidy kitchen in the background. 'I tried to ring, but it was engaged. You really should have contacted me,' she said, talking to Liz as if she was one of the four-year-olds she taught.

Liz bit back a retort. 'I'm terribly sorry, Miss Harvey. The phone doesn't seem to be working, and like I say, I haven't been too well. I fell asleep. It must have been the tablets the doctor gave me.' God, lies tripped off her tongue so easily these days! She muttered some more apologies and finally closed the door on the disapproving but slightly mollified teacher.

'Go and wash your hands, Lucy, and then we'll go to McDonald's.'

Lucy gave her a funny look. Mummy didn't approve of McDonald's, but they were going there an awful lot lately. 'But Mummy, maybe we shouldn't go out if you're sick.'

Liz hugged her daughter tightly, feeling truly sick about the worried look she'd put on her little girl's face. 'Now you're home, love, I feel much better. Would you prefer it if I made you a special lunch?'

Lucy nodded in delight. Mummy's food was always great. It was ages since she'd made anything nice. Beans on toast didn't count.

'Mummy, do you hate Daddy now?' Lucy asked later through a mouthful of pasta.

Liz paused in the middle of ironing Lucy's pink top and stared at her daughter in shock. 'No, love, of course

I don't. Daddy and me are just angry with each other at the moment. It's nothing for you to worry about. I love you and Daddy loves you.'

Lucy wasn't satisfied. 'But Mummy, when is Daddy coming home?'

Liz sighed. If Lucy was like this at four, what would she be like when she was a teenager? 'I don't know, love.'

'Doesn't he want to live with us any more?'

'Yes, he does, pet, but I don't want him to live here at the moment.'

Lucy stuck her lip out, a sure sign that she was ready to throw a tantrum.

'Listen, love. Grown-ups have rows sometimes. It's better that Daddy's not here right now, because we'd only fight. You wouldn't like that, would you?'

Lucy shook her head reluctantly. 'But why would you fight?'

Liz was losing her patience. 'We just would. It's nothing for you to worry about, Lucy. Now finish your lunch.' Liz picked up her coffee and went into the living-room. She switched on the TV and lit a cigarette, the ironing forgotten.

Steph brought the tray of coffee over to Joe and Edward and sat down to join them. It was just gone three and there was only one other party left in the restaurant.

Edward looked up and smiled. 'That was a lovely lunch, Stephanie. Who was responsible for the rack of lamb?'

'Conor,' she said, delighted that he was pleased. 'I'll give him a shout in a few minutes and introduce you.'

'Is Chris about?' Joe asked.

'No, he's headed off for the afternoon. Probably banging on Liz's door as we speak.'

'She still hasn't talked to him?' Joe was surprised. He'd thought Liz would cave in much sooner than this.

'Nope. She talks to him about Lucy, but that's it.'

'How's she coping?' Edward asked lightly.

Steph shrugged. 'Not well although she'd never admit it. I'm very worried about her but I don't know what to do. Any ideas?'

'There's nothing you can do, Steph, until she's ready to talk,' Joe told her. 'Don't you think so, Edward?'

'What? Sorry, I was miles away.'

'I was just saying to Steph that Liz will talk when she's ready.'

'Yes, I'm sure your right. Different people handle things in different ways. Liz might need to be alone right now. Don't worry too much, Steph.'

'Easier said than done,' Steph said with a heavy sigh. 'Anyway. We need to go over the contracts before we get Chris to sign. How are you two fixed on Saturday afternoon? We could work in my place.'

Joe nodded. 'Fine, but aren't you working?'

'Nope,' she said happily. 'I'm off for a full week. So come out to my place around two. We should have it all wrapped up within a couple of hours. Is that okay, Edward?'

'No problem.'

Joe stood up. 'Well, I'd better be getting back. Can I give you a lift, Edward?'

'That's okay, Joe. I'll walk. It's the only exercise I get these days.'

Steph looked at his athletic frame and thought otherwise. After Joe left she offered Edward more coffee.

'Yes please. I'm not in any rush.'

Steph returned his smile. God, he really was gorgeous.
His eyes were the strangest colour. They appeared to be
grey but sometimes they looked almost brown. She wondered why he was hanging on? Maybe he was going to
ask her out! Oh but she couldn't – what about Sean?

'Do you think Liz will take Chris back?' he broke in
on her thoughts.

'I don't know, Edward, but either way, I believe Chris
will go to Galway. Don't worry, he won't back out of
the deal.'

Edward smiled at the reassurance. 'I'm sure he won't.
Now why don't you introduce me to Conor? I can't wait
to meet our new head chef.'

'Oh okay.' Steph struggled to hide her disappointment. She thought that they'd have a little time together
alone. 'I'll go and find him. Won't be long.'

Edward and Conor hit it off immediately. Edward
asked intelligent questions about Conor's training, and
Conor answered enthusiastically, glad of the interest.
Stephanie left them together and went up to the office.
She was a bit nervous about how fast things were moving.
Now that Edward was her partner, and Chris had agreed
to stay on, there was nothing to stop the deal going
through. She hadn't expected things to go quite this
smoothly. She hoped it wasn't the calm before the
storm. She still hadn't told Sean what was happening.
Any time they'd talked, one of them had been interrupted and despite all her good intentions, she hadn't
had the heart-to-heart with him she'd been promising
herself.

Edward poked his head around the door. 'I'm off now. See you on Saturday?'

'See you,' she called brightly and then slumped back in her chair. So much for asking you out, big head! He's only after you for your restaurant!

Chapter Eleven

Stephanie brushed the hair back off her face impatiently and reached absently for her cigarettes. She was sitting cross-legged in the middle of her sitting room floor surrounded by files and papers. In her faded denims and white cotton shirt she looked more like a teenager than a successful businesswoman. Edward and Joe were at the dining-room table in the alcove, heads bent over a document.

Stephanie reached for her mug and took a mouthful of tepid liquid. She winced. 'Are you ready for more coffee?' She stood up and stretched, massaging the crick in her neck that seemed to be permanent these days.

Edward looked up at her, his eyes raking her long slender frame appreciatively. 'No. I've got a better idea. Let's go for a pint. I think we deserve one.'

'We certainly do,' Steph said lightly, but she could feel the flush on her skin.

Joe, oblivious to them both, tapped mercilessly at his calculator.

Edward gave him a dig in the ribs. 'What about it, Joe? A pint?'

'What? Oh, no. You two go on. I have to get my head around this. I won't be happy until I'm finished.'

'Steph?'

'Yeah, why not? Just let me get some shoes on.' She hurried off to the bedroom, put on her desert boots, grabbed a sweatshirt and checked herself in the mirror. She could do with touching up her lipstick but she resisted. They were, after all, only going to the local for a pint.

'You won't be able to wear gear like that for much longer,' Edward warned as she returned to the sitting room. 'You'll have to wear little designer numbers when you're a famous restaurateur and the paparazzi want to come out and photograph you at home.'

Stephanie looked around ruefully. 'I'll have to decorate the place first. It wouldn't do much for my image if they saw it at the moment.'

'I like it as it is.' Edward looked around the airy, peaches and cream room. It was decorated with comfort in mind. The large sofa was inviting and cushions in a variety of pastel shades crowded it and the matching armchair. Apart from the suite the only furniture was a coffee table and a sleek black-ash dining room suite. Sunshine flooded in from the balcony window, casting a warm golden glow throughout the room. The overall effect was one of comfort and space.

Steph grinned. 'It has that lived in look! Now are you buying me that drink or not? Sure you won't come, Joe?'

Joe muttered something unintelligible.

'Come on, Steph. Let's leave him to it. He won't even notice we're gone.'

The phone rang just after they left. After ignoring it for a few rings, Joe remembered he was alone and picked up the receiver.

'Hello?'

'Hello? Joe? Is that you?'

'Sean?'

'Yeah, that's right. Don't tell me I'm getting an American accent?'

'Ah, no. There's a bit of Dub there yet. So how are things going in Arizona?'

'Really taking off, Joe, I'm glad to say. A few teething troubles, but I suppose that's to be expected.'

'Oh sure. You're better off having them now than later.'

'Yeah, you're right. Listen, this is costing me a fortune. Can I have a word with Steph?'

'Oh, sorry, Sean. She's just gone to the pub with Edward.'

'Who?'

Joe hesitated. 'Edward, a mate of mine. He's a lawyer. Steph's new partner?'

'Partner?' Sean echoed.

Joe groaned inwardly. He was in way over his head here. He'd kill Steph. 'Look, sorry, Sean, I have to run. I'll get Steph to call you later. I'm sure she's dying to tell you everything herself. Bye now. Look after yourself.' Joe rang off and sighed heavily.

'Hello? Hello? Joe?'

Sean took the phone from his ear and looked at it in bewilderment. What was going on? What kind of partnership was he talking about and why had Steph not told him about it? And why was she down in the pub on a Saturday afternoon with a lawyer called Edward? Who the hell was he? He wandered over to the window of his apartment. A pale morning haze hung over Phoenix and the sun was making its first appearance, promising another beautiful day. He'd been looking forward to going home but now he was beginning to wonder if he should bother. Steph certainly didn't seem to be missing him too much.

Edward negotiated his way through Gibney's, zigzagging through the rugby buffs. He placed Steph's lager in front of her and settled his pint carefully beside it.

'Is it always like this?' he said looking around.

Steph grinned. 'Nah. Usually it's busy.'

'I must be getting old,' Edward said with a wry smile.

'Come back after eight and you'll feel positively ancient! So tell me. Are you happy with the progress we're making?'

Edward took a gulp of his pint and nodded. 'Yes, I'm very happy. What about Conor? How's he adapting to the whole idea?'

'He's chuffed. When he isn't cooking, he's studying. He's spent a fortune on all the latest cookery books. I should really reimburse him.'

'Absolutely. When does he head over to London?'

'Next week.' Steph had been delighted that the great chef Albert Roux had agreed to take Conor under his wing for a few weeks. It would be wonderful experience for Conor and the lad had been on cloud nine ever since Steph had told him the good news. When he finished his stint in London, he'd be going to work in Belfast with Paul Rankin for a while. 'He's thrilled,' she told Edward now. 'And our timing was perfect for him. He'd been getting very depressed and thinking of leaving. He has so much talent and enthusiasm but Chris just kept closing him down.'

'A bit like he closed you down?' Edward asked quietly.

'I suppose so. Still, that's water under the bridge. Tell me something about Edward McDermott. We're partners now and I hardly know a thing about you, except that you're Joe's friend and you're a lawyer.'

'Have dinner with me tonight and I'll tell you my life story.'

Stephanie flushed. 'Will you tell me absolutely everything I want to know?'

He put his hand to his heart. 'I shall withhold nothing.'

'Fair enough. But there's just one condition,' Steph said with a teasing smile. 'I pick the restaurant.'

He looked at her in mock horror. 'You're not going to bankrupt me, are you?'

'Eh, no, not quite.'

'Then it's a date.'

Joe raised his head as the door opened. 'Sean's looking for you. He seems a bit . . . in the dark about things.'

Stephanie smiled brightly. 'No problem, I'll call him later. Now I want you two to get out of here. Annie will be furious with you, Joe. I appreciate all the work, but I don't want to be the cause of a divorce.'

Joe looked at his watch and sprang up. 'Jesus, I'd no idea it was so late. Come on, Edward, she'll kill me.'

'Okay, okay, don't panic.' Edward gathered up his

papers, slid them into his briefcase and followed Joe to the door. 'Pick you up about eight, Steph?'

'Eh, yeah, great,' she said, avoiding her brother's questioning stare. 'Thanks again, bye now.' She hustled the two men out and leaned against the door with a groan. Time to face the music. She picked up the phone and put it down again. Just a little Dutch courage. She went out to the kitchen and poured a glass of wine. She took a sip from the glass and dialled.

'Hello – Sean Adams. Sorry I'm not in right now. Leave a message after the tone.'

'Sean, it's me, Stephanie. Eh, sorry I missed you earlier. It's – eh – six thirty here, eh – talk to you later. Bye.'

Two hours later, as she walked down the steps to the car, laughing and talking with Edward, her telephone rang and the answering machine kicked in.

'Hi Stephanie, it's Sean. We seem to keep missing each other. I had no idea you were so busy. I'll try calling you at Joe's, if not I'll speak to you tomorrow. Bye.'

'Ruth! Who's he?' Stephanie strained to get a good look at the man standing at the door.

Ruth looked around. 'Oh, that's Sean. Sean Adams. Nice, isn't he?'

'Nice? Nice? He's gorgeous! Introduce me, but make it look casual. Well, go on!' she urged.

Ruth knew she'd get no peace if she didn't so she pushed her way through the crowd. 'Hiya, Sean,' she shouted over the noise of Led Zeppelin. 'Thanks for coming. I think you know everyone. Follow me and I'll get you a drink.'

'Howya, Ruth,' Sean grinned at her and proffered a six-pack. 'I brought some of my own.'

'Good man, but let me get you a cold one,' Ruth said as she crashed into Stephanie. 'Oh sorry, Steph. Didn't see you there. Have you two met?'

Steph looked up into a pair of gorgeous twinkling brown eyes and felt weak at the knees. 'I don't think so,' she said, smiling up at him. She was quite tall at five foot seven, but he still seemed to tower over her.

'Believe me, we haven't,' Sean murmured.

Ruth looked from one to the other and grinned. 'I'll get you that drink, Sean.' He didn't appear to hear her.

'I haven't seen you around the campus,' Sean said.

'Oh, I'm not a student. God forbid! I'm a working woman.'

'Really? What do you do?'

'I'm in the bank.'

'That sounds interesting. What do you do there?'

'Well, I'm usually on the front desk. Either at the cashier's desk or in the foreign exchange.'

'They must think very highly of you, to give you such responsibility at your age,' he said, his eyes full of admiration.

'Oh, I don't know,' Steph said, flushed with embarrassment and pleasure.

Ruth returned with Sean's drink. God, they really had it bad. Sean hardly noticed the can being shoved into his hand.

'Are you studying computer science too?' Steph thought it only polite to ask.

'Yeah. Ruth's in my year. She's a great girl. Definitely going to be top of the class. I'll probably get through by the skin of my teeth.'

Steph nodded sympathetically. 'That's the way I was at

school. I don't know how you could go on and do another four years of studying. It would kill me.'

'I'm sure you'd be great at anything you tried to do,' Sean murmured, moving closer. 'Has anyone ever told you that you have the most amazing eyes?'

Steph looked up into his face thinking his weren't so bad either. Chocolate brown, melting. They were certainly making her hot!

'It's hard to talk with all this noise, isn't it?' His mouth was almost touching her ear. 'Want to go somewhere a bit quieter?'

Steph felt her heartbeat quicken. 'That would be nice.'

'Where are you off to?' Ruth asked as she saw Stephanie sling her bag over her shoulder and head for the door.

Stephanie smiled dreamily at her. 'Just going somewhere a bit quieter. Where we can talk, you know?'

'Talk, huh?'

'He's okay, isn't he?' Steph asked anxiously. 'Not an axe-murderer, or anything?'

'Not that I know of,' Ruth said drily. 'No, seriously, he's a great guy. You could do a lot worse.'

Steph winked happily. 'I'll call you tomorrow.'

'You'd better,' threatened Ruth and then went off in search of the dishy history student who answered to the name of Trev.

Steph snuggled up to Sean on the sofa in his bedsit. 'Happy anniversary,' she whispered and kissed him on the ear.

'It's our anniversary?' he asked, raising an eyebrow.

'Yup. We've been going out together two and a half months.'

'Oh well, in that case we'd better do something to cele-brate. Any ideas?' He swung her onto his lap and kissed her slowly.

Steph drew back. '*Mmmnn. That's one idea, or we could go out.*'

'*Where?*'

'*Well, the gang are meeting up in the Baggot Inn.*'

'*The gang?*' he asked suspiciously. '*Would that consist of Ruth and Des Healy by any chance?*'

'*Oh, Sean, I know he's a pain, but what can I do? Ruth's my best friend.*'

'*For a clever girl, she sure has lousy taste in men. I thought Trev was bad enough. At least he was just a druggie. But Des Healy is such a prat. If I have to spend one more night listening to him talk about that damn car of his and all the commission he makes ... But you never see him put his hand in his pocket.*' He broke off as he saw Steph's expression. '*Oh, go on then. Just keep him away from me.*'

Steph hugged him fiercely. '*You are the best, Sean Adams. You know that?*'

'*It's true,*' he agreed.

'*Steph, over here.*'

Steph and Sean pushed their way through the crowd.

'*Hiya, Ruth.*'

'*Hi.*'

'*Howya, Ruth. Is Des getting the drinks, then?*' Sean ignored Steph's warning look.

'*No, Sean. He couldn't make it.*'

He grinned broadly. '*Ah, that's too bad.*'

'*No, he had important business down the country.*'

'*What else?*' Sean muttered with a meaningful glance at Steph. '*I'll get the drinks, then. Harp okay, Steph? Same again for you, Ruth? Right. Back in a minute.*'

93

Steph pulled off her coat and scarf and pulled up a stool beside Ruth. 'Well?'

'Well what?' Ruth asked.

'You and Des. Is everything okay?'

'Of course. I told you. He's away on business.'

'He seems to be away an awful lot.'

'What's that supposed to mean?' Ruth asked hotly.

'Nothing. Just saying. Is anybody else coming?'

'Robbie, Richard and Karen said they'd be here,' Ruth replied.

'Great,' Steph said brightly. Good. She'd get Sean to herself for a while after all.

Chapter Twelve

'Stephanie. How are you? Good to see you.'

'You too, Tony,' Steph noted the waiter's curiosity. Maybe it had been a mistake to take Edward to Lorenzo's.

'Your table isn't quite ready. Why don't you – and your friend – take a seat at the bar. I'll get some menus.'

Edward nodded. 'Yes, that's fine. What would you like to drink, Steph?'

'I think I'll have a Bloody Mary.' Steph climbed onto the high stool and thanked God that she hadn't worn her lycra mini-dress after all. Especially when Edward arrived in a smart navy blazer, lemon Calvin Klein shirt and beige chinos. She'd finally decided to wear her blue silk sarong that reached to her ankles.

'A Bloody Mary and a gin and tonic, please.'

'Certainly, sir.' Tony handed them the menus and went to get the drinks.

Edward bent his head towards Steph's. 'Is it my imagination or is there a certain "atmosphere" between you two?'

Steph laughed. 'Don't mind Tony. We go back a long way. I told him you were a business partner, but he obviously doesn't believe me.'

'Is that all I am?' Edward pretended to look offended.

Steph laughed with him but nevertheless could feel her cheeks getting hot. Damn, you weren't supposed to blush when you were in your thirties. But she seemed to do nothing else when Edward McDermott was around. She fumbled in her bag for cigarettes. 'Well, like I said, Edward, I hardly know a thing about you. So until you fill me in I'll have to reserve judgement.'

'I see I'm not going to be let off the hook but at least let's order first.'

They turned their attention to the menu and Stephanie started to relax as they discussed the food and made their choices.

They had almost finished their drinks when Tony approached, eyes twinkling. 'If you'd like to follow me?' He led the way upstairs and showed them to a table in a dark corner, avoiding Steph's eyes as he held out her chair. 'Enjoy your meal.'

When he left, Stephanie rolled her eyes. 'I'm sorry about this.'

'I'm flattered that he sees us as a couple.'

'Thank you,' Steph said, wishing she could read his thoughts for he seemed to say everything with a twinkle in his eye and a twitch of the lips. Was he just amusing himself or did he fancy her?

'This is a nice place.'

'Isn't it? I always thought it had a nice cosy atmosphere. And with the exception of Tony, the staff are very efficient and discreet.'

'You really love this business, don't you?'

Steph smiled. 'Sorry, am I boring you?'

'Not at all. It's nice to meet someone who enjoys what they do.'

'Do you? Enjoy your work, I mean.'

Edward considered the question. 'I suppose I do. Though not as much as I did when I first qualified.'

'You mean when you were broke and had to work ridiculously long hours?' Steph said incredulously.

Edward threw his head back and laughed. 'It does sound ridiculous when you put it like that. But in those days I thought I could change the world.'

'And now?'

His smile faded. 'Now, I'm not so sure it's worth the effort.'

A waitress interrupted them to take their orders.

'What did Annie say about me?' Edward asked when she'd left.

'Why do you ask?'

Edward smiled. 'Sometimes I get the feeling that she doesn't quite approve of me.'

Steph laughed. 'You're imagining it! Although she's probably not that keen on you hanging around with Joe.'

Edward looked wounded. 'Why not? I'm a nice guy.'

'A nice guy who's single, has a hectic social life and always has a beautiful woman on his arm.'

'Well, the last part is certainly true tonight,' he murmured.

Stephanie blinked. Was he actually coming on to her? She smiled coolly. 'So tell me something about Edward McDermott.'

'It's all quite boring, I'm afraid. My folks moved to Liverpool just after they got married. Both my sister and I were born there and then we came back to Dublin when I was ten.'

'Whereabouts did you live?'

'Terenure.'

'A south-sider!' Stephanie said in disgust.

'You are too, surely, or do you call yourself a Wicklow woman?'

Stephanie shook her head vehemently. 'Neither. Mam and Dad only moved to Wicklow when Dad retired. I was born and bred in Clontarf. Just up the road from here.'

'Oh. I didn't realise. Joe was in a flat by the time I met him, so I presumed . . .'

'Nope. North-side, born and bred. What did your dad do?'

Edward smiled apologetically. 'He was a lawyer too. You see I told you it was boring. It was taken for granted that I'd follow in his footsteps.'

He broke off as their starters arrived. Bruschetta for him and tiger prawns in a garlic and chilli sauce for her.

Steph eyed the food appreciatively. 'This is what I love about Lorenzo's. Proof that it isn't necessary to pay a king's ransom to get a good meal in Dublin.'

'That's good coming from the owner of one of the most expensive restaurants in the city!' he retorted with a laugh.

'Oh, you know what I mean. This is good, simple food for a reasonable price. No frills, no gimmicks, just good value.'

Edward bit into his bruschetta. 'Well, it certainly tastes good.'

Steph smiled triumphantly. 'Anyway. You were about to tell me about the juicier parts of your past,' she prompted.

'I was?' Edward prevaricated taking a sip of his wine.

'Oh, come on, partner. You know all there is to know about me,' Steph complained.

'Do I? Well, there isn't much more to say. I live alone with my two dogs. I visit my parents regularly – who still live in Terenure. I see a fair bit of my sister too. Oh, and I love rugby.'

'Isn't there anyone . . . special?' Steph asked, emboldened by the wine.

'No one,' Edward replied shortly, his eyes on his food.

'I'm sorry. Have I overstepped the mark?'

He looked up, almost surprised to see her there. 'No, no, of course not. I'm sorry. There was a girl – a very long time ago – but it didn't work out.'

'And you never met anyone else? What about the gorgeous redhead you were with in L'Écrivain?'

Edward looked blank for a moment. 'Oh, Gayle. She's just a friend. We keep each other company when she's between boyfriends, nothing serious. I'm not interested in getting involved.'

'I don't blame you,' Steph agreed drily.

'That sounds a bit cynical. What about Sean?'

Steph sighed. 'Sean's wonderful and we've known each other for years, but . . .'

'But?'

She shrugged feeling a bit uncomfortable and guilty discussing Sean like this.

'The restaurant's very important to you, isn't it?'

'Yes. It's an opportunity to turn things around and make something of my life.'

'And you don't think Sean would approve of you taking it on?'

'Oh no, I think he'll be very happy for me when I

eventually get around to telling him. It's not quite that simple.'

'Tell me,' Edward persisted topping up her glass.

Steph took a long drink. 'Well, you see, I'm happy the way things are right now. But I don't think he is.'

'He wants to marry you?'

She nodded, and was surprised to find tears pricking the back of her eyes. 'And I'm not really interested in being a wife or a mother. I don't think I ever will be.' She pulled out a tissue and blew her nose noisily. 'How did we get onto this? You're supposed to be telling me all about you, and instead, I'm the one spilling my guts.'

He smiled. 'It's my charm. No woman can resist it.'

'Modest, aren't we?'

'Me? Never!'

'Seriously, Edward. Thank you for this evening. It seems ages since I've had such a good time.'

'Glad to be of service.' He bowed solemnly and leaned forward, his eyes suddenly serious. 'I want this partnership to work, Stephanie. I want you to feel that you can come to me about anything. I won't interfere, but I'm there if you need me.'

Oh, dear, Steph thought ruefully, it seems I have another big brother. 'Thanks, Edward. I do appreciate that.'

He nodded contentedly and sat back. 'So tell me, how did someone who started out in a bank end up running a restaurant?'

'It was all down to pure luck and a good friend,' Steph laughed. 'I hadn't a clue what I wanted to do when I left school so I just applied for everything and ended up in the Allied Bank in town. That's how I met Annie. She started at the same time.'

'Oh, so *you* introduced her and Joe.'

Steph nodded, grinning. 'Just call me Cupid.'

'How did you meet Liz and Chris?' he asked casually.

'Liz and Annie grew up together,' she explained. 'A whole gang of us used to go to the rugby club dances every weekend and Liz, Annie and I always seemed to end up together. Liz was working in the Burlington hotel then and doing very well for herself. Then she met Chris on a training course.'

'Did you like him then?'

'He was okay,' Steph admitted. 'And he was nuts about Liz. They were married within two years and almost immediately decided to go out on their own.'

'And where did you come in?'

'Well, after a few months, Liz realised they couldn't possibly cook and handle all the admin work too. She knew I was totally bored in the bank, took a risk and asked me to come and work for them. I owe her so much.'

The main courses were set in front of them and they admired each other's plates before Edward finally returned to the conversation. 'And you liked working in the restaurant?'

'I took to it like a duck to water. It was like coming home. I loved the thought of being responsible for someone's enjoyment for a couple of hours. To feed them, help them to relax and then see them come back for more.' She looked up at him, slightly embarrassed. 'I'm afraid I don't explain it very well.'

Edward shook his head. 'You explain it very well indeed. It's a pity more restaurateurs don't feel as passionately about the business as you do.'

Steph smiled. 'That's the first time I've been called a restaurateur. I think I like it.'

'Good. It suits you. I look forward to working with you, partner.'

She smiled happily. 'Me too.'

Chapter Thirteen

'Sean? Sean, hi, it's me.'
  'Steph? Hi, thanks for getting back to me.'
Odd reply, she thought. You'd think she was a stranger. She decided to ignore it. 'Sorry I missed you yesterday – things are hectic here. I've got so much to tell you.'
'Really?' Sean sounded slightly mollified. 'I'm glad you're paying for the call so.'
Steph was relieved to hear the lighter note in his voice. 'I don't know where to begin. I haven't said anything before because, well, because I didn't know how you'd react. I thought you'd give me a hard time. Look, the fact is I'm buying Chris out. Me and Edward McDermott, that is. He's a lawyer and a good friend of Joe's.'
'But that's great! Why did you think I'd have a go at you?'
'I don't know. You wanted me to leave and I wanted to stick with the job. Then it turned out Chris was thinking of moving on anyway, so everything has kind of fallen into place.'
She told him about their progress and the plans for Conor's training in other restaurants.
'He's working his butt off already. Wait till you taste

some of his new dishes,' she told him. 'My mouth waters just thinking about them.'

'He must be over the moon. It's a great opportunity for someone so young.'

'Yes, he's delighted. We're hoping that will attract some good publicity. You know the sort of thing. Young, trendy, progressive.' She went on to give him a brief history of Edward's involvement and referred casually to their business dinner the previous night.

There was silence at the other end of the phone.

'So it was just the two of you?' Sean said finally.

'Yeah, Joe wasn't in the mood,' she lied. She had nothing to hide – as it turned out – but it was easier.

'Right. And this guy's come up with thirty per cent of the capital?'

'That's right.'

'Where did he get that kind of money? It's not the sort of thing you'd think a lawyer would want to invest in, is it?'

'He's very successful, Sean. I suppose he earned it. Anyway, why wouldn't he want to invest in a well-known restaurant?'

'Why didn't you ask me? I could have put you in touch with a potential investor. I've plenty of contacts. Have you checked this guy out?'

Stephanie was getting impatient. 'I told you, Sean. He's a friend of Joe's.'

'I've never heard Joe mention him before,' he remarked.

'Why would he? Look, they've known each other since college.' She paused but he said nothing. She continued more gently. 'I'm sorry I didn't tell you, but I didn't think you'd take me seriously. I thought you'd try to put me off and I couldn't handle that.'

There was another pause and she could almost see him raking his fingers through his hair, a habit of his when he was frustrated.

'I don't know why you'd even think that,' he said eventually. 'I only asked you to leave Chez Nous because you were cracking up before my eyes.'

'I know, love. I'm sorry. And you're right. I was cracking up. But I just couldn't have given up and walked away.'

Sean sighed. 'You're something else, you know that?'

Steph laughed. 'I know. Look, Sean, I'm really excited about this. I've never been so sure I was doing the right thing as I am now.'

'Then that's all that's important. Look, I've got to go. I have a meeting in five minutes. I'll call you tomorrow.'

'Okay.'

'Oh, by the way. I knew I'd something else to tell you. I'm coming home on Wednesday morning.'

'Oh, Sean, that's brilliant!'

'I'm glad you think so. Any chance of you taking the night off?'

'I'm actually off all week. Are you sure you won't be too tired after the flight, though?'

'Well, if I am, we could always have an early night.'

Steph smiled. 'I suppose we could.'

'Okay love, I'll talk to you tomorrow.'

'Bye Sean . . . and Sean?'

'Yeah?'

'I love you.'

'I love you too. Take care.'

The following morning, Stephanie was up early, moving quickly around the apartment tidying, polishing and scrubbing. She sang along with the radio as she worked. The windows and doors were thrown open to allow in the sunshine and sea air and washing swung on the line on the balcony.

Annie stood in the doorway, mesmerised by her sister-in-law's vitality and good humour. Steph was balancing on the windowsill, hanging on to the window frame with one hand and polishing furiously with the other. Her face was flushed with the effort and she hadn't noticed Annie. In her T-shirt and cut-off jeans she looked about sixteen.

'Any chance of you coming over and starting on my place when you're done here?' Annie put a hand up to steady Steph as she swayed precariously. 'Sorry. Didn't mean to startle you.'

'That's okay.' Stephanie climbed down and brushed her hands off on the seat of her jeans. 'Coffee?' She headed for the kitchen.

Annie followed. 'Just a quick one. I'm on my way round to Mam's. I was just wondering how things went with Edward on Saturday night.'

Stephanie put on the coffee and took two mugs from a shelf. 'Edward and I had a lovely evening.'

'Oh?'

Steph looked at Annie in amusement. 'Oh? Oh what? We had a nice evening, he's a nice man and I think we're going to make a good team. Working team,' she added hastily when she saw Annie's expression.

'Any word from Sean?' Annie asked innocently.

'Yes, as it happens. I was talking to him last night. He's coming home on Wednesday.'

'And what about Edward?'

Stephanie looked confused. 'What about him?'

'Did he see you home?' Annie persisted.

Steph wagged a finger at her. 'He dropped me off in a taxi. You've a dirty mind, Annie West!'

'Just asking.'

'The only things that interest me about Edward are his contacts and his money. Anyway, he's not interested in me either. Determined to remain footloose and fancy free and good luck to him.'

'Aren't you going in to the restaurant today? Joe says you've been working morning, noon and night lately.'

'I have and for that very reason I am taking this week off.'

'Wonders will never cease,' Annie said drily. 'So what are you planning to do?'

'I thought I'd go down to Wicklow this evening. I haven't seen the folks for a while.'

Annie eyed her suspiciously. 'And what about Sean?'

'I'm seeing him on Wednesday evening,' Steph conceded with a grin.

'Why don't you hit the road now, while you've got the light?'

Steph shook her head. 'No. Liz is coming to lunch. I've been trying to get together with her for weeks, but she always seems to find an excuse. Why don't you stay?'

Annie groaned. 'Oh, I wish I could but my mother's expecting me. I said I'd take her to town. She needs some curtains. Damn it, I would have liked to see Liz. How does she seem to you lately?'

Steph shrugged. 'I can't really figure her out. To be honest I think she's been avoiding me. I'm still in shock that she agreed to come over today.'

Annie drained her cup, one eye on her watch. 'Well, try and talk to her.'

'I will but I doubt if I'll get very far. If I even mention Chris she changes the subject.'

'And how is Chris?'

'Keeping out of my hair, thank God. He seems genuinely upset about Liz, but then, you never know with Chris.'

Annie stood up. 'Well, I'd better go. Tell Liz I was asking for her and give my love to your folks. Tell them we'll be down next week.'

Liz drove her Fiesta slowly and reluctantly along the Malahide Road. She'd racked her brains for excuses not to come out today, but Stephanie knew that Chris would be collecting Lucy from school – as he did every Monday when the restaurant was closed – and she'd be spending the rest of the day with him. So she had no excuses and there was no way out. She didn't want to get into any heavy conversations about her marriage at the moment. Mind you, Steph would probably take the hint. She hated being questioned about Sean. With Annie it was harder. She knew exactly how her mind worked and what questions to ask. Liz didn't think Annie would be too impressed with the way her mind was working lately. She was thinking of taking Chris back. What else could she do? How would she ever manage on her own? Lucy needed her daddy. The thought of resuming her life with Chris seemed almost attractive after the last couple of months. It would be easier if he came back. He wasn't perfect, he never would be and she'd never trust him again. But he was better than nothing.

She pulled up outside Steph's apartment. As she grabbed the wine and got out of the car Steph ran down the steps to meet her. She'd changed out of her jeans and into a lemon shift mini-dress and looked vibrant and pretty. Liz's heart sank even further.

'Hiya.' Steph threw her arms around Liz, then stepped back to examine her friend. Liz's dark eyes looked huge in her face and she'd lost weight. She'd taken care with her appearance though. A white shirt and flowery silk skirt showed off her slimmer figure and her bare legs already boasted a light tan. She'd even applied some eyeshadow and lipstick. But Steph's overall impression was one of a sad and fragile woman. 'You look well,' she lied. 'How are things?'

'Pretty good, Steph. Pretty good,' Liz lied back.

'Great. Look, I hope you're hungry. I've cooked way too much.'

'I'm starving,' Liz lied again and followed Steph into the kitchen. 'Smells good.' She sniffed the air appreciatively and forced a bright smile.

'Chicken kebabs, new potatoes and salad.'

'Lovely. Want me to do anything?'

'Just open the wine. There's a bottle of Macon Lugny in the fridge. That should be colder than yours.'

Liz took the bottle from the fridge, replacing it with the one she'd brought. 'Mine will be cold enough by the time we've finished this one.'

Steph laughed. 'Oh, dear. It's going to be *that* kind of an afternoon, is it? You're a very bad influence on me. I hope you realise that I wouldn't normally take a drink at this hour of the day. I'm just being polite.'

Liz pointed up at the ceiling. 'Look! There goes that pig again. Where are the glasses?'

'Outside. It was such a nice day, I set the table on the balcony.'

'Excellent.' Liz went outside with the wine. Small dinghies bobbed on the water. Two little boys played chasing along the promenade and a young girl was stretched out on a rock, her blouse tucked up to expose white skin to the sun. Liz sighed. Oh, to be young again without a care in the world! She poured the wine and carried the glasses back to the kitchen. 'You're so lucky to live beside the sea. I'd love to wake up to a view like this every day.'

Steph took her glass. 'It is lovely, isn't it? Right, I just have to make the salad dressing and then we're ready to eat. You go and enjoy the sunshine. I'll be there in a minute.'

Liz went back outside. It was still early in the year and the breeze was cool, but the balcony was sheltered and bathed in sunshine. It was the kind of day that made you feel optimistic, she thought as she stared miserably out to sea. But it wasn't working.

'Are you all right?'

Liz looked up to see Steph standing over her with two plates of food. 'Yeah, sure.'

Steph set the food down and looked worriedly over at her friend.

Liz caught Steph watching her and smiled. 'This looks great. Gosh, I could eat a horse!' She prayed that Steph wouldn't offer her a shoulder to cry on or she'd burst into tears for sure. She seemed to do that a lot lately.

Steph sensed her mood and changed the subject. 'Sean's home on Wednesday.'

'Oh, that's great, Steph . . . isn't it?'

Steph laughed 'Yeah, I've really missed him. Do you

know Annie thought I had my eye on Edward? Just because we had dinner together.'

'Well, didn't you?' Liz said shrewdly.

Steph smiled guiltily. 'Well, maybe it did cross my mind, but not seriously. Sean's my man and probably the only one who'd put up with me.'

'True.'

'Well thanks! You're as bad as Annie!'

Liz smiled. 'What do you think of Edward?' She hadn't told Annie or Stephanie about bumping into him and he obviously hadn't mentioned it either. But then he'd probably forgotten.

Steph thought about it. 'He's very suave, well-read and awfully sophisticated.'

'It sounds like he just stepped out of a Mills and Boon novel.'

'Exactly!' Steph agreed. 'Except he's good fun too. He doesn't take himself too seriously. I think he'll make a good partner.'

'Well, you could certainly do with a stabilising influence.'

'We are still talking about business, aren't we?' Steph said suspiciously.

Liz laughed. 'You tell me.'

'He is gorgeous,' Steph admitted, 'and while of course I love Sean, it was kind of nice being with someone else for a change. I haven't been out to dinner with another man in ages.'

Liz was surprised by the pang of envy she felt. Trust Stephanie. She could have anyone she wanted. It was just her luck that the only time she'd run into Edward, she'd looked like a dog's dinner. But then, what difference did it make? What man would show an interest in someone

like her when Stephanie was around? Liz was amazed at
her own feelings. Why, in God's name, did she care what
he thought of her? Maybe it was all down to the break-up
with Chris. She still felt a complete failure. She should
have made her marriage work. Her mother always said,
'You've made your bed, now lie on it'. She was of the
old school that believed marriage was for life no matter
what you had to put up with. She probably thought
Liz should be grateful that Chris hadn't knocked her
about! Thankfully her dad was a lot more supportive
and understanding and he was furious at how Chris
Connolly had treated his beloved daughter.

They finished their lunch and Steph cleared the
dishes away and returned moments later with straw-
berries and cream, and the second bottle of wine.

'I'm not so sure about dessert but I'll definitely have
more wine.' Liz held up her glass and eyed Steph
defiantly.

Steph smiled weakly and poured. Liz had drunk most
of the first bottle and had hardly touched her food. Oh,
well, if she had too much to drink she could always stay
the night.

They talked desultorily for a while and Liz finally
dozed off in the afternoon sun. Steph was drifting
in and out of consciousness herself when the intercom buzzed. She opened one eye, debating whether
or not to answer it. Probably just kids. Liz was out
cold. The buzz came again. Damn it. She stood up,
straightened her clothes and went to the door. She
looked through the peephole and saw Edward standing on her doorstep. Oh Lord, what on earth was
he doing here? She ran her fingers through her hair
and checked her reflection in the hall mirror. She

was flushed from the sun and her dress was a mass of creases. Damn!

She fixed a smile on her face and opened the door. 'Hi!'

'Hello, Stephanie. Sorry for dropping in unannounced. There are just a couple of things I need you to sign before you head off.'

As usual he looked immaculate in a lightweight suit of pale grey and his pristine white shirt accentuated his permanently tanned skin. He looked every inch the successful man about town.

'No problem. Come in. You caught us having a very indulgent afternoon.' She led the way into the living room.

'Us?' he asked.

She nodded towards Liz's inert body on the balcony. Edward laughed. 'Liz?'

Liz stirred as she heard her name and saw a tall dark figure coming towards her. She started to sit up and then remembered that she'd unbuttoned most of her blouse. 'Edward! Hi.' She fumbled with the buttons and tried to straighten her skirt.

Edward smiled and sat down in Steph's vacated seat. 'Hi, Liz. I envy you taking advantage of such a beautiful day.' His eyes wandered appreciatively over Liz's legs.

'Edward? The papers?' Steph interrupted. What on earth was he doing chatting Liz up?

'No rush, Steph,' Edward said easily, not taking his eyes off Liz. 'Any chance of a glass of wine?'

Liz smiled shyly. 'Get another glass, Stephanie.'

Stephanie looked indignant at the summary dismissal and stomped back inside.

'So how are you doing?' Edward asked gently.

'I'm doing just fine.' For a change she actually believed it. The wine had worked its magic and she felt quite relaxed.

'That's good. He's a bloody fool, you know.'

Liz looked puzzled. 'Who, Chris? Why do you say that?'

'To risk losing such a beautiful woman. If he's not careful, you'll be snapped up,' he clicked his fingers, 'just like that.'

Liz blushed like a schoolgirl. 'Very flattering, but a little over the top.'

'Not at all,' he murmured.

Stephanie returned with a glass, which she filled and pushed towards him ungraciously.

'Thanks, Stephanie. So how's Chez Nous going to manage without you for a whole week?'

'Oh, they'll be thrilled to get rid of me, for a while. I'm driving them all mad.'

'Rubbish. I'm sure they're delighted with their new boss.'

Steph glowed and decided to forgive him for chatting up Liz. He was just being polite.

They finished the wine, chatting companionably in the afternoon sunshine and Liz and Steph were disappointed when Edward finally rose to leave.

'I'd better be making tracks,' he said regretfully. 'I have to get back to the office, but why don't I come back tonight and take you two to dinner?'

Steph shook her head. 'Sorry, no can do. I'm due in Wicklow for dinner. Mam will have prepared the fatted calf, but thanks for the offer.'

'That's a pity. What about you, Liz?'

Liz looked up, startled. 'Me?'

'Unless you're doing anything else?'

She smiled. 'No, actually I'm not. Lucy is with Chris today. And she's staying overnight.'

'Then it's a date?'

'Why not?'

Steph stared at her. If she didn't know any better she'd swear that Liz was flirting. Oh, God, what the hell was Edward playing at? 'Shall we look at those papers now, Edward?' She glared at him and led the way inside.

He chuckled as she bent her head over the papers. 'There's no need to be ratty with me. I'm just taking her to dinner.'

'I am not being ratty,' she spat back. 'But Liz is very vulnerable at the moment. I don't want you taking advantage of her.'

'Did I take advantage of you?' he asked.

'No, but—'

'Well then. Trust me. She looks like she could do with a bit of fun.'

They fell silent as Liz joined them.

'I'd better get going too, Stephanie. Shall I meet you in town, Edward?'

'No, no. I'll pick you up. Give me your address.'

Liz scribbled her address down and also some directions from the school.

Edward took the piece of paper and studied it. 'Eight o'clock okay?'

'Fine. See you then.'

'I'll see you out,' Stephanie said tightly and walked him to the door.

He bent and kissed her cheek. 'Don't worry, I'll be a good boy. Enjoy your week off.'

Steph smiled reluctantly. 'Thanks. Bye.'

Liz sighed at the grim expression on Steph's face when she returned. 'Now don't give out to me, Steph. Like you said to Annie, it's only dinner. I'm not going to do anything. But he is very nice, isn't he? Easy to talk to.'

There was an almost dreamy expression on her face and there was a sparkle in her eyes that wasn't entirely due to the wine.

Steph groaned inwardly. 'Don't get carried away, Liz. He's just a man and he has his faults like all the others. Take off the rose-tinted glasses.'

'Oh, shut up, Steph. Don't you think I deserve a night out?'

Steph was immediately remorseful. 'Of course you do. I'm sorry Liz. I'm being overprotective.'

'Oh, you're probably right,' Liz said, the light leaving her eyes. 'What the hell am I doing going out with another man? It's ridiculous! I should have refused. Maybe I'll call and cancel . . .'

'You'll do no such thing,' Steph said firmly. 'You're a grown woman and it is only dinner. Go and have a good time. There's absolutely nothing to feel guilty about.'

Liz hugged her. 'Yeah, okay. Well, I'd better go. I have to dig out something sexy in lycra.'

'Wear something long with a very high neck,' Steph said severely, wagging her finger.

Liz shook her head sadly. 'It doesn't really matter, Steph. Edward wouldn't be interested in me even if I'd nothing on but a smile. It's you he wanted to go out with. He just feels sorry for me. He was just being kind.'

'I don't know the man that well, Liz, but one thing's for sure. He never does anything he doesn't want to.'

Chapter Fourteen

'You look lovely.' Edward smiled at Liz and led her out to the car.

Liz barely replied. She'd lifted the phone several times to cancel, but she'd lost her nerve each time. Eventually she'd accepted the fact that she'd have to go through with it and she went and got dressed. She'd chosen a black silk dress with a halterneck. She felt a bit bare so she slipped a gold embroidered shawl around her shoulders. A pair of gold hoop earrings was her only jewellery. She swept her hair back from her face, added the minimum amount of make-up and went downstairs to wait for Edward. Her stomach was sick and she felt guilty. She was still a married woman and here she was going out on a date! She took a deep breath. This was silly. Edward would never look on this as a date. He was just being polite. Stephanie had obviously been the target of his attention.

She shot him a quick sidelong glance as he pulled away from the kerb. He'd mentioned where they were going, but she hadn't heard. She tried hard to concentrate on what he was saying.

'Have you eaten in Peacock Alley?' he was saying.

Oh, right. Peacock Alley. 'Not recently. When they first opened Chris and I went to check it out.'

'Of course. And what did you think?'

'Chris was very impressed.'

'I asked what you thought,' Edward said mildly.

'Well, I thought it was good too.'

'Right.' Edward nodded grimly.

Liz looked at him nonplussed, conscious that she'd said something to annoy him. 'Steph likes it,' she added.

'Oh, Liz,' Edward breathed.

'What? What?' Liz's voice was high.

'I wanted *your* opinion. Not Stephanie's or Chris's.'

'And I gave it,' Liz said defensively.

'Yes, you did. I'm sorry.' They drove in silence for a moment. 'Do you think Conor will be able for the head chef's position?' he asked conversationally.

'Easily. He's probably been doing most of the work anyway.' She closed her eyes briefly. That sounded so disloyal. 'Most sous-chefs have to take over completely from time to time,' she added to soften her first comment. 'That's what they're trained to do.'

'I see,' Edward said, reversing smoothly into a parking spot outside the restaurant. 'Well, he's certainly enthusiastic. I must say I like the lad.'

Liz laughed. 'That makes you sound very old.'

Edward grinned. 'Well, I am very old.'

'What? All of thirty-nine, forty?'

'Forty, almost forty-one.'

'Oh, very old,' Liz teased.

'Well, it feels like it when I'm surrounded by the Chez Nous staff. They're all so incredibly young.'

'It's a young industry.'

Edward held the door open for her and minutes later they were seated at a round table in a quiet corner.

Liz looked around nervously. It hadn't seemed like a date until now. Now she was tucked into a discreet corner with an extremely handsome man.

'I like sitting with my back to the wall,' Edward said, aware of her discomfort. 'I can see everyone and no one can creep up behind me.'

Liz smiled. 'I love people watching.'

'Oh yes?'

'I try to guess who's married and who's not,' she explained. 'It's usually quite easy. If there's no conversation then they're married. If they're arguing then they're probably dating. And if they're besotted with one another then it's definitely an affair.'

Edward looked at her sadly. 'That's very cynical.'

'Can you blame me?' Liz bent her head over the menu.

Edward watched her thoughtfully. She was a total contradiction. It was obvious from the moment she'd opened the door this evening that she'd regretted agreeing to go out with him. She was defensive of Chris and, moments later, angry with him. All to be expected, really, given what she'd been through.

Liz, conscious of his scrutiny, tucked her hair behind her ear nervously and kept her eyes on the menu. She read it but her mind registered nothing The thought of food made her feel slightly sick.

'Can I get you a drink?'

She looked up at the waiter and then at Edward. 'Gin and tonic, please.'

'The same,' Edward said.

Liz hoped that the waiter hurried with their drinks. She needed something to calm her down.

'Do you like lobster, Liz?' Edward looked up from

his menu. 'It's something of a speciality here. They do it with a lemon-grass vinaigrette, it's really delicious.'

'I think I'll have the sole.' It probably wouldn't make her throw up.

Edward frowned. 'What about a starter?'

'Just a green salad.'

'No wonder you're so thin,' he said with a shake of his head.

Liz gave a nervous laugh. Thin? Her? Was he trying to be funny?

The waiter returned with their drinks and Liz took a gulp as soon as it was in front of her.

'Are you ready to order?'

'Yes. One mussels and one green salad to start. And sole and lobster for our main courses. And a bottle of number forty-three – the Chablis. Thank you.' The waiter departed and Edward turned back to Liz. 'So how's Lucy coping these days?'

Liz pleated and re-pleated her napkin. 'Not bad. She seems happy enough but just when I think she's settled into the new routine she turns around and asks me when Daddy's coming home.'

'And what do you say?'

'The only thing I can say. I don't know.' Liz took a gulp of her drink.

'It must be very hard.'

'It is.' Liz drained her glass.

'Do you want him back?'

'I honestly don't know,' Liz admitted and then wondered why the hell she was telling this man all about her private life. He was practically a stranger. 'Look, I really don't want to talk . . .'

'Of course you don't. Forgive me, I'm being much too nosy. Let's talk about something else.'

'Tell me about your sister. Where exactly does she live?'

'Jen is not that far away from you at all. You know the green at the top of your road? Well, her house is just opposite on the corner.'

'Oh, I know it. Does she have other children?'

'No, just Carol.'

Liz thanked the waiter as he put her salad in front of her. 'Does she plan to have any more? Chris wanted us to have another baby. He doesn't think it's fair to Lucy not to give her a brother or sister. Of course he would have liked a son. I suppose every man does.'

Edward didn't reply until the waiter had poured their wine and left. 'Jen's husband is dead. He was killed in a car accident.'

'Oh, the poor girl. When did it happen?'

'Nearly three years ago, now. Carol barely remembers him.'

'That's so sad.'

'Jen's doing okay. She's a great mother and Carol's a sweetheart.'

Liz watched the softening in his face when he mentioned his niece. He really was an incredibly nice man. And an extremely handsome one, too. She watched his strong tanned hands as he fiddled with the cutlery. The hands of a successful man with perfectly manicured nails. He wore a black and white check jacket, a white shirt and a paisley tie in muted grey and blue shades. She smiled. A tie that Chris wouldn't be seen dead in.

'What's amusing you?'

Liz reddened. 'Sorry. I was just admiring your tie and thinking how much Chris would hate it.'

'Why is that?'

'Too subtle.'

'Oh. It's one of my more flamboyant ones actually.'

Liz giggled. 'I'm glad to hear it.'

'I'll take that as a compliment.'

'How come you've never married?' Liz asked, emboldened by the gin warming her insides. 'You strike me as a family man and you're obviously good with kids.'

He shrugged. 'It just hasn't happened that way. And I'm probably too set in my ways now to get used to living with another person.'

'I can understand that, but it's such a waste. You'd be a great father. Why is it that the men who shouldn't do?'

Edward looked blank. 'You've lost me.'

'Well I mean, why do some men get married and have a family and then start playing around? Why the hell do they get married in the first place?'

'Because they fall in love?'

'You're a romantic!' she exclaimed.

'Maybe. Well, when I look at the likes of Joe and Annie I have to believe in the occasional happy ending.'

'Yes, they're perfect together, aren't they? So are Steph and Sean if only she'd realise it.'

'I haven't met Sean. What's he like?'

'He's great,' Liz said affectionately. 'And, I know it's an old-fashioned word, but he's also very nice.'

'I always associate nice with boring.'

Liz shook her head vehemently. 'Nope. Definitely not boring.'

'So you think Steph should settle down with him?'

'I've told her till I'm blue in the face. So has Annie. She's already lost him once.'

'Oh?'

Over the sole and the lobster, Liz told him about Sean's marriage and his son and how he'd only got back with Steph two years ago after a ten-year separation.

'And his son lives with his wife in Cork?'

'Yes. Sean visits Billy sometimes but not often.'

'That's sad.'

'Yeah. It is.' Liz fell silent. Lucy was in exactly the same position now. If Liz stuck to her guns, she'd be living in Dublin and Chris would be in Galway. They wouldn't see each other as often as they should. Lucy would miss out on having a full-time father. She pushed her plate away and finished her wine. Immediately a waiter appeared to refill it.

'A penny for them?' Edward said gently.

Liz shook her head.

'You're thinking that Lucy's going to be in the same boat as Sean's son, aren't you?'

'You should become a shrink.'

'It wasn't that difficult to follow your line of thought.'

'I just don't know what to do for the best.'

'Whatever will make you both happiest. There's not much point in taking Chris back just for Lucy's sake. You'd probably be at each other's throats morning, noon and night and that wouldn't do her much good, would it?'

'No, but does that mean I should just throw in the towel on my marriage?'

'Is that what you think you're doing?' Edward countered.

'No, oh, I don't know.' She tossed her hair back impatiently. 'I don't know what I'm doing half the time these days.' She looked at a man smoking at the next table and was tempted to bum a cigarette off him.

'You'll do the right thing,' Edward said calmly.

'How can you say that? How do you know?'

'Because you're a good mother and in the end you'll do what's best for Lucy and for yourself. Just remember, if you're not happy, she won't be either.'

'You make it all sound so simple,' Liz complained.

'That's because it is.'

Liz looked at him her eyes bright with unshed tears. 'And that's what's so scary,' she whispered.

Chapter Fifteen

Stephanie paced her parents' living-room, pausing every few minutes at the window. She knew that the woman was supposed to keep the man waiting but she didn't believe in all that. Sean wasn't due for another ten minutes, but here she was ready and waiting, eager for his arrival.

She'd spent over an hour going through her wardrobe. If only she'd brought her Paul Costello suit! Clothes were tried on and discarded. Finally she had settled on a midnight-blue satin trouser-suit with a v-necked jacket that revealed a hint of cleavage and narrow trousers that tapered in at the ankle. She chose a pair of very high silver sandals and the sapphire earrings and pendant her parents had given her for her thirtieth birthday to complete the outfit.

She inspected her make-up in the mirror over the fireplace. She'd applied a combination of grey and blues to her eyelids, defined her pale brows with a pencil and used mascara and eyeliner to make her eyes look larger. Her foundation was light and she'd used a very pale pink lipstick. Her hair was swept back off her face. She was pleased with the effect she'd created. This should stop Sean from going away for too long in future!

She turned from the mirror and walked to the window just as Sean pulled into the driveway in his black BMW. She ran to the front door and threw it open as he stepped from the car. Then she paused, suddenly shy.

He turned around and stopped in his tracks when he saw her. 'Hiya, gorgeous.'

Steph flew into his arms and turned up her face for his kiss.

'Oh, I've missed you,' Sean gasped when they finally came up for air. 'You're not really hungry are you? Couldn't we just go somewhere . . .'

'Sean? Is that you?' Catherine West called from the hallway. 'Come on in.'

'Coming Mrs W,' he called and rolled his eyes at Steph. 'I suppose I'll have to wait another ten minutes.'

Steph laughed. 'If you manage to get away from them that quick it will be a miracle!' She led the way into the dining-room where Tom and Catherine West were having dinner.

Catherine hugged him affectionately. 'It's good to see you, Sean. You look great. Doesn't he look great, Tom?'

'He does.' Steph's father stood up to shake his hand. 'The American air obviously suited you.'

'Everything about the place suited me, Tom.'

'So everything went well, then?' Catherine asked anxiously.

'It went great. Look, I'm sorry for interrupting your dinner. We'll get out of your hair—'

'You will not,' Catherine said, pulling up a chair. 'We've been dying to hear all your news.'

'We don't have much time, Mam,' Steph said quickly. 'I booked the Orange Grove for eight.'

'Plenty of time for a quick drink,' Tom said happily.

Catherine stood up immediately. 'You'll have a G & T, Sean?'

'I'll get the drinks, Mam,' Steph said resignedly. 'You eat your dinner.' She walked through the arch into the kitchen and took two glasses out of the press.

'There's some fresh soda in the fridge, love. The one Sean likes,' her mother called after her. 'I only got it this morning. Don't use the stale bottle.'

Stephanie grinned. 'Yes, Mam.' Talk about the prodigal son!

Steph fell into the passenger seat laughing. 'Lord, I thought we'd never get out of there. We're going to be late.'

'Oh you're not still talking about eating are you?' Sean said mournfully.

'Absolutely, I'm starving. And I need my energy.'

He leaned across and kissed her hard on the lips. 'You are definitely going to need energy, I can promise you that.'

Steph felt the familiar tingle of excitement run through her.

'It's good to be home,' he said stroking her thigh – God bless automatics.

Stephanie put a hand on his knee. 'I'm glad you're home.'

'So you missed me?'

'Well, a little bit.'

'I was beginning to wonder,' he said lightly. 'Between the restaurant and your new partner I was afraid you'd forgotten all about me.'

'It has been chaotic,' she admitted, 'but that made the time pass quicker. Oh, I've so much to tell you. And I can't wait for you to meet Edward.'

'Yes. I'm looking forward to meeting him,' Sean said grimly.

'You're jealous,' Steph said delightedly.

'Have I reason to be?' he shot back.

'Of course not, silly.' She leaned across and kissed his ear as he pulled up in front of the restaurant.

He switched off the engine and pulled her into his arms. After a long probing kiss he pulled back to look down into her flushed face. 'And you're absolutely sure that you want to eat?'

'I'm beginning to think you're trying to get out of buying me dinner.'

Sean smacked a hand to his forehead. 'Sussed! Oh, well it was worth a try!'

'Come on, idiot. If you're good I promise not to have a dessert.'

They got out of the car and walked inside arm in arm.

'When you say "if I'm good",' he murmured as they were led to their table.

'Shut up, Sean,' Steph hissed but she couldn't wipe the smile off her face.

They chatted easily as they ate their meal. About Phoenix, Conor's progress, Liz and Chris.

'I have a surprise for you,' Sean told her when they'd finished eating.

Stephanie's eyes lit up. 'What is it?'

'Guess.'

'Jewellery?' she asked nervously. *Not a ring. Please not a ring!*

'No. Guess again.'

'Something to wear?'

'Nope. Guess again.'

'Oh, stop it, Sean. Tell me. Please?'

'I'm taking you away for the weekend,' he said, triumphantly.

'You're being a bit presumptuous, aren't you? How do you know I'm free?'

Sean was unflappable. 'You said you were off all week. The restaurant's closed Sunday and Monday.' He shrugged. 'But I can always cancel . . .'

'Well, maybe I could manage it,' she said with a slow smile.

'You haven't asked where we're going.'

Steph didn't really care. 'Where are we going?'

'Paris. The same hotel, the same room . . .'

'Oh, Sean. That's fantastic!' she squealed, leaning over to kiss him.

'Does that mean I shouldn't cancel?' he asked.

'No way! Oh Sean. That's so romantic.'

Sean kissed her hand. 'I'm way too good to you.'

'You are,' Steph murmured leaning over, affording him an excellent view down her top.

Sean groaned. 'Look, do you want some dessert or can we get out of here now?'

'To my parents?' Steph asked with twinkling eyes.

'No bloody way! We're going to Clontarf.'

'I can't, Sean. The folks are expecting me back.'

'In that case we'll just have to find a discreet layby and pretend we're teenagers!'

Steph laughed. 'Okay. You've talked me into it.'

'Waiter. Bill please!'

Chapter Sixteen

'Steph? Niall Casey phoned. He says they can't deliver until Friday. Oh, and Chris said he won't be in until twelve. And there was an announcement on the news. There's some problem with pipes on Dame Street and they'll be switching off the water in the whole area from two until four.'

Steph groaned. 'Oh it's so good to be back.'

'So how was your week off?'

Steph smiled at Liam Dunne, glad that it was Sam's morning off. Liam was a total contrast. At twenty-five, he was enthusiastic, great with the customers and always cool in a crisis. In fact the only problem with Liam was the number of female staff who spent their days drooling over his dark good looks.

'I had a lovely break, Liam. But now I feel like I've never been away. Does George know about the water?'

'Yeah, but he says it's not his problem.'

'Does he now? Okay. I'll have a word.' She went to the top of the stairs. 'Jean,' she called down to the waitress. 'Do me a favour? Make me a huge pot of coffee and don't let anyone come near me before lunch.'

Jean grunted and slunk off to the kitchen. Steph rolled her eyes at Liam. 'Enthusiastic, isn't she?'

'A positive dynamo,' he agreed drily. 'Seeya later.'

Steph sat down in her chair and waited for the coffee to arrive. She couldn't think of starting work without some caffeine inside her. She allowed her mind to drift back over the weekend. Paris had been wonderful, not that they'd seen much of it! Most of the weekend had been spent in the large double bed with occasional trips to the restaurant and bar. And Sean hadn't brought up the 'M' word once, she sighed happily. It was wonderful to have a love life again. She'd come home physically exhausted but mentally she'd never felt better.

Jean arrived with her coffee and after the first cup Steph felt ready to tackle the huge pile of post. It really wasn't worth going away when there was this mess to face on her return. She'd have to get an assistant. Someone to look after the wages and the accounts and definitely the mail. She worked steadily through the day, drank copious amounts of coffee and smoked too many cigarettes. She tidied her desk at seven o'clock, stretched and went down to the restaurant.

'Everything okay?' she asked Jean as she looked through the reservations for the evening.

'Yeah.' She was lounging against a table, inspecting her fingernails.

Steph frowned. 'Haven't you anything to do?'

Jean cast an eye around the empty restaurant. 'Eh, not really, no.'

Steph picked up a glass from the nearest table, then a fork. 'These could be cleaner. Get a cloth and check every place setting.'

Jean opened her mouth to protest but closed it again when she saw the look on Stephanie's face. She sighed loudly and went into the kitchen.

Sam came out of the kitchen. 'What's the problem?'

Steph waved a hand at the tables. 'Some of the table settings are a disgrace. That girl is a lazy little bitch. It's not good enough, Sam, I'm surprised at you.'

Sam pursed his lips. 'I was just coming to check on things myself.'

'It's seven o'clock. Cutting it a bit fine, aren't you?'

'It is only Tuesday, for God's sake.'

'The standards should be upheld whatever day of the week it is. Now please see that the job is done properly.' She turned on her heel and went back upstairs.

Sam glared after her. 'Bitch,' he muttered to himself.

The phone rang just as Steph sat back down at her desk. 'Yes?'

'Steph? You sound a bit browned off. What's up?'

'Liz? Oh nothing important. I'm just having one of those days. How are you?'

'Fine. Sorry I didn't get back to you sooner.'

'That's okay. I was just calling for a gossip. I was just dying to know how you got on with Edward.'

'Very well. Like you say, he's a nice man.'

'Where did you go?'

'Peacock Alley.'

'Oh, really? Was it good? It got a great write-up in the paper last week.'

Liz grinned. Steph was successfully diverted. 'It was very good,' she confirmed and went on to give all the minute details that she knew her friend would enjoy.

'So, I hope Edward behaved himself,' Steph said lightly when she'd finished.

'Stephanie, of course he did! Anyway, enough about me. How was your break down in Wicklow? How's Sean?'

'Wicklow was fine and Sean is *still* great – if you know what I mean! We went to Paris for the weekend.'

'Paris. Very romantic. And . . . ?'

Steph laughed. 'And it was very nice.'

'Did he propose again?'

'No, he didn't actually.'

'Hah! Good. The man's getting sense. Mind you, you're better off,' she added cynically. 'Love, honour and cherish – that's a laugh!'

Steph was taken aback at the bitterness in Liz's voice. 'You sound very cynical, Liz.'

'I feel very cynical, Steph. I've had quite enough of being Mrs Connolly.'

'Promise me you won't make any rash decisions,' Steph begged.

'I don't think you're really in a position to set yourself up as a marriage guidance counsellor, do you?' Liz said caustically.

'Fair point. But while marriage wouldn't suit me, it certainly seemed to work for you. Well, until . . .'

'Yes, until,' Liz said shortly. 'I've been doing a lot of thinking and I think getting back with Chris would be a huge mistake. A night out with a nice, attentive man has made me realise just how stale our marriage had been. To be treated like an intelligent adult with opinions was a novelty. Quite a change from, "Where are all my bloody socks, Liz? Why can't you keep them in pairs? Surely rolling them up together isn't too challenging."'

'I'm sure that—'

'And another thing,' Liz was in full flow now. After not confiding in anyone for so long it was like the flood-gates had opened and she couldn't stop. 'I've finally realised that the fact that Chris fancied other women doesn't mean there was anything wrong with me.'

'Well of course not—'

'So I was a few pounds overweight, so what?'

'You're right of course, Liz,' Steph said when Liz finally paused to draw breath.

Liz was silent.

'Liz? Liz, are you there?'

'I'm here, Steph.'

'Are you okay?'

'That's the point, Steph, don't you see? I'm better than okay. I'm better than I've been in a long time. I'm just beginning to realise what a pig Chris was, treating me like a child, patronising me, even bullying me sometimes when he didn't get his way.'

Steph closed her eyes. 'That sounds familiar.'

'Yes, and you've solved your problem. Don't you think that it's time I solved mine?'

'Oh, Liz, I don't know,' Steph said helplessly. 'Walking away from a boss isn't quite the same as walking out on a marriage. And then there's Lucy to think of. Whatever your feelings, he's still her father.'

Liz exploded. 'Jesus! Would you listen to yourself?' she almost screamed down the phone. 'How the hell would you know what it's like? And as for Lucy, you think you know what's best for her? Just because you're her bloody godmother! You see her maybe once a month, if she's lucky. Why don't you just go to hell?'

Steph jumped as Liz banged down the receiver. She sat looking at the phone, shocked. How could Liz say such horrible things? She lit a cigarette with trembling hands and took some deep calming breaths. She couldn't ever remember having an argument with Liz before. They'd always been so close. Oh, God, this was terrible! Her hand hovered over the phone. Maybe she should call back and check to see if Liz was okay. What if she did something silly? Although maybe it would be better to let her calm down. She'd probably just hang up again anyway. Yes, she'd give Liz a little space and then she'd call. God, they were best friends. She wasn't going to let Chris come between them. He'd caused enough trouble already.

Sam stuck his head round the door. 'Ready for inspection.'

Stephanie looked up, confused, her face white and tense. 'What?'

Sam frowned. 'Are you okay?'

'Yes, of course,' she said briskly.

'I thought you might want to check up on Jean's work.'

'Fine, let's go.'

'So I was thinking, all going well, we could move your stuff in at the weekend. What do you think? Steph? Steph, are you listening to me?'

Steph turned in Sean's arms. 'Sorry, love. What was that?'

'You haven't heard a word I've said, have you? And you're always saying I don't listen to you!'

Steph kissed him. 'I'm sorry. I just can't stop thinking about Liz. Maybe I should call her.' She sat up in bed and reached for the phone.

He pulled her back down beside him. 'Give her some time, Steph. And don't be so surprised that she's hitting out. You said yourself that it wasn't natural the way she was handling everything so well. Let her throw a wobbly. Give her time.'

Steph settled back in his arms. 'You're right. You're always right. I hate that.'

Sean nuzzled against her ear. 'So what about it? Will you move in at the weekend?'

Steph took a deep breath. 'Yeah, great. Why not?' She had finally agreed to move in with Sean and while she didn't regret it she still felt slightly nervous at the prospect.

Sean smiled happily. 'I'll give the estate agent a call. They could meet us at your place on Saturday and have a look around.'

Stephanie stiffened. 'There's no rush, is there?'

Sean frowned. 'Well, it would be good to have the cash now you're self-employed.'

Steph looked away. 'True, but I could always rent the apartment and have a regular income. You know the price of property in Malahide. I think I should hang on to it.'

'Yeah, you're probably right,' Sean said easily.

Steph relaxed again in his arms. Though she might be moving in with him it was still nice to know that she'd have her own little apartment – just in case.

Ruth pushed Des away and straightened her clothes. 'Not here, Des.' She looked around the car park anxiously.

'Well, come back to my place then,' Des said, suppressing a sigh of frustration. He'd been dating Ruth for nearly

three months and she still wouldn't let him anywhere near her.

He was beginning to wonder if she was worth the effort. But, as he looked down into the dark eyes which looked back at him beseechingly from that pretty little face, he knew she was. If only she wasn't such a good girl. He'd topped up her wine glass a few times tonight in the hope that it might relax her but when he'd dropped his hand from her breast to the zip of her jeans, she froze.

'I can't come back, Des. You know I can't,' she pleaded for his understanding.

'Right so,' he said curtly, switched on the engine and pulled sharply out onto the road.

Ruth looked at him nervously. She knew he was annoyed. He'd been trying to get her into bed for weeks now. She was afraid she was going to lose him. He was a man of the world and he could have his pick of the sophisticated girls in his office. Ruth often wondered why he'd bothered with a poor student like her. She couldn't believe her luck when Des, easily the best-looking fella in the Baggot Inn, had approached her and bought her a drink. She'd been even more impressed when he'd insisted on dropping her home in his sporty black Capri.

He'd wined and dined her several nights a week since then, although he was often sent down the country on business. He wasn't too interested in going out with her friends. He said he wanted her all to himself, but she knew he didn't like the student scene. She couldn't really blame him. What had he got in common with them? Anyway, Sean Adams hadn't gone out of his way to make Des welcome. Jealous no doubt, Ruth decided. Still, it wasn't a problem. She got together with her friends when Des was away, and she saw Steph for lunch regularly. It all worked out quite well.

Des took a bend very fast and Ruth tightened her grip

on the edge of her seat. She hated it when he was angry with her.

'I'm sorry, Des,' she said, slipping into his arms when he pulled up outside her flat.

'I'm sorry too, pet. It's just I love you so much. I want to be with you.'

Ruth's heart soared at his words. He loved her! He really loved her! She turned her face up to his and kissed him. Des groaned and slid his hand down to her breast. He pulled impatiently at her shirt and dipped his head, his mouth finding her nipple. Ruth shivered with pleasure under his mouth and hands.

'Oh Ruth, I want you so much,' he said hoarsely.

'I want you too, Des,' she gasped. What the hell was she saving herself for? She loved this man. She wanted to spend the rest of her life with him. And hadn't he just told her he loved her? Her flatmates would be asleep by now. And she had a bedroom all to herself . . .

'Do you really want me, Ruth?' Des asked as he planted little kisses around her neck and throat.

'Yes, Des,' she said, raising his head so she could look deep into his eyes. 'Please come in and make love to me.'

Des kissed her hard, jumped out of the car and ran around to open her door. 'I'll be gentle, Ruth,' he murmured in her ear as she opened the front door with an unsteady hand. 'I'll make you happy. I promise.'

Ruth watched Mary nervously, as she slammed around the kitchen. Des seemed oblivious to her flatmate's mood as he sat at the kitchen table and sipped his coffee.

'I'm off to Mass,' Mary announced with a pointed stare at Ruth and a glance of disgust at Des.

'Say a prayer for us,' Des said cheerfully as Mary left, banging the door behind her.

'God, she's never going to let me forget this,' Ruth said morosely.

'Ah, she'll get over it. She's just jealous. Frustrated.'

Ruth glared at him. Mary might be a bit on the straight side, but she was a good friend. Sinead hadn't been too impressed either. She'd bumped into Des on her way to the bathroom earlier that morning. She'd asked Ruth, rather coolly, to let her know in future if she planned on having an overnight guest. Then she'd retreated to her bedroom and banged the door. Ruth was beginning to wonder if it had been worth it. Des had seemed to enjoy himself, but to Ruth it had seemed much ado about nothing. It had been quick and painful. Nothing like the romantic novels led you to believe. Afterwards, Ruth had fought back tears of pain and shame and longed for Des to take her in his arms and tell her how much he loved her. But he'd just given her a peck on the cheek, rolled over and promptly fallen asleep. He'd reached for her this morning for a repeat performance, but Ruth was afraid her flatmates would hear. It all seemed a bit sordid in the cold light of day and she felt ashamed and embarrassed.

'I think you'd better go, Des,' she said with an apologetic smile. 'Sinead won't come out until you're gone, and I'm in the bad books as it is.'

Des was happy to comply. It was a sunny Sunday morning and the golf course beckoned. 'Right, love, I'll be off.' He pulled her to him and kissed her soundly. 'You were great,' he whispered.

'You too,' she replied smiling up at him shyly. She'd get used to it. It was probably just because she was so inexperienced. No doubt it would be better the next time. 'Will I see you later?' she asked timidly.

'Probably not. I have to prepare for an important meeting tomorrow. I'll phone you. Bye, love.'

Ruth watched from the window, as he ran down the steps, hopped into his car and drove away at speed.

Sinead wandered into the room. 'So lover boy's finally gone.'

Ruth flushed. 'Leave me alone, Sinead.'

Sinead held up her hands. 'Hey, nothing to do with me, but for Christ's sake be careful. I hope you made him use a condom.'

Ruth's eyes widened in alarm. 'I never thought . . .' It had all happened so quickly. It hadn't even occurred to her that they should have been taking precautions.

'Oh really, Ruth!' Sinead looked at her in dismay. 'Better get yourself down to the doctor,' she advised grimly.

'Oh no, I couldn't. He'd tell my mother.' Ruth was horrified at the thought of discussing her sex life with Dr Lynch. He'd be shocked for sure.

'Well then, go to the Well Woman Centre. They won't ask any questions. Please, Ruth. It's safer,' Sinead pleaded.

Ruth dreaded the thought of discussing something so personal with a stranger, but what choice did she have? She'd make an appointment tomorrow. Before she lost her nerve.

Sinead thought Ruth wanted her head examined, hanging around with a creep like Des Healy. He was too smooth. Too good to be wholesome, to use a phrase of her mother's. She could have told Ruth to make Des use condoms, but it would be a lot safer if Ruth was on the pill. Then she wouldn't have to rely on Des.

Sinead had met him in a club in Leeson Street recently. He'd been smooching with a well-endowed, scantily clad girl, who'd had more than enough to drink. Sinead watched from *a distance, and went over when the girl tottered off, rather unsteadily, to the ladies'.*

'Having a good time, Des?' she'd said sarcastically.

Des looked up in alarm but quickly pulled himself together and gave her one of his practised smiles. 'Sinead! Hi! I didn't think a poor student could afford to socialise in a place like this.'

'No chance of you bumping into Ruth, you mean,' she said grimly. 'Relax, Des. She's not here, more's the pity. She's safely tucked up in bed, probably dreaming about you.'

'As I do about her,' Des answered smoothly.

'Yeah. Sure.' Sinead glared at him and went back to her friends. She slept late the next morning, and so it was the following evening before she saw Ruth. She wasn't sure whether to mention the incident or not. Ruth probably wouldn't believe her. She knew full well that Sinead couldn't stand Des.

Ruth solved her dilemma. 'I believe you met Des in Leggs last night.'

Sinead looked at her warily. 'Yeah, that's right. It was Bridget's birthday. We decided to make a night of it. What was Des's excuse?'

Ruth rolled her eyes. 'Oh, business as usual. It's not enough that he puts in all those hours at the office, they expect him to entertain as well. He told me you probably thought he was up to no good,' she added with a laugh. 'One girl got really pissed and was all over him like a rash.'

'Poor man,' Sinead muttered. One up to Des. If Ruth believed that story, there was no hope for her. Love was definitely blind.

Chapter Seventeen

Edward was striding past the kitchen when he caught sight of Conor. He doubled back. 'Conor. You're back. How did it go?'

'Fantastic, Mr McDermott. A great experience altogether. Albert's kitchen is amazing and the food – well, let's say I learned a lot!'

Edward nodded approvingly. 'That was the idea. A stint up in Belfast should round you off nicely. I assume all of these guys have their own ways of doing things.'

'Absolutely. And it's up to me to take the best from each of them and then add my own ideas.'

Chris snorted in the background.

Edward winked at Conor. 'Yeah, I think that's important. Put your own stamp on it. Modern, young, trendy – I'm sure you've got lots of ideas.'

'I certainly do,' Conor agreed loudly. 'There are lots of things I've wanted to try out for some time. I'm all for French cuisine, that's where my background is, but I do feel it can be livened up with other influences. North African, for instance.'

Chris snorted again. 'Well, right now, *Chef,*' he said sarcastically, 'I think our customers would settle for bangers and mash! Would it be too much to ask that you get back to work? And you,' he pointed his knife at Edward. 'Out of my kitchen. We've got work to do.'

Edward smiled but his eyes were steely. 'Certainly, Connolly. But you'd do well to remember that this is no longer *your* kitchen.' He turned on his heel and Chris attacked the pheasant on his board with a vengeance.

'Hi, Stephanie. How's it going?' Edward stretched himself out in the chair in front of her desk.

Stephanie looked up at her partner. 'Okay. I've put together a list of who I think we should invite to the press reception.' She passed an A4 sheet to him.

Edward scanned it quickly. 'I don't know half of these people, so I'll leave it to you. This is your forte. Any buttons you need me to push?'

'I don't think so – unless you've any contacts in television? I'd love to get Conor on a magazine programme or cookery show.'

'I may be able to help there. Leave it with me. When is the big night?'

'Tuesday, three weeks.'

'Maybe we should start spreading the word now. Work up the media so they're clamouring for an invite. What about inviting in one of the major wine buffs to advise on wines to complement the food?'

Steph nodded in agreement. 'That's a great idea. Are you after my job?'

'No. But just because I'm a lawyer doesn't mean I don't have the occasional creative idea. Anything else?'

'Ah, yes. There's something else, or rather someone else I wanted to talk to you about.'

'Oh yes? Who?'

'Sam.'

'The head waiter?'

'Yeah. I want to get rid of him. He's lazy and he's a whiner and he's been a constant thorn in my side from day one.'

Edward shrugged. 'You're the boss – I hardly know the guy. Would you want to hire someone to replace him?'

'I don't think I need to. I plan to spend a lot more time out front myself – I'll get in an assistant to look after the office work. And Liam Dunne is showing great potential. I think we could promote him to take over Sam's role.'

'Sounds perfect. What about the kitchen staff? Any trouble there?'

Stephanie shook her head. 'Not really. Most of the lads are delighted that Conor's taking over – Chris wasn't the most popular of bosses. John Quigly doesn't care who's running the show. He does his own thing anyway. George is another story.'

'Do you want to get rid of him too?'

'I don't, but I'm sure Conor would love me to,' she said, laughing. 'He's got a friend of his all lined up for the job! We think that George may decide to go himself. He's not going to like answering to Conor all of the time.'

'Well, at least you've someone to step in if he does decide to leave.'

Sean poked his head around the door of Steph's office. His smile faded when he saw the other man. 'Sorry to interrupt.'

Stephanie felt his tension immediately. She smiled brightly and waved him in. 'Not at all. Sean, this is Edward McDermott. Edward, this is Sean Adams.'

The two men shook hands.

'Glad to finally meet you, Sean. Sorry if you're not seeing too much of your girlfriend these days. There's still a lot to do before we're up and running.'

'Yes, well she always was a workaholic.' Sean turned to Steph. 'I was wondering if you were free for lunch, love?'

'I don't think so—'

Edward stood up and grabbed his briefcase. 'Don't refuse on my account. I have a lunch meeting. It was nice to finally meet you, Sean. See you, Steph.'

Sean closed the door after him. 'He seems okay,' he said grudgingly.

Stephanie reached up to kiss him. 'He is.'

'You get on well then?'

'We get on very well.'

'That's good, I suppose.'

'It is,' she agreed. 'Let's go to lunch.'

'Where would you like to go?'

'How about McDonald's?'

He looked at her in mock horror. 'A top restaurateur eating in a fast-food joint?'

She poked him in the ribs. 'Do you want to eat or not?'

'So you get on well with this guy?' Sean asked again through a mouthful of French fries.

'Sean, he's my business partner. That's all.'

'He fancies you.'

Stephanie laughed. 'You think every man fancies me. Anyway, I get the feeling Edward's involved with someone.'

Sean brightened. 'Really? Why don't we invite him and his significant other to dinner?'

Steph was amused. Sean wanted proof. 'I'll ask him,' she promised, 'but he's a very private person. Even Joe doesn't seem to know much about him.'

'Maybe he's gay,' Sean said hopefully.

'Definitely not,' Stephanie assured him with an innocent smile.

Liz looked at her watch. She'd ring Steph now. It was lunchtime. She was sure to be there and it was unlikely that Chris would answer the phone.

'Chez Nous, can I help you?'

'Sam? Hi, it's Liz. Is Steph there?'

'Hello, Liz. How are you? I think Steph's up in the office. Hang on and I'll put you through.'

Liz heard a couple of clicks and then the office phone rang, but there was no answer. She hung up. Stephanie had phoned several times but Liz had always found an excuse to ring off quickly. It had taken her this long to accept that Stephanie was only trying to help. Now she wanted to clear the air. Edward had wanted to intervene but she wouldn't let him. It was up to her to sort this out. Anyway, she wasn't ready for Steph to know how friendly she and Edward had become.

It had all happened so naturally. At first it had just been long phone conversations but now he dropped in at least once a week after Lucy was in bed. Liz had come to look forward to seeing his car pull up outside. He was so good to talk to and she didn't feel at all threatened by his interest. She'd learned a lot more about him over the last few weeks. He'd told her about his business and about his family. And because he was open with her, she relaxed with him. But she wouldn't talk about Chris. It was silly but she felt it would be disloyal to discuss her husband with another man. Especially when the man concerned had bought her husband's business.

But time with Edward had helped her get a lot of things back into perspective. She took more care with her appearance and she spent less time lounging in front of the television and more time with Lucy. For that she was very grateful.

Chris muttered to himself as he worked, barking occasional orders at his team. Pat and Marc exchanged nervous glances. Working with Chris was a bit like working with an unexploded bomb. You never knew when he was going to go off.

Chris was oblivious to them. All he could think of was that slimy bastard, McDermott. It was bad enough having to put up with him in the restaurant, but now it seemed that he was seeing Liz. Chris was fed up listening to Lucy going 'Uncle Edward this, Uncle Edward that.' He had a bellyful of 'Uncle Edward'. He'd tackled Liz about it but with no success. When he'd told Liz that it was disgusting to carry on an affair so openly in front of his daughter, she'd looked at him with distaste.

'Don't judge everyone by your own actions,' she'd said. 'Edward's a nice man, whose niece happens to be in Lucy's class. Nothing sordid is going on. I leave that kind of behaviour to you.'

Chris had tried to question his daughter once about the relationship. 'So do you see a lot of Uncle Edward?' he'd asked casually.

Lucy just shrugged and concentrated on her milkshake.

'Carol's your best friend, isn't she? Does she come over to play?'

'Sometimes,' Lucy said, uncharacteristically reticent.

'And does Uncle Edward come too?'

'Sometimes,' Lucy said again. 'Daddy? Can we go to the playground now?'

Chris abandoned his interrogation. He lifted her up in his arms and carried her out of the restaurant. 'Of course we can, princess,' he said swinging her over his head till she shrieked with laughter. 'We can do whatever you want.'

Chris whisked the sauce he was making with renewed vigour and wished it was McDermott's face he was scrambling. He didn't believe this relationship was as innocent as Liz made out. If nothing had happened yet, it wouldn't be long before it did. Chris knew Edward's sort. He was after something. Bloody cheek of him going after another man's wife. Chris hardly recognised Liz these days. She was so hard and cold. He'd tried charm, flattery, money, but nothing worked. Eventually his temper got the better of him and he'd tried to bully her into reconciliation, threatening all sorts of action concerning Lucy if she didn't come to her senses. He was giving up his restaurant for her. It was because of her that he was going to Galway. What more did the bloody woman want? McDermott was obviously influencing her. Turning her head. He'd have to do something to get rid of him or Liz would probably never take him back.

Chapter Eighteen

Stephanie flushed the loo, sat down on the side of the bath and wiped her mouth and face.

'Are you okay?' Sean asked from the other side of the bathroom door.

'Fine,' Steph said before leaning over the loo once more. Ten minutes later she emerged, white-faced and trembling.

Sean shook his head. 'You look awful. Hop back into bed. I'll make you a cup of tea and get you a hot-water bottle.'

'But I have to go to work.'

'You're not well enough to go anywhere today.'

'But, Sean, it's the press reception tonight,' she wailed.

Sean laughed. 'And Conor would really love you to be there. The owner running to the loo every five minutes to throw up – just the image he needs to present to the press!'

Steph groaned. 'Oh, I suppose you're right but I was so looking forward to it.'

'It's only one night, Steph,' he said firmly.

'But how will they manage—'

'Oh, for God's sake, Steph, you've organised everything down to the last detail. Now it's up to Conor. Anyway, won't McDermott be there?'

'Yeah, but he doesn't know anyone.' Steph sat up and reached for the phone. 'I'll call him. Tell him who he should talk to, who he should chat up.'

'I doubt if he needs any help there,' Sean muttered.

'What's that?'

'Nothing. I'll go and make that tea. Would you like some toast?'

Steph's stomach lurched again. 'God, no. I don't think I'll ever eat again.'

'Well we're definitely not getting anything from that Chinese takeaway again.'

Steph grimace. 'I thought that chicken tasted funny.'

'I'm going to call the doctor. If it's food poisoning you're going to need something to help you get over it.'

'I'll be fine,' Steph said half-heartedly.

'No arguments. You call Edward and leave everything else to me.'

Sean put the kettle on and used his mobile to call the local GP. Luckily he got him before surgery started and Steph was just taking a cautious sip of her tea when the doorbell went.

'That was fast.'

The GP was a young and very friendly Scotsman who cheerfully informed Steph that he'd had to treat a lot of people who'd eaten in the local Chinese. 'I'll give you an injection that should stop the vomiting. Apart from that just take plenty of fluids and stay in bed for a few days. You'll be fine.'

By the time Sean showed him to the door and went back upstairs, Steph was in the loo again.

'The injection should take effect soon, love,' he called in. 'And the doctor said it would make you sleepy.'

Steph groaned in reply as she staggered back into the room. 'I feel awful.'

Sean helped her into bed and tucked the duvet around her. 'Go to sleep. You'll feel better when you wake up.'

'Promise?' Steph said as her eyelids drooped.

'Promise,' he replied before closing the curtains and tiptoeing out of the room. The phone rang just as he got to the bottom of the stairs and he jumped on it so that it wouldn't wake Steph. 'Hello?' he whispered.

'Sean? Is that you?'

'Yeah, who's that?'

'It's Liz. Sorry if I disturbed you. It's just that I've being trying to reach Steph and all I ever get is her answering machine. I thought you might know where she is.'

'Liz, hi. How are you? No, well you wouldn't get Steph – not at her apartment anyway. She's moved in here.'

'Oh Sean, that's wonderful!'

Sean grinned. 'It is, isn't it?'

'Yeah. How on earth did you manage it?'

'A combination of threats, charm and brute force. Anyway, how are you? I haven't seen you since . . .'

'Yes, well, I'm doing okay, considering.'

'I was sorry to hear about you and Chris.'

'That's the way it goes. Steph seems to think I should take him back, forgive and forget.'

'She doesn't really, Liz. She just wants you to be sure that you make the right decision for you.'

'I know, Sean. I overreacted. I'm very touchy these days. Is she there?'

'Yes and no. She's asleep, Liz.'

'At this hour? Isn't she going into work today?'

'No, she's sick. Food poisoning, apparently. The doctor's just left.'

'Oh, poor Steph. Can I do anything to help?'

Sean smiled. 'You know, I think you can.'

He quickly filled Liz in on the reception planned for that evening.

'Will Chris be there?' Liz asked without preamble.

'No. It seemed more politic to pack him off to Galway for a few days. Steph didn't really trust him to show total support for Conor. And apparently he hates Edward McDermott.'

'Then there's no problem. I'll drop Lucy off at my mother's and I'll go straight in. Get Steph to give me a call when she wakes up and I'll be her slave for the day.'

'That'll really put her mind at rest, Liz,' Sean said. 'You're an angel. Why don't you drop over tomorrow night? I'm sure she'll be in better form and she'll be dying to hear how everything went.'

'I'd love that, Sean. And I'm delighted that you two have finally got it together.'

'Me too. See you tomorrow.'

When Steph woke her mouth was dry and she felt weak but, thankfully, when she moved, her stomach remained calm.

'Hello, sleepyhead,' Sean said from the armchair in the corner. 'How are you feeling?'

'Not too bad,' she said, sitting up gingerly. 'What time is it?'

'Almost five o'clock.'

'What? I can't believe I've been asleep all day!'

'The doctor said the injection would knock you out.'

She yawned. 'So what are you doing here at this hour?'

'I decided to work from home today.' He shut down his laptop and came over to sit on the side of the bed.

'Did you hear anything from the restaurant?'

'Not a dicky-bird, but Liz was on.'

'How is she?'

'Feeling guilty about having a go at you. You're to call her at the restaurant.'

Steph looked confused. 'What's she doing there?'

'She's gone in to help out and she says you're to ring her with instructions.'

'Oh, wow, that's brilliant! She knows a lot of the journalists and she can represent Chris. It will look great! Oh, Sean, this is wonderful.' She grabbed the telephone and called the restaurant. 'Liz?' she said hesitantly when she was put through to the office.

'Steph? Oh, Steph I'm so sorry for shouting at you.'

Steph breathed a sigh of relief. 'You've nothing to apologise for, Liz. I'm just glad you're talking to me again.'

'Of course I am! I was just a bit upset and—'

'You don't have to explain a thing, Liz. I'm just sorry for being so pushy.'

'You were just doing what you thought was right.'

'I'm going to throw up if you two keep this up,' Sean murmured as he came back into the room with a mug of tea.

'What was that?' Liz asked.

'Sean says we're making him sick.'

Liz laughed. 'Okay, enough of the soppy stuff. Tell me what you want me to do.'

After filling Liz in on her plans for the evening, Steph smiled happily at Sean, took a sip of tea and promptly fell asleep again. Sean closed the door gently and went downstairs to catch up on his work.

It was almost nine o'clock before Stephanie appeared in the doorway. 'Hi.'

Sean turned down the volume on the TV. 'Hey, how are you feeling?'

Steph shuffled across the carpet and sank down on the sofa beside him. 'Fragile.'

'Do you feel like eating? I got some chicken soup?'

Steph grinned. 'You're really turning into a Yank, aren't you?'

'Nah, then it would be home-made.'

'God forbid – I've tasted your cooking!'

'But I'm a dab hand with a microwave. So are you going to try some? It will give you strength.'

'Yes, Daddy.'

Minutes later Sean carried in a steaming bowl but Steph only managed a couple of spoonfuls before putting down her spoon. 'Sorry.'

'That's okay. You'll be feeling much better tomorrow.'

'I wonder how it's going.'

'I'm sure it's going just fine.'

'Do you think I should call?'

'No, they'll be too busy to talk now.'

'You're right,' she said with an impatient sigh and tried to concentrate on the documentary about heart transplants that Sean was engrossed in. Before long she'd dozed off again.

It was nearly eleven when Sean shook her gently. 'Steph? Conor wants to talk to you.'

Steph sat up and took the receiver. 'Conor? How did it go?'

'Brilliantly, Steph! They loved my food. The foie gras dish turned out better than ever, I used brandy instead of champagne . . .'

Stephanie heard some shouts in the background. 'What's that?'

Conor laughed. 'Liz says she'll strangle me if I tell anyone else about my foie gras. Here's Edward. Sorry you weren't here, Steph. We missed you.'

'Steph? It's Edward.'

'Well, Edward, be honest. Did it really go well?'

'Like clockwork,' he assured her. 'Congratulations, Steph. Conor outdid himself. The food was amazing and Liz and I really worked the room. She was sensational.'

Steph felt a pang of jealousy.

'Steph? Oh Steph, it was wonderful. You should be so proud of Conor – and of yourself. All your hard work paid off.'

Steph smiled at the excitement in Liz's voice. 'Hiya, Liz. Thanks for stepping into the breach. It sounds as if you did a great job. I'll get you back into this business if it's the last thing I do.'

When Stephanie eventually hung up, Sean took her in his arms. 'Well done, love.'

'But I didn't do anything,' she said miserably.

'You set it all up. You saw a talent in Conor and you gave him a chance. You organised this evening, you drew up the guest list, you did the PR. If it wasn't for you, tonight wouldn't have happened at all. I'm very proud of you, Steph and you should be too.'

Steph hugged him gratefully. 'Thanks, Sean.' She kissed him gently.

'That's nice,' he murmured against her lips and kissed her back.

Steph felt her body stir in response. 'I think I'm feeling a bit better.' She grinned at him and started to unbutton his shirt.

'Really? Is there anything that I can do to assist in the recovery process?' He bent his head and bit her nipple through the thin cotton night-shirt.

Steph shivered. 'Some tender loving care would be nice.'

He pushed her back against the cushions and bent his head to her other nipple. 'I think I can manage that.' His tongue traced the edge of her collarbone.

'Come here!' Steph whispered urgently and pulled his head up to kiss him hungrily.

'You seem to be feeling somewhat better,' he gasped as she reached down to open his fly.

'You know, I think I am?'

Chapter Nineteen

'Can I have a word?' George stood in the doorway of the office.

Steph looked up. 'Sure, George, take a pew. What's the problem?'

George sat down and lit a cigarette. 'I think it's time I moved on.'

Stephanie was glad Conor wasn't present. He'd never have been able to suppress his delight. 'Why's that, George? Is there a problem?'

'Ah no, love, but I'm too old for this caper. It's hard to teach an old dog new tricks. I don't think I fit into this new set-up.'

'I'm sorry you feel that way, George. You're a damn good chef. You know how highly I think of you.'

George warmed to the flattery. 'Nice of you to say so, Steph, but my mind is made up.'

'Have you something else lined up?' Steph asked, hoping he wasn't planning to walk out immediately.

'No, no. I just wanted to let you know. Give you a bit of notice. Chris says I'm welcome in Galway, but I don't fancy leaving Dublin – what would I do in the middle of nowhere?'

Steph smiled. Only a die-hard Dubliner could think

of a cosmopolitan city like Galway as the middle of nowhere! 'Well, I'll be sorry to lose you, George. Thanks for the notice. I appreciate it. Let me know when you've found something. Have you mentioned this to anyone else?'

George looked surprised. 'Of course not, Steph. I told you first. Aren't you the boss now?'

Steph held out her hand. 'Well, good luck, George. I hope you find something to suit you.'

George shook her hand and left the office.

A few hours later, Steph grabbed a quiet moment to call Conor in Belfast. She closed the door of the office before dialling.

'You're kidding,' Conor said. 'The old bastard's leaving?'

Steph laughed. 'Try to sound a bit disappointed when you talk to him, will you?'

'I'll even buy him a drink,' Conor promised. 'This is great news. I'll phone Kevin and put him on notice. God, he'll be chuffed. Listen, I have to go, Steph. It's pretty busy here. I'll call you when I've talked to Kevin.'

'Fair enough, Conor. See you next week. Bye.' Steph hung up. Well at least she'd made one person happy today. Maybe it would help her through her next unpleasant duty. She picked up the phone and dialled zero. Liam answered.

'Liam? Could you ask Sam to drop in, please?'

Steph sat down at the table in Annie's kitchen and pulled out her cigarettes. 'God, I'm gasping for a cuppa.'

'I'm not surprised.' Annie poured the tea and sat

down. 'You seem to be constantly on the go these days.'

'It is a bit mad.'

'And George is leaving?'

'Yeah.'

'And you've given Sam the push.'

'I have.'

'Lord, whatever next?'

Steph exhaled a cloud of smoke. 'Next, I get myself an assistant.'

'How about Liz?'

Steph shook her head. 'No, I'm looking for someone at a very junior level to take over the routine office work. If I ever hire Liz, it'll be as a chef.'

'Do you think she'd be interested?'

'Well, it doesn't look like she's planning to go to Galway so she may well need to get a job. You know we could do with an extra pair of hands part-time. Maybe I'll mention it casually and see how she reacts.'

Annie nodded. 'I think you should. I know things are tough for her right now but I think she'll be better off without Chris in the end. She changed so much after she married him.'

'I don't think she changed until Lucy came along.'

'Yes, but it was Chris who insisted they start a family. I honestly think he wanted her out of the way. That he couldn't handle the competition. I always thought Liz was the better chef.'

'Well, she was definitely more professional,' Steph agreed. 'So you think Chris wanted her out of the restaurant and chained to the kitchen sink?'

'Well, maybe not consciously,' Annie conceded.

'I wonder if she'll ever meet someone else?' Steph mused.

'Not if she doesn't get out more. If we can't talk her into going back to work, we're at least going to have to work on her social life. Speaking of which, I was thinking of having a bit of a get-together for Joe's birthday.'

'Oh, great! It's ages since I've been to a party. Who are you going to invite?'

'Well, that's one of the problems. All our friends are couples. How will that make Liz feel?'

'She won't come,' Steph said glumly. 'Could we fix her up?'

Annie raised an eyebrow. 'Are you tired of living?'

'Well, then maybe we could invite a few single people. We must know some. What about Edward?'

Annie frowned. 'I thought you said he was seeing someone?'

'I'm not so sure now. Any time I've talked about us getting together as a foursome, he's dodged it. But if he wants to keep the mystery woman to himself, let him. Invite him on his own.'

'Liz would think I was setting her up. Maybe if we invite a few others too . . .'

Stephanie clapped her hands. 'I've got it! Conor! He's between girlfriends and he gets on well with Liz. In fact we could kill two birds with one stone. He could talk Liz into going back to work.'

'I like it! But that still leaves me with an odd number. We need another woman. What about Jean?'

Steph nearly choked on her tea at the mention of the surly waitress. 'You've got to be kidding! She's next on my hit list.'

'Well then, it'll have to be Jackie. She's a bit much after a few drinks but beggars can't be choosers.'

'Who's she?'

'Oh, you know the one. Two doors down. Her husband ran off with the nanny.'

'Oh, great. You'd better keep her away from Liz or it could turn into a wake!'

'No, Jackie's okay. She's living it up these days – making up for lost time. She's good company as long as you don't mention his name. Now another problem. What night can I have the party if Conor's coming?'

'As long as Chris is still with us, any night except Saturday will be fine.'

'Well then, we'll go for a Friday. Joe's birthday's on a Sunday, so the Friday before. He won't be expecting it. I just hope I can keep the kids quiet.' Annie knew there wasn't a chance of hiding the preparations from her children. The best thing was to get them involved. They'd love that.

Steph rooted in her bag and pulled out her diary to check the date. 'That's the fifth, isn't it? Yes, that should be – oh!'

'What?'

Steph frowned. 'That's odd.'

'What is it? Steph?'

Steph's face paled. 'I should have got my period three days ago.'

'Give or take,' Annie joked.

'No, seriously, Annie. It's the pill, you see. My period always starts three days after I stop taking it. I could set my watch by it.'

'Maybe you're just run down. After all, you've been working very hard. And then there was that time you were sick—'

'Oh, God.'

'What?'

'I was vomiting for nearly twenty-four hours, Annie. And afterwards – well, Sean and I, we – how could I be so bloody stupid?'

Annie grinned. 'I see.'

'It's not funny, Annie!' Steph's voice started to rise. 'What the hell am I going to do?'

'Calm down, for goodness sake. Why don't you buy one of those tests? There's no point in getting all worked up until you know for sure. And even then, well, you and Sean are together . . .'

'I can't have a baby, Annie. Are you mad?'

Annie winced at Stephanie's ferocity – she was practically hysterical. 'Stephanie, it wouldn't be the end of the world. Anyway, there's no point in even worrying about this until you take a test. There's a chemist on the corner. I'll go.'

'No!' Steph barked. She took a deep breath and struggled to speak more calmly. 'No, it's okay. I'll pick one up on my way in to work.' She stood up and slung her bag over her shoulder. 'Sorry, Annie. It's just a bit of a shock. I'd better go.'

'Call me later and let me know.' Annie watched anxiously as Steph sped away.

Stephanie sat in the car trying to work up the courage to go into the chemist. She'd always been so careful, how could this happen to her? She was almost sure that the test would prove positive. She was regular as clockwork. Her period was never late. Still, she shrank from proving herself right. What a terrible mess. What lousy, rotten luck.

Ruth ran into the bathroom for the third time that morning. Luckily classes were in full swing and there was no one around to hear her retching. When the nausea passed she sat back against the toilet door and wiped her face with a bit of toilet paper. How had she got herself into this mess? Her dad would be so disappointed. He'd wanted a wonderful career for her, and that had looked more likely after the interview she'd had last week. Now it seemed that she was fated to become a housewife and mother. Tears welled up in her eyes. She'd always wanted to be a mother, but not quite so soon. She'd imagined a few years of good living and partying with Des. She'd planned to buy herself a car – nothing as flashy as his – just a banger that would get her from A to B. She'd imagined holidays in Spain, with Des rubbing oil into her tanned skin. She sniffed and blew her nose. No point in feeling sorry for yourself, Ruth. You got yourself into this mess, you're just going to have to deal with it. She made her way out of the loos and down to the telephones. She rummaged for coins and dialled Des's office number. She cursed the snobby receptionist as her money wasted away while she was left on hold listening to 'Edelweiss'. Eventually she was told that Des was in a meeting and couldn't be disturbed. She hung up, disappointed. She picked up the phone again and dialled Steph's office.

Steph agreed to meet immediately she heard the panic in her friend's voice. That bastard Des must be the reason. He usually was. She wondered what he'd done this time. She pushed her way through the crowd in Bewley's to the table where Ruth sat staring into her coffee.

'Hiya, how's it going?' she said, dropping into the chair opposite her.

Ruth looked up at her friend and immediately burst into tears. 'I'm pregnant, Steph,' she managed eventually.

Steph sat back in her chair, her mouth open.

Ruth started to sob again. 'I've been so stupid, Steph. What are Mam and Dad going to say? They'll be so disappointed in me. They had such high hopes. I know they'd have wanted me to have a husband and family at some stage, but not yet. Not for a long time.'

'You've talked to Des? He's going to marry you?'

Ruth smiled through her tears. 'Of course he'll marry me, Steph. Don't be silly. He loves me. I haven't told him yet, but he'll be fine once he gets used to the idea.'

Steph was amazed. How was it that such an intelligent girl was so dense when it came to men. 'I hope you're right, Ruth. But maybe you should prepare yourself, in case . . .'

'In case what? Of course he's going to marry me. He's got to marry me.' Ruth's voice rose in panic and Steph put an arm around her.

'It's going to be okay, Ruth. Don't worry. Everything's going to be okay,' she said soothingly. Please God she was right.

Chapter Twenty

Stephanie stared at the test-stick in her hand. It was incredible to think that one blue line could change her entire life. She tucked the evidence away in her bag, touched up her make-up and went back to her office. Calmly, she reached for the phone book and found the number she was looking for.

'Hello, Marie Stopes Clinic. Can I help you?'

Stephanie quickly wrote down some details and thanked the girl. Before she had time to think, she rang the number in London and booked an appointment for the following week. She could only be a couple of weeks pregnant. Better to do it before she started to notice any changes. She'd have to stay over for a couple of days. She was to attend a counselling session and then go in for the procedure the following day. She would opt for the local anaesthetic. That way she'd be in and out in a couple of hours. Anyway, the thought of being conscious appealed to her Catholic mind. She knew that what she was doing was wrong. The least she could do was go through it consciously, acknowledge her sin.

She booked a British Midland flight. Now all she had to do was think of an excuse for going to London. But what was she going to tell Sean? She sighed heavily.

She couldn't tell him she was pregnant because she knew he'd want her to keep it. She'd have to make sure Annie kept her mouth shut. Sean would never understand. And things were so good between them lately she didn't want anything to spoil it.

Keeping the secret was harder than she'd imagined. Every time Sean smiled at her or told her he loved her she cringed inside. He wouldn't feel that way if he knew what she was planning to do. So she avoided him, convinced that guilt shone out of her eyes. She managed to keep him at bay for two days, leaving the house earlier in the mornings and arriving home long after he'd gone to bed. When Sean wanted to make love, she pleaded tiredness – it wasn't really a lie. The combination of work and the burden of her secret left her exhausted. And anyway, she couldn't face the thought of making love. It seemed wrong. She refused to take Annie's calls, knowing exactly how her sister-in-law would react. But Annie wasn't so easily put off.

Steph looked up from her desk one day to see her standing in the doorway.

'We're going out,' Annie said without preamble.

'I can't—' Steph began.

'Do you want to have the conversation here?' Annie looked pointedly at Liam who was rummaging through a filing cabinet in the corner.

Steph picked up her bag. 'I'm going out for a while, Liam. I won't be long.'

Ten minutes later they were settled with coffee in a quiet corner of a nearby pub.

'It was positive?'

Steph nodded.

'And what are you going to do?'

'I'm going to get rid of it, of course,' she said abruptly.

Annie swallowed hard. She struggled to find the right words, the right tone. 'Why?'

Steph looked at her in surprise. 'What?'

'Why are you – getting rid of it?' Annie stumbled over the last words. This was a new life they were talking about.

'I don't want children,' Steph said flatly. 'There's no place in my life for them.'

'And what does Sean think?' Annie asked, knowing full well that Stephanie hadn't told him.

'It's nothing to do with him.' Steph folded her arms in front of her, her mouth settling into a stubborn line.

'I'm not sure he'd agree with you. It takes two to make a baby. It isn't up to you to make this decision on your own. It's not your right.'

Steph glared at her. 'It's my body, for Christ's sake. I'm the one who'd have to carry it for nine months.'

'True,' Annie agreed as calmly as she could manage. 'But we're not talking about some bastard who wouldn't stand by you. We're talking about Sean, the man you love, who loves you. You trust him, don't you? Even if you've made up your mind, you must realise that you have to tell him. If he found out afterwards he'd never forgive you.'

Stephanie lit a cigarette and puffed on it silently.

'You love him, Steph. Don't hurt him.'

'He'd want the child. What if he leaves me when I tell him what I'm going to do?' There was a tremor in Steph's voice.

'He might,' Annie agreed. There was no point in

lying. 'But at least you'll be able to live with yourself.' Stephanie seemed to have softened slightly, so Annie decided to probe further. 'Do you really not want kids, Steph, or does all of this come back to Ruth?'

Steph buried her face in her hands. 'I don't know, Annie. I don't know. I don't think I'm normal. I can't imagine being responsible for something so small and defenceless. I don't think I could handle it.'

Annie laughed. 'You're not abnormal. All prospective parents feel that way. It's perfectly natural. It's the biggest job you'll ever take on in your life.'

'No, Annie. It's more than that. I just know it's not for me. I'm not in the least maternal. Maybe it is to do with Ruth. When she died, something inside me died too. It's like I lived a lifetime over that weekend.'

Annie put a hand out to her friend. All these years, drunk and sober, she'd tried to get Stephanie to talk. And now out of the blue . . . 'You were only a kid, Steph. Of course it had a traumatic effect on you. And then you kept it all to yourself. You never talked, never told anyone her secret. You were a great friend, Steph.'

Steph shook her head impatiently. 'Not good enough.'

'You did everything you could have done. Ruth made a mistake and now you're in a similar position. Don't make the mistake of shutting Sean out. Even if you're determined to do it, tell him first.'

Steph nodded sadly. 'I will but I know it will be the end of us. It's hard enough that he doesn't see Billy. He'd never be able to forgive me for this.' Tears welled up in Steph's eyes and misery engulfed her. What was wrong with her? Why was she hell-bent on self-destruction? She wiped the tears away and patted Annie's hand. 'Thanks, Annie. I'd be lost without you. Now I must get back. I'll finish up early and I'll tell Sean tonight. No point in putting it off any longer.'

'Have you, eh, made any arrangements?' Annie shrank from the words.

'Yes. Next Wednesday in a clinic in London. I fly back Thursday evening.'

'So fast,' Annie said sadly. 'Would you like me to go with you? I'm sure Joe would want me to.'

'Oh no, that's okay. And please, don't tell Joe.' She paused when Annie looked away. 'Too late, huh? Oh dear. He'll never understand this, will he? Try to explain for me, will you Annie? I couldn't stand it if he turned against me too. And Mam and Dad must never know.'

'I'll talk to Joe,' Annie assured her, 'and your folks will never hear it from us. I promise you that.'

Stephanie gave her a quick hug and left.

Sean was surprised to see Steph's car already in the driveway. It was supposed to be one of her late nights. He hoped she wasn't sick again. She'd been so tired lately and very withdrawn. He was getting quite worried about her. He wondered if he could persuade her to take a break. He was due to go back to the States at some stage and it would be wonderful if she came with him. He'd ask her tonight.

'Honey, I'm ho-ome,' he sang out as he let himself in, dropped his briefcase in the hall and flung his jacket over the banisters.

Steph smiled despite herself. Oh, why couldn't she run to him and tell him there was good news? Why couldn't she rejoice in the new life growing within her? Eat too much ice cream, read baby books and let Sean spoil her? Stop it, Steph. Get a grip. This is no time for feeling sorry for yourself.

'Hello, love. You're home early. Is everything okay?' Sean planted a kiss on her forehead and sat down beside her. She'd changed into a tracksuit and removed all her make-up and she was looking very young and very vulnerable.

'I need to talk to you,' she said quietly.

'Okay. Why don't we go out to dinner? Somewhere quiet.'

'I don't really feel like it. Maybe we could get a takeaway later.'

'Not Chinese,' he quipped.

'No, not Chinese,' she agreed with a weak smile.

'Why don't I open a bottle of wine?' He was out of the room before Steph could reply. This wasn't going to be easy.

'I've had a lousy day,' he said, returning with the wine and two glasses. 'You wouldn't believe how stupid—'

'Sean, I've got something to tell you.'

He poured the wine and handed her a glass. 'I'm all yours,' he said lightly, sitting down beside her.

'There's no easy way to say this, no point in beating around the bush. I'm pregnant.'

Sean looked at her blankly.

'Sean, did you hear me? I said I'm pregnant.' Steph looked at him, wishing he'd say something.

'You're pregnant?' he cried and pulled her into his arms. 'Steph, I can't believe it! My God, when? How?' He laughed. 'Well, of course I know how – how do you feel? Are you okay?'

Stephanie quaked at the concern in his eyes. 'I'm okay. But I, I . . .'

'What is it, love? Nervous? That's natural, believe me. You'll get used to the idea. You're going to be a fantastic mother, and a very sexy one.' He trailed kisses across her face and down her neck.

Steph pulled away abruptly. 'No. You don't understand, Sean. I can't do it.'

His smile was sympathetic. 'Of course you can, Steph. You'll be fine. I'll look after you.'

'No, Sean, you're not listening! It's not going to happen. I don't want it to happen. I'm flying to London next week for a termination.'

'No, you're bloody well not!' he ground out. 'What the hell are you talking about?'

Steph flinched at the cold fury in his eyes. 'I'm sorry, but I've made up my mind.'

Sean clenched his fists and took a deep breath. 'Look, love. I know this is a shock but give it a bit of time to sink in. Believe me, no one can make you as happy as your own child. You don't understand how much you'd be giving up. Please think about it.'

Steph shrugged him off and turned her face away. She couldn't bear him like this. His fury was easier. 'There's nothing to think about. I've made up my mind.'

'And what about me? Don't I have a say? I am the father – or am I?'

Steph stared at him. 'How could you even say such a thing? You know there's no one else. God, is that what you think of me?'

'I don't know what to bloody think any more.' Sean raked his hand through his hair. 'I don't know how you could even think of doing this.'

'I'm sorry but a termination's the only answer.'

'Termination? Termination?' he shouted at her. 'Call

it what it is, for God's sake. Abortion. Murder. This isn't just some neat little operation. You're not deciding on a "termination"! You're deciding to kill our child.'

'Don't say that!' Steph screamed and ran upstairs. She curled into a ball on the bed, crying into her pillow and waiting for Sean to come and tell her it was all right. She listened for his step on the stairs but it didn't come. Minutes later the front door slammed and she heard the screech of wheels on the gravel. 'Oh, God help me,' she whispered and sobbed herself into a restless sleep.

When she woke the room was dark and the house was silent. She took off her clothes and after a moment's hesitation unlocked the bedroom door. She climbed into bed and waited for Sean to come, eventually falling into an exhausted sleep but she was plagued by nightmares.

When she opened her eyes the next morning she was still alone. She groaned as the memory of last night's horrible scene came flooding back. She dragged herself out of bed and went in search of Sean. The other bedrooms were empty. Maybe he'd spent the night on the sofa. But downstairs was as empty and silent as the rest of the house. She padded into the kitchen, the terracotta tiles cold underfoot. She'd make some tea and then call him on his mobile. But what would she say? She wasn't going to change her mind and that was the only thing he'd want to hear. She couldn't blame him for attacking her. She understood his horror, but was powerless to do anything about it. She crossed to the patio door and looked out on the large unkempt garden. She'd been nagging Sean for weeks to do something with it. He'd laughed and told her to call her dad. She made a mug of tea and carried it over to the table and for the first time noticed the note propped up against the sugar bowl. She picked it up and read it. Short and to the point.

I've gone to my folks. I'm going back to the States as soon as I can arrange it. Please move out before I get back.

Steph rested her head in her arms and cried like a baby. She'd prepared herself for his anger and for the possibility that he might not want anything more to do with her, but nothing had prepared her for the pain that was ripping her apart.

Chapter Twenty-one

Stephanie leaned back, closed her eyes and ignored the flight attendant giving the safety routine. It had been the longest week of her life. She hadn't seen Sean again and he wouldn't take or return her calls. She'd never have got through the week without Annie. Even Joe had been great – despite his obvious disapproval – and moved all her stuff back out to Malahide. She felt sad as she closed the front door of Sean's lovely old house. In the few weeks she'd lived there, she'd come to look on it as home. By contrast, her apartment seemed cold and empty.

Joe had a quiet word with Edward, filled him in on the situation and asked him to look after things for a while. Edward didn't let on to Stephanie that he knew what was going on. He accepted her lame reason for going to London, and assured her he'd be available if any crisis arose in her absence.

Steph avoided Liz, afraid that in her emotional state she'd blurt everything out. She didn't know how Liz would react. She probably wouldn't be as sympathetic as Annie was. Anyway, she didn't want to tell anyone else. It was hard enough coping with Sean's rejection.

She turned as the hostess stopped beside her with the drinks trolley.

'Cognac, please,' she said. She tossed back half the glass defiantly. 'I'm doing the right thing. I'm doing the right thing.' She repeated the words to herself like a mantra.

'Des, I'm pregnant,' Ruth said before she lost her nerve. She was still breathless after their swift and intense lovemaking. She'd tried to talk to Des earlier, but he was hell-bent on making love and it was easier to go along with it.

'You're what?' Des rolled over in bed and stared at her.

'I'm pregnant, Des. It must have been that first time. I've been on the pill since.'

Des stared at her. 'Christ.'

Ruth laughed nervously. 'I know it's not what we wanted, but if we get married quickly, we can get away with it. My dad will probably go nuts, but he'll calm down eventually. I'm sure he'll give us his blessing in the end.'

Des looked at her, panic-stricken. 'I don't think we should rush into anything, Ruth,' he said, struggling to keep his voice calm. 'Marriage is a big step.'

'But we love each other. We would have married sooner or later, this just means it has to be sooner.'

Des pulled on his trousers and reached for his shirt.

Ruth looked at him nervously. 'Des? You do love me, Des, don't you?'

He hesitated and then gave her a quick, awkward hug. 'Course I do, silly. But like I say, marriage is a big step. I think it would be better if you had an abortion. You have your whole life ahead of you, not to mention a very promising career. You don't want to throw it all away, do you?'

Ruth shook her head.

Relieved, he took her hand and continued more gently. 'There you go then. There'll be plenty of time for babies. You're only nineteen, for God's sake. It would be very hard, Ruth. Too hard. Trying to bring up a child on my salary alone. And we'd have to get somewhere decent to live. It's really not a great idea.'

Ruth looked at him solemnly. 'So you want me to have an abortion?'

'Don't say it like that,' he said angrily. 'That's not what I said. I just want you to do what's best.'

For who? Ruth wondered.

'So what do you think?' he asked anxiously.

She smiled weakly. 'You're probably right.'

The look of relief on his face was like a knife through her heart.

'Good girl!' He hugged her. 'Why don't you get in touch with one of those clinics and I'll take care of your travel arrangements? I think you should fly. The boat might be a bit much if you're not feeling well.'

'I can't afford it . . .'

'I'll pay. Don't you worry about a thing.'

'Thanks, Des,' she said quietly.

'You're doing the right thing, love. I promise you. You won't regret it.'

Ruth stared into the distance. 'No. No, I won't regret it.'

Steph consulted her *A to Z*. The clinic was quite near the hotel so she set out on foot. Ten minutes later she walked up the steps, pushed open the swing door and found herself in a bright reception area. It could be any ordinary office building, she thought idly. Somehow that didn't seem right to Stephanie. The receptionist was kind but businesslike. She showed Stephanie into an office and another woman stood to greet her.

'Good afternoon, Ms West. I'm Eve Wilmot. Please sit down.'

Steph shook her hand and perched nervously on the edge of a chair.

'There are just some details I need about your general health and family history.'

Steph nodded and answered the questions. It was all very weird. The woman hadn't even mentioned the baby.

With all the details out of the way, Eve Wilmot took off her glasses and smiled at her. 'So, Ms West – Stephanie. Why have you decided to terminate your pregnancy?'

Stephanie was ready for this question. She'd no intention of telling the truth. It was too complicated. 'It just wouldn't work. I've broken up with my partner and I'm in the throes of setting up a new business.'

'Does your partner know you're pregnant?'

'Yes, but he's not interested,' Steph lied, silently begging Sean's forgiveness.

'What about your family?'

'There are only my parents who are elderly and live in County Wicklow. They wouldn't be able to help out.' Steph lowered her eyes as she thought of the vibrant couple who lived life to the full.

'Could you afford a child-minder?' Eve Wilmot asked pleasantly.

Steph flushed. 'Well, yes, I could, but I don't see much point in bringing a child into the world and then handing it over to someone else to raise. Do you?'

'I'm not judging you, Stephanie. It's my job to make sure that you've made the right decision.'

'Well, I have,' Steph said defiantly. 'I don't want to be a single mother, not now, not ever. I've a business to run and that's my top priority.'

Eve asked some more questions and then explained the procedure for the following day. 'You'll see my colleague, Doctor Knight first – just in case you have any more questions or have second thoughts overnight.'

'I won't,' Steph said shortly. She felt guilty as the counsellor reassured her that she was probably making the right decision and she left the clinic feeling uneasy. She'd planned to go and do some shopping. Buy a present for Lucy and pick up something nice for Annie in Harrods, but she couldn't face it. She walked slowly back to the hotel where she ordered a bottle of wine from room service and ran herself a hot bath.

She undressed and slipped on a hotel robe while she waited for her wine. She lit a cigarette and then stubbed it out. You weren't supposed to smoke when you were pregnant. She laughed out loud. It was a bit silly worrying about that now! The harsh, slightly hysterical sound took her by surprise. There was a knock on the door and she took the tray from the waiter. She poured herself a large glass of the Côtes du Rhône and lit another cigarette, pulling deeply on it. Maybe she'd get drunk. It might make her feel better. Maybe she'd even miscarry naturally and she wouldn't have to go through with tomorrow. Wouldn't have to feel guilty. She pulled a clean blouse out of her overnight bag and hung it on the bathroom door to let the creases fall out. It would do for dinner.

Two hours later she walked into the dining-room and was led to a table near the window. She sat with her back to the room. She wasn't in the mood for company. The waiter handed her a menu and she scanned it quickly. 'Consommé followed by the fish with a side salad,' she said. She selected a wine and then settled back in her seat to wait. She'd never ordered a meal so fast – Sean would be in shock. But tonight she didn't care. She was just going through the motions. Killing time.

The waiter arrived back with the wine, and she waved at him to pour away – another deviation from the norm, but she didn't much care what she drank as long as it knocked her out. She lit a cigarette and ignored the dirty look she got from a neighbouring table. She turned her thoughts to Chez Nous and the weeks of work ahead but she kept going back to the ordeal facing her, the look of disgust on Sean's face that night . . . She shivered and took a gulp of wine. When the soup arrived she took a couple of spoonfuls before pushing it away. The main course got much the same treatment, but the wine got a quick death.

She signed for her meal and headed back to her room where she channel-hopped for an hour, paced for a while and then went back to the TV. Eventually she got into bed and turned off the light. It was only eleven and she was wide-awake. The drink had neither dulled her senses nor made her sleepy. It looked as if it was going to be a long and restless night.

Ruth picked up the phone and dialled Steph's number.
  'Hello?'
  'Steph? Hi, it's me.'
  'Ruth? Hi. What's happening?'

'Nothing much. Still pregnant.' Ruth gave a short humourless laugh.

'Did you tell Des?'

'Yep.'

'And?'

'He was . . . shocked.'

'I'm sure he was. Is he going to stand by you?'

'Yes. Of course.'

'Oh, Ruth. That's great. So when are you going to tell your folks? When are you getting married?'

'We're not. I've decided to get an abortion. I'm not going to tell Mam and Dad.'

Steph stared at the receiver in her hand. How in God's name was Ruth able to talk so calmly? She was dead against abortion – always had been. This had to be Des Healy's idea, the bastard. 'Are you sure that's what you want, Ruth?'

'Of course it's not,' Ruth said impatiently, 'but it's for the best. Listen, can you come over? Mary and Sinead are still away and this place is like a bloody morgue.'

'Oh, I'm sorry, Ruth. I can't. Sean's taking me out. We're meeting some of his friends. Look, I'll meet you for lunch tomorrow. Bewley's at one, okay?'

'Okay,' Ruth said her voice flat. She hung up the receiver, wandered into the living-room and switched on the TV. An image of a woman in labour with a concerned husband bending over her swam onto the screen. Ruth groaned and switched it off. She went back out to the phone.

'Hi, Gary? It's Ruth, is Des there?'

'Oh, hi, Ruth. Eh . . . no . . . I think he's out at some business do.'

Ruth smiled grimly. 'Okay. Thanks, Gary. Bye.' A work do on a Sunday evening. Unlikely. She thought back over the last few months and the number of strange and rather weak excuses

Des had given for his absence. No wonder Steph thought she was dumb. It had been obvious to everyone except her that Des wasn't serious about her. But she'd only seen what she wanted to see. She was in love and she desperately wanted him to love her too. Oh, well.

She unplugged the phone from the wall and then locked the front door. Sinead and Mary had gone home to Tullamore for the weekend. They weren't due back until Monday evening. She went into the bathroom and opened the press. Mary's medication for her migraine was neatly lined up. There was also a bottle of aspirin and a half pack of paracetamol. Ruth regarded them thoughtfully and then gathered them all up with trembling hands. She went into the kitchen and set them down on the table. She fetched a jug, the breadboard and a rolling pin. She paused to turn on the radio. She needed some kind of noise. 'I'm Not in Love' by 10CC. That was appropriate, she thought grimly. She emptied out each pack of pills onto the board, crushed them and then carefully scraped the powder into the jug. When she was finished, she went to the fridge. There was only one can of beer and a half bottle of cheap wine. That wouldn't do at all. She checked all the cupboards and found a vodka bottle with a drain in the bottom and half a bottle of whiskey. She'd never get that down her – she hated the stuff. She went in search of her purse. Fifteen quid. That would do.

She put on her jacket, picked up her keys and went down to the off-licence.

'Howya,' the owner said cheerfully.

'How's it going?' Ruth replied with a smile. 'A bottle of brandy please.'

'Sure. Any particular brand?'

'Oh, whatever you recommend. It's a special occasion.'

'It's well for you,' he said, selecting a dark green bottle from the top shelf. 'That's eleven-fifty, please.'

Ruth handed over the money.

'Well, enjoy,' he said and handed her the brown bag and her change,

'I will. Seeya,' she said with a cheerful smile. She walked back to the flat, feeling calm and almost relaxed.

After depositing the brandy on the counter in the kitchen she went into her bedroom and opened the wardrobe. She started flicking through the stuff on the shelf. Her red leather belt. Sinead loved that. And then there was her new hairdryer. Sinead could have that too. Mary wouldn't mind. Her new gypsy skirt – that Steph liked. It would fit her perfectly. Look better on her too. She went through all her stuff adding selected items to different piles. All the shoes were Mary's to keep or discard. She was the only one who was the same size.

Ruth moved to the bedside table and flicked through her small collection of books. The Jane Austen and the book of Irish poetry for Steph. The joke book for Sinead, and the pristine good-as-new Pru Leith cookbook was added to Mary's bundle. It might actually get used now. She put all her trendiest stuff into another pile for her sisters and added her extensive collection of earrings. After the wardrobe was clear, she carefully labelled the piles and went back out to the kitchen. She poured some of the brandy into the jug and mixed the concoction with a spoon. She emptied it into a tumbler and carried it and the bottle into the living-room. She settled down on the lumpy sofa and set her concoction on the coffee table in front of her. Now. Was there anything else to do? Should she leave a note for Des? No. There was nothing left to say. Should she ring her folks? No, too risky. They might come over. She'd have to leave them a note, but what would she say? Tell her parents that the daughter they'd been so proud of had got herself knocked up? It was so hard. How could she make them understand? Still, if she didn't leave a note, they'd always wonder. She found a pen and took a piece of Mary's pretty, scented notepaper from the drawer in the sideboard. When she'd finished writing, she folded the page neatly and put it in the matching pink envelope. On the front she wrote 'Mam and Dad'.

She put down the pen, stirred her drink and took a deep breath before lifting the glass to her lips. She managed to swallow half of it without gagging. She winced at the bitter taste and took a slug from the brandy bottle before emptying the glass. Then she settled back and waited for the darkness to engulf her.

Chapter Twenty-two

Stephanie walked into reception and the same girl welcomed her. 'If you'd like to follow me, Ms West.' She led the way towards the double doors. 'Ms West?'

Stephanie tried, but she couldn't move. The simple act of putting one foot in front of the other seemed impossible. 'I can't,' she whispered.

The receptionist nodded, unfazed, and excused herself, returning moments later with the counsellor.

'Why don't we go into my office and have a nice cup of tea?' Eve Wilmot said, taking Steph's arm.

'Feel better?' the counsellor asked, an hour and half a box of tissues later.

'Yes, thanks,' Steph smiled shakily. 'You've been very kind. I'm sorry for messing you about.'

Eve dismissed her apologies with a wave of her hand. 'Every time a woman decides to keep her baby, I go home happier.'

'It happens a lot?'

'Oh my, yes. A lot of women can't go through with it. Some come back the following week, but others send me their baby pictures. I hope you will.'

'Of course.' Steph smiled shyly. It was still hard to come to terms with the idea of being a mother. It terrified her, but she knew she couldn't get rid of her baby – Sean's baby. Oh, he'd be so happy! She couldn't wait to tell him.

'Please consider counselling,' Eve said seriously. 'You had a terrible experience when you were very young, and it's being eating you up for a long time. You've taken the first step towards dealing with it, but you've still a long way to go.'

'I'll have a word with my GP,' Steph promised. She stood up and held out her hand. 'Thank you so much, Eve. You've been very kind.'

'My pleasure. Now why don't we get you checked out while you're here? Have you any idea of your due date?'

Stephanie floated down the steps of the clinic, one hand touching her stomach almost reverently. She was seven weeks pregnant! It was amazing! She couldn't quite believe it all. She'd been so sure that termination was the only way but, when it came to the crunch, she couldn't do it. Now it was as if an enormous weight had been lifted from her shoulders. The future suddenly seemed bright. She could manage work and motherhood – plenty of other women did. Women who weren't nearly as well off as she was. She couldn't wait to tell her mother. She'd be thrilled. She'd be more thrilled if Stephanie was married of course, but that would happen soon enough. Steph hailed a taxi and directed him to Mothercare. It might be a bit early to buy, but there was no harm in looking.

Steph wandered through the shop with a silly smile on her face. She paused to touch a Moses basket, finger a lace quilt and linger over a tiny peach satin dress that was an outrageous sixty-five pounds. She went into the maternity section and looked in wonder at the smocks and dungarees. Maybe she should buy some. It wouldn't be long after all . . . She forced herself to move on. It was too early to buy anything. She didn't want to tempt fate. She made her way to Hamleys and satisfied her sudden, surprising, maternal instincts by buying toys for Shane, Danielle and Lucy. Then she went to Harrods where she bought some pretty lingerie for Annie, perfume for Liz, table linen for her mother and a polo shirt for her dad. Her final stop was at the food hall, her favourite department. She spent an hour wandering around before finally making her way to the restaurant laden down with goodies.

She ordered tea and a scone and resisted the temptation to light a cigarette. She had to be careful now. No more cigarettes, and only the occasional glass of wine. Now that was going to be hard! She'd only one purchase left to make. Something for Sean. What would make up for all the heartache she'd put him through? It came to her as she sipped her tea. A ring. Not a wedding ring, that would be presumptuous. No – a signet ring. She gulped back her tea, gathered up her bags and made her way to the jewellery department.

It was an hour and two frustrated salesmen later before she emerged, satisfied with her gift. She hailed a taxi and sat back feeling happy and excited at the prospect of telling Sean her news and presenting him with her peace offering.

Sean stood up as his flight was announced and strode towards the gate. He was glad to be getting out of the country for a while. Thinking about Stephanie and what she'd done, or was about to do, tore him to pieces. He felt very depressed and suddenly he missed Billy more than ever. He phoned Karen and arranged to visit on his way back from Phoenix. At least that was something to look forward to.

Even Annie hadn't been able to take away the pain. He'd been surprised when she'd phoned him at work and asked him to come over. His first instinct was to say no. He didn't need to rake over the whole business again. He'd accepted Steph's phobia about marriage, but this was too much. He'd finally given in to Annie. She'd been so insistent.

She opened the door as soon as he pulled up.

'Thanks for coming, Sean.' She led the way into the kitchen. 'Coffee?'

'Yeah, okay. Look, I don't have much time, Annie. And I'm not too sure why I'm here.' Sean leaned against the counter and watched Annie spoon instant into two mugs.

'It won't take long, Sean. But there's something I think you should know. I think it might help you understand why Steph . . .' She faltered.

'Why she's killing our child?' he said coldly. 'I doubt it.'

'I know it's hard, Sean. I'm a mother, remember. But no woman makes this decision lightly. There's always a reason.' She handed him a mug and waved him to a chair before taking the one opposite. 'It all goes back to Ruth. You know how upset Steph was.'

'We all were. She seemed to take it harder than most, but then that's because they grew up together. I thought at the time that she should talk to someone about it. You know, a counsellor or doctor because she wouldn't talk to me and her mother said she'd clammed up with her too. Did she talk to you?'

'Yes – oh not much, and certainly not willingly,' she added hurriedly when she saw the hurt in his eyes. 'I happened to be in the right place at the right time. You see, the thing was, Ruth was pregnant when she died.'

Sean lowered his mug. 'What?'

'Yes. She'd found out a few days earlier.'

'Oh, Christ. Is that why she took the overdose?'

'It looks like it. Apparently Ruth had expected Des to rush her down the aisle and they'd live happily ever after. Des wasn't so keen.'

'I never did like the bastard. But what has this got to do with Steph wanting an abortion?'

'Well you see, Steph was the only one Ruth confided in. She came to her for help and advice.' Annie watched him steadily. 'And the day that Ruth died she called Steph. She wanted her to come over. But Steph was, eh . . .'

'She was meeting me,' Sean said, staring into space.

Annie looked at his stricken expression and wondered if she'd been right to tell him. 'Yes. Steph said she couldn't see her but they arranged to meet the next day for lunch.'

'But Ruth was dead by then – oh, shit,' Sean gasped, raking his hand through his hair.

Annie sighed. 'So, you see, Steph blames herself. In

fact I think – though my husband says I'm mad – that she's been punishing herself ever since.'

'What do you mean?

'She sent you away at the time. And even when she got back with you she still wouldn't consider marriage. And now this. Maybe because Ruth couldn't have a family, Steph felt she didn't deserve one either. Does that sound ridiculous?'

Sean sat down heavily and put his head in his hands. 'Sadly no. It actually makes a lot of sense. How did her parents find out? Did Steph tell them?'

'No. Apparently Ruth left a note. They had never even heard of Des up until then.'

'How come Steph told you all this, Annie? No offence but why you? Why couldn't she talk to me?'

'Don't take it to heart, Sean. She'd never have told me anything either. I just happened to be with her one night when Ruth's dad phoned. He was in a terrible state, shouting and crying on the phone. He wanted her to tell him about Des. He was looking for his address.'

'I hope she gave it to him.'

Annie nodded. 'Of course she did but she was in an awful state after that call and she just blurted it all out. But she's never mentioned it since.'

'What about Des?'

'He left his job and went to England. Maybe he had a conscience after all.'

'I find that hard to believe,' Sean said grimly. 'It's more likely that Ruth's dad caught up with him. I certainly hope so. What am I going to do now, Annie?'

She shook her head, her eyes sad. 'That's up to you, Sean. All I can tell you is that I really don't believe she's responsible for her actions.'

Sean rubbed his eyes wearily. 'I love her, Annie. But this – I'm not sure I can get past this.'

Annie squeezed his hand. 'You need time, Sean. It's a lot to take in. You're grieving for your child. But just remember that whether she admits it or not, Stephanie is grieving too. She'll be home tomorrow night. Talk to her.'

'I'll be on a plane to Arizona by then. Maybe it's just as well. I don't think I could face her yet. It's too soon.'

Annie swallowed back her tears. 'How long will you be away?'

'Who knows?'

Annie raised an eyebrow. 'You are coming back, Sean?'

He shrugged. 'I don't know any more, Annie. I just don't know.'

As the plane rose into the sky Sean stared down at the Dublin coast and thought of his words to Annie. Though he pitied Steph and realised that she'd been punishing herself for all these years he still wasn't sure he'd ever be able to forgive her. And if he did come back to Dublin, what was he coming back for?

Stephanie let herself into her apartment and immediately made for the phone. She got Sean's machine. No point in leaving a message – she knew he wouldn't call her back. She'd catch up with him in his office tomorrow. She'd march right in there and he'd have to talk to her. The phone rang and she pounced on it.

'Hello?'

'Hi, Steph. It's me. How are you?'

'Oh hi, Annie. I'm great. How about you?'

'Eh . . . fine.'

'Wait till you see what I got the kids in London. And I bought you a little something too.'

'Oh, thanks,' Annie said faintly. 'You shouldn't have. And you're sure you're – okay?'

'Yeah. Just tired.'

'Of course you are. I'll let you go. By the way, Sean left for Phoenix today.'

Steph's heart sank. 'Already? How do you know?'

'He called me and asked me to let you know,' Annie fibbed.

'How long is he gone for?'

'I'm not sure.'

'Blast! Okay, Annie. Thanks. Bye.'

'How is she?' Joe asked.

Annie stared at the phone in her hand. 'Fine. Too fine. She sounded as if she were just back from a holiday. Until I told her Sean was gone. She wasn't too happy about that.'

Joe frowned. 'Maybe she's "in denial", as the Americans say.'

'Great. That's all we need.'

Joe put an arm around his wife and hugged her. 'Don't worry, love. She'll be all right.'

Annie smiled at him, but she couldn't stop thinking about her sister-in-law. She'd just gone through a terrible ordeal. She had to be going through hell. She couldn't possibly be okay.

Annie was right. Steph wasn't happy at all, but only because she couldn't talk to Sean and tell him the good news. Lord, he must be so miserable. She'd have to call his office and get a number where she could reach him in Phoenix. She'd burst if she didn't talk to him soon. She moved her hand protectively to her stomach. How was she going to manage to keep the wonderful news to herself? She'd have to. Sean had to be the first to know. She'd have to avoid Annie and Liz – she'd never be able to keep her mouth shut otherwise. Annie wouldn't be that surprised. Between the abortion and breaking up with Sean she'd expect Steph to be miserable.

She smiled ruefully as she remembered their telephone conversation. How dumb of her to chatter on about the presents when Annie thought she was just back from having an abortion! God, what must she think? Still, she'd forgive her. When she knew the truth. Everyone would.

Chapter Twenty-three

Liz took Lucy by the hand and walked back towards the car.

'Hello, Lucy. Hi, you must be Liz.'

Liz turned to the pretty woman smiling at her. 'Jennifer?'

The other woman nodded. 'That's me. Finally we meet. I was beginning to wonder if you actually existed!'

'A neighbour has been taking Lucy to school for the last few weeks,' Liz explained.

'Oh, I see. Well, it's nice to meet the woman that's finally hooked my brother.'

Liz gaped at her. 'You must be mixing me up with someone else. Edward and I are just friends.'

Jennifer smiled brightly. 'Sorry. I must have got hold of the wrong end of the stick. Ed's always saying I should put my brain in gear before I open my mouth.'

Liz raised an eyebrow. 'Ed? Is that what you call him?'

'Only when I want to annoy him. He hates it but it keeps him in his place.'

Liz laughed.

'Do you fancy a coffee?'

Liz hesitated for only a moment. 'Yes, okay. Why don't you come back to my place?'

'Lovely. I'll follow you in my car. Just give me a minute to find Carol. She was here a minute ago.'

Liz opened the car and helped Lucy in.

'Jenny's real nice, Mum. I like her.'

'She seems lovely, pet,' Liz agreed. She was amazed at herself. The invitation had been out before she realised it. She'd never asked any other mother home for coffee before. Still, Jennifer was Edward's sister, and he'd been very kind to her. She wondered what exactly he'd told his sister about her.

As soon as they got back to the house, Lucy dragged her friend upstairs to play in her room and the two women were left alone.

While Liz made coffee, Jennifer wandered around the kitchen admiring the oak-panelled units, the large workstation in the centre of the room and the array of shining knives and utensils dangling from hooks above it. The kitchen table was in a corner by a large window that looked out on the small pretty garden. An oak dresser, with an alarming stack of cookery books and a row of shining copper pots and pans, stood in the corner.

'Wow! This is an amazing kitchen. But of course you're a chef. I forgot.'

Liz smiled and poured steaming coffee into two mugs. 'I do too sometimes.' She looked ruefully at the books. 'Looks impressive, doesn't it? But most of the time, baked beans and fish fingers are all that's on the menu. Especially since, well, since my husband moved out. I never entertain any more.'

Jennifer ignored Liz's embarrassment. 'Oh, you should. I'd crack up if it weren't for friends coming over. I don't cook anything grand – a lasagne or chilli, but it's fun to have a crowd in.'

Liz imagined that just being around this woman would be great fun. She was much more out-going that Edward. Though the eyes and colouring were the same, Jennifer's eyes twinkled with fun and her mouth was turned up in a permanent smile. How sad that she was a widow.

'I used to be like you,' Jennifer continued. 'I didn't go outside the door after Finbarr died. I didn't want to see anyone. But eventually you have to pick yourself up, dust yourself off and start again. Sorry. Sermon over.'

'That's okay. It's nice to meet someone who actually understands,' Liz said. 'Though of course it must have been much worse for you. Your husband died in terrible circumstances. I just lost a creep to his mid-life fantasies.'

'Finbarr may have died, but he was no angel,' Jennifer said drily.

Liz stared at her, slightly shocked. She'd been taught never to speak ill of the dead.

'Edward didn't tell you?' Jenny said when she saw Liz's face.

Liz shook her head.

'Finbarr died in a car crash on the Wicklow to Dublin road. He was supposed to be at a conference in Cork at the time. He was with another woman. They were both killed instantly.'

'Oh,' Liz said inadequately. 'I'm sorry. Maybe there was a simple explanation . . .'

'No. It was just as seedy as it appeared. We were able to trace them to a hotel in the area. I'm surprised Edward didn't tell you.'

'I don't see why. It's your business, after all.'

Jennifer looked at her curiously, but said nothing.

'It must have been awful for you.'

Jennifer shrugged. 'I'm over it. It was almost three years ago and Carol hardly remembers Finbarr. I keep photos around the place and talk about him, but it's not the same. It's a pity. Whatever his faults, he was a great dad and he worshipped Carol.'

Liz shook her head wearily. 'Why the hell do they do it? Why are they ready to throw away so much for a quick fling?'

'Now that is the six-million-dollar question,' Jennifer said as Liz refilled their cups. 'I always thought we were blissfully happy. Oh, let's talk about something else before we start crying into our coffee. Look, I'm having a bit of a get-together next week. Some of the neighbours are coming – none of the gossips, I promise. Why don't you come along?'

'Oh, I don't know . . .' Liz shifted uncomfortably.

'I'll ask Edward too. That way you'll have at least two people to talk to if you hate everyone else.'

Liz brightened at the idea of seeing Edward. 'Well, okay then. Why not? But let me help. I could cook something.'

'Would you? God, that would be great. Some real food for a change. But look, I don't want you going to too much trouble,' she warned. 'Ed would kill me.'

'I promise. I'll keep it simple. Please, I'd enjoy it.'

Liz went over to her cookery books and selected two. She quickly ran through a few menus, while Jenny sat gobsmacked. They finally decided on three dishes that they would serve buffet-style.

'We better leave it at that, Liz, or we'll never be invited

back. You'll scare them all off with your talent. Have you ever thought about going back to work?'

Liz shook her head. 'My friend Stephanie is always at me to go back to work, but I hate the idea of leaving Lucy.'

'Stephanie West? Edward's partner?'

'Yes. She's always telling me that I'm wasting my talents. I wouldn't mind doing something, but now it's going to be more difficult than ever. You see, Chris, my husband, is moving to Galway. Lucy's only going to have me. Well, full-time, that is.'

'So you're definitely splitting up?'

'Yes, we are,' Liz said and for the first time she knew she really meant it. 'And it'll be hard enough on Lucy, without me going back to work.'

'You're probably right,' Jennifer agreed. 'Kids can get really screwed up when parents separate. They start thinking they did something wrong. You probably have a tough time ahead of you.'

'Thanks,' Liz said drily. 'You're really cheering me up.'

Jennifer laughed loudly. 'Oh, I'm sorry. Don't mind me. Subtlety was never my strong point. I'd better leave before you throw me out.' She went out into the hall and banged on the staircase. 'Carol? It's time to go home now.'

Liz followed her out. 'I'll give you a call next week, Jennifer, and we can go shopping for supplies.'

'Great. Whenever suits you. I really appreciate this. Just do me one more favour? Call me Jenny or Jen. I've always thought Jennifer was such a mouthful. Jennifer and Edward. My parents have a lot to answer for.'

Liz and Lucy waved as Jenny and Carol drove away. Liz was still smiling as she prepared Lucy's lunch. It was nice to have a new friend. One who understood exactly what she was going through. She was very glad she liked Edward's sister and she knew that he'd be delighted that they'd hit it off.

The phone rang and to Liz's delight it was Edward.

'You'll never guess who I just met,' she said, settling herself on the bottom stair.

'My sister?'

'How did you know?'

'I just got a call from her. She couldn't wait to tell me how great you are.'

'Well, she's very nice too,' Liz said, gratified that Jenny had liked her.

'I think she's decided we're perfect for each other.' There was a smile in Edward's voice.

'I don't know why,' Liz said shortly. 'We only talked about menus and lousy husbands.'

'She told you about Finbarr?'

'Yes. It must have been awful for her. It's bad enough to find out your husband's been killed, but that he was with another woman at the time . . .'

'Yes,' Edward agreed quietly. 'It was a terrible time. So I believe she's bullied you into doing the cooking for one of her little soirées.'

'Not at all. It was my idea. It's a good excuse to hide in the kitchen,' she added with a grin.

'In that case, I'll be your waiter. I could do with a hiding-place. Some of Jen's female friends can be a bit overbearing.'

Liz laughed. 'That's because you're so eligible. If you were with someone you'd have some protection.'

'Do you think so? Well, in that case I'll have to cast long loving glances in your direction and maybe they'll get the message.'

'Don't be silly, Edward,' Liz said brusquely. 'I'm a married woman.'

'Only on paper,' he pointed out.

'I don't agree with that. Call me old-fashioned, but I happen to believe in the vows I took. Even if Chris doesn't.'

'Well, of course. Quite right, too. But it doesn't mean you have to live like a nun, does it?'

'No,' she agreed with a smile. 'Not quite like a nun. But I'm not interested in anything serious.'

'Of course you're not,' Edward's tone was reassuring. 'But surely you'd like some company occasionally?'

'I don't know how I'd have got through the last couple of months without you,' Liz said shyly. 'You've been great. And it's done my ego the world of good to go out with a good-looking man.'

'Good-looking eh?'

'Well, you're not bad.'

'Too late. You said good-looking. Now I'm hanging up before you say anything else. I'll see you at Jenny's next week.'

'You will. Talk to you then. Bye.'

'Bye, Liz. Love to Lucy.'

Edward put down the phone and stared into space. Why, when he finally fell for another woman, did it have to be one as nice as Liz? He still wasn't convinced she wouldn't go back to Chris. He knew that in her mind it would be 'the right thing to do'. He'd been delighted when Jenny had called to give her vote of approval. He was very close to his sister – even more so since the crash.

Jenny had immediately seen the qualities in Liz that had attracted him. Not least, her innate honesty, a virtue they'd both learned to value. He'd have to go gently, though. He knew Liz was fond of him, maybe even more than that, but if he came on too heavy, she'd run. What she needed now was a friend, and that's what he'd be for as long as it took. He hadn't believed he'd ever feel this way about a woman again. He wasn't going to blow it. Liz was worth waiting for.

Chapter Twenty-four

Stephanie tucked her blue silk camisole into the cream linen trousers and studied her profile in the mirror. No sign of a bump, no matter how hard she looked. Her stomach was as flat as ever and she hadn't put on any weight. If it weren't for the aching heaviness of her breasts she wouldn't believe she was pregnant at all. She couldn't wait to see some sign of the life within her, but it would probably be a few weeks yet. And then there was her eighteen-week scan. With a bit of luck Sean would be home by then and he could come with her.

If he wasn't she was going to have to disguise her condition as long as necessary. He had to be the first to know. It would be a lot harder to explain why she continued to avoid alcohol and why she'd given up smoking. Conor was amazed at her will power. Steph explained that she'd got a chest infection and it was doctor's orders. This was also her excuse for giving up the drink. She couldn't with the fictitious tablets she was taking. My God, but life was complicated!

She still hadn't talked to Sean and that was the only cloud on her horizon. His secretary, Elaine, wouldn't give her an office number in Phoenix. It was against his express instructions, she said. He was also staying in a different hotel – Elaine conveniently forgot which one. She offered to relay messages, but Sean never returned them. Steph was getting embarrassed calling Elaine, and Elaine was definitely fed up being caught in the middle.

Stephanie was frustrated and annoyed that she was unable to give Sean the one bit of news that would make him happy. She'd go crazy if she didn't talk to him soon. In the meantime, she avoided her family and friends.

Liz phoned a few times, but Steph usually managed to dodge the calls. When they did talk, Steph confined the conversation to Lucy, Chris and the restaurant and got off the phone as quickly as possible. Annie was easier to handle. She called once a week to see how Steph was, but she didn't ask any questions, or pry. Steph knew how uncomfortable Annie was with the whole situation and was grateful for her discretion – even if it was misplaced!

She slipped on the jacket of her suit, slung her Chanel bag over her shoulder and let herself out of the apartment. It was sunny, and the air was already warm. Steph was making an earlier start than usual. She was hoping to slip out this afternoon and do some shopping. She sang along to the radio as she turned the car onto the Malahide Road. All was well with the world. Well, it would be. As soon as she talked to Sean.

'Steph? It's Dad. He's had an accident.'

Steph clutched the phone tighter. 'Joe? How is he? What happened?'

'It's nothing serious. He fell off the ladder. They think his arm's broken. The bloke next door drove him and

Mam to the hospital. Can you get down there? I'd go myself but I'm due on a flight to London in a couple of hours . . .'

'It's okay, Joe. I'm on my way. What hospital?'

She scribbled down the details and, after assuring her brother that she'd call Annie as soon as there was any news, she went in search of Chris.

'I've got to go. Family crisis. I'll call in later.'

Chris raised an eyebrow and muttered something about boyfriends.

Steph glared at him and left, slamming the door behind her. She cursed in frustration as she made her way out to the Merrion Road. It was only twelve, but already the lunchtime traffic was building.

Thirty minutes later she walked into Casualty and approached the desk.

'Stephanie? Over here.'

Steph turned to see her mother approaching, smiling. Well, that was a good sign.

'Hiya, Mam. How is he?' she asked, kissing her cheek.

'He's fine, love. The arm isn't broken. His wrist is just badly sprained, but you know him. With all the moaning, you'd think they were going to amputate!'

Steph laughed with relief. Her dad was great, but he wasn't the easiest patient in the world. She linked her arm through her mother's and they made their way to his cubicle.

'Oh, hello, love. You shouldn't have come. I'm fine. A lot of pain, you know, but I think they're going to give me an injection for that.'

Stephanie kissed her dad and stepped back as a nurse arrived.

'All right, Mr West. Just take these and then we'll strap you up and you can go.'

Tom West looked disappointedly at the two capsules. 'Is that it, then?'

The nurse smiled brightly. 'That's it.'

'What are you giving him?' Steph asked.

'Ponstan,' she told her before disappearing behind the curtain.

'Are they any good, Steph?' her dad asked. 'Are they strong?'

'Oh, yes, Dad, very strong. They should make you feel a lot better.'

Tom West swallowed the tablets satisfied that his condition was being treated seriously.

Steph winked at her mother. 'Why don't I go and get us some tea? We could be here for a while.'

'I've had enough bloody tea,' Tom said grumpily. 'And it's no fun trying to go to the gents' like this.' He indicated his swollen arm.

'Just tea for two so,' Steph said. 'I'd better call Annie while I'm at it and let her know you're okay. Joe was frantic when I talked to him.'

'Well, I suppose you can tell them that it's not *too* serious,' her dad agreed reluctantly.

Steph suppressed a smile and made her way outside. After she'd called Annie she went to the canteen and collected two plastic cups of grey tea. She was keeping clear of caffeine these days, but one cup wouldn't hurt. Mind you, looking at this stuff . . .

Her mother was leaning against the wall outside the ward when Steph came back.

'They're putting a bandage on,' she explained. 'What do you think, Steph?'

'He'll be fine once the swelling goes down. It'll be uncomfortable for a while, but that's all.'

'What were those tablets that the nurse gave him?'

'Just mild painkillers,' Steph assured her. 'Standard hospital issue, but don't tell him that. Anyway, tell me what happened.'

Catherine sighed. 'Oh the silly man was up the stepladder, trying to trim the top of the hedge. I told him to leave it, but you know what he's like.'

Steph smiled. She knew. 'Well, thank God he didn't do any real damage. We should be out of here soon enough. He'll be more comfortable when he's at home. At least it's his left hand otherwise you'd be on toilet duty.'

Catherine West looked horrified. 'I would not! He could wear tracksuit bottoms.'

Steph laughed. 'There's true love for you!'

'Oh, Steph, I got an awful fright when I found him. He was very pale.'

Steph silently agreed. Her dad had looked surprisingly vulnerable lying on the trolley. This little accident could have been a lot worse. 'He didn't have a dizzy spell, did he?' she asked tentatively.

Her mother frowned. 'I don't think so. He said he was reaching over and lost his balance.'

'That's good then. Still, maybe we should have a word with the doctor. Just to make sure.'

'Yes you're right.' Her mother set down her tea and went over to the desk.

Steph called Liam while she was waiting and explained that she wouldn't be back.

'Nothing serious, is it?' he asked.

'No, thank goodness, but I've got to drive them back

out to Wicklow and I don't want to leave them alone for a while. You can manage, can't you?'

'Yeah, sure. Want to talk to Chef?'

'No,' she said quickly. The last thing she wanted to do was talk to Chris. 'He can call me on the mobile if he needs me. Talk to you later, bye.' She rung off as her mother approached smiling.

'He's fine. They checked him out and did a couple of X-rays and they're happy to let him go. He's got to check in with the GP next week and they've given me a prescription for those painkillers.'

'Great, then let's get him home.'

Two hours later, Stephanie sank down into a kitchen chair. Her GP, Maeve O'Farrell, had warned her she'd tire easily and she wasn't kidding. The journey down had been a nightmare. Tom West had groaned at every bump and complained that Steph pulled up too suddenly and took the corners too hard. She'd said nothing, but her grip had tightened on the wheel, and she was a nervous wreck by the time she pulled into the driveway. They'd finally settled her dad in front of the TV with his dinner chopped up into bite-sized pieces.

'You look tired,' her mother commented. 'Everything all right?'

Steph looked away from her mother's searching gaze. 'I'm fine, Mam. Just not sleeping too well.'

'You're very thin, Stephanie. I hope you're not neglecting yourself. You have to eat properly.'

'I do, Mam,' Steph assured her. She hadn't suffered from any morning sickness but she hadn't much of an appetite either. 'Never mind me. You could do with putting on some weight yourself.' She looked worriedly at her mother. She looked tired and drawn, but then it had been a tough day. 'Finish your dinner and then you can go and have a nice bath. I'll stay with Dad.'

'That would be nice, love. I'll make some tea first. I'm sure he'd like a cup. He should be able to manage the loo now he's wearing pyjamas!' She chuckled as she went over to fill the kettle.

'Catherine? Stephanie?' Tom West's plaintive voice interrupted them.

'I'll go,' Steph said, rising slowly.

'What is it, Dad?' she said wearily from the doorway of the living-room.

'Oh sorry, love. But I dropped the remote control.'

'Oh, for God's sake, Dad! You only have a sprained wrist. There's nothing stopping you moving around. I don't want you letting Mam run after you all the time. She's not able for it.'

Her father snorted indignantly. 'Sorry I'm so much trouble. Don't worry about me.'

Steph suppressed a sigh. 'You're no trouble, Dad. I'm sorry.' She bent and kissed his cheek before picking up his tray and carrying it back outside.

'Dad seemed to like – aargh!' Steph yelped as she slipped on the tiles, her thigh collided with the corner of the kitchen table and the tray soared into the air.

'Mother of God, what happened? Are you all right, love?' Her mother hurried over and helped her to her feet.

Steph gave a shaky laugh. 'I slipped.' She groaned at the pain in her leg. 'I'm okay,' she said bravely but her face crumpled and the tears started to fall.

Catherine looked at her worriedly. 'Oh, love, what is it? What's the matter?'

'Nothing,' Steph laughed through her tears. 'I just cry a lot these days.'

Catherine looked bemused. 'Steph?'

'I'm fine, Mam. Honestly. Blooming, in fact.'

'Oh, Stephanie! You're pregnant?'

Steph nodded and Catherine West gathered her daughter into her arms. 'That's wonderful. I'm so happy for you. Sean must be over the moon.'

'He doesn't know yet,' Steph sniffed and rummaged in her pockets for a tissue.

'What? Oh, you just found out?'

'No. It's a bit complicated.' Steph's eyes filled up again. God, she hoped she wasn't going to be this emotional all the time.

Her mother settled her in a chair and then sat down beside her. 'What is it, love?'

Stephanie hadn't meant to tell her everything, but somehow the words just tumbled out. About Sean, their split, Ruth's pregnancy and finally about her own aborted abortion. They both cried and Catherine West gripped her daughter's hand hard while she talked.

Why didn't you talk to me, Stephanie? I'm your mother. You know you can always come to me. Poor little Ruth.'

Stephanie sniffed and wiped tears from her cheeks with the back of her hand. She'd abandoned her search for a tissue. 'I don't know, Mam. As far as Ruth was concerned, well, I suppose I thought you might be shocked that she'd got herself pregnant. You were always so fond of her. I didn't want to tarnish her memory.'

Her mother shook her head sadly. 'It's terrible that she took her life over something like that. Of course there would have been trouble, scandal, but once the baby was born, everyone would soon have forgotten all that. Babies have a way of bringing people together. Peter and Joan McCann are good people. They'd never have turned their backs on their daughter.'

'I know you're right, Mam. I can see that now, but then . . .' She shrugged.

'The poor girl. It's such a waste.'

They sat in silence for a moment, Catherine drinking her tepid tea, Stephanie fiddling with a teaspoon and longing for a cigarette.

'Why?' her mother said eventually.

Steph frowned. 'Why what?'

'Why were you going to get an – abortion?' Catherine West nearly choked on the word.

Steph was silent for a moment. How could she ever explain this to her mother? She wasn't sure she understood it herself.

'I was afraid.'

'Afraid of what, love?' her mother asked, desperate to understand.

Steph stood up and went over to the window. She looked out on the neat rows of roses and hydrangeas that skirted the perfect green lawn. The colours blurred as her eyes filled again.

'I don't know. I just don't know, Mam.' She buried her face in her hands.

Her mother went over and put her arms around her. 'Shush, don't cry, love. It's not good to get upset in your condition.'

Steph smiled through her tears. Her condition. Her

wonderful condition. 'I think I was guilty, Mam. About Ruth. I wasn't there for her. I should have been. I should have stopped her. I could have, you know? I could have gone over there, instead of going out with Sean. If I'd gone, if I'd said the right words, she might be here today. Her and her baby.'

'If, if, if,' her mother said dismissively. 'You can't live in the past, Stephanie. You can't change things. You have to accept them and move on. And what about that new life growing inside of you? Doesn't it deserve all your attention now?'

Steph's hands went automatically to her stomach and she nodded.

'Right then. You nearly did something terrible – I'm sorry, but that's the way I feel about it. I would have stood by you, of course, just as Ruth's mam would have stood by her. But you didn't do it, love. And I'm very happy that you didn't. Now you have to look to the future. Everything's going to be all right. Sean will be a wonderful father. And husband?' she added tentatively.

Steph nodded eagerly. 'Oh, I'll marry him, Mam, if he'll have me.'

Catherine hugged her daughter tightly.

'Catherine? Stephanie?' Tom West's plaintive voice broke the mood.

'His Master's Voice,' Catherine murmured. 'I'll go. Now you dry those tears. Everything's going to be fine. And remember, Stephanie. I'm your mother. I'm always here for you, whatever happens. Always.'

Stephanie kissed her mother and watched as she hurried off towards the living-room.

'Coming, Tom, coming.'

Chapter Twenty-five

$\mathbf{A}$ nnie made the children wipe their shoes on the mat, took off her coat and went into the kitchen. 'Hi, Liz? How's it going? Can I do anything?' She ran slender fingers through her auburn locks and leaned over to peer into a pot.

'Nope. It's all under control,' Liz said as she tasted the sauce. 'Hiya, kids.' She smiled down at Shane and Danielle.

'Hiya, Auntie Liz,' they chimed.

'Mummy, can we go out to play?' Lucy looked up hopefully at her mother.

'Just for a little while. Lunch will be ready soon.'

Lucy pulled open the door and the three raced off.

'Have you seen Steph recently?' Liz asked Annie as she wiped her hands on her apron.

Annie busied herself with setting the table. 'No, why?'

'Oh, I just haven't heard from her lately. Whenever I ring the house, I just get Sean's answering machine. They really should change the message. You'd never know Steph lives there too.'

Annie thought quickly. She didn't want to lie to Liz, but she didn't want to let Stephanie down either. 'Sean's back in the States again so maybe Steph is staying in Malahide while he's gone. She mentioned something about redecorating.'

Liz brightened. 'Oh, she should have said. I'd give her a hand. But surely she's got enough on her hands with the restaurant? What a funny time to start decorating.'

Annie cursed silently. God, she was no good at lying. 'Maybe I got it wrong,' she said lamely.

Liz frowned. She still didn't understand why Steph was so hard to get hold of. Maybe she hadn't really forgiven her for their run-in a few weeks back. Or maybe she knew that Liz was seeing Edward. Could she be interested in him herself? But no – she was living with Sean now. 'Did she say anything about me?'

'What do you mean? What about?' Annie asked, confused.

'Oh, I don't know. Anything,' Liz said vaguely.

'No. Well, only that she was wondering if you'd ever consider going back to work.' At least Annie was able to be honest about that! 'Look, Liz. I'm sure there's nothing wrong. She's just very busy. I haven't talked to her myself in ages. Well, except when she rang about her dad.'

'What about her dad?'

'He had an accident. Oh, it's okay, nothing serious,' she added hurriedly as Liz's eyes widened in concern. 'He fell off a ladder and sprained his wrist.'

'Maybe Steph's down in Wicklow. I'll phone the restaurant again later and see what the story is.'

'Good idea.'

'So what are you buying Joe for his birthday? It's next week, isn't it?'

Annie nodded, only too glad to change the subject.

Any idea of having a party had gone out the window after the events of the last few weeks. Annie had decided on a small family dinner instead. Just Joe's Mam, Dad and Steph – if she felt up to it. 'I was going to buy him some new golf shoes. The only problem is he's so damn fussy. Maybe I'll ask Edward to get them for me. I could rely on him to get nothing but the best.'

'What do you mean by that?' Liz said defensively.

Annie looked at her curiously. 'Only that he'll know the best ones to get.'

Liz flushed. 'Oh, right. You better call the kids. Lunch is ready.'

Annie went to the back door. 'Shane, Lucy, Dani. Lunch is ready.'

'Mum, are we having sausages?' Lucy ran into the kitchen with her two pals hot on her heels.

'No, love,' Liz said. 'We're having pasta.'

'Oh goody! I love pasta. So does Uncle Edward. Is he coming for lunch too?'

Liz bit her lip and looked away from Annie's open-mouthed stare. 'Wash your hands, Lucy, and stop chattering,' she said curtly, turning back to the oven.

Annie rolled up Dani's sleeves and then helped Lucy dry her hands. What on earth was all that about? Liz seemed very embarrassed. 'Uncle Edward' indeed. It had to be Edward McDermott – who else? Annie hoped that Edward wasn't moving in on Liz. She was much too vulnerable at the moment. But then why else would he be hanging around? Why couldn't he stick to single women? Or at least to women she hadn't introduced him to!

'Uncle Edward, eh?' she said mildly when the children had finished and gone inside to watch *Pokémon*.

'What?' Liz said absently.

'You heard.' Annie watched Liz closely. She was looking an awful lot better these days. She'd got her hair trimmed again and it swung in a soft, silken sheen around her face. Her eyes were bright and her figure was trim in white jeans and a tight red top. 'What's going on?'

'For God's sake, Annie, you sound like my mother. Nothing's going on. Carol, Edward's niece, is in Lucy's class. They play together.'

'Right. And Edward plays too?'

Liz scowled at her. 'Don't be smart, it doesn't suit you. Edward happens to be a very good uncle. His sister Jenny's a widow and he spends a lot of time with them.'

'Oh,' Annie said, surprised. It didn't fit in with her image of him at all.

'Hah! That's taken the wind out of your sails, hasn't it?' Liz laughed triumphantly.

'Well, I didn't even know he had a sister,' Annie defended herself. 'God, men are useless. Joe's been his friend for years, and he doesn't know a thing about him. So what's the sister like?'

'Very attractive and really nice. Like I said, she's a widow. Her husband was killed in a car crash.'

'That's terrible,' Annie said sympathetically.

'She and Edward seem very close and he dotes on Carol. He's like a father to her.'

'So there's nothing going on then?'

'Nothing,' Liz confirmed.

'But you do see him?'

'Only when he brings Carol around to play or we're over at Jenny's,' Liz lied.

'Very cosy.'

'Annie, stop it! Look, Edward's very nice and I like him a lot but there's nothing going on. I wouldn't do anything like that.'

'Sorry,' Annie said meekly. 'So how are things with Chris?'

'Lousy. He's being very understanding and patient.'

Annie frowned. 'And that's lousy?'

'Yeah. It makes it harder for me to tell him it's over.'

'Oh. You've made up your mind then?'

'Yes, I have. I just can't have him back, Annie. It would never work. The more we're apart the more I realise how unhappy I was. And though I was a mess when I first threw him out, I'm a lot stronger now. In fact, sometimes I think I'm actually happier without him. Lucy was the only reason I'd have taken him back, but I've decided that it's not a good enough one. She won't be happy if Chris and I are arguing all the time.'

'How is she?'

'Fine. She loves going out with Chris and she's stopped asking me when he's coming home. She probably sees more of him now than she did when he lived here!'

'So will you get a divorce?' Annie asked wide-eyed.

Liz shook her head. 'Not unless he wants one. I'm not bothered. I certainly won't be getting married again.'

'You're a bit young to make a statement like that, Liz.'

'No, I'm not,' Liz said firmly. 'I may not be able to give Lucy a normal family life, but I'll never inflict a stepfather on her.'

Annie decided not to argue. 'Have you told Lucy? Does she understand?'

COLETTE CADDLE

'I haven't actually spelled it out, but I've told her that Daddy is going to work in Galway. She was happy enough about that, once I told her she'd be able to go and visit him. I can't really say much more than that until I've talked to Chris.' She sighed wearily. Getting through to her husband was the hard part.

'You'd better do it soon,' Annie advised.

'I know, but it's almost impossible. He has this amazing knack of only hearing what he wants to hear. When I've hinted at it, he talks about giving me more time. Honestly, I could strangle him sometimes. He just can't accept that I would dump him.'

'When does he leave for Galway?'

'Next month, thank God.'

'Why don't you go and see a lawyer about organising a legal separation. I mean what about this house? You need to make sure that you're financially secure.'

Liz sighed. This was the part she dreaded. It seemed so cold and official. 'I was going to ask Edward about it. It probably wouldn't be a good idea for him to represent me given that he's the new owner of the restaurant but maybe one of his partners could. What do you think?'

'Good idea.'

'There's also the money from the sale of the restaurant. Some of that should come to me. I put all my savings into it.'

'Well, Chris wouldn't try and con you, would he?'

'I suppose not,' Liz said, not entirely sure. There was no knowing how Chris would react when he heard she wanted a separation. He wasn't likely to accept it calmly. He was possessive and jealous and unpredictable. She shivered involuntarily.

Annie looked at her, worried. 'Do you want Joe to talk to him?'

'No, no. I must do this myself.'

'Well, I'm not sure you should do it alone.'

'He's not going to get violent, Annie!'

'No, of course not,' Annie said doubtfully, 'but, well, moral support, you know?'

'Yeah, maybe. We'll see.'

Joe agreed with his wife. From what she'd said and from what Steph had told him, he didn't entirely trust Connolly. He was full of hot air most of the time, but there was no doubt he was a bit of a bully. It would be wise to keep an eye on Liz until Chris was safely out of the city. 'Have you heard from Steph?' he asked.

Annie shook her head. 'Not this week. I don't want to keep ringing her. I'm sure she just wants to forget all about it. She knows where I am if she needs me.'

'I suppose you're right. Mam seemed to think she was on great form.'

'Well, I suppose Steph was putting on an act for them.'

'I suppose. What do you think will happen when Sean gets back?'

'It's hard to know. Sean was pretty devastated but at least now he understands why.'

'Does he?' Joe muttered. 'I wish I did.' He couldn't get his head around what his sister had done. He looked at his two children and he simply couldn't understand any of it.

'You don't have to,' Annie said firmly. They'd had

this conversation many times. 'You just have to keep your mouth shut.'

Joe nodded. 'Of course I will. What's for dinner?'

'Nothing. The kids were at a party so they're stuffed silly. I thought we might get a takeaway.'

'Grand,' Joe said. 'Will I get us a video as well?'

'Okay. Joe?'

'Yeah?'

'You don't think Chris would actually *do* anything, do you?'

'What do you mean?'

'Well, you know, hurt Liz.'

'God, no. He's all talk.'

'I suppose you're right.'

'Of course I am. Don't worry.'

Chapter Twenty-six

Stephanie ran through the flat, searching. Where was that awful crying coming from? It was pitch dark and she kept stumbling and bumping into things. The cries turned to screams and got louder. She reached the sitting-room and fell over something lying in the middle of the floor. She looked down to see Ruth, whose eyes stared at her unseeing. She screamed and jumped away, bumping against a cradle. She looked down into it and a tiny faceless baby screamed through an orifice that should have been a mouth—

'No!' Stephanie jumped up in the bed bathed in sweat, her face wet with tears. She reached for the light-switch with a shaky hand and took a few deep breaths. It had been so long since she'd had the dream, she'd hoped it had gone away for good. Why had it come back now? Was Ruth coming back to haunt her? She cupped her hands protectively around the slight bulge in her stomach. But Ruth had been her best friend. She wouldn't wish anything bad to happen to her or her child. She decided to make herself some hot milk. It might help her to get back to sleep. Getting upset like this couldn't be good for the baby. She padded out to the kitchen, heated some milk in the microwave and carried the mug back to bed.

It was only ten o'clock in Phoenix. She wondered what Sean was doing. If only he'd call her. Oh well, at least now she had Mam to talk to. She smiled. One person she could indulge in baby talk with. She finished her milk and snuggled down once more. She said a prayer for Ruth, for Sean and for her baby, wrapped herself into a protective ball and fell into a dreamless sleep.

Sean closed the lid of his laptop and looked out of the window. Lights twinkled on the pool below and a couple were relaxing in the bubbling jacuzzi. As he watched, the man leaned over and kissed the woman. Lord, he seemed to be surrounded by happy, loving couples. Or maybe he was just more aware of them because he felt so miserable. He still hadn't returned any of Steph's calls. Elaine was not impressed. But then she didn't know the facts.

He was still trying to come to terms with the loss of their child. In a way, it had been a blessing that he had so much business over here now. He wasn't sure he could have handled living with Steph, watching her go about her daily life as if nothing had happened. Billy had been on his mind a lot too. Sean was eaten up with guilt thinking how he'd let his son down. Just because his marriage had broken up, didn't mean he had to break up with Billy too. It seemed sensible at the time to leave him with Karen. Whatever her faults, she had been a good mother. Some of his happiest memories were of their family outings. Now he'd practically dropped Billy from his life. Sure he always remembered his birthday and Christmas and he picked up the odd toy when he was on his travels, but that wasn't enough. He was a lousy father. He had been disgusted with Steph for getting rid of their baby, but was what he'd done any better?

Things would have to change. He'd go down to Cork more often, it wasn't that far. He could be down and back in a day. And he'd decorate the attic room for his son. He'd show him that he had a home in Dublin whenever he wanted to come and visit. He cheered up at the thought and was happy that he'd arranged to see Billy on the way back to Dublin. He couldn't wait to get to Cork and talk to Karen. He was sure she'd be open to the idea. She wanted what was best for Billy and had always encouraged Sean to see him.

Sean jumped up and went down to the restaurant. He normally ate in his room, but tonight he felt like a bit of company. It was a business hotel, so he was bound to run into a few guys in the bar. He ordered a steak and a beer and settled back, feeling slightly happier.

'Liz? Hi, it's Steph.'

'Well, well, well. The Scarlet Pimpernel.'

'I'm sorry I haven't been in touch. It's been a bit hectic. What with the restaurant and Dad's accident—'

'And the redecorating?'

'Redecorating?'

Liz sighed. 'What's going on, Steph? You don't return my calls. And Annie keeps giving me cock and bull stories. Is everything okay?'

Steph thought for a moment. 'I'm sorry, Liz. Look, the fact is that Sean and I had a row before he went away. I've moved back to Malahide.'

'Oh, Steph, I'm sorry.'

'Thanks. Look, I really wasn't avoiding you; it's just that I needed a bit of time to myself. And I wasn't ready to talk about it.'

'Oh, Steph. You know me better than that. All you ever have to do is say "shut up, Liz".'

Stephanie laughed. 'Yeah, sorry. Forgive me?'

'There's nothing to forgive, silly. Now do you want to get together or will I leave you alone for another while?'

Steph felt strong enough to meet Liz without spilling the beans. It was more difficult with Annie, who'd expect her to be depressed and sad. 'I'd love to meet.'

'Great! Well, why not come over here later? I'm cooking some stuff for a party tomorrow. You can keep me company.'

'What party?' Steph was surprised.

'I'll explain later. Come over about four.'

'Right so. Seeya then.' Steph hung up and sat smiling at the phone. It was good to hear Liz sounding so relaxed.

Annie had told her that she'd decided to split with Chris for good. 'Well, she can't have said anything to him yet,' Steph assured her. 'We'd have known all about it by now.'

'You think he'll take it badly?' Annie had asked, worried. 'I don't think she should be on her own when she talks to him. Joe says I'm overreacting.'

'I'll talk to her,' Steph had promised and finally picked up the phone to her friend. And now she'd be able to see for herself how Liz was. She'd missed her these last few weeks – Annie too. She'd better call her mam before she went over there and get a fix of baby talk. That way there was some chance of her keeping her mouth shut! Lord, Sean had better come home soon!

The phone rang bringing her back to the present with a jolt. Liam informed her that there was a double booking for that evening. Apparently a local businessman had booked a celebration dinner with Sam some weeks ago and Sam, God bless him, had failed to put it in the book. Steph wondered idly if Sam's lapse of memory had coincided with his dismissal. 'I'm on my way, Liam.' At least Conor was back and she didn't have to worry about the kitchen staff any more. That was his responsibility now.

Steph parked the car and walked up the driveway past the small garden with its border of roses and trim lawn. Liz certainly seemed to be managing fine without Chris. Mind you, Chris had usually left most of the domestic chores to Liz. She rang the doorbell and smiled as a flour-smudged Liz opened the door.

'Sorry I'm late, Liz.'

Liz wiped her hands on her apron. 'To be honest I've been too busy to notice the time.'

Steph followed her into the kitchen and gasped at the array of food on the kitchen table and the bubbling pots on the stove. 'My God. Are you feeding the five thousand?'

Liz laughed. 'Only about thirty, actually.'

Steph dipped a crab claw in the sauceboat and popped it in her mouth. 'Yum, lucky them. This is gorgeous.'

'That's a Moroccan lamb casserole,' Liz said pointing to one pot, 'and this is a Cajun chicken dish that I'm trying for the first time.' Liz watched Steph's expression anxiously as she tasted the two dishes.

'They're great, Liz. You're wasted, you know that, don't you?'

'Don't start that again,' Liz moaned but she was pleased with her friend's praise. Steph never lied about food.

'Anyway. Who's all this for?'

'Jennifer McDermott, Edward's sister. She's a neighbour. She invited me along to this party tomorrow and I agreed to come if she let me do the cooking.'

Steph looked confused. 'Let me get this straight. Edward's sister is your neighbour? God, it's a small world.'

'Isn't it? Her daughter, Carol, is one of Lucy's best friends. I've known the child for ages, but I didn't know who she was. It all came out when I ran into Edward outside the school one day.'

'So what's the sister like?'

'Really nice. Not at all like some of the nosy old biddies around here. She's a widow, you know, but she's only about my age and she's very pretty.'

'Oh, that's sad. What happened the husband?'

'Car crash.'

'Oh dear, the poor woman. So you're getting well in with the family then?' she added with a sly grin. 'Edward's sister, his niece – when do you meet Mummy and Daddy?'

Liz looked cross. 'You and Annie are as bad as each other! I assure you that it's all very innocent. We meet sometimes when the children are playing together and I've asked him for advice about my separation.'

'No more dinner dates then?'

'Of course not,' Liz said quickly, keeping her head buried in a cookbook.

'So when is D-Day? When are you going to talk to Chris?'

'Friday.' Liz closed the book and sank into a chair. 'I'm dreading it, Steph. I truly am. What's he going to say?'

'He won't be happy. Where's Lucy going to be? In fact, where is she now?'

'Jenny's minding her while I organise the food. She's going to my mother's on Friday. I thought it was best. Just in case.'

'Damn right. But I'm not sure you should be alone, Liz.'

Liz tossed back her hair impatiently. 'That's what Annie says, but I think you're both overreacting.'

'Well, I hope you're right but why take the chance? You know what his temper is like.'

Liz did, but while Chris had always had a quick temper he'd never hit her. 'No, Stephanie. I at least owe it to him to do this privately. He's not a bad man and he loves Lucy. In his own weird way, he probably still loves me. So I want to make this as painless as possible. If anyone else were here it would be a further humiliation.'

Stephanie hugged her. 'You know best. Just keep the phone nearby in case you need to call in the cavalry.'

Jenny McDermott pushed open the kitchen door with her hip and carried in a pile of dirty plates. 'Liz, you're amazing! This stuff is going down a bomb. They're all asking for a recipe for the chicken.'

'Can't tell them that,' Liz said with a wink. 'Trade secret. Tell them they'll have to hire me instead.'

Edward turned from the sink where he was rinsing glasses. 'That's not such a bad idea.'

'What?' Liz asked.

'Well, think about it. You're a great chef. You'd like to work but you don't want to leave Lucy.'

'So?'

'So why not start up a private catering service? You could work from home, apart from the actual events, which will nearly always be in the evening . . .'

'After Lucy's in bed,' Jenny finished. 'That's a great idea! You could limit your availability to two or three times a week. All you need is a reliable baby-sitter.'

Liz looked from one to the other a bit flustered at how fast this conversation was moving. 'Oh, I don't think so . . .'

'What's the problem?' Edward asked. 'Don't you think you're up to it?'

'Damn right I am!'

'There you go,' Edward said smugly.

'It's a great idea,' Jenny said excitedly. 'There's a lot of people around here that I'm sure would be interested.'

'And I have business contacts, single men who'd like to entertain at home but beans on toast doesn't exactly cut it.'

Liz laughed, intrigued by the prospect. It would be perfect. She could do most of the preparation in her own well-equipped kitchen and as Jenny pointed out, Lucy would be asleep for most of her working hours. It would bring in some regular money too and give her a chance to get out more. If there was one thing she'd found out tonight it was that she missed adult company. It was good to get out and have a laugh and she was enjoying the praise she was getting for her food. The limelight had been on Chris for so long, she'd forgotten how good a chef she actually was.

'Do you really think it could work?' She looked anxiously at brother and sister.

'Yes!' Jenny said.

'Absolutely!' Edward said. 'We could set up a couple of dinners to allow prospective clients to sample your cooking. I've been meaning to take out some clients for a while. I could invite them to my house instead. They like the personal touch.'

'That's a good idea,' Jenny nodded approvingly. 'And we could put the word around tonight that you do this professionally.'

'Tonight? But that's too soon! I'd have to talk to an accountant and lawyer.'

'No problem.' Jenny waved away her concerns. 'If anyone asks, you're booked up for the next couple of months. They'll want you even more then! Now I'd better get back in and mingle. Come on, Liz. I need to introduce you to our more affluent neighbours!'

Chapter Twenty-seven

Liz paced the living-room, pausing occasionally to look out of the window. Chris was due any minute and her heart raced at the thought of the ordeal ahead. The slight hangover didn't help matters. She was so high at the prospect of a new career last night that she had drunk more than usual. She'd enjoyed herself enormously, and was amused by the envious glances of some of Jenny's neighbours when Edward remained by her side for most of the evening. He seemed oblivious to the effect he had on women. His dark good looks and those startling grey eyes were guaranteed to draw every woman's eye from eighteen to eighty. The fact that he was also single and definitely not gay made him positively irresistible.

'You could have a different woman every night,' Liz had said, only half joking as he walked her back to her house.

'I do,' he'd assured her. 'But I rest on Sundays.'

She started as Chris swung his Peugeot into the driveway. She felt a flash of irritation at his presumption. He didn't live here any more. She opened the door and watched him as he climbed out of the car. She noticed the thickened waist and the sagging flesh around his throat. He was letting himself go.

'Hello, love. How are you?' Chris shoved a bouquet into her hands and planted a wet kiss on her cheek.

'Fine,' she said with a fixed smile. The flowers reminded her of churches and funerals. She left them on the hall table. 'I'll arrange them later. Would you like some tea?'

Chris checked his watch. 'Oh, the sun's over the yard-arm. I think a little drink would be nice.'

He headed for the drinks cabinet and poured himself a large whiskey. Again, Liz bristled at his familiarity.

'Can I get you one?' he asked.

What the hell, it might give her some courage. 'Just a sherry, please,' she said settling herself in an armchair.

He handed her a glass and settled himself on the sofa. 'Where's Lucy?'

'With Mam.'

'So it's just the two of us.' His eyes roved over her appreciatively. She was looking really great. She'd lost weight – that was it, and her hair was shorter. His eyes dropped to the generous curve of her breasts. She hadn't lost weight from there, thank God!

Stupid bastard, Liz thought, reading his mind. 'I wanted to talk to you about the future, Chris. I've been doing a lot of thinking.'

'Yes?' Chris downed his whiskey.

Liz fidgeted with her glass. 'I've decided to stay in Dublin.'

'What? You want me to pull out of the Galway deal? But it's a great package, Liz, and we could buy a wonderful house with the money we got from this place . . .'

'No,' Liz interrupted. 'That's not what I mean. Sorry, I'm not doing a very good job of this. I've decided that

I want a legal separation.' There, she'd said it! She watched his face nervously.

Chris looked confused, then incredulous and then angry. 'What the hell are you talking about?'

'It's over, Chris.'

He crossed the room and slopped more whiskey into his glass. 'Don't be bloody ridiculous, you're my wife. And what about Lucy? You're not thinking straight. What is it, has McDermott screwed all the sense out of you?'

'Chris!' Liz flushed, shocked at his coarseness.

'Oh, come on. Do you think I'm stupid? You throw me out for having a drink with a woman and then you carry on an affair, in my house, in front of my kid.'

Liz swallowed hard. She must remain calm. 'Firstly, I'm not having an affair. I have never been unfaithful to you. Can you say the same thing? I very much doubt it. And secondly, this is *our* house and don't you forget it. As for your "kid". Your beautiful daughter's name is Lucy and Edward McDermott is the uncle of her best friend. That's all.' She gulped down some sherry and watched Chris pace the room.

'She will always be your daughter, Chris,' she continued more gently. 'I would never try to come between you. But there's no future for you and me, and I'm afraid I couldn't play at happy families. It would be living a lie and it would make us all miserable in the end.'

Chris sat down on the arm of her chair and took her hand. 'But, Liz, we've been together so long. How can you just throw it all away?'

Liz pulled her hand from his. 'You did that, Chris, not me.'

'Oh, for God's sake! I tell you I did nothing!'

'You humiliated me. You left me at home with Lucy and you lived the life of a bachelor. Frankly it doesn't matter whether you slept with that girl or not. You left me behind. You left us behind.'

'What the hell are you talking about? I built up the business. I did it for you and Lucy. I worked my butt off, for God's sake.'

'And what did you do when you weren't at the restaurant and you weren't here?' she asked.

Chris shifted uneasily. 'I had to socialise sometimes. It's expected.'

'Really,' Liz said drily. 'How hard on you! Forcing yourself to go out on the town and drink with young girls. Tell me. How did that promote Chez Nous?'

'You're twisting everything. Just because you've turned into a boring middle-aged housewife doesn't mean you have to drag me down with you.'

Liz gasped. Her eyes filled with tears, but she struggled to control them. She wasn't going to cry. 'I think you should go now. My lawyer will be in touch. We need to work out our finances and there's the money from the restaurant to think about.'

Chris looked at her, scornfully. 'You're not getting your hands on that.'

Liz stared back in alarm. 'I put money into it, I'm entitled to my share.'

'Tough. I have to buy a house in Galway and if you're going to stay in this place . . .' He shrugged.

'You have to support us,' she said, panicking.

Chris smiled, coldly. 'No, I don't. You threw me out for no good reason. You needn't think I'm going to give you a penny. I'll support Lucy, but that's it.'

'There's no point in carrying on this conversation. I think we should let the lawyers sort this out.'

'I suppose your precious McDermott is handling it.'

'Not him personally, but his firm is,' Liz agreed quietly.

'Very bloody cosy,' Chris said bitterly. 'Just keep that bastard away from Lucy or I'll make you sorry you ever laid eyes on him.'

'Don't threaten me, Chris, it doesn't work any more. Look, I don't want this to turn into a bitter feud. We have to think of Lucy. I don't want her torn between us.'

Chris snorted. 'Really? I'm going to Galway and you're keeping her here in Dublin. You deliberately waited until I was committed to taking that job, didn't you? You wanted to make sure I'd be out of your hair.'

'No, of course not! I didn't plan this, Chris. I wanted us to get back together. I wanted to go to Galway, you know that. But now . . .'

'But now you've found someone else. You're a stupid bitch, Liz. McDermott will soon get tired of you and move on to a younger model.'

'Like you did?' Liz retorted.

'Yes, dammit! You bored the hell out of me! All you could ever talk about was Lucy. You weren't interested in me or in what was going on in the real world. I had to keep the restaurant going on my own. And what support did I get from you?'

Liz looked at him in shock. 'You never said anything.'

'When did you ever listen?' he said bitterly.

'Don't you dare try and turn this around! Don't try to make me feel guilty – you broke this marriage up. I'm sorry I wasn't interesting or glamorous enough for you. Minding a child isn't a very glamorous occupation.'

Chris sighed. 'Enough of all this, Liz. I'm angry and more than a little hurt and we have both said things we shouldn't have. But there's too much to lose. Let's put this behind us. Come to Galway with me. Give it a go.'

'No, Chris.'

'You'll never manage here on your own. I'm not going to support you. You'll have to move out of this house.' He paced the room, red-faced, sweating.

'I'll manage.' She was sorely tempted to tell him about her new business venture, but she held back. He'd only ridicule her and tell her that she could never pull it off. Or he'd probably figure it another good reason not to give her any money from the sale of Chez Nous. 'Please go,' she said instead.

'You stupid bitch, you'll regret this,' he said, turning on his heel. He paused in the hall, threw the flowers on the floor and ground them into the carpet with his heel. 'You'll never survive on your own. You'll turn into a sad and twisted old bitch! Well, good riddance!' He slammed the door after him and pulled out of the driveway with a screech of brakes.

Liz slumped in a heap at the bottom of the stairs and let the tears come. She grieved for the end of her marriage, for her lost youth and her lost love. She felt empty and old. Maybe Chris was right. Maybe there was nothing in her future but sadness and loneliness.

Edward watched Chris leave. It was obvious from the tyre marks on the road that he was not a happy man. He took out his mobile and dialled.

'I'm just outside if you want to talk about it,' he said quietly, when Liz eventually answered.

'Yes, please,' Liz said through her tears and went to open the door.

Chris drove to the nearest pub and ordered a double. He lifted the glass with a shaking hand and knocked back half of it. He bought a pack of cigars and took his drink to the quiet end of the bar. He couldn't quite believe it. His quiet, easy-going Liz – what had happened to her? No doubt Stephanie West had something to do with it. She was probably delighted that Liz had thrown him out. She'd probably talked her into it. Liz would never have had the strength to do it on her own. And then there was Edward McDermott. What the hell was going on there? Despite what he'd said, he didn't believe that Liz was involved with him. She'd never do that. He was pretty sure, for all her protestations, that she still loved him. He threw back his drink and stood up. He'd go back there and try again. Make her listen. Get her to see sense.

Chris drove around the corner just in time to see Edward step out of the house. Liz followed and reached up to kiss his cheek. Chris felt his blood run cold as he watched the other man stroke his wife's cheek and look tenderly into her eyes. Chris fired up the engine and took off. The road blurred as tears of anger and self-pity filled his eyes. The bitch! He was only out the door and she had him in there. Christ, maybe he'd been there all of the time. Up in the bedroom just waiting for her to get rid of him. The tart! The lying, filthy tart. Well, she wouldn't get a penny out of him, no chance. Let her lover look after her. He wasn't going to finance her love life. He wiped the tears away angrily. How could she treat him like this? What had he ever done to deserve it?

Chapter Twenty-eight

L iam looked up uneasily as Chris called for another bottle of wine.

Jean looked at him beseechingly. 'What do I do?' she hissed.

Chris had arrived an hour earlier and attached himself to a party of businessmen who were enjoying a late lunch. Judging by his high colour and loud voice he'd had quite a lot to drink already.

'Give it to him,' Liam said. 'There's not a lot else we can do.'

Jean delivered the wine and Chris took it and waved her away. 'I'll open it. If you want something done properly, gentlemen, do it yourself. Women are only good for one thing.'

Two ladies, dining nearby, looked up in disgust. Liam shook his head, and headed for their table. 'Can I get you a liqueur with our compliments, ladies?'

'No, thank you,' one replied curtly. 'We're leaving. Some of us have work to do. Tell me, isn't that Chris Connolly, the owner?'

Liam fidgeted uncomfortably. 'It is Mr Connolly but he's no longer the owner.'

'I'm glad to hear it.'

After they'd left, Liam hurried out to the kitchen in search of Conor. 'Chef? We've got a bit of a problem.'

'What is it, Liam?'

'It's Chris. He's out front and pissed as a newt.'

Conor wiped his hands and walked to the door. 'Shit. Who's he with?'

'The Callaghan party.'

Conor groaned. They were good customers and he couldn't really afford to offend them. 'Has he upset anyone?'

Liam nodded. 'Yeah. Two ladies left when he said that women were only good for one thing.'

'Bloody idiot. Go and get Stephanie.'

'She's gone out.'

'Well then,' Conor said, putting on a fresh apron, 'it's up to me. Stay close by. I might need you.'

Conor went into the restaurant and made his way to Chris's table. 'Excuse me, gentlemen. I need to borrow Mr Connolly for a moment.'

'What is it?' Chris said irritably.

'Just need your advice on the dinner menu,' Conor said, swallowing his pride.

Chris grinned and slapped him on the back. 'Ah, what are you going to do without me?'

'I really don't know,' Conor said with a tight smile.

Chris wove his way out of the room with Conor close behind him. When he got through the door, Conor grabbed him by the collar and pushed him up against the wall. 'What the hell do you think you're doing?' he hissed.

Chris tried to focus on him. 'Take your hands off me.'

'You've already frightened off two customers, Chris.

Now go home and sober up and don't ever come in here in this state again.'

'Don't you talk to me like that, you cheeky little bugger!' Chris took a swing at him.

Conor saw the clumsy punch coming and ducked. Chris, caught off balance, slid to the floor.

Liam crouched down beside him. 'He's out cold, Chef.'

'Shit!' Conor looked around the tiny hall. 'We can't leave him here. Let's bung him into the storeroom. He can sleep it off. Take his legs.' The two men tugged Chris into the back room, pulled the door closed and went back to work.

'Your blood pressure's fine, Stephanie.' Maeve O'Farrell took off the stethoscope. 'Now, hop up on the scales.'

'I don't think I've put on any weight,' Steph told her doctor anxiously.

'That's not necessarily a problem. Women vary greatly in how the weight goes on. You'll be back here in a few weeks moaning because nothing will fit you!'

'No, I won't,' Steph said fervently. 'I can't wait. How long do you think it will be before I feel the baby move?'

'Probably two to three weeks.'

Steph's face fell and Maeve laughed. 'When do you go for your scan?'

'Friday fortnight. And I see the obstetrician immediately afterwards.'

'Great. You'll really enjoy the scan. It will make everything seem so much more real. Have you thought any more about seeing a counsellor?'

Steph had told her all about Ruth after she'd returned from London. 'No,' she admitted. She'd been so busy thinking about the baby she'd forgotten all about Eve Wilmot's advice.

'Well, I think we can leave it for the moment. Pregnancy will do you more good than any amount of counselling.'

Steph beamed at her. 'I do feel wonderful.'

'Then that's all that matters. Make an appointment to see me again in three weeks. Other than that, carry on as normal, but don't work too hard.'

Steph left the surgery and dropped into Mothercare on her way back to work. She couldn't resist it. It was late afternoon when she finally let herself into the empty restaurant. She went straight upstairs, tiptoeing past the kitchen. She didn't want to bump into anyone – not with a Mothercare bag in her hand! She reached the sanctuary of her office and closed the door quietly. She emptied the contents of her bag onto the desk, smiling as she surveyed her purchases. She'd hesitated over the maternity trousers, but she was sure she'd need them soon and they'd be a lot more comfortable as the weeks progressed. She smiled ruefully as she examined the extra support bra. A real passion killer, but again, a necessary evil. Her breasts were very tender these days and she'd already gone up a cup size. Sean wouldn't complain about that!

The last purchase was a mobile of farmyard animals. She felt a bit guilty about that one. She'd promised herself that she wouldn't buy anything for the baby until she was at least six months pregnant but she just couldn't resist the pretty little mobile with its bright colours and lovely melody. She tucked everything away in a drawer and turned her attention to the pile of CVs in front of her. She'd finally advertised for an assistant and was eager to find someone quickly. Once Chris left, there would be a lot more pressure on her and she'd need some back-up. She also wanted someone to be trained in before she had to leave to have the baby. She didn't plan to take too much time off, but she needed to be ready in case there were any complications.

Chris woke up and looked around him, disoriented. Where in hell was he? It took him a moment to get his bearings and another moment to remember the events from earlier in the day. The argument with Liz, Conor having a go at him – cheeky little bastard! He'd sort him out later. When his head cleared. He reached into his pocket and pulled out a cigar, lighting it with unsteady hands. Bloody hell, McDermott! The memory of the bastard holding his wife came flooding back. Chris stood up unsteadily and reached up to the top shelf for a bottle of whiskey. He opened it and took a swig. The bastard. He'd sort him out.

He'd been pretty sure that Edward was screwing Stephanie – Jesus, maybe he had both of them on the go. Poor old Sean – another decent bloke being taken for a ride. A ride, ha, there was a Freudian slip for you! Chris puffed on his cigar and took another swig from the bottle. Women were all the same. They were nice to you as long as you were giving them things. Although Liz didn't appreciate all that he'd done for her. She wouldn't have her fancy house in Stillorgan if it weren't for all his hard work. And now she was demanding money from the sale of his business.

Well, she could whistle for it! He took another drink. He was better off without the money-grabbing bitch. McDermott was welcome to her. She was over the hill anyway. And then he passed out again, the cigar slipping from his fingers.

'Marc? What the hell's burning?' Conor sniffed the air.

Marc looked at Pat who shrugged. 'We're not cooking, Chef. Nothing's burning here.'

Pat sniffed. 'You're right, though, something is burning. But not in here.' He followed the smell and saw smoke coming from the storeroom. 'Oh fuck! Chef! We've got a fire in the storeroom!'

Conor jumped up. 'Jesus! Chris is in there!'

Pat grabbed a fire extinguisher and moved cautiously towards the door. He kicked it open, took a deep breath and sprayed in the general direction of Chris.

Conor went over to a sink, doused himself in cold water and soaked some cloths. 'Dial 999, Marc. Get the fire brigade and an ambulance. Quick!' He made his way towards the storeroom. The hallway was thick with smoke now and he couldn't even see Pat.

'Pat? Are you okay?' he called. 'Where are you?'

'Over here!' Pat shouted and then had a fit of coughing as the smoke hit his lungs.

Conor moved towards him and threw the cloths around his head and shoulders. 'Can you see Chris?'

Pat nodded towards the corner, not willing to open his mouth again.

Conor followed his gaze and saw a large dark shape. Chris. The fire was behind him, but the smoke billowed around. Conor felt it tear at his throat and his eyes, mercilessly. 'Okay. You aim the extinguisher at him. I'm going in.' He made a lunge through the flames, grabbed Chris by the ankles and started to drag him towards the door. He cursed Chris for his weight. It was like moving a beached whale. When he'd got a safe distance from the room he stopped and took a breath, but all he got was another mouthful of smoke. 'Come on, Pat,' he gasped. 'Let's get out of here.'

When they got outside, Marc and Liam took Chris from them and set him down carefully on the pavement.

'Is everyone out?' Conor said, taking in gulps of clean air and coughing uncontrollably.

'Yes, Chef. The fire people, they come soon.'

Pat stumbled out onto the street, wheezing and coughing, the tears streaming down his face.

Chris seemed to be unconscious, his face and hands blistered, but he was breathing. Conor sent up a silent prayer of thanks that no one else had been hurt.

'Chef! Chef! Stephanie! She is upstairs! *Mon Dieu!* She cannot get out!' Marc was jumping up and down, pointing at the upstairs window.

'Oh, my Christ!' Conor looked up in horror. Stephanie's white, terrified face was at the barred office window. 'I'm going back in.'

'Conor! No! The stairs are behind the storeroom. You'll never get near her. Wait for the firemen . . .' But Pat was talking to thin air. Conor had gone.

When Conor opened the kitchen door, the smoke hit him like a brick wall. He took a last gulp of fresh air and went in. He felt as if he was drowning. The smoke was thick in his mouth and in his eyes and he had to feel his way through the room. After what seemed like an eternity, he found the door and made his way towards the stairs.

'Stephanie?' he called hoarsely.

'Conor!' she screamed and then broke down in a fit of coughing. 'I can't get down,' she managed finally. 'The stairs are on fire.'

'It's your only hope, Steph. Don't worry – it's mostly smoke. It looks worse than it is,' he lied, praying that he was doing the right thing. 'You'll have to jump. I'll catch you. I promise.' He broke off as the smoke ripped his throat apart. How in hell was he going to catch her? He couldn't even see her!

Steph moved gingerly across the landing. She could feel the heat of the floor right through her shoes. The old wooden floorboards cracked ominously. She hesitated for a moment and then started down the stairs. She screamed as she felt the second step give way. Conor caught her as she fell forward and dragged her down the rest of the way. 'I've got you, Steph. I've got you.'

He half-carried, half-dragged her back through the kitchen. At this stage he was just moving blindly in what he hoped was the right direction. When he got out into the yard Marc ran forward and lifted Steph out of his arms, putting her down gently on the pavement beside Chris. She struggled to speak, her eyes wide and frightened, but her breathing was laboured and she didn't have the strength. Finally she gave up the struggle and closed her eyes.

'Chef! Chef!' Marc looked worriedly up at Conor.

Conor knelt down and shook Stephanie. 'Steph? Steph? Oh, Jesus.'

Pat pushed him out of the way and checked for a

pulse. 'She's breathing. Where the fuck is that ambulance?' He looked anxiously at Chris who hadn't moved since they'd brought him out.

It seemed like hours, but within minutes the fire brigade and two ambulances arrived. Chris and Stephanie were whisked away in the first and Pat, Marc and Conor were loaded, under protest, into the second. A few of the kitchen staff had returned from their break in the middle of all the drama and were wandering around aimlessly. Conor called George over before allowing them to close the ambulance doors. 'Can you send everyone home, George? There's nothing they can do here. But would you hang on with the firemen and the police?'

'I'll take care of everything,' George said gruffly. 'Go on now. Don't worry about anything.'

Conor grabbed his hand gratefully and then slumped back exhausted on to the seat.

George had a quick word with the staff, promising to get in touch if there was any news on the injured. When they'd wandered off, he went to the pub across the road and called Edward. It was probably better to let him get in touch with Chris's and Steph's families. That done, he went in search of the fire chief to see what he could do to help.

As soon as he hung up on George, Edward phoned Joe and gave him the few details that he knew. After a moment's hesitation he called Liz and told her the news too. 'If you like, I'll pick you up on my way in to the hospital,' he offered.

Liz hesitated. 'I'll have to call Chris's dad and I

need to let my mam know that I won't be able to collect Lucy.'

'It'll be okay, Liz.'

'Will it?' she said dully before hanging up.

Joe and Annie were on the way to the hospital when he phoned his parents on the car phone. Annie's fingers dug into her seat as she listened to Joe haltingly explain to his mother what had happened.

'Don't worry, Mam. It seems to be just smoke inhalation. I'm sure she'll be okay.'

'And the baby?' his mother asked anxiously.

Joe and Annie looked at each other in confusion. 'What baby, Mam? What are you talking about?'

Liz sat fidgeting at Edward's side on the journey to the hospital.

'But what was he doing there?'

'I don't know, Liz,' Edward repeated.

'And in the storeroom – it doesn't make sense.'

'I'm sure he'll be able to tell you himself,' he said calmly.

'Will he? Do they know if Steph will be all right?'

'I don't know, Liz. I'm sorry. George couldn't give me any real details about either of them.'

'We should try to get in touch with Sean.'

'Joe may have already taken care of that. If not, I'll call his office.'

Catherine and Tom West sat silently in the back of the taxi. Suddenly, Wicklow seemed an awful long way from Dublin. Joe had insisted on sending the taxi for them. He'd said it was because of Tom's wrist, but he was more afraid of his dad driving like a demon to get to his daughter's side.

'A baby, you say,' Tom said quietly.

Catherine squeezed his hand and swallowed back the tears that threatened. 'Yes, love.'

'Oh, please God look after them both.'

'Amen to that.'

Jack Connolly refused when Liz offered to pick him up on her way to the hospital.

'No, love. I hate those places. Anyway, I'd only be in the way. You give me a call when you know how he is.'

Selfishness runs in the family, Liz thought drily. Chris and his dad had never been close, but had stopped making any effort at all after Chris's mam died three years ago. Liz tried to bring them together a number of times, but had eventually admitted defeat. Now they only saw Jack Connolly a couple of times a year, and that was at Liz's insistence. She was determined that Lucy should see something of her grandfather.

She rung off, promising to call him later, and offered up a grateful prayer for her own close family.

Sean Adams was in JFK when he was paged and Joe's message was relayed. He ignored the call for his flight and went to the nearest phone. No answer at Joe's or at the restaurant and he didn't have any of their mobile numbers. He heard his name being called and he abandoned the phone, running for the gate. Shit! This flight only brought him as far as Cork. He doubled back to the Aer Lingus desk. There was a direct flight to Dublin in two hours. The thought of waiting frustrated him, but he knew it would be quicker in the long run. He headed for the bank of telephones.

Karen was very understanding and he promised to get in touch as soon as he knew what was happening. He talked to his son for a few minutes before making his way to the gate. He found a quiet corner and sat down wearily. 'Please let her be all right. Please God, let her be all right.'

Chapter Twenty-nine

M arc stood at the front door of the casualty department, chain-smoking.

Edward went out to join him. 'Why don't you go on
home, Marc? There's nothing more you can do. I'm
sure Conor and Pat are going to be fine.'

Marc shook his head and managed a weak smile. '*Non,
merci*, Monsieur McDermott, but I would like to see them
before I go.'

Edward patted the pale young man on the shoulder
and went back to the waiting-room. 'Can I get anyone
tea or coffee?'

'Tea would be nice.' Catherine West smiled gratefully.

Annie nodded. 'I'll have a cup too.'

Joe stood up. 'I'll give you a hand. What about
you, Liz?'

Liz looked at him blankly.

'Tea? Coffee?' he repeated gently.

She shook her head.

Catherine West leaned over and squeezed her hand.
'He'll be all right, love. Don't worry.'

Liz nodded dumbly.

Edward looked at her worriedly before heading for
the canteen with Joe.

'I hate these bloody places,' Joe said as they made their way down the corridor.

'I think everyone does. My mother always wanted me to be a doctor. I said I'd consider it if I didn't have to meet any sick people.'

Joe laughed and then felt guilty as the sound echoed around him. 'It's not looking too good for Connolly, is it?'

'Fuck him,' Edward said coldly. 'If it wasn't for him, your sister wouldn't be in here.'

Joe stopped. 'What do you mean?'

Edward sighed. It probably wasn't the right time for this conversation but he couldn't handle Joe feeling sorry for that shit. 'Well, from what Marc says, it looks like Chris may have started the fire.'

'The bastard! What happened?'

'I'm not too sure. Marc's English isn't the best and my French is a little rusty. From what I can gather Chris was having a boozy lunch with some customers, passed out and they put him in the storeroom to sleep it off. That's where the fire started.'

'But how?'

'That we don't know, but he was probably smoking.'

'The bloody fool,' Joe muttered angrily.

'I feel sorry for Liz. She told him this morning that she wanted a separation. I think she's blaming herself now for the whole thing.'

'What a mess. I just hope Steph's going to be okay. And the baby.'

Edward blinked. 'Baby?'

'Yeah. Mam just told us. Apparently Steph never went through with the abortion after all.'

'Oh, that's good news.'

'Well, it is as long as their both okay,' Joe said worriedly.

'Does Sean know?'

'No. And he probably hasn't heard about the accident yet either. His office tried to get in touch with him but they think he was already on a plane home. Someone's going to meet his flight and take him straight here.'

'Poor bastard. That's some welcome home.'

They collected the drinks and brought them back to the waiting-room. Annie sipped the hot liquid but Catherine West just sat staring into her cup.

Tom West stood up suddenly. 'I can't stand this place any longer. I'm going for a walk.'

Annie looked pointedly at Joe. 'I'll come with you,' he said and followed his father outside.

Edward sat down next to Liz. 'Are you okay?'

'Not really. I keep thinking about how angry he was with me.'

'It wasn't your fault, Liz.'

'He's my husband and he could be dying.'

'No one said he was dying. In fact the doctor said he was stable.'

'Edward's right, Liz. There's no point thinking like that. I'm sure he'll be fine,' Catherine said kindly, although she was finding it hard not to blame Chris. What if Stephanie ... and then there was the baby ... oh please God.

'Mrs West?'

She stood up as the nurse came into the room. 'How is she?'

'She's going to be fine. If you'd like to come with me, the doctor would like to talk to you.'

'I'll go and find Joe and Tom,' Edward told her.

Catherine smiled her thanks and followed the nurse.

Tom and Joe were shown into the office where Catherine was already seated.

'I'm Stephanie's brother,' Joe introduced himself to the impossibly young Asian doctor.

The doctor shook hands with the two men. 'I'm happy to report that Stephanie is going to be fine. She has some burns on her face, hands and legs, but they're superficial and it's unlikely there will be any scarring. The main problem was smoke inhalation. Her lungs are a bit raw and she'll feel sore for a couple of weeks, but there's no permanent damage.'

'Thank God,' Tom said.

'I'm afraid it's not all good news.'

'The baby?' Catherine said, her voice barely a whisper.

'Yes. I'm afraid she lost it.'

Tears streamed down Catherine's cheeks and she clung to her husband's hand. 'Oh, poor, poor Steph. Does she know? Can I see her?'

The doctor shook his head. 'She's sleeping now. She was unconscious when the miscarriage started and we went straight in and did a D & C. She's been given a strong sedative now so she will probably sleep until morning.'

'I understand, but I'd like to be here when you talk to her.'

'Of course, Mrs West. I think that's a good idea. I start my rounds at ten. Now I suggest you all go home and get some sleep. There's nothing more you can do tonight.'

'Thank you, Doctor,' Joe said gruffly, before guiding

his parents out into the corridor. 'Why don't you stay with us tonight? It's closer,' he suggested to them.

Tom nodded. 'Thanks, Joe. I think that would be a good idea.'

'We should go to Malahide and get some of Stephanie's things.' Catherine struggled to concentrate.

'That's okay, Mam. Annie can lend her whatever she needs.'

They returned to the waiting-room and collected Annie. Joe gave Edward a brief update on Stephanie's condition and Edward assured him that he would stay with Liz. Marc decided to leave too. He'd been allowed in to see Conor and Pat. They were recovering quickly and would be let out the following morning. Marc was going to collect them and he'd also promised to call George and give him an update on everyone's condition.

'Stephanie's going to be okay,' Edward said, sitting down beside Liz.

'Thank God for that,' Liz said. 'It doesn't look so good for Chris though.'

'Why? Did you talk to someone?'

'No, but it's been such a long time.'

Edward put his arm around her. 'Don't jump to conclusions. I'm sure he'll be fine.'

Liz shrugged off his arm. 'Why don't you go on home, Edward?'

Edward watched her carefully. She hadn't looked him in the eye all day. 'I'm fine here.'

'You don't understand. I don't want you here.' Liz stood up and walked out of the room.

Edward stared after her. He went in search of a nurse. 'I'm going down to the canteen. If there is any news on Mr Connolly, would you give me a shout?'

The nurse smiled and glanced speculatively at the ring finger of his left hand. 'Of course. I'd be happy to.'

Liz pushed open the door of the ward and looked in. There were three patients. An elderly woman in the bed nearest her lay still and white, with tubes attached to her nose, mouth and arms. Liz crept past and peered at the man in the second bed – definitely not Chris. The form in the bed looked slight and frail. She moved on to the last bed. Chris lay on his back, very still. Half his face was covered with a bandage. The part that was exposed was an angry red. His right hand and arm were also bandaged. There were no tubes or machines, just a drip going into his left hand. That had to be a good sign.

'Mrs Connolly?'

Liz turned to look at the young girl in the white coat. 'Yes? How is he? Is he going to be okay?'

The girl smiled. 'He's a very lucky man. He has some minor burns and he inhaled a lot of smoke, but he'll be fine.'

Liz glared at her. 'I don't understand this. I've been worried sick. Why didn't someone come and tell me this? I've been sitting out there for ages.'

The girl smiled sympathetically. 'I'm sorry about that, Mrs Connolly. I was actually just coming to talk to you. You see, your husband had been drinking and we didn't know how much of his, eh, unconsciousness, was due to the smoke and how much to the effects of alcohol.'

Liz glanced at her husband's inert form. 'You mean he's sleeping it off?' she exclaimed.

'Eh, yes, you could say that.'

'I'd like to talk to a doctor,' Liz said shortly.

'I am a doctor.'

'Oh, right. Sorry.'

'That's okay. Look, why don't you go home and get some sleep? I'm sorry for keeping you hanging around for so long, but we had to be sure.'

Liz smiled weakly. 'Of course. Thank you. Thank you very much.'

When Liz left the ward, Edward was waiting in the corridor. 'How is he?'

Liz took a deep breath and let it out slowly. 'He was drunk,' she said angrily. 'They thought he was unconscious, but the bastard's just been sleeping it off!'

Edward reached out and gripped her by the arms, trying to calm her. 'Well, shouldn't you be grateful that it's not serious?'

'Grateful? He could have killed someone. He could have killed Stephanie.'

'We don't know that he caused the fire,' Edward pointed out, although he'd stake his life on it.

Liz gave a short laugh. 'Oh, come on. The fire started in the storeroom. He was the only one in the bloody storeroom. And he was pissed – you don't have to be Sherlock Holmes to figure it out.'

Edward slipped an arm around her shoulders. 'Let's get out of here.'

'Her blood pressure's fine. I'll just check Mrs Molloy and then I'll go and make us a cuppa.'

Stephanie stirred as the two nurses moved on to the next bed. It took a few moments for her to figure out where she was and why. She moved her arms and legs gingerly. They seemed to work, though her left hand was sore where a drip was attached. Her breath was short and rasping, despite the oxygen mask, which made her feel slightly claustrophobic. She struggled to remember what had happened. The flames rising up from under the stairs had terrified her. She remembered Conor's voice, pleading with her to jump. It had taken all her courage. Her last memory was Conor's strong arms around her. 'I've got you, Steph. I've got you.'

Conor – God, was he okay? She looked around to ask a nurse but the ward was quiet. She noticed a call button on the wall but as she twisted to reach it, she became aware of bulky padding around her crotch. She slipped a hand down under the covers . . .

The screaming went on and on. Nurses came running, lights were switched on, blinding her.

'Stephanie? Stephanie? You're okay. You're safe now.'

Steph suddenly realised that the noise, that inhuman wailing, was coming from her. She became aware of a nurse bending over her and a doctor preparing a needle. 'My baby,' she gasped. 'My baby. What have you done to my baby?'

The nurse stroked her cheek. 'Calm down, love. Everything's going to be okay. You poor pet. I know how terrible you must feel. But you're going to be okay.'

The doctor stuck the needle in her arm. She looked up into his sad brown eyes. 'My baby,' she said reaching out to him.

He squeezed her hand. 'Rest now. You need to rest.'

She fell into an uneasy sleep, still holding his hand. And then she was back on the burning staircase. Flames licking at her ankles.

'Throw me the baby,' Conor called to her.

'I can't.'

'Throw the baby, Steph. I'll catch it. I promise.'

She looked down at him and then at the bundle wriggling in her arms and threw for all she was worth. It flew up into the air, unravelling, and she screamed because there was no baby.

Chapter Thirty

Liz ran up the steps of the hospital and crashed straight into Annie. 'Oh, sorry, Annie. How's Steph?'

'I don't know, Liz. Catherine and Tom are with her. I thought I'd give them some time alone.'

Liz looked at her strained, tired face. 'Come on. Let's get some coffee.'

'Aren't you going to see Chris?'

'Chris can wait,' Liz said grimly.

Annie found a table in the crowded canteen while Liz queued at the counter. She carried two steaming mugs to the table and handed Annie a Kit-Kat. 'Thought you might need a bit of sustenance.'

Annie smiled and sipped her coffee appreciatively. 'It tastes so much better when it's not in one of those awful plastic cups.'

'Sure does. God, I wish I had a cigarette.'

Annie nodded towards the no smoking signs. 'A cigarette wouldn't be much good here. It's funny. I remember going to visit Jackie, my neighbour, in St Patrick's.'

'Isn't that a nut-house?'

Annie grinned. 'Honestly, Liz, it's a psychiatric hospital. She had a bit of a breakdown when her husband left. But, it's just so different from other hospitals. There was a haze of smoke throughout the whole building. You could hardly see through it in the canteen. Poor sods, I suppose they needed something to keep them going.'

Liz shivered. 'I've never been in a place like that. It must be very depressing.'

'Oh, I don't know. There must be comfort in the knowledge that you're not alone. We all lose the plot occasionally. Anyway, tell me about Chris.'

'Apparently he's fine,' Liz said grimly. 'Though the bugger doesn't deserve to be.'

Annie didn't comment on this. Joe had told her the part Chris had played in the fire. 'Did you get to talk to him last night?'

'You're joking,' Liz said harshly. 'Sure he was comatose. Out cold. Drunk.'

'You will go in to see him though, won't you?'

Liz nodded. 'Yeah. I'll go. And I'll tell him exactly what I think of him too. Then I'll go home and tell Lucy that poor Daddy is sick. And tomorrow I'll take her in to see him. And we'll play happy families. And after that, the sooner I can pack him off to Galway the better!'

Annie grinned.

'It's not funny, Annie!' Liz glared at her.

Annie looked penitent. 'Oh, I know it's not, Liz, it's awful. But it's done now. There's no point in going on about it.'

'I wonder will Steph feel like that.'

Annie fidgeted with her spoon. She should really tell Liz about Steph's miscarriage. But if she told her now, Liz would probably kill Chris. It was so awkward. What would Stephanie want? No one had even known she was pregnant – except for Catherine. Annie didn't envy that poor woman now. Sitting up there with her daughter while she was told that she'd lost her baby. She sighed heavily.

'What?' Liz looked at her.

'Oh, nothing,' Annie said with a forced smile. 'It's just so sad. Things were going so well for Steph and Conor, and now this.'

'Is there much damage?'

Annie shrugged. 'I don't know. Edward and Joe are going in this morning to have a look. The fire was in the storeroom, so obviously that's gone. And apparently the stairs gave out completely just after Steph got out.' She shuddered as she thought of what might have happened.

'The insurance will cover it all, though,' Liz pointed out. 'And at least no one was seriously hurt.'

Annie said nothing.

'They'll need to get an assessor in quickly and figure out how long it's going to take before they can reopen.'

Annie rubbed her eyes wearily. 'God, it's a bloody nightmare.'

'Steph will have it sorted in no time,' Liz assured her. 'She's a great organiser. Look, I'd better go and visit this man.' Liz gave her friend a quick hug. 'Give Steph my love. I'll drop in and see her later.'

'Better not,' Annie said quickly. 'They said family only for now.'

Liz frowned. 'But I thought you said she was okay?'

'She is, they just want her to get as much rest as possible.'

'Oh, okay. Well, I'll call you later then. Bye.'

Annie watched her leave. Liz was going to be really pissed off when she eventually discovered the truth but Steph had to come first for the moment. She finished her coffee and made her way up to the third floor. Stephanie had been moved into a private room and Tom West was standing outside, staring into space.

'How is she?' Annie asked.

He shook his head, his eyes full of tears. 'She's very upset. It's awful watching her. There's nothing you can do or say to make it better. I've left her with her mother. Catherine's better at this. She'll know what to say.'

Catherine didn't. Her heart ached for her daughter. Steph looked beseechingly at her from distraught, red eyes. She wanted answers that Catherine couldn't give her. She wanted reasons, but there weren't any. She thought it was punishment because she'd considered abortion but Catherine assured her that God wasn't cruel. She cried because Sean had never known the joy of this pregnancy. Catherine had no words of comfort. She held Stephanie, rocked her in her arms, kissed her hair and wished that she could take the hurt away.

Steph felt like she was floating through some kind of nightmare. Everything seemed so unreal. One minute she was in this plain, clinical room and the next, she was reaching for Conor on the staircase. Then she was back in the London clinic, lying to the counsellor about her background and her circumstances. Then she was wandering through Mothercare.

Her hands constantly moved to her stomach, as if she could change things. Maybe they'd made a mistake. Maybe the baby was still there. Stupid, stupid, stupid.

The doctor had explained about the D & C. He'd told her that they'd taken everything away. He'd told her that they'd done a scan and that there had been no heartbeat. He assured her that there was no reason why she shouldn't have a successful pregnancy in the future. She'd looked at him blankly. He thought she was going to replace her baby, just like that? But then it was just one of those things to him. It happened to a lot of women. What had he said? One in four pregnancies ended in miscarriage. But why did she have to be the one in four? Anyway, there was nothing natural about what had happened to her. Her baby had died because of the fire.

A young girl banged open the door and shoved in a trolley. 'Lunch,' she announced, sliding a tray onto the table at the end of the bed. 'It's fish. The woman who was here yesterday ordered it.'

'I don't want it,' Steph whispered, wincing at the pain that shot through her chest.

The girl ignored her and left, leaving the tray behind her.

Catherine inspected the meal. 'It looks all right, Stephanie.'

'I couldn't.' It seemed wrong to eat, to drink, to live when her baby had died.

'Maybe some soup,' her mother persisted.

'No! I don't want it, okay?'

'Sorry, love.'

Steph immediately regretted her outburst. She reached out and took her mother's hand. 'Sorry, Mam.'

Catherine nodded. 'That's all right. Everything's going to be all right. Sean should be here soon.'

Steph looked surprised. 'Sean?'

'Yes, he's on his way home. We left word with his office and they're going to bring him straight here.'

'Why?' Steph said sadly. 'What for?'

'Don't be silly, love. He'll want to be here with you.'

'I don't want to see him.'

'But Stephanie, why? You need him now. You need each other. I know things seem very black now, but in time . . .'

'What? In time I'll forget?' Steph's eyes filled up and she snatched her hand away angrily.

'No. No you'll never forget,' Catherine said firmly. 'But you'll learn to live with it. Now you've driven Sean away enough times. Don't do it now. You need him. You know you do.'

Steph nodded, tears streaming down her face.

Annie knocked on the door and put her head in.

'Come in, Annie,' Catherine said, standing up. 'I'll just go and stretch my legs. I'll bring you back some ice cream, Stephanie. That will soothe your throat.'

Steph dabbed at her tears with a sodden handkerchief and accepted her mother's kiss with a weak smile. 'Thanks, Mam,' she whispered.

Annie exchanged looks with Catherine and then pulled up the chair she'd vacated. 'How are you doing?'

'Lousy,' Steph said, unable to stop the tears rolling again.

'Oh, come here to me,' Annie climbed onto the bed and took Steph in her arms. 'I'm so sorry, Steph. I'm so very sorry.'

Edward and Joe stood and looked at the devastation around them. The fire hadn't reached the restaurant or the kitchen, but it had destroyed the hall, stairs and landing. They'd no idea of the extent of the damage upstairs. The prompt arrival of the fire brigade had saved the day, but the resulting water damage was unbelievable.

'You won't be opening for a while,' Joe said, wrinkling his nose at the stench of smoke and damp.

'No,' Edward agreed, taking his jacket off. 'Oh well. The sooner we start to clean up, the sooner we can sort things out. I'd better get on the phone.'

'What do you want me to do?' Joe asked.

'Call Liam and George and ask them to ring around the others. If we have enough people, we can get the worst of this muck cleaned up today. I'll call the broker and see if we can get an assessor out. We won't be able to start until he's seen the damage.'

They were both talking on their mobiles when Conor, Pat and Marc walked in.

'What the hell are you doing here?' Edward asked, putting his hand over the mouthpiece.

Marc shrugged. 'I try to take them home, but they insisted they come here first.'

'Jaysus, this is a right mess,' Pat said, picking his way through the hall.

Conor followed, silently. His dream had gone up in smoke. 'How soon can we open, Mr McDermott?'

'I don't know, Conor, we'll have to see what the assessor says. I'm holding for him now.'

Conor nodded and went out into the kitchen. It was a mess. The firemen had dragged their hoses through it, knocking food and crockery from the worktops. The floor was a mishmash of dirty water, food and broken crockery.

'*Merde*,' Marc swore softly. 'We'd better get stuck up.'

Conor laughed. 'Stuck *in*, Marc.'

'We can't clean up yet,' Joe told them. 'But you can throw open every window in the place. We need to get rid of this God awful smell.'

Edward had finished his call and followed them in. 'Well, good old George is way ahead of us. The assessor was here last night and we can start cleaning up straight away. But Conor, you and Pat should go home and rest.'

Conor shook his head stubbornly. 'I'm staying. This is my kitchen. You go, Pat.'

'Not at all, Chef. I'm grand.'

Edward smiled at them. 'In that case, let's get to it!'

'Or as Marc would say,' Pat said with a wink, 'let's get stuck up!'

They laughed at Marc's confused expression and got to work.

Sean strode through customs and out into arrivals. Michael Walsh, his General Manager was waiting for him.

'How is she?' Sean asked without preamble, not breaking his stride.

'She's fine,' Michael assured him. 'Joe called this morning. She has some superficial burns and she's suffering from smoke inhalation, but it's not serious.'

'Thank God,' Sean breathed. 'Where's your car?'

Thirty minutes later, he walked into the hospital.

'Sean?'

He swung around to see Tom and Catherine sitting in a corner of reception. 'Hello.' He bent and kissed Catherine's cheek and shook Tom's hand. 'She's okay, then?'

Tom looked away and Catherine's smile faded.

'What is it? What's wrong with her?'

'Nothing, nothing at all, Sean,' Tom assured him.

'Why don't you sit down, love?' Catherine said quietly. 'We do have something to tell you.'

Sean pulled up a stool and waited.

'Stephanie didn't go through with the abortion,' Catherine said simply. 'She had a change of heart when she was in the clinic.'

'Oh my God – but that's wonderful.' Sean's eyes lit up, but Catherine and Tom weren't smiling. 'What?'

'She lost it, Sean. As a result of the fire.' Catherine looked at him sadly. He was such a good, kind man. It really wasn't fair.

Sean raked his fingers through his hair. 'Oh Jesus. Poor Steph.' He looked at Catherine. 'I didn't know you knew.'

'She told me when she came home. Oh, Sean! She was so happy. She couldn't wait to tell you.'

He nodded, his face stricken with grief.

'I'm so sorry, Sean. It's a terrible thing. But you have each other. You'll get through this,' Catherine said, repeating the words she'd said to Stephanie.

'I'd better go up,' he said finally. 'I'll see you later.'

Catherine watched him walk away, his shoulders hunched. Dear God, would this day get any easier?

Chapter Thirty-one

Sean pushed open the door softly and looked at Stephanie. She seemed so tiny and frail, her hair hung limply on the pillow, and her pallor was emphasised by angry red patches on her cheek and forehead. Her eyes were closed. He walked over and sat down in the chair at her side, moving as quietly as possible so as not to disturb her sleep. His eyes fell to her right hand. It looked sore. She must have held it up to protect herself. He closed his eyes and sank back in the chair. It was all so hard to take in. When he'd found out that Steph hadn't got rid of the baby, his heart had jumped in his chest, with excitement and love. But when Catherine had told him that they'd lost the baby anyway, it was as if someone had punched him in the gut. He felt disoriented, tired and sad. What else could go wrong, for Christ's sake?

'I'm sorry.'

Sean looked up to see Steph staring at him from eyes bright with tears. He immediately stood up and took her gently in his arms. 'You've no need to be sorry, love. It's not your fault. You're not to blame.'

She leant against him, letting the tears roll down her cheeks. 'I was so happy, Sean,' she whispered, holding her throat in pain.

'Hush, don't try to speak.'

Steph ignored him. She had to talk, no matter how much it hurt. 'I was dying to tell you, but you wouldn't take my calls.'

Sean groaned. 'I'm sorry, love. I didn't know.'

'I know that – I don't blame you. I wouldn't blame you if you never wanted to see me again.'

Sean pushed her away so that he could look her in the eyes. 'Listen to me, Steph. You changed your mind about the abortion and that makes me very happy. The fire, well, that was awful. Losing the baby is awful. But it wasn't your fault. We'll get through this. Together.'

Steph hugged him to her tightly. 'I hope you don't regret it.'

Sean kissed her hair. 'When are they going to let you home?'

'Probably tomorrow. The obstetrician wants to see me before I go.'

Sean looked at her in concern. 'There's nothing wrong, is there?'

'No, it's just routine.' She coughed and winced as pain shot through her chest.

Sean held her while she coughed and then handed her a glass of water. 'I wish there was something I could do to make you feel better.'

'You're here,' she whispered.

Chris had also been moved to a private room. He sat up in bed, watching TV, and rang the nurse's bell on average every twenty minutes.

Liz approached the nurse's desk. 'I was looking for Chris Connolly.'

'Room 225,' the young nurse said grimly. 'Down the corridor on your left.'

The staff nurse stood up and looked after Liz. 'Is that the wife, do you think? Poor woman.'

Liz took a deep breath and pushed open the door. When he saw her, Chris lay back and closed his eyes. Liz stood looking down at him. His eyelids fluttered and he looked up at her with a slight, pained smile.

'Oh hello, love. Didn't see you there.' He turned off the TV and made a production out of sitting up, grimacing in pain.

'How are you, Chris?'

Chris winced again. 'Oh, not too good, Liz. I'd a very bad night – a lot of pain. This is a terrible place. They wouldn't give me painkillers. Just left me to suffer.'

Liz suppressed a smart retort. 'I'm sure they didn't mean to.'

'They don't give a damn. God, they're always on strike saying they don't get paid enough. Rubbish! This isn't hard work! They should come into my kitchen. I'd show them hard work!'

'What happened, Chris?' Liz ignored his ranting. She wanted answers.

He looked puzzled. 'What? What do you mean?'

'The fire, Chris. How did it happen?' Liz watched him steadily.

'I'm not sure – it's all a bit fuzzy. God, I was damn lucky though.'

'You were,' Liz agreed. 'The story goes that you were drunk, you passed out and Conor left you in the storeroom to sleep it off.'

Chris looked taken aback.

'And that the fire started in the storeroom,' Liz continued.

Chris flushed. The combination of burned flesh and reddened skin made him look like a circus clown. 'Well, I remember having one of my cigars,' he said hesitantly.

Liz glared at him. 'You stupid bastard! You could have killed someone. As it is, Stephanie's down the corridor in a bad way, and Conor and Pat have only just been let home. You owe those two your life.'

'If it wasn't for Conor I wouldn't have been in there in the first place!' Chris shot back.

'You wouldn't have been in there if you hadn't got pissed and made a show of yourself. You've done a lot of dumb things in your life, Chris, but this . . .'

Chris was annoyed. This wasn't going the way it should. Liz was supposed to be fussing over him. Telling him how worried she'd been. Telling him she wouldn't leave him after all.

'I've got to go,' she said. 'I'll take Lucy in to see you if you're still here tomorrow. Otherwise, give me a call and we'll set something up. By the way, your dad sends his best.'

'Isn't he coming in?' Chris said petulantly.

'No,' Liz said from the doorway. 'He doesn't like hospitals. Seeya.' She closed the door and leaned back against it. It had been hard to resist the urge to thump him. He was so caught up in himself. He didn't seem to feel any guilt. He hadn't even asked how Steph was and he showed no gratitude to Conor and Pat who'd risked their lives for him. She shook her head in disgust and, on impulse, made her way down the corridor to Steph's room. When she peered in she saw Sean draped across the bed, his eyes closed. Steph gave her a shaky smile. Liz blew her a kiss and withdrew quietly. Thank God some good had come of this. It looked like Sean and Stephanie were definitely back together again.

Edward hung up after talking to the assessor and returned to the kitchen. The room had been cleaned up as much as it could be for the moment and the men sat around the preparation table, eating burgers and fries and drinking coffee.

'Well?' Conor looked up expectantly.

'Not good news, I'm afraid.' Edward sat down. 'Apart from the obvious damage to the storeroom, there are a few other problems. The assessor thinks we need to replace all the floorboards of the landing and the ladies' loo.'

Conor groaned. 'God, that'll mean tearing up all the floor tiles. They cost a fortune, Steph will go spare.'

Edward shrugged. 'Look on it as an opportunity to get the place exactly the way you want it, Conor.'

Conor brightened a little. 'How long before we can reopen?' he asked for probably the tenth time that day.

Edward frowned. 'Hard to say, at least a month I should think – and that's only if we can get some reliable contractors.'

'That's an oxymoron,' Joe said drily.

'A what?' Pat asked.

'A contradiction in terms,' Edward explained with a grin.

Pat shrugged and went back to his burger.

'I have my secretary ringing around some contractors,' Edward continued. 'I've told her to stress the time factor. Still, the insurance will cover us for our lost earnings and expenses for the time we're closed.' He glanced around at the crew. 'Everyone will be paid.'

A murmur of appreciation went around the room.

'Being closed that long isn't going to do us any good though,' Conor said worriedly.

'No,' agreed Edward. 'And of course we'll have to postpone the official reopening.'

'Is your insurance adequate?' Joe asked, ever the accountant.

'I haven't seen the policy,' Edward admitted. 'Presumably it's in the office and I won't be able to get hold of the broker before Monday.'

'Steph would know all about it,' Pat said.

There was silence in the room. All the staff had heard about Stephanie's miscarriage.

'What about Chris?' Pat persisted.

'Maybe,' Edward agreed. He wasn't entirely sure he could manage a civilised conversation with Connolly. He wondered how Liz was. He hadn't talked to her today. 'Joe? Can I have a word?' he said, and led the way out into the yard. 'It's about Liz. She didn't know anything about Steph's pregnancy – well, I know no one did. But it's only a matter of time before she finds out and I was wondering if it would be okay if I explained it to her?'

Joe frowned. 'Yes, yes of course. Well, I'd better get over to the hospital – unless there's anything else I can do?'

Edward clapped him on the back. 'No. Thanks for your help. I don't think there's much more we can do. It's over to the professionals now. Well, just one thing . . .'

'Yes?'

'I need to talk to Stephanie and agree with her where we go from here. I was going to drop in to the hospital later but at the same time I don't want to seem insensitive.'

Joe scratched his head. 'I don't think there's going to be a good time, Edward. Drop in if you like. You can always back off if she's not up to it.'

'Fair enough.'

'I'll go so. I'm a bit worried about Mam and Dad. This whole business has taken a lot out of them. I might talk them into staying in town for another couple of nights.' Joe bid the crew goodbye and left.

'We may as well call it a day, lads,' Edward said. 'Thanks for all the hard work.'

Conor nodded his agreement. 'Yeah, thanks lads. I'll give you a call in a couple of days and let you know what's happening. Remember, your wages are safe, so don't go looking for a new job. Relax and enjoy this unexpected holiday.'

Pat grinned. 'That's not a bad idea. Anyone for a pint?'

There was a murmur of agreement and they all trouped off to O'Neill's, while Conor and Edward locked up. Conor looked up miserably at the blackened walls.

Edward saw his expression. 'Don't worry, Conor. You'll have your restaurant. This is just a hiccup. Use the time to work on your recipes and menus.'

'I will. Look, give Steph my best, will you? I'd go in and see her myself but I don't want to intrude.'

'I'll pass on your message, Conor. Go and have a pint. I'll call you tomorrow.'

Edward watched the lanky young man lope down

the road. He hoped another restaurant didn't take this opportunity to make him an offer he couldn't refuse. That was all they needed. He hated the idea of going up to the hospital and bothering Stephanie at a time like this, but he didn't know enough to sort everything out on his own. There was the whole business about the Michelin Star, for one thing. Then, despite his assurances to the staff, he was a little concerned about their insurance cover. Edward got into his car and started the engine. No point in putting it off any longer.

Chapter Thirty-two

L iz tucked the duvet in around Lucy and tiptoed out of the room. The phone rang as she closed the door gently. She picked up the extension in her bedroom.

'Liz, it's Edward.'

'Hi,' she said softly.

'How are you doing?'

His voice echoed on the line. On the car phone, Liz surmised. 'I'm fine.'

'Could I come over later?' he asked. 'I'm on my way up to the hospital to see Stephanie so it'll be late.'

'That's okay. I don't feel much like sleeping. See you later.'

Edward pulled into the hospital car park with a heavy sigh. He didn't know what to say to Stephanie. What were you supposed to say to a woman who'd just been through what she had? He was sure the last thing she wanted was to talk about Chez Nous. The prospect of seeing Liz afterwards didn't appeal to him either. He usually enjoyed sitting at her kitchen table watching her throw an amazing meal together in half an hour. He liked the way she moved, the way she smiled. But tonight what he had to tell her would make her sad. He hated being the bearer of bad news, but he was afraid she'd find out accidentally and he'd prefer Liz to hear the full story from him. He sighed again. This was proving to be a very long and miserable day.

Sean stood up and shook hands with Edward. 'Steph's in the bathroom,' he explained.

'I'm very sorry, Sean,' Edward said awkwardly.

'Thanks.'

Edward looked at Sean. He looked terrible. His eyes were red and his face was drawn. Grief and jet lag didn't go well together. 'How is she?'

'Bearing up. She's coming home tomorrow.'

'That's good. These places are very depressing. I need to talk to her about the insurance, Sean. Do you think that would be all right?'

Sean shrugged. 'She'll probably be glad of the distraction, though I'm not sure if she'll be much use to you. She's finding it hard to come to terms with—'

'Edward.' Steph emerged from the bathroom and kissed his cheek before sitting up on the bed.

'How are you, Steph?'

'Not so bad,' she said. 'How are the boys?'

'Grand. They were in today helping us clean up – came straight from the hospital. They're a good bunch, Steph.'

She smiled faintly. 'Yes. So what's the damage?'

Edward was relieved that she'd broached the subject first. He gave her a quick summary of the situation.

'Sounds bad,' she said glumly.

'Well, it won't be too bad if we're fully insured.'

Steph frowned. 'Chris used to take care of all that. I

275

did get in touch with the broker when we took over, to check if the change of ownership affected anything.'

'So whatever cover we have is what Chris put in place on day one?' Edward asked.

'I suppose so. You don't seem too happy about that.'

'I suppose Connolly doesn't instil me with confidence,' he admitted. 'Anyway there's nothing we can do until Monday.'

'Why don't you check the policy. It's in the filing cabinet in my office.'

Edward looked embarrassed. 'Eh, yeah. We can't get up there. The other matter is the *Michelin Guide*. What do I need to do about that?'

'I'm not sure. I suppose we just need to let them know what's happening. They're going to want to pay a couple of visits once we're up and running again.'

Edward frowned. 'Well, that's not a problem, is it?'

'No, but it doesn't give Conor much time to settle into the job.' Steph chewed her bottom lip and felt a flicker of interest spark inside her. 'We've got a lot to do.'

'Don't you worry about it,' Edward said hurriedly. 'Just point me in the right direction.'

'Don't be silly. I'm fine. I'll get on to the Michelin people on Monday and then I think I should pay our broker a visit. He should have a copy of the policy.'

'But you can't possibly go back to work so soon,' Sean protested.

'I'll take it easy tomorrow and by Monday I'll be fine. Anyway a couple of phone calls and one meeting is hardly going to exhaust me,' she croaked.

Edward looked apologetically at Sean who shrugged helplessly. He wasn't pleased at the idea of Steph going back to work so soon, but on the other hand, it would probably be better if she didn't have too much time to think about the baby.

'Right,' Edward said. 'I'll call you tomorrow then. Oh, eh, where?'

'You'll get me on my mobile,' Steph told him.

Edward stood up. 'Right then. I'll talk to you tomorrow. Take care. Bye, Sean.'

'See you, Edward.'

When he'd gone, Sean stretched and yawned. 'I should really be making tracks myself.'

'Yes, you must be exhausted.'

'I'm fine.' He bent and kissed her. 'I'll pick you up tomorrow and then we can go out to Malahide and pick up some of your stuff.'

Steph studied her fingernails. 'Oh, Sean, I think it would be easier if I stayed in Malahide for the moment.'

'Why?'

'Well, it makes sense. With all my stuff there.'

'Steph, I want you to move back in.'

'Yes, and I will,' she said impatiently. 'Just not tomorrow. You said yourself that I need to rest.'

Sean bit his lip. 'Okay then, but I'm not leaving you there alone.'

Steph smiled. 'You'd better not.'

Liz opened the door. 'You look terrible.'

'You do wonders for my confidence,' Edward said drily.

'Coffee? Drink?' she asked, hovering between the living-room and the kitchen.

'I could do with a drink,' he admitted. He was going to need it and so was Liz.

'How's Lucy?' he asked as Liz made two G & Ts.

'Fine.' She handed him his drink and curled up on the sofa. 'I didn't tell her about the fire though. I thought it might give her nightmares. I just said Chris had burned himself and that the doctors were looking after him. I told her he was dying for her to come in and kiss him better.' She made a face. 'It's terrible the crap you have to come up with when you have kids.'

Edward laughed. 'How is Chris?'

'Infuriating. Honestly, Edward, he never even asked how the others were.'

'So you're not having second thoughts then?' he asked, watching her intently.

She looked confused. 'About the separation? God, no! Now I'm sure I'm doing the right thing!'

Edward smiled, happy with her answer. He took another sip of his drink and wondered how to tell her.

'A penny for them?' Liz broke in on his thoughts. 'What is it, Edward? Something's wrong, isn't it?'

'Not really. Well yes, I suppose so. There's something I have to tell you, Liz. It's about Stephanie.'

'Is she okay?' Liz looked at him in alarm.

'She's fine,' he assured her. 'Something happened a few weeks ago that she didn't tell you about – she didn't tell me either,' he added hastily when he saw her face.

'For God's sake, Edward, spit it out.'

'Okay. Before Sean went to the States, Steph discovered she was pregnant.'

'What?' Liz looked at him in astonishment.

'She decided to have an abortion,' Edward continued. 'Remember that time she went to London?'

'Well, yes. Oh my God . . .'

'But it seems at the eleventh hour she had a change of heart.'

'Oh, thank God.' Liz's face lit up.

Edward lifted his hand. 'I'm not finished. Last night as a result of the fire, she lost it.'

'Oh my God.'

Edward moved over onto the sofa beside her and put his arm around her.

'This is awful. How far on was she?'

'I don't know any of the details.' He thought for a moment. 'It must be at least three months though.'

Liz shook her head. Poor Steph. She'd lost her baby because of the fire. The bloody fire. Chris. 'I'll kill him,' she said bitterly.

'You may have to get in line,' Edward said, thinking of the pain in Sean's face.

'How is Steph? Did you see her?' Liz said, dabbing at her eyes with a tissue.

'Yes. She's not bad, considering. I had to talk to her about work. It seemed terribly insensitive, but what could I do? We need to move quickly. Still, as soon as we started talking business, she was like her old self.'

Liz smiled sadly. 'That's Steph for you. When is she getting out of hospital?'

'Tomorrow.'

'Maybe Sean will take her away for a few days. A break would do them both good.'

'I'm afraid she's going straight back to work.'

Liz shot him an accusing look. 'Surely there's no need for that. Can't you handle things?'

Edward looked uncomfortable. 'Most things, yes. But there are areas that I'm not familiar with. But Steph could take some time off once the work is under way.'

COLETTE CADDLE

Liz nodded, resignedly. 'Is there anything I can do? Or could Chris help out? He owes her that at least.'

Edward thought for a moment. There was no doubt that Chris would be able to step in for Stephanie. His wounds seemed superficial and he should be up and about in no time. But Edward wasn't sure he could work with Connolly. And Conor would probably kill him. He couldn't very well say that to Liz, though.

'I think it might be good for Steph to get back to work. Apart from which, I believe she's made up her mind.'

'And nobody would really want to work with Chris after what's happened,' Liz surmised.

Edward sighed. 'Probably not.'

'Then I think my job should be to make sure Chris moves to Galway as soon as possible,' she said grimly. 'He'll probably be safer there. The further away from Sean the better.'

Edward squeezed her hand but said nothing.

'So tell me. How come you knew everything that was going on and I didn't? Why didn't you tell me? Did Annie know?' Liz was a bit hurt that Steph hadn't confided in her.

'Yes, Annie knew. I think she was the only one Steph told. Annie told Joe and Joe told me. He wanted me to cut her some slack and look after things at the restaurant while she was in London. I didn't tell you, Liz, because it wasn't my secret to tell. Steph had intended to get an abortion and she didn't want anyone to know.'

'I understand. I feel so sorry for her, but I'm glad she didn't go through with the abortion. That must be a terrible thing to live with. Is everything okay between her and Sean?'

'Well, they were together when I went in. A tragedy

like this will either bring you closer together or drive you apart. Let's hope it's the former in their case.' He stood up and stretched. Every bit of him ached. He felt closer to eighty than forty. 'I'd better go home. Do me a favour?'

'What?'

'Don't mention any of this to Chris when you visit him tomorrow.'

Liz bit her lip. 'I couldn't even if I wanted to. I'll have Lucy with me. I wish I didn't have to go near the man at all.'

'He's still Lucy's dad,' Edward reminded her gently. He leaned down and kissed her forehead. 'I'll phone you tomorrow.'

'All right. And Edward? Look after Steph when she gets back to work. She might put on a tough front, but she has to be going through hell.'

'I'll keep an eye on her,' he promised.

Sean opened the door and watched Chris quietly for a moment. He was munching biscuits and watching a film, laughing at Steve Martin's antics. 'Enjoying yourself?'

Chris jumped and then smiled uncertainly. 'Sean, hi. It's not a bad film. Distracts me a bit from the pain. How are you?'

'Not good, Chris. My girlfriend's struggling to breathe properly and she's just lost our baby, so, no, I'm not too good at all.'

Chris opened and closed his mouth like a goldfish. 'I didn't know . . . I never . . . nobody told me . . .'

'No. When are you off to Galway, Chris?'

'Well I'm not sure . . .'

'As soon as possible, I think. That would be best, don't you agree?' His eyes were steely and there was a menacing note in his voice.

'Don't threaten me, Sean,' Chris said nervously.

'It's no threat,' Sean said grimly. 'You've outstayed your welcome, Chris. Time you moved on. Make sure you do. And quickly.'

Chapter Thirty-three

Steph shut the hall door and breathed a sigh of relief. She thought Sean would never go to work. His concern and solicitousness were beginning to suffocate her. He wanted to talk things through, analyse everything, but it was just too raw. All Steph wanted to do was forget. She walked across her living-room, enjoying the silence and threw open the balcony doors. It was a beautiful day and small boats were already heading out into the bay, taking advantage of the breeze that would probably abate before noon. It would be nice to have a day to herself, but it wasn't to be. Edward would pick her up in less than an hour. They had an appointment with the broker, Pat Mulvey, at eleven thirty. She took one last deep breath and went back inside to get ready. Going into the bathroom, she started the shower and slipped out of her clothes. She wrinkled her nose. She still smelled of hospitals and smoke, despite the long bath she'd taken when she got home yesterday. She got into the shower, careful to keep the temperature down so as not to aggravate her burns. She soaped her arms and legs but her hands shook when she ran them over her stomach and abdomen. She felt the sadness well up inside of her. *Stop, don't think, you've a job to do.* She stepped out of the shower and dried her hair with a towel. She couldn't handle using a hot hairdryer – even the thought of the warm air blowing on her skin made her shudder. Instead she slicked it back with some gel. It would have to do. She lightly applied some powder – not ready to put too much make-up over the burns – and selected a cream Paul Costello suit. The high v-neck meant that she didn't have to wear a blouse. She added a chunky gold necklace and earrings and cream leather court shoes and felt ready to face the world. She studied her image. She was a far cry from the red-eyed wreck of two days ago. She jumped as the phone rang. She was tempted to let the answering machine pick it up, but it was probably her mother.

'Oh, hello, love. How's your throat?' Catherine's voice was full of concern.

'I'm fine, Mam. Don't worry.'

'Is Sean there with you?'

'No. He's gone to work.'

'Well, we'll come over, so.'

'No, Mam. I'm going out. I have a meeting.'

'A meeting? For God's sake, Stephanie! You're only out of hospital and you sound terrible.'

'I'm fine,' she lied. Talking was proving to be even more difficult today. 'And there's a lot to sort out. It's only one meeting.'

'Are you driving?' Catherine persisted.

'No. Edward is picking me up.'

Catherine was slightly mollified by that. 'Well don't stay out too long, love. It's only your first day. Don't push yourself.'

'I won't. There's the doorbell, Mam. I have to go. Bye.'

Steph hung up, collected her bag and went out to meet Edward.

Edward glanced at her surreptitiously. She looked fine, if a little pale and weary around the eyes but she'd said very little since she'd got into the car and the silence was uncomfortable.

'So how are you?' he'd asked finally. He wasn't quite sure what he was supposed to say.

'Fine.' She stared out of the window.

'I'm very sorry, Stephanie, about – about the baby.'

'Thank you.' She continued to study the scenery.

Edward gave up and they completed their journey in silence.

'Sit down, sit down. Very sorry to hear about your trouble.' Pat Mulvey patted Steph's hand. 'Mr McDermott? Nice to meet you. Coffee?'

'No, thank you. Have you had a chance to look at our policy?' Edward asked without preamble.

The broker rummaged through the papers in front of him. 'I have. There will be no problem in relation to damage cover. You need to submit quotes for approval, and any hospital charges will be taken care of under you employer's liability cover. Will any of your staff be claiming against you?'

Steph looked at Edward who shook his head. 'I don't believe so. Two suffered smoke inhalation but they were only kept in overnight.'

'Good, good.' The broker made a note.

'So what's the bad news?' Steph asked, her voice barely a whisper.

'Well, I'm afraid you've no consequential loss cover.'

'What's that?' Steph looked at Edward.

'It covers your expenses and expected profit for the period the business is closed,' Edward said wearily.

'But why aren't we covered?' Steph shook her head in confusion.

The broker shrugged. 'Chris thought it was too expensive. He decided to take the risk.'

Steph and Edward sat in stunned silence.

'You never mentioned this to me when I called to tell you I was taking over,' Steph said finally.

'I assumed you knew,' Mulvey said defensively.

'You're paid to advise your client,' Edward said coldly. 'Surely you should have advised Stephanie to increase her cover?'

'As I said, I assumed she knew. After all, she worked in the restaurant for long enough.'

Edward glared at him. 'I think it's time we reviewed our insurance arrangements, Steph.'

'I think you're right.' Steph stood up and walked to the door.

'That's up to you,' Mulvey said smoothly. 'But you won't get a better deal anywhere else.'

'Maybe not, but we might get a proper service. Goodbye, Mr Mulvey.' Edward resisted the temptation to bang the door.

'What on earth are we going to do?' Steph said when they got back to the car.

'Let's get some lunch,' Edward said grimly, starting the engine.

Steph took a sip of her wine and looked around the bright, airy room appreciatively. 'This is nice.' They sat in Trastevere, an Italian restaurant in the heart of Temple Bar and Steph was feeling a bit better. The chilled Pinot Blanc was soothing on her throat and she'd ordered a creamy pasta dish that she would be able to swallow quite easily.

'I like it,' agreed Edward. 'You and Sean should drop in some evening. There's always a great buzz. I like sitting at the window and watching the world go by.'

Two girls passed. One had blue hair, elaborate eye make-up and a tanned midriff and the other had rings through her nose, lip and eyebrow. 'I see what you mean,' Steph said with a croaky little laugh. 'So what do we do now?' Her smile faded as she thought about their predicament.

Edward tapped his nails against his glass. 'Well, I think we have to pay the salaries. I'm afraid I'd already promised them.'

Steph sighed. 'We can't afford to pay all of them. We'll have to let some of the waiters go. Not Liam Dunne though. I want to keep him. We'll pay all the chefs.'

'We don't have to worry about George. He's handed in his notice.'

Steph smiled. 'He'll get another position quite easily.'

'I hope so. He was wonderful the night of the fire. I don't know what we would have done without him. Even Conor said so.'

Steph gave a croaky laugh. 'Amazing!' But her laughter was soon replaced by a worried frown. 'I don't see how we're going to survive this, Edward. We're dead in the water before we even start.'

Edward frowned. 'Most of my money is tied up. But I do have one idea.'

'Yes?' Steph wished he'd stop tapping the damn glass. It set her teeth on edge.

'Well, Chris isn't due the second half of the payment until he leaves.'

'That's in two weeks' time,' Steph pointed out. 'We can't use that money. We won't be up and running by then.'

'Maybe we could persuade him to wait.'

Steph laughed harshly. 'Yeah, right. And he'll do that out of the goodness of his heart.'

Edward smiled. 'Maybe not, but he might do it to protect his reputation. Or out of guilt and remorse.'

'What do you mean?' Steph looked at him curiously.

'There's no doubt that he started the fire, Steph. It wouldn't be very good for his image if that information got out.'

Stephanie gripped her glass until her knuckles went white. 'Chris started the fire?' Strange, but she hadn't thought to ask anyone how it had started. She'd been so caught up in her miscarriage that it hadn't really mattered. 'Tell me,' she said quietly.

Edward cursed under his breath. He couldn't believe that no one had told her. 'He was with Liz that day. She told him that she wanted a separation and he didn't take it well.'

'I told her she should have had someone with her. He didn't hit her, did he?'

'Oh, no. It seems he decided to drown his sorrows

288

instead. He appeared in the restaurant later and joined some customers who were having a boozy lunch. He started to get a bit loud, and some other customers were getting upset. Conor had enough and brought him into the back to tell him off but apparently Chris just passed out. They put him in the storeroom to sleep it off.'

'Then what?'

'Well, it gets a bit hazy after that. Chris admits to waking up at some stage and lighting a cigar, and the remains of a whiskey bottle was found nearby. We assume that he fell asleep again and dropped the cigar. He was very lucky, really. He could have been killed.'

'Pity he wasn't,' Steph said bitterly. 'He should be charged for this. Can we sue him?'

Edward looked taken aback. 'We couldn't do that, Steph. It was an accident. And think of what that would do to Liz.'

Steph nodded. 'I don't want Liz hurt any more than she has been already. So instead you're suggesting that we blackmail him?'

'I wouldn't put it quite like that,' Edward said with a small smile. 'But we could appeal to his sense of . . . decency.'

Steph found it hard to believe that Chris had a decent bone in his body. But he would be concerned about his future employer finding out that Chez Nous had gone up in smoke as a result of his drunken antics. 'What have you got in mind?'

'I think we should look for a delay of three months before the final payment. I also think we should renegotiate the amount – say a reduction of ten per cent?'

'Twenty,' Steph said, her face hard.

'Cutting the price will cut Liz's share too,' he reminded her.

Steph sighed. 'Okay. Ten per cent.'

'I'll give him a call tomorrow. Is he still staying with his dad?'

'No, I'll take care of this.' Stephanie's eyes were hard and determined.

'I don't think that's such a good idea,' Edward said gently. For all her composure, he wasn't convinced she could handle a confrontation with Connolly.

Steph glared at him. 'I said I'll handle it.'

Edward sighed. So much for him promising Liz he'd look after her. 'Okay. If that's what you want. Now what about the Michelin people?' He topped up their wine and sat back.

'I'll call them and set up a meeting. They'll want reassurances that we're going to restore it to the same quality. Then they'll want to inspect it before we reopen.' Steph made a note on the pad by her plate.

'I think we should see them together.'

'Fine. I'll try and set something up for this week. It'll have to be in their offices.'

Edward shook his head. 'No, get them to come to my office. Then we can take them over to the restaurant afterwards and show them what we're doing.'

'Let's hope we *know* what we're doing. Any luck with contractors?'

'Yes. I'm meeting three this afternoon at Chez Nous.'

'I'll sit in on that.' Steph shivered involuntarily. She wasn't looking forward to going back, but it was better to get it over with as soon as possible.

Edward's eyes narrowed. 'There's no need,' he insisted. 'It's only for preliminary quotes.'

'Nevertheless. It's important that I know the full extent of the damage when I talk to Chris. My argument will be more forceful.'

Edward gave in again. 'Fair enough. But Sean is going to throttle me for keeping you out so long.'

'I'm not a child, Edward.'

'Fine. Let's go.' Edward called for the bill and they walked the short distance to Chez Nous. From the outside it looked all right, but as soon as Edward opened the door, a dank acrid smell enveloped them.

'We had every window in this place open all weekend, but that bloody smell is still here.' He wrinkled his nose in disgust.

Steph had walked on through to the back. She stood looking at the remains of the staircase. Edward came up behind her and put a hand on her shoulder. 'Are you okay?'

She nodded dumbly. It all looked so normal now. Ugly and dirty, but normal nonetheless. Not the terrifying inferno of two days ago. She shivered and moved into the area that had been the storeroom. It had been cleaned up, but the walls were black, the ceiling a gaping hole and the light timber wall that had divided it from the hallway was no more. Steph's heart sank as she imagined the damage to the rooms upstairs. She forced herself to move on into the kitchen. It was a lot better. A good scrape and a fresh coat of paint and it would be fine. 'Does all the equipment still work?' she asked Edward, who'd followed her in.

'There's no electricity at the moment, so we don't

know. We had to empty the freezers and fridges. I told Conor to divide the food out among the staff.'

Steph smiled. 'They must have thought all their birthdays had come together. Did you itemise the contents first?'

'All done. And it is covered by the insurance.'

'I'm glad something is.'

There was a rap at the front door. Edward checked his watch. 'That'll be the first builder.'

Steph pasted a businesslike smile on her face. 'Then let's get started.'

Chapter Thirty-four

Sean watched Stephanie push her pasta around the plate. 'My cooking's not that bad.'

'What? Oh sorry,' Steph gave him a weak smile. 'I'm not very hungry.'

'Tough day?'

'Not too bad. I feel exhausted though. There's such a lot to do. And then there's this business with the insurance.' She sighed.

Sean frowned. 'Do you really think Chris is going to agree to wait for his money?'

'I don't know.' Steph looked worriedly around at her apartment. 'If he won't I may have to sell this place.'

'Do you want me to come with you when you talk to him?'

'No, that's all right,' Steph said firmly. 'I can handle Chris.'

'Are you sure? I don't want him upsetting you.'

'If anyone's going to get upset it will be Chris.'

Sean grinned. 'I almost feel sorry for him.'

'Don't.' Steph stood up to clear the plates away.

'We should move your stuff back to my place.'

'I suppose,' Steph said doubtfully.

'There's no need to sound so happy about it,' Sean snapped.

'Sorry, love.' Steph moved to the back of his chair and slipped her arms around his neck.

'Are you sure you're okay?' He twisted around so he could see her face.

She nodded.

'Look, the hospital gave me some pamphlets,' Sean said tentatively. 'There's a miscarriage association. They have a helpline, group therapy sessions, that sort of thing. Maybe you should contact them.'

'I don't think so.' Steph couldn't see herself pouring out her heart to a therapist or sharing her pain with a whole group of miserable women.

'You should talk to someone, Steph,' Sean persisted. 'You've been through a lot.'

'I'm fine, Sean. Please don't fuss.'

Sean rubbed his eyes wearily. 'I'm worried about you, Steph. Don't blame me for that.'

Steph felt a pang of guilt. 'I don't, it's just that I don't want to talk to anyone. What's done is done. There's no point in dwelling on it.'

Sean pulled her to him and kissed her. 'Whatever you want, Steph. Just promise you'll talk to me if things are getting you down. Don't shut me out.'

'I won't, love,' she murmured. 'I promise.'

Steph lay still listening to Sean's steady breathing beside her. She hadn't really lied to him. She was all right. It was just at night that she got scared. During the day she could keep herself occupied and with so much to do to get the restaurant up and running again there wasn't time to think. But at night, when she was alone in the darkness, all the memories flooded back. She plumped her pillow and rolled over onto her side. She closed her eyes, willing herself to sleep. 'Think nice thoughts,' she instructed herself. She thought about her parents' garden in Wicklow. She imagined herself stretched out on a sun-lounger with the sun beating down on her face. She heard insects buzzing, the clip-clip of her father cutting the hedge and the distant sound of the radio in the kitchen. She thought about her mother and the chats they enjoyed, sitting in the large airy kitchen, drinking copious amounts of tea. And then she thought about the day when she'd told her mother she was pregnant. She moaned softly and her eyes filled up as misery engulfed her once more. Maybe she should go and talk to someone. Maybe she did need help. Still the thoughts of talking to some shrink didn't appeal to her. Anyway, what did women do fifty years ago? They got on with it, that's what. There were no helplines or therapists then. There was too much emphasis on therapy these days, Steph decided. If she needed to talk, she had Sean, she had her mother, and she had Liz and Annie. Wasn't that what family and friends were for? Okay, so she hadn't actually talked to any of them but everyone had their own way of dealing with things. She just wasn't the sort to spill her guts. What was the point in continually going over the past? Regurgitating, analysing, examining. It was a waste of time and energy.

No, she didn't need to talk to anyone. She was bound to get upset occasionally. It was completely natural, but it would pass. Eventually. She flipped over onto her other side and shut her eyes tightly. She had to sleep. It was going to be a long day. And there was Chris to face. 'Sleep,' she urged herself. 'Sleep.'

∽∾

'Come on, sleepy head.' Sean prodded Steph's sleeping form. 'It's almost eight o'clock.'

Steph groaned. She felt as if she'd only just closed her eyes. 'Maybe I'll grab another couple of hours.'

Sean frowned. 'I thought you were seeing Chris at ten. It'll take you over an hour to get out to Dun Laoghaire.'

'Oh shit.' Steph threw back the covers and padded out to the bathroom. 'Put on the kettle, would you, Sean?'

∽∾

'Are you sure you'll be okay?' Sean asked through a mouthful of cornflakes.

Steph nibbled on a piece of toast. 'What?'

'Chris. Are you sure you can handle seeing him?'

'Of course. Will you be late tonight?'

'I don't think so. Why?'

'I thought we might move my gear back to your place.'

Sean beamed at her. 'In that case I'll make sure I'm early. Your bed is awful bloody hard. I hardly slept a wink.'

Steph thought of his comatose state last night while she lay wide-awake beside him. 'Poor you. Well, I suppose I can't have your insomnia on my conscience. Tonight it is. It shouldn't take too long. I never really unpacked since, well since . . .' She flushed as she remembered the reason for her leaving.

Sean hugged her tightly. 'Gotta go. Give me a call and let me know how you got on.'

'I will. Bye.'

An hour later, Steph was on the road to Dun Laoghaire. It was a horrible day. Rain lashed the windscreen and a strong wind buffeted the car on the coast road. 'Lovely summer weather,' Steph said to herself.

By the time she'd pulled up outside the Connolly home, the rain had passed off and the sun was trying to break through the clouds. Steph walked up the path, picking her way through the puddles. She rang the doorbell, noticing the chipped paint on the doorframe and the tarnished brass fittings. Chris's dad was obviously as handy around the house as his son.

'Stephanie, hi.' Chris opened the door and gave her a nervous smile.

'Chris.' She brushed past him.

Chris closed the door, eyeing her warily. 'Let's go into the lounge,' he said indicating the door to her right. Steph went in and perched on the edge of a shabby wingback chair beside the gas fire.

'So how are you?' Chris asked nervously. 'I was sorry to hear about – your miscarriage.'

Steph looked at him coldly. A riot of emotions ran through her. He was sorry? He'd made her life hell for years, almost destroyed her livelihood and now he'd killed her baby and all he could say was he was sorry? She swallowed hard and closed her eyes as a wave of nausea engulfed her.

'Steph? Are you okay?'

She managed to nod and took a deep breath.

'So what can I do for you?'

'You've left us in a bit of a fix,' she said faintly.

'How's that?'

'You didn't have full insurance cover.'

'Of course I did.'

'No,' Steph assured him. 'You didn't take out consequential loss cover. Apparently it was more than you wanted to pay.'

Chris reddened as he remembered that particular 'discussion' with Pat Mulvey. 'Well, sure it's no big deal, is it? What is it anyway? It mustn't have been important or I'd have bought it.'

Steph pursed her lips. 'It covers the profits we would have made while the restaurant is closed for repairs.'

'Oh?'

'Yes. And we're going to be shut for over a month.'

Chris looked away. 'Oh.'

'Yes "oh". So we need your help.' Steph swallowed hard. It was tough having to ask this man for help.

'What can I do?'

'We need to postpone your final payment.'

Chris gave a short laugh. 'Forget it! You owe me that money. We have a contract.'

Steph took another deep breath. 'Yes, we do, but as our predicament is a consequence of your actions—'

'You've been running things for the last few months. The insurance was your responsibility,' Chris said hotly.

'True,' Stephanie said quietly, keeping a tight rein on her temper. 'But I couldn't do anything to stop you getting drunk and setting fire to my restaurant.'

'It wasn't my fault.'

Steph raised an eyebrow. 'The evidence says otherwise. I'm sure your new partner would be interested in hearing about the incident.'

Chris stared at her. 'Are you threatening me?'

Steph's eyes widened. 'Of course not. Just thinking aloud. It's such a small industry and word travels fast.'

A look of panic crossed his face. 'I don't like your attitude, Stephanie,' he said quickly, 'there's no need for it. Of course, I'd be glad to help out under the circumstances. What did you have in mind?'

Steph looked at him steadily. 'We want an extension of six months.'

'That's a long time,' he said cautiously.

'And we propose to reduce the payment by fifteen per cent, to reflect the part you've played in this whole business.'

'Now look here. That's not on. That's not on at all,' he blustered.

'It's a small price to pay for the total support and backing of your colleagues,' Steph said quietly.

'Five per cent,' Chris said abruptly.

'Ten,' Stephanie shot back.

'You'll make sure they say nothing? Conor? Pat?'

'I will,' Steph promised.

'Okay,' Chris said resignedly. 'Draw up the papers and I'll sign them.'

Steph opened her briefcase and handed him two sheets of paper.

Chris glared at her. 'Presumptuous, weren't you?'

Steph shrugged. She'd actually printed out two versions of the contract, with five and ten per cent. She signed her name to the documents and handed Chris his copy. 'Nice doing business with you,' she said coldly. 'I'll see myself out.'

Edward smiled at her broadly. 'Well done, Stephanie. I'm impressed.'

Steph grimaced. 'I can't say it was easy. I nearly hit him. We'd better make sure we can keep to our side of the bargain now.'

'Indeed. It's in all our interests to keep this under wraps.'

Edward's secretary arriving in with a tray interrupted them.

'Thanks, Louise.' Edward poured steaming coffee into two delicate china cups. 'Have you been in touch with Michelin yet?'

Steph helped herself to cream and sugar. 'What do you think I am?'

Edward laughed. 'Sorry. I'm just eager to get things moving.'

'Me too. Actually I did contact them. They've to call me back.'

Edward nodded. 'Great. The builders are moving in tomorrow and they've promised to be out in two weeks.'

'That's not bad. Except the decorators won't be able to move in until they're finished.'

'Probably not, but the builders are going to arrange the rewiring. At least then we can restock the freezers.'

'That's true,' Steph acknowledged.

'So what's next?'

Steph frowned. 'I'm worried about the staff. We could replace any of the younger lads no problem, but if we lost John Quigly, or Pat or Marc or – God forbid – Conor, we'd be in a right mess.'

'I don't believe we'll lose Conor,' Edward said. 'He's very keen on running his own kitchen and it's unlikely that anyone will offer him a better deal in the short time that we're closed. I don't know about the others. What are the odds?'

Steph thought for a moment. 'John might well be headhunted. He's an excellent chef and a good worker and he's got a good reputation in the city. Pat and Conor are good mates so I don't believe Pat would want to leave. Kevin Nolan – you know, the lad that Conor was bringing in to replace George? I don't think he's given in his notice yet, so we're all right there. Marc is hot property and I'd hate to lose him. His mother has been ill so I was going to suggest that he goes home for a while.'

'Good idea.'

Steph's mobile phone rang. 'Excuse me,' she said to Edward. 'Hello? Stephanie West? Michelin,' she whispered to Edward. 'Three o'clock tomorrow?' she raised an eyebrow at Edward who nodded. 'Three will be fine. You know where we are? Good. Thank you. See you then.' She switched off the phone and smiled at Edward. 'Well, that's another one to knock off the list. Now I think we need to sit down with each of the chefs and lay our cards on the table. Oh, and Liam too.'

'Agreed.' Edward flicked open his diary. 'Let's call them now and set up appointments for the next couple of days.'

They worked steadily for two hours, and when Stephanie finally walked down the steps onto Merrion Square she was feeling tired but a lot more optimistic. If only she could be sure of a night's sleep. She dreaded the thoughts of another night lying awake in the darkness. Maybe she should talk to her GP about getting some sleeping pills. It was going to be a busy few weeks and she was going to need her rest. She checked her watch. If she hurried, she'd catch Maeve before she went out on her calls.

Chapter Thirty-five

'Mummy, Mummy! Daddy's here.' Lucy ran to the door and tugged it open.

'Great,' Liz muttered drily. She checked on the lasagne and then joined Lucy in the hall.

'Hiya, Luce!' Chris waved at his daughter before ducking back into the car and pulling out some bags.

'Are they for me?' Lucy asked excitedly.

'Maybe,' Chris teased.

Liz managed a thin smile. 'Come on in. I've made some lunch.'

Chris smiled at her gratefully. 'That's nice, Liz. Thanks.'

'No problem.' Liz led the way into the kitchen.

'The smell is great.'

'It's only lasagne.' She deliberately hadn't gone to any trouble as Chris had always found fault with her food. Either she hadn't added enough seasoning or the sauce was too thick or some other petty criticism. She eyed him suspiciously as he pulled Lucy onto his lap and allowed her to rummage in the bags.

'Barbie!' she cried delightedly.

'Another one?' Liz said and immediately regretted her bitchiness. She smiled at her daughter. 'She's lovely.'

Lucy pulled the other bags apart impatiently and squealed in delight as she found two outfits for Barbie and a miniature Barbie office – complete with computer. 'Thanks, Daddy. You're the best.' Lucy planted a loud kiss on his cheek before dashing upstairs with her new toys.

'That was nice of you,' Liz said.

Chris shrugged. 'Well, it'll be a couple of weeks before I see her again. I'm leaving for Galway tomorrow.'

Liz sat down opposite him. 'I thought you weren't going until the end of the month.'

'There's no point in hanging around now that the restaurant's closed.' He didn't tell her about his little chat with Sean. 'Besides, I'm not exactly popular at the moment.'

'You caused a lot of damage. Not only to the business but to Steph—'

'I know, I know, Liz. And I'm sorry, believe me.'

Liz couldn't help feeling sorry for him. 'Do you need some stuff for the flat?' Apart from some CDs and his trophies Chris hadn't taken anything from the house when he left.

'Well, I wouldn't mind taking a few of the books.' He eyed the stack of cookery books on the dresser greedily. 'And I'd love the desk lamp from the study.'

Liz smiled. 'No problem. Take the nest of tables too.'

'Oh, no. That's okay,' Chris said.

'No, please. They were a present from your mother. It's only right that you should have them.'

Chris smiled. 'Thanks, Liz.'

Liz looked away, embarrassed at this new, gentle Chris. She opened the oven door. 'This looks ready.

Would you call Lucy?' Chris went upstairs to get his daughter and Liz set the food on the table. She took a bowl of salad and a bottle of Chablis from the fridge. She was opening the wine when Chris returned, with Lucy chattering at his side.

'None for me,' he said when Liz went to fill the glass in front of him.

Liz said nothing but served the meal and sat down to eat. Chris asked Lucy about school and her friends and Liz started to relax and almost enjoy this precious, peaceful moment with her family. It had never been like this in the past, she realised sadly. On the few occasions that Chris ate with them, his head was usually buried in a newspaper. But today he was attentive and funny and Lucy loved every minute of it. There was one dodgy moment when Lucy mentioned Edward, but Chris just smiled tightly and said nothing.

'Lucy, I'm going down to Galway tomorrow,' he said as Liz cleared away their plates.

Lucy's face clouded over and her bottom lip trembled. 'But I thought you weren't going for weeks.'

'Things have changed. I have to go now.'

'I don't want you to,' Lucy said stubbornly.

'Don't be like that, Luce. We talked about this, remember? I've got to get down there and decorate your room. It's going to be the nicest bedroom in Ireland – fit for a princess. I bet you'll be the only girl in school with her own holiday home.'

Lucy brightened slightly at that. 'What colour are you going to make it?'

'Whatever colour you want it to be,' Chris promised, his eyes suspiciously bright.

'And can I bring my toys when I come and visit?'

'Of course, although I think we should keep some toys down there too. What do you think of that?'

Lucy nodded happily and Chris thanked God that she was still at the age where bribes worked. He hugged her and winked at Liz over her head. 'We'll have a great time together.'

'Can Mummy come to Galway too?'

'Of course she can,' Chris said quietly, watching Liz. 'Whenever she wants to.'

'Will you, Mum?' Lucy watched her mother solemnly.

'We'll see.' Liz fought back the tears as she scrubbed the casserole dish furiously.

'Have you heard how long it'll be before Chez Nous is up and running again?' Chris asked, breaking in on her thoughts.

'At least a month I think,' she said, repeating what Edward had told her.

'It'll never be the same again. Michelin will be keeping an eye on them. It will probably affect their rating in the guide.'

Liz turned in time to see the smug look on his face and her heart hardened. 'Why don't you decide what books you want,' she said coldly. 'I'll have a look around and see if there's anything else belonging to you.'

'Great. Come on, princess,' Chris said, sweeping Lucy up in his arms. 'You can help Daddy.'

∞∞

Two hours later, Liz stood in the doorway, waving Chris off while Lucy ran down the road after the car, waving and shouting.

'What's all that about?'

Liz turned to see Jenny McDermott standing at the end of the driveway. 'Hi, Jenny. Come on in.'

Carol had run down the road after her friend, and now the two of them were skipping back towards them hand in hand.

'That was Chris,' Liz explained, leading the way back inside. 'He's leaving for Galway in the morning.'

'Oh.' Jenny's eyes widened.

'Let's go and sit in the garden,' Liz suggested, collecting the bottle of wine from the fridge. 'Lucy. Why don't you show Carol what Daddy gave you?'

It was one of those unusually warm late summer days and the garden looked beautiful. Jenny settled herself in a large garden chair, adjusted her sunglasses on her nose and accepted the glass from Liz. 'This is the life,' she said contentedly.

Liz set the bottle down in the shade and sat down beside her. 'I almost told him I'd go with him,' she confided.

'Really?' Jenny breathed.

Liz nodded. 'Yep. But then he said something really nasty and I came to my senses.'

Jenny laughed. 'Thank God for that.'

Liz frowned. 'You don't even know him. Why are you so sure that I'm doing the right thing?'

Jenny shifted uncomfortably. 'Just from the things you've told me and from what Edward's said.'

Liz's eyes narrowed. 'What has he said?'

'Very little – you know what he's like. But he was worried about you the day you told Chris about the separation.'

'There was never any reason to worry about my safety. Chris has never laid a finger on me.'

Jenny sipped her wine and said nothing.

'I just feel sad about the way it's all turned out,' Liz explained after a while. 'Sitting having a meal together today, just the three of us, laughing and joking – it was nice. Why couldn't it have been like that when we were together? I can't help feeling guilty for not making it work.'

'It takes two,' Jenny said firmly. 'Stop beating yourself up about it. It's a waste of time.'

'I suppose you're right,' Liz said sadly.

'Oh, come on, cheer up! Have you done anything more about setting up your business?'

Liz flushed with pleasure. 'Her business'. It sounded wonderful. 'I haven't really been able to concentrate on it, what with the fire and everything.'

'How's Stephanie?'

Liz shook her head. 'I wish I knew. I haven't really talked to her. What would I say? "Sorry my husband killed your baby"?'

Jenny squeezed her hand. 'It was nothing to do with you. You're her friend. Call her.'

Liz nodded, swallowing back tears for the second time that day. 'I will.'

Jenny gave her hand another squeeze. 'So what about the business? You are going to go ahead with it, aren't you?'

Liz gave her a watery smile. 'I think so. I've been going over some recipes but it's not as straightforward as working in the restaurant. I have to consider how much preparation I can do at home, how long the food will keep for and how to cost the whole meal. That's the tricky part.'

'Whatever you do, don't sell yourself too cheap,'

Jenny warned. 'You're providing an up-market service.'

'I agree, but if I go for expensive ingredients, the cost could be prohibitive. I think I'll need to come up with three menus, standard, special and deluxe. That way I can tweak the recipes to suit.'

Jenny frowned. 'I don't understand.'

'For the standard menus I can cut costs by going for cheaper ingredients,' Liz explained. 'Use hake instead of turbot, lumpfish roe instead of caviar, that sort of thing.'

'Oh, I see.' Jenny looked at her admiringly. 'What about a name?'

'Sorry?'

'What are you going to call the business? It should be something catchy, but classy.'

'I suppose so. I hadn't thought about it.'

'What about "Dinner Service"?'

Liz wrinkled her nose. 'I don't think so. How about "Meals On Wheels"?'

Jenny laughed. 'It doesn't sound classy somehow!'

'Silver Service?' Liz offered.

'Not bad. But maybe you should use your own name. After all, you were well-known and certainly the Connolly name means something.'

'Liz Connolly Catering?' Liz asked doubtfully.

'Maybe. Why don't you ask Steph what she thinks?'

Liz nodded. 'That's an idea, and it's a good excuse to ring her.'

'There you go then,' Jenny said smugly. 'I've earned my glass of wine.'

Liz reached for the bottle and topped up their glasses. 'You've earned two!'

Jenny raised her glass. 'Well, for the moment, here's to Liz Connolly Catering.'

Liz smiled broadly. 'Cheers.'

Chapter Thirty-six

'Steph? Phone,' Sean called from the hallway.
She stood up from the desk and went to the top of the stairs. 'Who is it?'

'Liz.'

'I'll take it up here.' Steph went into their bedroom and lifted the phone. 'Liz?'

'Hi, Steph. How are you?'

'Fine, how are you?'

'Grand. Listen. I need to talk to you. I want your advice.'

Steph frowned. After what happened the last time Steph had offered advice this didn't seem such a good idea. 'What about?' she said cautiously.

'Business.'

Steph smiled. 'You're going back to work?'

'Maybe, well, probably. Look, I don't want to get into this over the phone. Will you meet me for a drink?'

Steph hesitated. She had so much to do but then she had been the one pestering Liz to get a job. 'Sure. When?'

'Well, I can get a baby-sitter for Wednesday night.'

'Wednesday it is, so. Let's meet in the Bailey at eight?'

'Great. Seeya then.'

Steph went down to Sean who was sitting in the kitchen, drinking coffee and reading the *Irish Times.*

'Liz wants to meet me on Wednesday. She wants to talk business.'

Sean looked at her over his paper. 'Is she thinking of coming back to Chez Nous?'

Steph poured herself a cup of coffee and sat down. 'I don't think so, but she's certainly got something up her sleeve.'

'That's good,' Sean said, stretching lazily. 'What will we do today?'

'I've got to work.'

'Oh, Steph, it's Saturday! I was looking forward to having you all to myself. I never get the chance when the restaurant's open.'

'Sorry.' Steph grinned at his woebegone expression. 'I know what you can do, though.'

'What?'

'The garden.'

Sean groaned. 'Oh, no! It's my day off, for God's sake! I've been working hard all week.'

'Oh, go on, Sean,' she wheedled. 'It's such a lovely garden. And you should get it sorted before the bad weather sets in. And it would be nice for Billy to have somewhere decent to play.'

Sean scowled at her. 'That's blackmail. Anyway, he'd prefer it like this. He could pretend that he's in the jungle hunting wild animals.'

'He'd probably find some too,' she said drily. 'Oh, go on, Sean. Please.'

Sean flicked her with his paper. 'Okay, okay. God, you're an awful nag.'

'But you love me,' Steph assured him.

Sean grunted and stood up. 'I wonder if the lawnmower still works.'

Steph laughed. 'I'd better get my act together too. Conor's due in half an hour.'

'What wonderful things are you teaching him today?'

'I'm showing him the costing system on the computer.'

'Sounds riveting. When his eyes start to glaze over send him out to the garden.'

'No chance,' Steph told him. She went back upstairs and looked ruefully around the boxroom that Sean had turned into an office. It had been so neat and tidy before she'd taken it over. Now it looked like a bombsite. The builders had rescued all the files and filing cabinet from her office in the restaurant. The blackened cabinet stood next to Sean's pristine one. Some blackened, smelly ledgers sat on his lovely mahogany desk and a bulky black sack full of files was propped up against the wall. Sean's sleek modern laptop was pushed to the back of the desk and Steph's old IBM sat in its place – but at least it still worked. All her computer files were intact and the packages were working.

She switched on the PC and started up the costing program. It was a great time-saver and it was a lot easier for Conor to learn than the manual version. Steph remembered the early days when Liz and Chris used to sit in the kitchen trying to cost a dish. They had to take everything from electricity, wages, rent into account down to the basic ingredients. It was a very cumbersome job. They'd been thrilled when Steph had discovered this computer program. It was a simple spreadsheet that prompted the user with all the possible factors, automatically added in the overheads and calculated the cost per portion. Conor should pick it up easily enough. And as long as he was with her, he wasn't out getting himself another job.

Marc had gone home to his family, so she didn't have to worry about him – unless of course he decided to stay there. She sighed. There was always something. The doorbell interrupted her thoughts and she hurried downstairs to open the door. 'Conor. Hi. You found us okay?'

'No problem. Nice place.' He looked admiringly around the large bright hall. 'One of these days, I'm going to buy myself a house. There's just no privacy in the flat.'

Steph raised an eyebrow. 'You're the first twenty-something that I've heard complain about privacy.'

Conor laughed. 'It's the job. It's ageing me! So what are we doing today, boss?'

Steph made a face. 'Costing I'm afraid. Come on. I'll make you a cup of coffee before we get started.'

Conor followed her into the kitchen. 'Where's Sean?'

Steph nodded towards the garden and Conor walked over to the patio doors.

'Looks like he's got his hands full,' he observed as he watched Sean wrestle with a large bush.

Steph joined him. 'God, it looks like he's losing. Come on. We'd better get out of here before he ropes us in.'

'It might be better than costing,' Conor said gloomily.

Steph grinned. 'That's what he said. But if you're a good boy and you pay attention I'll buy you a pint when we're finished.'

Conor brightened. 'Fair enough. Let's go.'

Sean leaned on his spade, breathing heavily. He was knackered but exhilarated. He'd succeeded in clearing away all the overgrown shrubbery, weeded the flower-beds and mowed the lawn. Now the garden was looking a lot more like a garden. All he had to do now was plant some flowers. He chuckled at the thought. No, maybe on second thoughts he'd leave that to Steph and Tom. He wouldn't have a clue where to start. He'd cut back the hedges at the back of the garden, exposing the tree in the corner. It looked good and sturdy. He wondered idly what kind of tree it was. He could build Billy a tree house. Sean had always wanted a tree house when he was a kid. He and his brother had erected little houses out of tin and wood in the corner of their small backyard, but it wasn't the same. Yeah a tree house would be great.

Sean was thrilled when Steph had mentioned some-where to play for Billy. She obviously expected him to come and visit. He hadn't told her about his plans for the attic but he'd mention it to her later this evening. He was going down to see Billy next week and it would be nice if he could tell him about his special room. He wouldn't mention the tree house though. That would be a surprise.

'Yo! Sean!'

Sean looked up to see Conor standing in the doorway, waving a can of lager. 'Nice one, Conor. I'll be right there.' He picked up the shears and carried it and the spade back to the garage. Then wiping his hands on his jeans he went into the kitchen.

Steph groaned as he left a trail of muck from the

door to the fridge and swallowed half a can of lager in one go.

'So how did it go, Conor? Are you an expert now?'

Conor grinned confidently. 'No problem.'

'Oh, really? Maybe you should be in the software industry.'

Steph flicked him with a teacloth. 'Don't you start poaching my staff, mate.'

Sean winked at her. 'It would be handy though. He could write a couple of programs in the morning and then whip us up a four-course meal for lunch!'

'That sounds too much like hard work. I think I'll stick with Steph.'

'Why don't you get cleaned up, Sean, and we'll go for a pint?' Steph closed the back door and threw her empty can in the bin.

'Excellent but I need to take a shower. Why don't you two go on down to the Yacht? I'll see you there.'

Conor stood up. 'Sounds good to me.'

Steph kissed Sean's cheek. 'Ugh, you stink,' she said, wrinkling her nose.

Sean swatted her on the bum. 'Good, honest sweat. You love it really.'

Steph rolled her eyes. 'Yeah, right. Seeya later.'

Sean smiled after her. It was great to see her so light-hearted. Maybe she'd be able to give up those damn sleeping tablets soon.

'So, Conor. Do you think any of the lads are going to leave us?' Steph watched Conor over the rim of her glass.

'Nah, they're having too much fun. It's ages since they've been able to go clubbing.'

'Good. I hope they party all night and sleep all day. That should keep them out of harm's way. It was a bit of luck that your friend Kevin hadn't given in his notice.'

Conor laughed. 'That was a close one. He was going to do it the day of the fire, but the boss took a half-day.'

'Thank God for that. What are we going to do about a replacement for you, Conor?'

'Sous-chef? I'd like to use Pat. Marc's good too, but Pat has a bit more control over the lads.'

'Yeah, I'm inclined to agree. I think Marc is going to be a force to be reckoned with some day, but not yet.'

'Okay then, we'll give the job to Pat. He'll be delighted.'

'Well, I'm glad you didn't want to bring anyone else in. I'm not sure we could have handled another salary.'

Conor frowned. 'You're not stuck for money, are you, Steph?'

'No, no,' she said quickly. 'The insurance company will cover all the repairs, but I thought I'd push the boat out on some of the decor. And that will come out of our pocket.'

'What did you have in mind?' Conor drained his glass.

'Well, I thought we could clear out the back room upstairs and turn it into a private dining-room.'

Conor lit a cigarette. 'That's an idea but wouldn't that mean we'd need more loos?'

Steph shook her head. 'No, the number of loos isn't affected until the capacity goes over a hundred.'

'Well, it's sixty-three at the moment and the back room would sit twenty tops, so we should be okay. That would be a nice little earner.'

'That's what I thought,' Steph said, happy that he

liked the idea. 'Is there anything you need for the kitchen?'

'We could do with a second fryer and what about putting a second door in?'

'You mean an "In" and "Out"?'

'Yeah. It's safer.'

'Already agreed with the builders.'

Conor grinned. 'Nice one. Another drink?'

'I'll get that.' Sean appeared beside them,

'That was good timing,' Conor said. 'Mine's a pint.'

'What about the storeroom?' Steph continued after Sean had gone to the bar.

Conor thought for a moment. 'I think we just need a better shelving system and I think we should put the drink under lock and key from now on.'

'Agreed,' Steph said grimly. 'Maybe they could build a lockable cupboard into the room. I'll ask them on Monday.'

Sean put the drinks down in front of them and pulled up a stool. 'You should be sitting outside. It's too nice to be stuck indoors.'

'My God, all this outdoor activity must be getting to you,' Conor laughed.

'Sunstroke,' Steph said solemnly. 'There was nowhere to sit, Sean.'

He stood up immediately. 'There is now. Come on before someone else grabs it.'

They carried their drinks out to the table in front of the pub. Steph leaned back in her chair and slipped on her sunglasses. The sea was calm, and kids were skateboarding along the promenade in front.

Conor looked about him appreciatively. 'This is really nice. I think I'd like to live here.'

Steph shook her head. 'First you want to buy a house, now you want to move to the suburbs. Next you'll be telling me you're getting married.'

Conor flushed.

She sat up and took off her glasses. 'What's this? My God! The man's in love.'

'Ah, leave me alone, Steph,' Conor said, swallowing a mouthful of lager to hide his embarrassment.

'Who is she?' Steph persisted.

'No one you know,' Conor mumbled.

'So when are we going to meet her?' Sean chipped in.

'Dunno. We'll see.'

'God, you're a dark horse. Why don't you phone her? She could join us.'

Conor shook his head. 'She's in Kilkenny. She goes home at the weekends.'

'A country-girl? You're going out with a culchie!' Sean exclaimed.

'Ah, don't you start, Sean.'

'What's her name?' Steph asked.

'If I tell you, will you leave me alone?'

'Promise.'

'Concepta.'

Sean burst out laughing. 'Concepta from Kilkenny!'

Conor glared at him.

'Stop it, Sean,' Steph said suppressing a grin. 'That's a lovely name. You'll have to introduce us, Conor. Bring her over some night for a drink.'

'Oh, I will,' Conor said. *No bloody way*, he said to himself. These pair would scare Concepta off for sure.

'Ah, young love!' Sean stretched in his chair. 'Isn't it wonderful?'

Conor stood up. 'I'll get the drinks in,' he muttered.

Steph laughed. 'Leave him alone, Sean. You were young and in love once.'

'I'm certainly not young any more.' He stretched gingerly. 'I think I've injured myself. That bloody garden.'

'You did a great job.'

'Wait till you see it with a tree house.'

Steph stared at him. 'A tree house?' Maybe he really did have sunstroke.

Chapter Thirty-seven

Stephanie turned up the speed and the gradient on the treadmill and pounded on. She was still groggy from the sleeping tablets and the exercise helped to clear her head. Before the tablets, night-time had been the hardest. Now it was mornings. There was always those first few moments when she woke when she forgot what had happened. Then a feeling of unease would steal over her and she would know there was something wrong. And then it would all come flooding back and the dull ache would return to her gut, to stay with her until the release of the sleeping tablets that night. Sean wasn't happy with her taking them – he hated any kind of medication. But right now she wasn't sure she'd be able to carry on without them. The thoughts of returning to those dark, sleepless nights terrified her. No, it was better this way. She hardly had time to think. Except when she was alone. She turned up the speed again, wiped her face on her sleeve and checked the clock. She had an hour to finish, shower and change, then a full day of meetings at Edward's office and then drinks with Liz. She grimaced at the thought. She wasn't looking forward to that. Liz said she wanted to talk business, but Steph knew they'd end up talking about the fire, about Chris and about the baby. Apparently Edward had told her everything – though how he knew the full story still wasn't clear to her. Still, Liz would have heard it from somebody eventually and it saved her from having to explain. But she wasn't sure she could handle talking yet. It was too raw. She pushed the thoughts to the back of her mind and made her way back to the changing room. She had a business to run.

'This is really a brilliant idea, Liz.' Steph stared at her friend in open admiration.

Liz glowed with pleasure. She'd explained her plans and was delighted when she'd been able to answer all of Steph's questions. Her hard work had paid off. She'd spent hours working out costs and overheads and she'd developed an impressive menu of dishes that would travel well.

Steph set the file down on the table. 'I'm not sure why you need my advice. You seem to have everything covered.'

'Not everything,' Liz said. 'I'm not sure how to market the business or where to advertise. And then there's the name. I think I should use my own name, but it's not exactly catchy.'

Steph took a sip of her wine. 'I see. Well, as far as advertising is concerned, word of mouth will be your greatest earner. Mind you, that can work against you too.'

Liz rolled her eyes. 'Don't I know it! I remember the early days in the restaurant. There was always someone important in the night the freezer broke down, or two staff didn't show. Murphy's Law!'

Steph laughed. 'It hasn't changed.' She thought for a moment and then looked intently at Liz. 'What about linking yourself to Chez Nous?'

Liz stared at her. 'Are you serious?'

'You're a damn good chef, Liz. We'd be proud to be associated with you.'

Liz flushed. 'Well, I certainly wouldn't object, but I think you should discuss it with Edward and Conor first.'

'Of course, but I'm sure they'll agree. Conor has heard all about your amazing pastries and Edward thinks you're perfect full stop.'

'So we could call the business "Liz Connolly of Chez Nous"?'

'Sounds impressive. We should really contribute to your costs, though.' Steph frowned. They couldn't really afford to throw money around at the moment.

'Not at all.' Liz shook her head. 'Recommend me to your customers, leave my cards lying around and let me pinch some of Conor's ideas. That's more than enough.'

'We'll see,' Steph said. 'We need to have a proper meeting about this. Work out all the details. When will you be ready to start up?'

'In the next few weeks,' Liz said. 'I've had a chat with Mary – you know the girl next door who baby-sits for me? She's delighted at the idea of extra work.'

'Great. I could design the menus for you, if you like, and we could buy some fancy paper to print them on. Fifty copies should do you for the moment.'

Liz made a note. 'Good idea. I'll get the paper. I'll need some cards and some letterheads, but I suppose we should delay that until we talk to Conor and Edward.'

'Yes. Well, let's arrange that soon. How are you fixed at the weekend?'

'A baby-sitter might be a problem. Mary needs a bit more notice at weekends. I know. Why don't you all come to me? I'll cook something from my menu. After all, the proof of the pudding . . .'

Steph clapped her hands. 'Brilliant! They'll agree to anything once they've tasted your food, though I suppose Edward already has.'

Liz avoided Steph's teasing gaze. 'Nothing fancy.'

'Okay. How about Saturday?'

'Fine,' Liz agreed excitedly.

'Great.' Steph took out her mobile and punched in Conor's number. Ten minutes later it was all agreed. Edward would pick up Conor and Steph and be in Stillorgan for eight.

'What about Sean?' Liz asked.

'He'll be in Cork visiting Billy.'

Liz watched Steph carefully. 'Are you okay about that?'

Steph looked surprised. 'Of course. I wish Sean saw more of him. We're hoping that Karen will let him come and stay for a while. Sean's started clearing out the attic and he's talked to a building contractor about converting it into a bedroom.'

Liz looked at her. She seemed happy enough about it all, but yet she seemed edgy. She didn't look too good either. Very pale and awfully thin! Liz had often been envious of Steph's looks but not tonight. She was as elegant as ever in a beautifully cut, charcoal-grey suit. But the jacket hung loosely on her shoulders and her eyes seemed huge in her small face.

Liz reached out and took her hand. 'Steph, we haven't

had a chance to talk since the fire. I know about your miscarriage. I'm so sorry.'

'Thanks.' Steph managed a weak smile.

'It's so unfair. You didn't deserve it. It's an awful thing to happen. And if it wasn't for Chris . . .'

Steph swallowed hard. 'Well, what's done is done. Anyway, that's why it's important Sean gets to know his son better. Billy's all he's got now.'

'Sean's got you. And someday, who knows, maybe you'll try again.'

'I don't think so, Liz. I couldn't go through that again. I'd always be scared I'd lose it too.'

'That's natural, Steph. Every expectant mother feels like that. I panicked every time I had so much as a twinge. It was usually just indigestion. All the bloody doughnuts my mam kept feeding me, no doubt!'

Steph giggled. 'I got a real hankering for fruit gums. I hadn't eaten them since I was a kid. But when I was pregnant, I must have eaten five packets.'

Liz looked at her slim figure. 'It doesn't show.'

'The gym,' Steph explained. 'I'm working out like a maniac. It helps me forget.'

Liz frowned. 'You don't have to forget, Steph. It's okay to grieve.'

Steph sighed inwardly. Here we go. Lecture time. She put out a hand. 'Let me see those menus again, Liz. We have to decide what you should cook on Saturday.'

Liz took one look at Steph's face and obediently opened the file.

Steph pored over the menus, ignoring Liz's silence. Why couldn't they understand that she had to deal with this in her own way? Why did everyone want her to talk?

Talk wouldn't bring her baby back. 'What about the crab cakes to start?'

Liz shook her head. 'Too simple. Conor wouldn't be impressed. What about the globe artichokes stuffed with prawns?'

Steph wrinkled her nose. 'I don't like artichokes. What about a warm salad?'

Liz took the file and flicked over a couple of pages. 'There. Chicken liver salad. It's difficult to get the livers just right. Too much cooking and they're chewy and tasteless. Conor would be impressed with my chicken livers. They're always great.'

'Modesty becomes you,' Steph said drily. 'Right, now we've got that sorted, what about a main course?'

'Lamb or beef,' Liz said firmly.

'Is that not a bit boring?'

'Maybe, but it's what most customers want and it's always a challenge to come up with a new or more interesting way of presenting a traditional dish. How about shoulder of lamb with an apricot and walnut stuffing?'

'Mmmn. That sounds nice. And with your special gravy?'

Liz pulled a face. 'Yes, with my special gravy. You only like it because of the amount of booze in it!'

'Thas a malishus rumour,' Steph slurred.

Liz laughed. 'What about dessert? How about a coffee and orange soufflé?'

'No, no. It has to be a pastry or gâteau, Liz. That's what you're famous for.'

Liz flushed. 'I suppose. Well, maybe I'll make my Baileys and chocolate gâteau.'

'I don't think I've tasted that, but it sounds perfect. I'll buy the wines to go with it.'

'No, I'll take care of it, Steph. It's my show.' Liz was looking forward to choosing the wines. She looked forward to choosing something to complement her food. Chefs rarely got the opportunity to choose their customers' wine – more's the pity. It was terrible to see someone wash down a delicate fish dish with a robust Cabernet. Or team a strong game dish with a light burgundy. Sacrilege. No, this was one job that she was definitely going to enjoy. She was looking forward to impressing Edward. 'Oh, Steph. This is so exciting. I can't believe I'm actually doing this.'

Steph smiled. 'Believe it. This time next year you'll be expanding.'

'I don't know about that. I like the idea of staying small and select.'

'You've got a point,' Steph acknowledged. 'People always want you if they think you might be unavailable. Daft, isn't it?'

'Suits me,' Liz said happily.

'Hang on a minute. What about transport?' Steph didn't think that Liz's clapped-out little Fiesta was up to the job. And it certainly wouldn't promote the right image.

'I'm buying a van,' Liz replied. 'Dad's taking me to see one on Friday. It's five years old but the mileage is low. It would be grand for carting around the food.'

Steph looked at her in amazement. Liz had always left all the decision-making to Chris and now here she was, setting up in business, buying vans – whatever next? 'You're really on top of things, Liz. I'm impressed.'

'Thanks, Steph. It's funny but I feel ten years younger. It's like the early days in the restaurant. I feel in control and I like it.'

'Good on you.' Steph raised her glass. 'To Liz Connolly of Chez Nous.'

Liz lifted her glass. 'To better times ahead.'

'How's Liz?' Sean asked sleepily.

'Unrecognisable.' Steph stepped out of her skirt.

'What do you mean?'

'She's setting up a home-catering business. She's even buying herself a van!'

Sean turned around to face her and opened one eye. 'Do you think she's thought it through? It's a big step.'

'She's got menus, costing sheets, projected profit and loss statements – yes, I'd say she's thought it through.' Steph patted some cleansing cream on and wiped it away with a tissue before slipping into bed beside him. 'I'm telling you. She's a different woman.'

'I'm glad. What does Chris think of all this?'

'I never asked.'

'I bet she hasn't told him,' Sean said.

Steph felt the familiar knot in her stomach at the mention of Chris. She didn't want to talk about him any more. 'I want her to link her business to the restaurant. She's giving a dinner on Saturday for me, Edward and Conor so that we can discuss it and sample her cooking.'

'God, I'm not gone yet and you're planning dates with other men,' Sean complained.

Steph laughed and snuggled down beside him. 'I like it when you're jealous.'

'Don't flatter yourself. I'm just sorry I'm missing out on one of Liz's dinners.'

Steph kissed his neck. 'Rubbish. You can't wait to get to Cork.'

'Is it that obvious?' Sean said with a sloppy grin. 'Yeah, it'll be good to see Billy again. I just hope he's okay with me. I haven't seen him in ages.'

'He'll be fine. Especially when he sees the size of your goody bag.'

Sean groaned. 'Did I overdo it?'

'No, of course not. Stop worrying. It's going to be fine.' Steph kissed him and turned to get her sleeping tablet.

Sean frowned. 'Would you not try and do without one tonight? I'm sure you'd be fine.'

Steph's expression tightened. 'Oh, don't start, Sean.'

'I'm sorry, but I don't think they're the answer—'

'They're only sleeping tablets, for God's sake. Stop overreacting.' She settled down as far away from him as possible. 'Good night.'

Sean turned his back on her with an impatient sigh. 'Good night.'

Chapter Thirty-eight

Sean caught a glimpse of red hair at the upstairs window as he walked up the driveway towards his ex-wife. He bent down to kiss her cheek. 'Hiya, Karen. You look great.'

Karen tossed back her auburn mane and smiled up at him. 'Hi, Sean, it's good to see you. I'm afraid Billy's done one of his disappearing tricks.'

'Has he? No point in bringing in the toys so,' he added loudly.

Karen grinned. 'No, probably not. But you may as well come in now that you're here. I'll make some tea.' She led the way into the large sunny kitchen and put on the kettle. 'How's Stephanie?'

'She's fine,' he said as he always did when people asked. If only he could believe it.

'And you?'

'Sad,' Sean admitted. 'I think a baby would have been good for us, forced us to settle down.'

Karen raised an eyebrow. 'I think you've got that the wrong way around. You should be settled before you bring a child into the world. Surely you've learned something from our mistakes?'

Sean flushed angrily. 'We'd have done okay if . . .'

'If I wasn't such a flighty piece who wanted to enjoy life,' Karen finished for him.

'I didn't say that.'

'You didn't have to. Look, Sean, I know that I screwed up but I'm a different person now.' She smiled. 'Older and hopefully wiser. And Billy's happy.'

Sean looked out at the pretty little garden, strewn with toys. 'You're doing fine,' he told her, sorry for bringing up the past. 'How's Mike?'

She sat down in the chair opposite him. 'He's asked me to marry him.'

Sean's eyes widened. 'Congratulations.' Why was he surprised? Karen was only thirty, beautiful and now that their divorce had come through there was nothing standing in her way. Why shouldn't she marry again? She'd been dating Mike Grogan for a long time now and he seemed okay. Billy liked him. He frowned. God, he'd be like a new dad to Billy.

Karen watched the worried expression cross his face. 'You'll always be Billy's dad, Sean. That will never change.'

'Yeah. I suppose.' Sean gave her a sheepish grin. Karen was a very understanding woman. When they'd broken up he'd hared off back to Dublin, anxious to put his failed marriage behind him and only too happy to leave Billy in her custody. It was a wonder that she'd ever let him see Billy again.

'Can I have some lemonade?'

Sean looked up to see his son standing sullenly in the doorway.

'There's a word missing,' Karen said, crossing to the fridge.

'Please,' Billy mumbled.

Karen poured some lemonade into a Power Rangers mug and handed it to her son. 'Aren't you going to say hello to your daddy?' She tousled his hair.

Billy took a long, noisy drink and stared moodily at Sean over the rim.

Sean returned his stare, dumbstruck. This tall skinny, boy with the fiery mop of curly red hair was his son. Angry brown eyes, just like his own, stared accusingly at him. 'Hiya Billy, how's it going?'

Billy said nothing and moved closer to his mother. Karen threw Sean an apologetic look. 'Why don't you show your dad your new football boots?'

Sean grabbed the lifeline. 'You play football, Billy? Who do you support? Liverpool?'

Billy looked at him in disgust. 'Manchester United. They're the best.'

Sean laughed. 'Do you think so? What about rugby? Do you like that?'

Billy shook his head.

'Gaelic, hurling?'

Billy shook his head again.

Karen laughed. 'Soccer's his game. When he's not watching it he's playing it, or swapping cards. Football mad, aren't you?' She grabbed her son and tickled him.

Billy giggled helplessly and Sean felt a lump in his throat. 'Why don't we all go for a walk?' he suggested with a nervous smile.

Billy perked up. 'Can we go out to Kinsale?'

'Sure, if you want to,' Sean said, anxious to please.

'And go to McDonald's on the way home?'

'Don't push your luck, young man,' Karen warned. 'Go and put on your jacket.'

'Ah Mum, I'm roasting.'

'No arguments, Billy. Go.' Karen pushed her son towards the door.

'He's got so tall. You'd think he was eight, not six.'

'Almost seven,' Karen reminded him.

'Time goes so quickly. He'll be a grown man before we know it.'

'God, I hope not,' Karen groaned.

Sean led the way out to the car and when Billy was safely belted into the back seat, he drove out of the narrow lane and onto the Bantry Road. 'Will we open the roof?'

'Cool!' Billy answered, his former moodiness forgotten.

Sean grinned at his son in the mirror and opened the sunroof. 'Kinsale, here we come!'

Sean and Karen wandered along the waterfront while Billy skipped ahead of them.

'Daddy, can I have an ice cream?' Billy cried, stopping beside the Mr Whippy van.

Sean's heart lurched. 'Daddy.' It sounded great. 'Sure, son. We'll all have one.' Sean bought three cones and obediently poured strawberry flavouring all over Billy's.

'He'll probably throw up later,' Karen remarked as their son ran ahead, his ice cream wobbling precariously.

'Oh, sorry,' Sean said guiltily.

Karen laughed. 'That's okay. It won't kill him. He's thrilled you're here, Sean. He's always talking about you.'

'Really?' Sean found it hard to believe that his son had any time for him at all. 'He didn't seem too happy to see me.'

'Oh, that's just an act. He's punishing you for staying away for so long.'

'I don't blame him.'

'No, it's always, "What team do you think Daddy supports?" and "Do you think Daddy would teach me to play golf?"'

'I'd love to,' Sean said fervently. 'Karen, I know I've been a lousy dad, but I'd like to make up for it. I want to start seeing more of him.'

Karen didn't answer for a moment and Sean watched her anxiously.

'I think that would be great,' she said finally. 'But only if you're going to keep it up. You can't drop him when the novelty wears off. I won't let you hurt him.'

'I won't, I promise. I just want to be a part of his life again.'

Karen smiled. 'I'm glad to hear it. Don't say anything to him yet, though. Let him get used to you again. He may be wary at first. He's only a little boy.'

'I'll handle it whatever way you think best,' Sean assured her. 'I don't want to screw this up.'

Karen squeezed his hand. 'I'm sure you won't.'

Billy ran up, breathless. 'Dad? Can you make a stone hop across the water? Mike can.'

Sean suppressed a wave of jealousy and crouched down beside his son. 'Well, let's see.' He selected a flat pebble and skimmed it across the water, making it skip three times.

'All right!' Billy squealed in delight. 'Now it's my turn.' He picked up a pebble and threw it, but it plopped in. 'Oh no!'

'Here, Billy. Hold it like this.'

Karen sat down on a bench and watched father and

son playing. Sean looked well. Older, but it suited him. She remembered her reaction when she'd first met him. He was gorgeous and she'd had to stretch her head back to look into those amazing brown eyes. His height and broad shoulders had always made her feel safe. He was wearing his hair much shorter these days, but the tight crop didn't disguise the strong natural wave. He was a good-looking man, but if she was honest with herself, she'd never been really in love with him. They should never have got married but if they hadn't, she wouldn't have Billy and that was unthinkable.

There'd been no bitterness or anger when they'd finally broken up. Just resignation and sadness. But it was different with Mike. Mike was definitely her type. Still, she was nervous of marriage and how it would affect Billy. Her son was the most important person in her life. Sometimes she thought she'd burst with love for him. It would be wonderful for him to see more of Sean. Whatever their differences, Karen was still very fond of Sean and knew he'd be a wonderful dad once he put his mind to it.

'Just one more story, Dad,' Billy pleaded.

'No,' Karen said before Sean caved in again. 'You have to get some sleep. You've got a big day tomorrow.'

'Okay,' Billy agreed reluctantly. He didn't want to do anything to jeopardise his outing to Fota Wildlife Park. Maybe there'd be some lion cubs. It was going to be great. 'Night, Daddy, night, Mum.'

Karen kissed him and walked out of the room.

Sean bent down and hugged him. 'Sleep well, champ.

See you tomorrow.' He turned off the light and closed the door quietly.

'Would you like a drink?' Karen asked when he joined her downstairs.

'No, I'm meeting some colleagues in the hotel bar. Are you sure you won't come with us tomorrow?'

Karen shook her head, laughing. 'No, thanks, I'm planning a very selfish day of pampering. First I'm going shopping, then I'm getting my hair done and I might even meet my sister for lunch.'

'Good for you. Why don't you arrange something with Mike for tomorrow evening? I'll baby-sit.'

Karen stared at him. 'Really?'

'Sure. I came down to spend time with him, didn't I?'

'Well, okay, if you're sure. I'll give Mike a call, see if he's free.'

'Great. That's settled then. I'll see you tomorrow. And Karen?'

'Yes?'

'Thanks for being so understanding. I'm not sure I deserve it.'

'We've both had our moments, Sean. The important thing now is to put it all behind us and concentrate on Billy.'

Sean kissed her cheek. 'Agreed. Good night, Karen.'

'Mum, you should have seen the baby tiger. It was real small but it'll probably grow up to be bigger than me.'

'Amazing,' Karen said for the umpteenth time. Billy hadn't stopped chattering since he'd got home. He was always like this after a visit to the Wildlife Park. Maybe he was going to be a vet. 'Why don't you get ready for your bath?'

Billy made a face. 'Ah, Mum, *Gladiators* is coming on. Can't I have my bath after that?'

'No, Billy, you know I'm going out.'

'I'll give him his bath,' Sean said from the armchair in the corner. 'You go on and make yourself beautiful.'

'Yeah! Great, Daddy!'

Karen frowned. 'Are you sure, Sean?'

'I promise I'll try not to drown him,' Sean said, grabbing his son and tickling him.

Billy giggled. 'I'll drown you!'

'Oh, will you now?'

Karen looked at them doubtfully. 'I'm not sure I can trust either of you.'

Sean winked at Billy. 'Of course you can, can't she?'

Billy nodded, giggling again. 'We'll be good, Mum.'

'Well, okay. I'll trust you. But bed by nine, young man.'

Billy started to complain but Sean nudged him to keep quiet. 'Bed by nine,' he promised Karen.

Karen left them in front of the TV, eating crisps and drinking lemonade. She looked back at the two heads close together. She hoped for Billy's sake that this was the beginning of a new relationship with his dad. She'd kill Sean if he messed this up.

When Karen left and *Gladiators* ended, Sean hauled Billy upstairs and ran a bath.

Billy, up to his neck in bubble bath, suddenly looked a lot younger and more vulnerable. 'Daddy, why don't you live with us?'

Sean was taken aback at the question. Karen had probably answered it dozens of times already. It was important that he gave the right answer now. 'Well, Billy. Mum and I weren't getting along too well. If we lived together we'd probably fight all the time. You wouldn't want that, would you?'

'No,' Billy said reluctantly. 'But why did you fight? Was it because of me?'

'Oh no, son.' Sean was horrified. He looked steadily into his son's eyes. 'It was nothing to do with you. We tried to make a go of it because we loved you so much. But it didn't work.'

'Is Mum going to marry Uncle Mike?'

'Maybe,' Sean said hesitantly. 'How would you feel about that?'

Billy shrugged. 'I suppose it would be okay. I'd still be able to see you, wouldn't I?'

Sean felt a lump in his throat. 'Of course. There's one thing you have to remember, Billy. I'm your Dad and I always will be. And I'll always be there if you need me. Mike isn't trying to take my place. He'll be like your best friend. And he'll look after you, just like me and Mum would.'

Billy digested this for a moment. 'Are you going to marry Stephanie?'

'I don't know,' Sean said honestly. 'Do you think I should?'

'Maybe. She's nice. Not as nice as Mum, of course,' he said loyally.

'Of course,' Sean agreed solemnly.

He told Karen of the conversation when she returned.

'I'm glad you're on the receiving end of the difficult questions for a change,' she said smugly.

'He seems to have accepted the situation.'

'He's a good kid,' she said proudly.

'I'd like him to come and visit.'

Karen shifted in her seat. 'I'm not sure that it's a good idea at the moment.'

Sean frowned. Karen had been fine all along. 'Why not?'

'Billy's at a very impressionable age, Sean. I've brought him up to appreciate family values. As far as he's concerned mummies and daddies live together. They're married. If Billy sees you and Steph living together it will confuse him.'

'So you object to Stephanie?' Sean said shortly.

'No, of course not. I just want to do what's best for Billy.'

Sean stood up. 'Of course. Look, I'd better get going. I'll drop by in the morning to say goodbye.'

Karen nodded. 'I'm sorry, Sean. But I do feel strongly about this. You're welcome to visit us any time you want.'

Sean tried to hide his disappointment. 'Right. I'd better go. See you tomorrow.' He sped away in his car feeling angry and frustrated. But having left her to bring up his son alone, he could hardly expect her to stand aside and let him take over now. So where did that leave him? Begging Steph to marry him so he could spend more time with his son? Or was he going to be forced to choose between Steph and Billy? He shook his head miserably. Why was life always so bloody complicated?

Chapter Thirty-nine

Liz set down two bottles of 1982 Hermitage on the counter and went off to study the white wines. She'd decided on Pouilly Fuissé but now she wasn't so sure. Maybe a Riesling would be more suitable. She put off the decision, selecting a Sauterne to go with the dessert. One bottle should be enough. She grabbed three bottles of Riesling before she changed her mind and carried them back to the counter. A bottle of cognac and a vintage port completed her purchases. She blinked when the assistant told her the total figure. Oh well. It was an investment. She carried her bags carefully out to the car, where her dad sat waiting patiently.

'I thought you'd got lost,' he said good-naturedly as she slipped in beside him.

'Sorry, Dad. At least this is your last chauffeuring job. I'll have the van next week.' She'd already sold her car and was delighted when her dad pronounced the little Peugeot van they'd spotted a good buy. He'd negotiated the price down another hundred pounds and Liz had happily left a deposit and agreed to pick it up the following Tuesday. She could hardly contain her excitement.

'Where to now?' her dad asked cheerfully.

'The Merrion Centre, Dad. I've just a few things left to get.'

'That's okay, love. I've nothing better to do.'

Two hours later, Liz waved him goodbye and went into her kitchen, eager to begin her preparations. Jenny had collected Lucy first thing and was keeping her overnight.

'Are you sure?' Liz had asked guiltily.

'Of course,' Jenny said cheerfully. 'I have to do my bit. After all, I was the one who pushed you into all this.'

'And I'm so glad you did,' Liz said fervently.

'Good. Well, the best of luck. I'll pick Lucy up at nine and you can collect her sometime on Sunday. In fact, come to lunch and tell me how it went.'

Steph grinned. 'I'd love to. Thanks, Jenny.'

True to her word, Jenny had turned up on the doorstep at exactly nine, and took an excited Lucy off for the weekend.

Liz consulted her list. Her first job was to prepare the salad and vegetables. She'd bought three types of lettuce that would be tossed in a simple French dressing and the lightly cooked chicken livers would be added at the last moment. She lightly rinsed the salad leaves, and left them to dry.

For the main course vegetables, she was making carrot and courgette batons with baby corn. Boiled tiny new potatoes completed the meal. She'd considered doing a more complicated potato dish, but it would be too much with the stuffed lamb. She worked quickly, slicing and chopping the carrots and courgettes and wrapped them in cling film. Next, the apricot and walnut stuffing and the crumb coating for the lamb.

When the initial food preparations were complete, Liz

turned her attention to the table setting. She was considering offering clients a choice of themed evenings, extending the service to include special table arrangements. Steph had thought it was a great idea. Liz decided on a silver and midnight-blue colour scheme for tonight. It would go well with the Wedgwood blue of her dining-room walls. She'd bought silver and dark blue satin ribbon to tie around the white linen napkins and picked up some dark blue place cards, silver paint and a tiny paintbrush. After some practising, she'd done a reasonable job painting the names onto the cards, and now they sat drying in the kitchen window. Dark blue candles stood solemnly in her silver antique candelabra – a wedding present from a Chez Nous supplier. She'd spent an hour carefully pressing the white linen tablecloth yesterday and it now covered the large table, pristine and elegant. A variety of candles stood around the room, different sizes and shapes, but all blue. Liz opened the door of the dining-room cabinet and surveyed the glassware. She decided on a traditional look and selected four matching white-wine and red-wine goblets. She washed and polished them and set them on the table, standing back to admire the effect. The silver and glassware would look beautiful in the candlelight. She went back into the kitchen and put the lamb in the oven. Now all she had to do was shower and change. She'd slice up the breads and cook the chicken livers while they were having drinks. She took one last look at her table, poured herself a sherry and went upstairs to dress.

She'd chosen a formal navy blue velvet cocktail dress – she'd blend in with the decor, she thought smiling. The severe cut of the dress was relieved by a slit that revealed a generous amount of thigh when she walked. She'd splashed out on a pair of ultra-sheer tights and with the addition of a pair of very high suede shoes, she looked positively sexy. Her hair swung in waves around her face and her dark eyes shone with excitement. She put on gold earrings, sprayed herself with Chanel and ran downstairs. She had just finished lighting the candles when the doorbell rang.

'Liz, you look marvellous!' Steph handed her a bottle and took off her jacket. 'And something smells great!'

'Hi, Steph. Oh, Champers! Very nice!'

Edward stood in the doorway staring at Liz and then came forward to kiss her lightly on the cheek. 'You look lovely, Liz,' he murmured.

Liz blushed and took the bouquet of yellow roses. 'Thank you, Edward.'

Conor pushed past his boss and waved a box of handmade chocolates at Liz. 'Steph said these were the ones you liked.'

'I love them, thanks, Conor.' Liz smiled and ushered them into the sitting-room. 'Drinks?'

'Sherry would be lovely,' Steph said.

'G & T for me,' Edward said.

'Me too. God, it's great to have someone else doing the cooking.' Conor stretched himself out in an armchair.

Steph sank down on the sofa. 'It is, isn't it? And wait till you taste Liz's cooking, Conor.'

Liz appeared with the drinks. 'Please don't build me up, Steph. You'll only disappoint them.'

'Not a chance.' Edward smiled at her.

Liz smiled back. 'Right. Well, I'll just go and check on things.' She escaped to the kitchen, put on the vegetables, and melted some butter in the pan for the chicken livers. While it was warming, she sliced the breads she'd made that morning. White soda, brown and walnut. She arranged them in a long basket and carried it and the butter dish into the dining-room. Steph was in the kitchen when she returned.

'Everything okay? Can I do anything?'

'God, no. I'd never forgive myself if you got yourself dirty.'

Steph twirled around. 'Do you like it?' She was wearing a richly embroidered golden knee-length cocktail dress with a mandarin collar. With her shining golden hair, she looked like an angel.

'You look stunning,' Liz said without a trace of envy. She slipped on her oven gloves and lifted the lamb out of the oven.

'That looks great.'

'Well, that's a good start. Let's hope it tastes good too.' Liz slipped some silver foil over the joint and left it to rest. Next she poured the dressing over the salad leaves and tossed them briskly. 'Have you heard from Sean?'

'Yeah, he called this morning. He was taking Billy off to Fota Park for the day.'

Liz divided the salad onto four plates. 'That's a great place. We brought Lucy last year. She loved it, though she was a little afraid of the lions.'

Steph grinned. 'Billy's favourites, apparently. Typical little boy.'

'So they're getting on okay?'

'Seem to be. Sean's baby-sitting tonight and letting Karen go out with the new man in her life.'

'Gosh, It all sounds so cosy. I can't imagine ever having that kind of a relationship with Chris.'

'It's early days, Liz. Who knows?'

Liz nodded. 'Call the guys, will you? This is ready.'

Steph went in to Conor and Edward and led them into the large dining-room. 'Wow!' She paused at the door to take in the effect. 'How about this?'

Liz arrived in from the kitchen with the starters. 'Do you like it?'

Edward gave a low whistle. 'Very elegant.'

'Cool,' Conor said.

Liz smiled. 'Would you pour the wine, Edward?'

'Of course.' Edward lifted a bottle from the ice bucket at his side and inspected the label. 'Very nice. You are really spoiling us tonight, Ambassador!' he said in a corny foreign accent.

'Just buttering you up.'

'You can butter me up like this anytime,' Conor said, having sampled a mouthful of salad. 'This is great. The chicken livers are melt-in-the-mouth.'

'Try some of the walnut bread,' Steph urged.

Liz beamed happily at them, but they didn't notice. They were too busy eating.

'How many psychiatrists does it take to change a light bulb?' Edward asked.

Steph shook her head.

'Only one, but the light bulb has to *want* to change.'

Steph laughed. 'That's a good one, isn't it, Conor?'

'What?' Conor turned to her.

Steph rolled her eyes. 'Never mind – when are you two going to stop talking about food?' She turned back to Edward. 'A drunk and a giraffe walk into a pub . . .'

Liz groaned loudly. 'Oh, no, not that one again. I'm

going to get the cheese. Steph, make yourself useful and get the port and brandy.'

'It's a good joke,' Steph protested but obediently went to get the drinks.

'Nothing for me,' Edward said. 'Unless Liz can put us all up for the night.'

Liz came back in and set the cheese board and basket of home-made crackers on the table. 'No problem, as long as you don't mind sharing with Conor.'

Edward shuddered 'I'm sure he snores.'

'I've never had any complaints,' Conor told him.

'We'll have to ask Concepta about that,' Steph said mischievously.

'Who's Concepta?' Edward watched his chef blush like a teenager.

'Never you mind. I'll have a brandy, Steph.'

'Liz?'

'Port for me.'

'That was a truly magnificent meal, Liz,' Steph said as she served them their drinks.

'The lamb was cooked to perfection,' Edward agreed. 'I just love it when it's still pink and moist.'

'And the stuffing was excellent,' Conor added.

'What about the dessert?' Steph asked.

'Oh, we should put that on our menu – with your permission of course, Liz.' He looked at Edward and Stephanie. 'Look, why mess about any longer? Let's make a decision right now. Are we all in favour of Liz linking her business to Chez Nous?'

Liz looked nervously around the table.

'Well, I think it's a brilliant idea – but then of course it was mine – and no one could make it work as well as Liz could.'

Liz smiled gratefully at Steph.

Edward nodded solemnly. 'I agree. I think Liz can only add further to the success and prestige of Chez Nous.'

'So we're agreed,' Conor pronounced.

Steph jumped up to hug Liz. 'Welcome back, darling.'

Edward shook her hand and then leaned forward to kiss her cheek. 'Congratulations, Liz.'

'Can we open the champagne now?' Conor asked hopefully.

Liz almost ran to the kitchen. 'Absolutely!'

When they were sipping their champagne she turned shyly to Conor. 'I'd really appreciate it if you'd have a look through my menus.'

'I'd love to. Let's do it now.'

'Oh no, you don't,' Steph warned. 'We've listened to you two talk food for long enough. Get together some other time. Let's relax and enjoy the rest of our evening.'

Conor shrugged. 'Fair enough. Give me a shout anytime, Liz. I'm sort of at a loose end these days.'

'More's the pity,' Edward grumbled.

'Any sign of the builders finishing?' Liz asked.

Steph frowned. 'Not really. They seem to keep discovering more problems. Whether they're real or imaginary is anyone's guess.'

'At least the stairs are finished and we can get back up to the office.' Edward helped himself to a piece of Stilton. 'And we should be able to get the decorators in on Monday to start work on the loos and the new dining-room.'

'Well, that's not so bad,' Liz said, looking at their glum faces. 'Cheer up, lads, for God's sake!'

Edward smiled. 'You're right of course, Liz. It could be worse. Let's talk about your business instead.'

'You know, I was thinking,' Steph said thoughtfully. 'There's one drawback to you associating yourself with Chez Nous.'

Liz frowned. 'What's that?'

'Publicity. Promoting your business is going to draw attention to your split with Chris.'

Liz looked at her in dismay. 'I never thought of that.'

'Any ideas on how to deal with it, Stephanie?' Edward asked.

Steph chewed her bottom lip. 'It's probably best to be up-front about it. There'll still be talk, of course, but it will be short-lived. If we say nothing, the press will have a field day.'

'I couldn't handle that,' Liz said, panicking slightly. 'The last thing I need is journalists ringing the house, or worse, calling at the door. What about Lucy?'

'Maybe a joint interview with you and Chris would be the best answer. If you're open about it, it takes away the mystery. "The couple who decide to go their separate ways but remain good friends", that sort of thing.' Steph twirled her glass thoughtfully. ' "Starting up your own business after a marriage break-up. Triumph over adversity." That'll go down really well with other women.'

Liz gave a wry grin. 'That's not exactly an accurate picture.'

Steph shrugged. 'They want a story so you may as well turn it to your advantage.'

'Steph's right, Liz,' Edward said. 'It'll be a storm in a teacup.'

'It's a good idea to do it with Chris,' Conor joined in. 'That will kill any gossip before it starts.'

Liz looked around at her new business associates. 'Okay then, I'll talk to Chris. I'm sure he'll agree. After all, it's important for him to get good press too.'

'Good girl.' Edward squeezed her hand.

'I think it's time we called it a night,' Steph said with a yawn. 'I've a load of work to do tomorrow.'

'On a Sunday?'

Steph laughed. 'It's all ahead of you, Liz. Weekends will be a thing of the past.'

'True – oh, what the hell, I'm looking forward to it!'

'You're going to be a huge success,' Conor assured her. 'Give me a call during the week and we'll go over those menus.'

'Thanks, Conor. And thanks to all of you for letting me use the name.'

Steph waved away her thanks. 'You helped make that name what it is today, Liz. Look on it as coming home.'

Liz smiled. 'Coming home. I like the sound of that.'

Edward picked up his car keys. 'Okay folks, let's hit the road and let the lady get some well-earned rest. I'll call you tomorrow,' he added quietly as he bent to kiss her cheek.

'Okay,' she whispered back. 'But I'm having lunch with your sister.'

'Are you, indeed? Maybe I'll invite myself along.'

'Night, Liz. Thanks again.' Conor wrapped Liz in a bear hug.

'Seeya, Liz. Call me.' Steph blew her a kiss and followed Edward and Conor – rather unsteadily – out to the car.

Liz waved as they drove away. She returned to the kitchen and surveyed the pile of washing-up. Then she laughed and closed the door. It could wait until morning. Going into the living-room she poured herself a cognac and curled up in an armchair. She went over the evening, savouring each moment as she sipped her drink. The food couldn't have turned out better and Conor was particularly complimentary about the lamb. Steph had loved the table decorations, especially the place names. And, as she'd hoped, Edward had been very impressed with her choice of wines. All in all, it had been a great success. Liz felt quite pleased with herself. If she could please three such discerning and knowledgeable people, she could please anyone. 'Liz Connolly of Chez Nous,' she murmured. 'Watch out catering world, here I come!'

Chapter Forty

'Shane. Put on your jacket if you're going outside.'
'Oh, Mum.'

'You heard me.' Annie ignored her son's dramatic moans.

Shane grabbed his jacket and tugged Tom West's hand. 'Come on, Granddad!'

'Leave your granddad alone.'

'It's okay, Annie. A bit of exercise won't kill me.' Tom West went out into the garden with Shane. Joe and Sean were already kicking the ball around and Dani was running between them, shrieking with laughter. 'I'll be the goalie,' Tom announced.

Catherine West shook her head in despair as she watched from the window. 'My God, that man won't be happy until he breaks something. Sixty-six going on four!'

Stephanie laughed. 'He looks fine, Mam.'

'What about you, Steph? Are you fine?' Catherine West surveyed her only daughter. She looked lovely in a pale green trouser suit but she was as thin as a reed and very pale despite the expertly applied make-up.

'Sure. Can I do anything to help, Annie?' Steph asked

her sister-in-law in an effort to avoid any more probing questions.

'No, thanks. Everything's done.' Annie stirred the gravy and slipped the dish in beside the roast.

'You shouldn't have gone to so much trouble.' Catherine smiled at her daughter-in-law.

'It's nothing fancy, Catherine. I just hope there's enough to go round!' She sat down at the table beside them. 'Tell us about Liz's dinner party, Steph.'

'It was amazing, Annie. She's going to be a huge success.' Steph described the meal and the dining-room in minute detail.

'Oh, I wish I'd been there,' Annie groaned. 'What's she going to call the business?'

'"Liz Connolly of Chez Nous". Edward and Conor were keen on the idea from the start but when they tasted her food they were sold! It was great because once it was all agreed we were able to relax and enjoy the night. Conor and Liz never stopped talking about food, and recipes.' Steph rolled her eyes. 'You'd think Liz had never left the business.'

Annie laughed delightedly. 'That's brilliant. The transformation in Liz is amazing, isn't it? Honestly, Catherine, I know it's sad to see a marriage break up, but I truly believe it will be the making of Liz. And Lucy seems happy. I don't think she's going to have too many problems.'

Steph nodded. 'Yes, it's not like Chris was ever around that much anyway. That was part of the problem.'

'Well I hope you're both right,' Catherine said doubtfully. 'At least Liz has got you two and her parents.'

'Her dad's been great,' Steph agreed. 'She sold her old car and he's been ferrying her everywhere she needs to go. And he went with her to buy the van too. Now that she's mobile he'll be able to take a well-earned rest!'

'Van?' Annie looked at her, wide-eyed.

Steph laughed at her expression. 'Yeah, that was pretty much my reaction too. She wanted something sensible for carting the equipment and food about.'

'Well, good luck to her – oh!' Catherine jumped as the football hit the window beside her.

'Sorry!' Sean grinned in at her. 'Your grandson doesn't know his own strength.'

Steph watched Sean throw the ball back to Shane and shout instructions to him. This was the happiest she'd seen him since he'd got back from Cork. He hadn't said much about his visit and she'd wondered if Billy had rejected him. But that didn't make sense. When Sean had phoned on the Saturday, he'd been over the moon at how well he and Billy were getting on. She frowned. Maybe he'd had a row with Karen. Something was definitely wrong and he wasn't telling her.

Annie took the roast out of the oven. 'Lunch will be ready soon.'

'Just as well,' Catherine said drily. 'Tom won't last much longer!'

Steph looked out at her father. 'Oh, he's not doing too badly. How's his wrist?'

'It bothers him in cold or wet weather – rheumatism, I suppose.'

'Well, it's not bothering him today,' Annie said as Tom leaped up and stopped the ball from going into the neighbour's garden. She started to carve the beef.

'Will I call them?' Steph asked.

'Please, Steph. It will be at least five minutes before they pay any attention to you.' Annie was well used to her family's selective hearing when there was a game of football in progress.

Steph laughed and let a roar out the back door. Annie was right. Adults and children alike ignored her. She put two fingers in her mouth and whistled. 'Food!' she roared when she'd got their attention.

Minutes later they trooped in, red-faced and breathless.

'I'm starving!' Shane slipped in beside Annie and took a piece of meat.

'Hands!' Annie said, slapping him away.

Shane went off to the bathroom, chewing happily on his stolen beef.

'You okay, Dad?' Steph asked as he sat down heavily beside her.

He took a mouthful of wine. 'I am now,' he gasped.

Catherine shook her head. 'Silly man. You're a bit old for running around like a maniac.'

Tom looked affronted. 'I saved two goals and I could run rings around that pair any day.' He nodded at Sean and Joe, who'd headed straight for the fridge and were now downing cans of cold beer.

'No argument there,' Sean agreed.

Annie served up the meal and everyone tucked in, the children talking excitedly between mouthfuls. Catherine looked around her. It was nice to see everyone together, happy and healthy. Her eyes fell on Stephanie and she frowned. She'd have to get her alone later. She balked at the thought. She wasn't sure how Stephanie was going to react to her news. It wasn't the best of timing. She was only just getting over losing the baby. She sighed.

'Are you all right, Mam?'

'Fine, Steph,' Catherine assured her. 'Just full.'

'Leave room for dessert,' Annie warned. 'It's Baked Alaska. Your favourite.'

'Lovely.'

When the meal was finished, the men disappeared to watch the football and the women started to clear up.

'How come none of our fellas are these new men we hear so much about?' Steph complained.

Annie laughed. 'Because we have them spoiled. I blame the mothers.'

'Cheek!' Catherine looked affronted. 'I bet you'll be just as bad with Shane.'

'I already am,' Annie admitted. 'He gets away with murder.'

'Did you finish decorating his bedroom?' Catherine asked as she dried the last plate.

'Oh, yes, I'm very happy with it. The carpet arrived yesterday. Go on up and have a look while I make us some coffee.'

Catherine and Stephanie made their way up to Shane's room. 'Oh it's lovely,' Steph exclaimed as she pushed open the door. Annie had painted the walls a warm mustard, and the door and skirting-boards a deep cream. The carpet was a tweed effect with brown and gold tones.

Catherine smiled at the football posters over the bed. 'A real boy's room. Imagine he's nearly eight now. God, they grow up so fast.'

Stephanie turned to leave the room.

'Wait a minute, Stephanie. I have something to tell you.'

Catherine sat down on the side of Shane's bed.

'What is it, Mam? Is there something wrong? Are you sick?' Steph looked worriedly at her mother.

'No, nothing like that. I got a phone call during the week from Joan McCann.'

Stephanie sank down on the bed beside her. 'Ruth's mother?'

Catherine nodded.

'But what did she want? Why call you – you hardly knew each other?' The questions tumbled out of Steph as she tried to take in the news.

'She was trying to contact you.'

'So what did she say? What did she want?' Steph wasn't sure why, but she felt very uneasy. Why was Mrs McCann looking for her? What would she want to talk about after all these years?

'She didn't say. She did tell me that Peter died last month.'

'Oh. He wasn't that old.' Steph had a very faint memory of Ruth's dad. He'd never had a lot to say, retreating behind his newspaper most evenings when he finally got home from the office. Joan McCann warned the children to leave their father in peace because he worked so hard.

'Cancer,' her mother said. 'Apparently he'd been sick for some time.'

'And she didn't say what she wanted to talk to me about?' Steph plucked nervously at the duvet.

'No. I didn't give her your number. I told her I'd get you to call her.'

'Right,' Steph said.

'You will call her, Stephanie, won't you? She probably just wants to reminisce. Death has a way of reminding you of the past.'

'I'm not sure I can handle it, Mam. What the hell will I say to her? "Hiya, Mrs McCann. I went out with my boyfriend instead of going round and stopping your daughter from killing herself." That should really console her.'

Catherine patted her hand. 'Don't be so melodramatic. Surely you talked about all that already?'

Steph shook her head. 'No, we never talked at all. The only time there was any real conversation was when Mr McCann called me to get Des's name and address.'

'Well, that's probably it, then. Maybe she wants to know all the details. I know I would.'

'You think? But why now?'

'She's just lost her husband, Steph. This is a very tough time for her.'

'I suppose. How did she sound?'

'All right, but then it was a very short call. Anyway, here's her number.' Catherine produced a scrap of paper.

Steph took it and shoved it in the pocket of her jacket.

Catherine frowned. 'You will call her, won't you, Stephanie?'

'Yeah. Sure.' Steph stood up. 'We'd better go down.'

'You're very quiet,' Sean said, with a sidelong glance, on the drive home. 'What's up?'

'Nothing. I'm just a bit tired.'

Sean gritted his teeth. That was a load of crap. There was definitely something wrong. She'd been in a mood all afternoon. 'Oh come on, Steph. I know there's something wrong. Did you have a row with your mother?'

'No, of course not. Look, I don't want to talk about it.'

'You never do,' he muttered.

'Well, you've been pretty secretive yourself lately,' Steph retorted angrily.

'What's that supposed to mean?'

'You know damn well. You haven't told me anything about what went on in Cork and suddenly you've dropped any mention of converting the attic.'

Sean said nothing. How could he tell Steph what Karen had said? She'd think he was trying to press-gang her into marriage. He was in a lose-lose situation whatever way he looked at it.

Steph took his silence as a rebuff. 'Fine. If that's the way you want it.' She turned her head away and stared out of the window. What on earth was he hiding from her? She sighed heavily. God, she couldn't handle this. Not on top of the bombshell her mother had just dropped. Why did Joan McCann want to talk to her now? Steph felt a shiver run down her back. Maybe she wanted to have it out with her. Tell her off for letting Ruth down. Well, she'd every right to. But it just seemed so weird after all this time. And for some reason, it seemed more sinister and terrifying than it would have fifteen years ago. Who was she kidding? She'd have been terrified of this confrontation at any time. In a way she'd always been waiting for the phone to ring. It was like unfinished business. She'd probably never rest until Mrs McCann screamed at her and told her what a lousy friend she'd been. She glanced over at Sean's grim expression. Now she'd even managed to alienate him. No one can screw up life quite like you, kid, she thought.

Chapter Forty-one

Edward picked his way through the workmen and went upstairs. Two more were working up here, one painting the ladies' loos and the other wallpapering the new dining-room. Things were looking a lot better and that awful stench had been replaced by the smell of fresh paint. He joined Stephanie in the office. 'Well? What do you think?'

'It looks wonderful. I'll get them to give the walls in here a lick of paint too and the place will be as good as new.' She groaned as Edward leaned against the blackened filing cabinet. 'For God's sake, mind your suit, Edward. That cabinet is filthy.'

As usual he was impeccably and expensively dressed. Edward dusted down his jacket with a careless hand and sat down. 'You don't have a stamp, do you, Steph? I need to post this letter today.'

'There should be some here somewhere – although they might be black!' She pulled open the drawer of her desk and stopped short. 'Oh.'

'What is it?' Edward watched as the colour drained from her face.

Steph pulled out the Mothercare bag. 'I forgot that I did a little shopping the day of the fire.'

'Oh, Stephanie. I am sorry.'

She gave a small shrug. 'Don't worry about it. I knew it was bad luck buying things so soon.' She drew the colourful mobile out and twirled it around.

'That's superstitious rubbish, Stephanie, and you know it.'

'I suppose.' She shoved the mobile back in the bag and threw it in the bin. She rummaged in her drawer and produced a book of stamps. 'Here we are.'

'That's great, thanks. Have you heard anything about our insurance money yet?'

'Not a dicky-bird. They're very quick to take money but not so good at paying it back.'

'Not to worry. We're on top of the financial situation now, thanks to Chris.'

Steph frowned. 'Let's not go overboard. I've nothing to thank that man for.'

'Has Liz talked to him yet about doing an interview?' Edward said, changing the subject. He knew the answer already, but Liz didn't want to broadcast their relationship so he had to pretend he didn't know things that he did. It was all very confusing.

Steph shook her head. 'No. She hasn't told him about the catering business yet and she doesn't want to do it over the phone. He's due up at the weekend so she'll talk to him then.'

'The sooner the better. Now what about the reopening reception?'

Steph sighed. 'What about it? This place doesn't look as if it will ever be ready.'

'They've promised us they'll be out in two weeks.'

'If there are no complications,' Steph pointed out.

'Umm, true. Still, we have to be prepared. We ought

to talk to the staff and let them know when we'll need them back.'

'Okay. Did I tell you Jean got a job in the Italian place across the road?'

Edward raised an eyebrow. 'You must be gutted.'

'Devastated,' Steph agreed with a grin.

'Have we lost anyone else?'

'No, amazingly enough. I think they're too busy enjoying the time off. I had a postcard from Marc. He's looking forward to coming back.'

'That's good. Oh, come on, Steph, bite the bullet. Let's name a day for the reopening.' Edward reached up and pulled a dusty calendar off the wall. 'What about the end of the month?'

'But that's only three weeks away.'

'Yes, and the builders will definitely be finished by then. If they finish early we can open for regular business before then but keep the official reopening as planned.'

'I suppose.'

'So what date do you think?'

Steph chewed her pen and considered the calendar. 'It needs to be mid-week. There's more chance of the press coming along.'

'Early evening?'

'Yes, about six thirty or seven. That way we catch the business people coming from work, who aren't willing to travel back into town.'

'Right. So how about Tuesday, the thirtieth?'

'It's as good a date as any. We'd better start interviewing waiting staff and kitchen porters.'

'Yes, and we need to organise a staff meeting.'

'Okay, how about Thursday evening? About seven?'

COLETTE CADDLE

Edward stood up. 'That suits me. Right then, if there's nothing else I'd better get back to my real job!'

Steph laughed. 'They must think you've retired.'

'They should be so lucky.'

'Edward?'

He paused in the doorway.

'Thanks for everything. You've been great.'

'Hey! It's my business too, you know. I believe in looking after my investments.'

Steph ignored his flippancy. 'I mean it, Edward. I'm very grateful.'

'No problem, Steph. What are friends for?'

Steph smiled after him. It was true he had become a friend and a very good one at that. It was hard to believe that she'd only met him six months ago. Her thoughts were interrupted by the shrill of her mobile phone.

'Stephanie West,' she answered.

'Stephanie? It's Mam.'

'Hi, Mam. Are you okay? Is Dad all right?' It was very unusual for her mother to call her on the mobile.

'Yes, love, we're both fine. I just had another call from Joan McCann. She said you hadn't been in touch.'

'Oh.'

'She thought I'd forgotten to give you the message.' Catherine West was a bit annoyed at this – as if she'd forget to pass on a message.

'I lost her number, Mam,' Steph fibbed.

'I thought it must be something like that. Well, I've got it here. Have you got a pen?'

'Yeah, go ahead.' Steph doodled while her mother called out the number.

'Have you got that?'

'Yes, thanks.'

'Okay, love. See you at the weekend. Bye-bye.'

'Bye.' Steph hung up the phone and sat staring at it. She'd thought about calling Mrs McCann every day, but she just couldn't bring herself to do it. What was she going to say to the woman? They'd never been exactly close. Not like Ruth and Catherine West.

Joan McCann had had her hands full with a young family and didn't have time to sit down for a gossip with the two girls the way Catherine had. Ruth spent a lot of time at the West's and so Steph very rarely saw or talked to Ruth's parents.

So why did Mrs McCann want to talk to her now? Steph bit her lip anxiously. Her mam must be right. It must be the death of her husband that had brought it all back. She took her wallet from her bag and extracted the crumpled piece of paper with Joan's phone number. She picked up her mobile and then put it down again. It rang, making her jump.

'Stephanie West.'

'Steph, it's me.'

'Hi, Sean,' she said, relieved at the interruption.

'I was wondering if you'd like to meet for lunch?'

Steph smiled with relief. Things had been very frosty between them since Joe's birthday. 'That would be nice. Where do you want to go?'

'Wait and see,' Sean said and she could hear the smile in his voice. 'Just don't bank on getting much work done this afternoon. I'll pick you up in an hour.'

Sean rang off before she had a chance to protest. Oh, what the hell? She deserved a break. And it would be nice to share a tension-free meal for a change. Feeling slightly happier she decided to call Joan McCann. She dialled the number.

'Hello?' The voice was faint and tired.

'Mrs McCann? It's Stephanie West.'

'Oh, hello, dear. It's lovely to hear from you.'

Joan's voice immediately sounded brighter and stronger.

'I was so sorry to hear about Mr McCann.'

'Thanks, Stephanie, but he'd gone through a terrible time. It was a happy release.'

Steph struggled for something to say. 'And how are the family?'

'Grand, grand. John's working for a stockbroker in London and Celine just had twins. A boy and a girl.'

'Celine!' Steph thought of Ruth's baby sister. But then she must be twenty-five now. 'That's great news. Does she live in Dublin?'

'Oh yes, she's only around the corner. I get to see the children most days. I'm afraid I'm spoiling them, but then isn't that what grannies are for?'

Steph laughed. 'It certainly is.' She searched her memory for the names of the other children. 'What about Brenda? Is she married?'

'Oh no, I don't think any man is brave enough to take her on!'

Steph remembered how strong-willed Brenda could be. Or 'downright bold', as Ruth would complain.

'Her career comes first. She's a senior manager in IBM now and spends most of her time in the States.'

'Really! That's brilliant. Ruth always wanted to work for IBM—' Steph cursed silently. The words were out before she'd realised.

Joan was relaxed. 'That's right, I'd forgotten. You know, Steph, she could have been anything she wanted.'

'I know that. She always made me feel so brainless. She knew exactly where she was going, what she wanted to do. I never knew what I wanted.'

'You've done all right,' Joan remarked drily.

Steph laughed. 'I have, but through accident rather than intention.'

There was a small silence and Steph began to feel uncomfortable.

'I'd love to see you, Steph.'

Steph swallowed hard. 'Yes, we must get together sometime.'

'Soon?'

Steph felt her throat go dry. 'Of course, it's a bit difficult for me at the moment. I don't know if Mam told you, but we had a fire—'

'I'd really like to talk to you.' Joan was insistent.

'Right. Okay. Well, I'll call you and we'll arrange something.'

Joan was silent.

'Mrs McCann?'

'How about next week?'

'I'm afraid I can't next week.'

'Oh.'

Steph sighed wearily at the obvious disappointment in her voice. 'Look, I'll call you Monday or Tuesday and we'll set something up.'

'Thanks, love. I'll look forward to it. You see, we need to talk.'

'Bye Mrs McCann.' Steph put down the phone with a trembling hand. We need to talk. What did that mean?

'I think I'll have the spider's legs followed by the duck's armpits.'

Steph looked up at Sean. 'Sorry?'

Sean laughed. 'You haven't heard a word I've said. And you say that I never listen to you!'

'Sorry, love.'

'I don't know. I bring you to one of the nicest restaurants in the city and this is the thanks I get.'

Steph looked around her at the splendour of the Clarence hotel dining-room. 'It's lovely.'

Sean's smile faded. This wasn't like Stephanie. She usually came to life in a place like this. 'What's wrong, Steph? You've hardly said two words since we got here. You're not still annoyed with me, are you?'

Steph shook her head. 'No, of course not. I'm just a bit preoccupied.'

'I can see that. Talk to me.'

Steph sighed. 'It's Ruth's mother.'

'Ruth? Ruth McCann?'

Steph nodded. 'Yes. Her mother contacted me. She wants me to come and see her.'

'Why?'

Steph shrugged. 'I wish I knew. She contacted Mam a while ago asking me to get in touch but I kept putting it off.'

'Until today.'

Steph nodded. 'Yes. She called Mam again so I couldn't put it off any longer. Her husband died recently and Mam says that's probably what brought all the memories back.'

'So when are you going to see her?'

'I told her I'd call her next week, but I'm not sure that it's a good idea.'

He frowned. 'You can't let the woman down, Steph.'

'That's easy for you to say, Sean, but what am I supposed to say to her?'

Sean shrugged. 'Whatever she wants you to say. Whatever she needs to hear. You'll feel better once you get there. It will probably do you good.'

'Maybe,' she said doubtfully.

'Definitely,' he assured her, squeezing her hand. 'Do it for Ruth, Steph. Do it for your best friend.'

Steph stared at him for a moment and then nodded resignedly. 'Yes. Yes, okay, I will.'

Chapter Forty-two

C hris looked out into the garden. The lawn was trim, the barbecue tucked in beside the shed for the winter in its all-weather cover. Everything was in its place. He felt sad as he realised that he was completely dispensable. Liz was moving on without him. There would be no reconciliation. He hadn't realised how much he'd loved his home until Liz had thrown him out. Now as he tried to make a life for himself in Galway, he understood the difference between a house and a home. The only thing he'd really got enthusiastic over was Lucy's bedroom. Liz would have laughed if she'd seen his attempts at decorating. Still, after botching a couple of sheets of wallpaper he'd got the hang of it and the end result didn't look bad at all. He turned around as Liz walked into the kitchen. He couldn't get over how well she was looking. When she'd first opened the door he'd been dumbstruck. She seemed so vibrant and happy. Yes, that was it. She looked happy.

'Sorry about that. The phone never seems to stop these days. But I've put the answering machine on now, so no more interruptions. Would you like a coffee?'

'Yeah, great.' Chris sat down in his usual seat at the

kitchen table. Since when did Liz need an answering machine? 'So how are things? Any news?'

'Yes, quite a lot actually.' Liz busied herself with the mugs. She felt unaccountably nervous about telling Chris about the business. She was expecting him to ridicule the idea and she wasn't sure she'd be able to handle it. She made the coffee and carried the mugs to the table. 'I'm starting a new business, Chris. Catering for private dinner parties, that kind of thing.'

'You're what?'

Liz bristled. 'You heard,' she said curtly, fidgeting with a spoon.

'That's a great idea. It would suit you to perfection. You never did want to work full-time while Lucy was small. This way you can do most of the work at home.'

Liz stared at him. 'That's right. I promise, Lucy won't be neglected.'

Chris laughed. 'God, I know that, Liz. You've always put Lucy first. You expected me to be against this, didn't you?'

'Well, yes I did,' she admitted.

Chris sighed. 'Well, I suppose if I'm to be honest, I wouldn't have liked it if we were still together. Would you like me to take a look at your menus? I could give you a few pointers.'

Liz grimaced. This was more like the Chris she remembered. 'I think I'm on top of it.'

'Well, I'd be happy to give you some advice—'

'I'll call you if I'm in trouble,' she promised, thinking Chris was the last person she wanted advice from. But she wasn't going to annoy him by saying that. This was too good to be true.

'So when do you start? Where are you going to advertise?'

Liz explained her arrangement with Chez Nous and how the idea had started the evening at Jenny's. She neglected to mention that Jenny was Edward's sister. He didn't really need to know that, did he?

'That makes sense,' Chris said grudgingly. 'Using the name will give you a lot of prestige. So have you any bookings yet?'

'Three. The first is for Edward McDermott. He wants to entertain some of his business associates.'

Chris grunted.

'Then there's a friend of Jenny's, a lady who was at the party that night and then I've a provisional booking from Madge McCarthy – do you remember her? She owns the newsagent's in the village.'

'Word of mouth. That's going to be your best advertisement.'

'Yes, that's what I thought.'

'You should talk to someone in the press too. When Steph reopens there's sure to be a few of them knocking around. Make sure and get a plug in for your business.'

'Ah, yes. Well, I wanted to talk to you about that. Steph thinks we may become the focus of some of the gossip columnists. When they know I'm starting my own business, they'll realise that we've broken up and that you've gone to Galway alone.'

'Oh, shit. I hadn't thought about that.'

'No, neither had I.'

'Still, any publicity is better than none.'

'Yes, but what about Lucy? I don't want her to hear stories about us in school. Steph thought we might avoid all of that if we gave a joint interview to one journalist. Someone we could trust.'

Chris snorted. 'Modern Ireland and the couple who support each other in separation?'

Liz laughed nervously. 'Something like that. It does sound a bit silly.'

'No, it's a good idea. I'll give Adam Cullen a call. He's fair and he won't print anything that we haven't agreed. I'll see if he can talk to us tomorrow.'

Liz was taken aback. 'So soon?'

'The sooner the better. But we'd better get our stories straight and decide what we want to discuss.'

'He'll probably want to talk about the fire,' Liz said nervously.

The press had spent a few days trying to get to the bottom of the Chez Nous fire. Stephanie had announced – following the renegotiation of Chris's contract – that it had been an unfortunate accident and no one was to blame. The press had reluctantly accepted this, but there were still some rumours flying around.

'I'll deal with that,' Chris said firmly. 'Adam's a mate. He won't push it.' He stood up. 'Right then. I'll try and organise that and I'll drop back later and we'll prepare our script.'

'Thanks, Chris. And Chris?'

He paused in the doorway.

'When I get the business going, we'll talk about the maintenance again. I shouldn't need as much.'

'That's okay, Liz,' he said gruffly. 'Lucy's my daughter. I want the best for her. Don't ever worry about money. It's not important.' He patted her arm awkwardly and let himself out of the house.

Liz sank back into her chair. Who'd have thought

a couple of months ago that they'd be able to have such a reasonable conversation? Chris had even been reasonable about her starting her own business. She'd been sure he'd laugh at her, tell her she'd fail. Support was the last thing she'd expected.

Maybe she should give him another chance and consider going to Galway. Her heart sank at the thought of leaving her business behind. She didn't want to go back to just being somebody's wife. No, damn it, if she took him back, it would only be for Lucy's sake. Anyway, leopards didn't change their spots and it wouldn't be long before Chris reverted to his old ways. It would be great if they could be friends but their life together was over. It was time that Liz Connolly moved on and stood on her own two feet.

At three o'clock in the Shelbourne the following day, Chris stood and shook hands with Adam Cullen. 'Thanks for coming, Adam. We appreciate it.'

'Not at all.' Adam bent and kissed Liz's cheek. 'I'll fax you a copy of the article before I print it. Best of luck in Galway, Chris. And think about what I said, Liz. It would make a great article. See you both.'

When he was gone, Chris signalled the waiter and ordered more drinks. 'Well, I thought that went well.'

'Great,' Liz agreed. 'I can't believe he wants to spend a whole evening following me around just to do an article.'

'It would be even better on television,' Chris mused.

'God, no. What if something went wrong? I'd be ruined!'

Chris laughed. 'Maybe. Still, it's worth thinking about. I told you he'd be okay, didn't I?'

'I'll reserve judgement until I see the article.' Liz was nervous around journalists although Adam was obviously a very nice guy.

'It will be fine. Come on. Let's drink to success.'

Liz smiled and raised her glass. 'To success then. For both of us.'

Chapter Forty-three

J enny walked into the dining-room and gave a small gasp. Edward chuckled. 'Great, isn't it?'

She walked slowly around the polished mahogany table, her eyes round like a child on Christmas Day. The silverware gleamed, the crystal glasses sparkled in the candlelight and the rich crimson-coloured napkins were complemented by a vase of dark red tea roses. 'It's marvellous,' she breathed. She'd always felt this room was a little too austere, what with its dark wood, crimson walls and heavy cream drapes. But the candles around the room created a soft, warm effect. 'Where's Liz?'

Edward raised an eyebrow. 'Where do you think?'

Jenny went out to the kitchen. 'How's it going?'

Liz jumped. 'Oh! Jenny! Not too bad, I think – oh, I don't know!'

'The dining-room looks magnificent,' Jenny reassured her.

'Do you think so?' Liz asked anxiously. 'It's a beautiful room. I hope I didn't overdo it.'

'Not at all. What are we eating? It smells gorgeous.'

'Brill and crab terrine to start, followed by confit of duck, then cheese and orange liqueur soufflés.'

Jenny licked her lips. 'Sounds wonderful. Do you need any help?'

'I don't think so.'

'Will you be joining us?'

Liz looked horrified. 'God, no.'

'For coffee,' Edward said smoothly from the doorway.

'Oh, I don't think . . .'

'The point of the evening, Liz, is to introduce you. You can join us after you've served the dessert.' Edward looked her straight in the eye.

Liz looked away from the intensity of his gaze. 'Okay,' she said faintly.

'So who's coming?' Jenny asked. 'Am I going to be bored out of my mind?'

'It shouldn't be too bad. Tim and Susan Wallace will be there.'

'Oh, good.' Jenny liked Edward's partner.

'John Moriarty and partner.'

Liz gasped at the name of one of the largest property developers in the country.

'And a guy called Philippe Bacoux and his wife. He's a restaurateur from Antwerp,' Edward continued calmly.

'Oh, Edward! How could you? Talk about throwing me in at the deep end!'

'I wouldn't do it if I didn't think you were up to it,' he said smoothly.

The doorbell rang and Liz jumped.

'Come on, hostess, let's do it!'

Jenny winked at Liz and followed her brother out to the hall.

Liz closed the door after them and consulted her list once more. Her hands were shaking. 'Calm down,

Liz. Calm down. Everything's under control.' She cut the bread and carried it and some golden butter curls into the dining-room. She took a quick look around, polished a knife, rearranged a rose and went back into the kitchen. Edward wanted the starter served twenty minutes after the last guests arrived, and the duck needed another fifteen minutes so there was nothing to do but sit and wait. She wondered what it would be like to work for Edward. She'd seen a different side of him this week. He had very fixed ideas about what he liked. He'd organised the wines himself, though he'd discussed them with her first. She was delighted when they'd agreed on the selection.

The doorbell rang again and Jenny's head appeared around the door. 'Everyone's here, Liz.'

Liz jumped up nervously. 'Fine. I'll call you in twenty minutes.'

When the starters were ready, Liz took a deep breath and opened the double doors between the dining-room and living-room.

Edward stood up. 'Ah, Liz. People, I'd like you to meet our chef, Liz Connolly of Chez Nous.'

Liz smiled shyly. 'If you'd like to move inside . . .'

She stood aside as the guests entered the room, and then she went to collect the tray of starters.

There were murmurs of approval as she set the plates down in front of them. 'Enjoy your meal,' she said quietly and withdrew.

The next hour went by in a whirl of activity for Liz, but the dining-room was calm and relaxed.

'Lovely meal, my dear,' John Moriarty remarked as she took his plate.

'Excellent sauce,' the restaurateur said with respect.

Edward beamed at her. 'Why don't you bring in the cheese and desserts together, Liz, and join us?'

Liz looked doubtful but Tim smiled at her. 'Please do.'

Liz smiled back. 'I'd love to.'

She put on the coffee and took the soufflés out of the fridge. She added some grapes to the side of the cheese board and filled a silver basket with home-made biscuits. Edward's Denby china coffee service and a plate of petits fours stood on a silver tray in readiness. She carried in the tray of desserts first and went back for the cheese. Edward had already set the heavy crystal decanter of vintage port and the bottle of Beaume de Venise on the table. Decorum was forgotten as the guests eyed the dessert and Liz smiled as she served.

When he'd finished eating, Edward slipped out of the room and returned with the coffee tray.

After scraping up the last morsel of her dessert, Jenny put down her spoon and sank back in her chair. 'I don't think I'll be able to eat for a week.'

'It was a lovely meal,' Mrs Bacoux agreed seriously.

'You used to work in Chez Nous?' her husband asked.

'Liz started the business with her husband,' Edward interjected quickly. 'I firmly believe that it was her desserts that secured them the Michelin Star!'

Everyone laughed and Liz felt her cheeks get hot. 'I left the restaurant some years ago to look after my daughter. Now I'm interested in a different challenge. Also, in the current economic environment, I believe there are a lot of people who want to entertain at home but just don't have the time.'

'Amen to that,' Susan Wallace said. 'I'm long overdue

COLETTE CADDLE

to give a dinner party but with all my commuting to London I just don't have time. We must have a little chat later, Liz.'

Liz nodded eagerly and Jenny flashed her a triumphant smile. Philippe asked her about the restaurant scene in Dublin and Liz talked knowledgeably, forgetting her shyness now they were on a topic that she loved.

Three hours later, tired but happy, she packed away the last of her equipment in the back of the van. Edward was helping Jenny into her coat when she returned.

'Well done again,' Jenny said. 'You were amazing. I'll call you during the week.'

'Drive carefully, Jen,' Edward said as he held the car door for her. 'And thanks again.'

'No problem,' Jenny assured him. 'I'll be your hostess any time if I get to eat food like that! Seeya.'

They waved her off and returned to the kitchen.

'I'd better be off myself,' Liz said, regretful that the evening had come to an end.

Edward took her hand and led her into the living-room. 'Not yet. Let's have a cognac first. I'm too wound up to sleep.'

Liz curled up on the sofa while he poured the drinks. 'Was it really okay, Edward?'

'Stop fishing for compliments. You know it was.' He handed her a drink and stretched out beside her. 'You were a big hit with Philippe, that's for sure.'

'He's an interesting man, though a little overbearing.'

Edward laughed. 'He's not an easy man to do business with. He thinks we're all philistines who don't understand the restaurant business.'

Liz frowned. 'He can't say that about you. You're part-owner of one of Dublin's most successful restaurants.'

'Well, until tonight he thought that was merely a wise investment. Now he knows different. Thanks, Liz. It's all down to you.'

'I think that might be an exaggeration, Edward, but thank you. I've really enjoyed myself.' She looked around the living-room appreciatively. The fire was nothing more than glowing embers now, but it cast a warm glow on the rich buttermilk walls and cream rug. 'This is a lovely room. Did you decorate it yourself?'

There was a small silence. Liz looked at the closed expression on Edward's face. 'I'm sorry, I didn't mean to pry.'

'Not at all, Liz. Christina, my fiancée, decorated it.'

Liz stared at him. 'I didn't know you had one,' she said, feeling slightly shocked. How come Annie or Jenny had never mentioned her?

'I don't. That is, I did.' Edward passed a weary hand across his eyes. 'She died.'

'I'm sorry,' Liz said, not knowing what else to say.

Edward looked at her over the rim of his glass. 'She was killed in a car crash. She was with my brother-in-law at the time.'

It took Liz a moment for the pieces to click into place. 'Jenny's husband? Oh, God, Edward. I'm so sorry.' She reached over and touched his hand.

Edward gave a short laugh. 'Yeah, well. It's a long time ago now.'

'Had you any idea? Did you suspect anything?'

'No. Like you I thought we were perfectly happy. Don't get me wrong, it was a stormy relationship. We broke up more than a dozen times. Christina used to say it was what made us so great together. I kept asking her to marry me, to settle down, but she said life was too short. Then after one particularly angry bust-up, she came back, we made up yet again and she said she wanted to get married. In hindsight, I realised that her change of heart coincided with my becoming a partner.'

Liz looked at the bitterness in his eyes. 'Don't think like that, Edward. You were together a long time. I'm sure she must have loved you.'

'Maybe, but the money and status definitely helped. It was harder for Jen. She was crazy about Finbarr and couldn't believe he'd been unfaithful. It took her a while to accept it. She came up with all sorts of excuses as to why they might have been together. Then she blamed Christina. Mind you, she's probably right there. Christina loved to live dangerously.'

Liz squeezed his hand. 'I can't begin to imagine how you felt. I was devastated over Chris, and I don't even know that he actually did anything.'

Edward watched her steadily. 'You do know, Liz. You knew that night.'

Liz thought for a moment and then nodded. 'You're right. The bastard!'

Edward laughed. 'That's a good healthy attitude.'

Liz laughed too and gestured to the elegant room they were sitting in. 'Well, whatever else about Christina, she had good taste. But I'm surprised you wanted to stay in this house. It must have a lot of painful memories.'

Edward shrugged. 'It's been my home for fifteen years. I love it here. I was quite happy with the decor the way it was but Christina thought it was boring. It was easier to give in.'

Liz looked at him with raised eyebrows. 'I can't imagine you ever giving in to anyone!'

Edward pulled her close and smiled down into her eyes. 'Oh, you'd be surprised.'

Liz held her breath. His lips were very close and she had a sudden urge to pull his head down to hers. 'I'd better be going.'

'Oh, no.' Edward held her as she attempted to stand up. 'Not like that, Liz. I played all my games with Christina. I want everything to be out in the open between us.'

She watched him silently.

'I am very, very fond of you, Liz, and I know you're not ready for a relationship yet. I can understand that. That's why I wanted to tell you about Christina. I've been there. And I would never do anything to hurt you or Lucy.'

Liz's eyes filled up and she hugged him quickly. 'I know that, Edward, and I'm very grateful. But I won't lie to you. I'm not ready to get involved with anyone. I feel so much better these days, but right now I want to concentrate on Lucy and my new business. I need to feel in control again.'

Edward took her hand and kissed the tips of her fingers. 'I really admire you, Liz. You're an amazing woman.'

She flushed. 'I don't know about that but I'm certainly going to try and make a go of things and then, well, maybe . . .'

'Sssh. Don't. I'm not going anywhere. Let's agree to be best friends and just take things as they come.'

Liz smiled. 'Best friends. I'd like that.'

Chapter Forty-four

Stephanie walked through the restaurant, tweaking the odd napkin and polishing a place setting. Except for the faint smell of paint, everything was back to normal and they would reopen their doors tomorrow. It was good to have a few normal days before the official reopening next week. It would give them time to iron out any glitches. She moved into the passage that had been fully redecorated and now boasted a new storeroom. The banisters of the new mahogany staircase gleamed and a rich dark green carpet covered the stairs. The same carpet was used in the new private dining room upstairs. Stephanie went into the kitchen and smiled in satisfaction at the hive of activity before her. Kitchen porters were running everywhere, and Conor was going through the vegetable order.

She picked her way through the madness. 'Isn't Kevin here yet?' It was supposed to be the new chef de partie's first day.

Conor grinned. 'Been and gone. I've sent him out to get a few things from the Asian Market.'

'I see. How's it going?'

'Not too bad. One of the freezers is on the blink, but there's a guy on his way over to take a look at it. The meat is due in half an hour and the fish will be here first thing in the morning.'

'Right. Well, if you need me, I'll be in the office.' She went upstairs and paused to check the ladies' toilets. The cleaners had got rid of all the dust and paint marks and polished everything until it shone. A pile of new fluffy lemon towels sat on a wicker shelf next to the washbasins, and tissues, handcream and perfume stood on the dressing table. Several lemon satin cushions sat in the matching wicker chair. Stephanie looked around her, pleased with the overall effect. She left the room and went into the new dining-room. She'd asked a friend in the antiques business to watch out for a suitable table and Terry had done her proud. The dark mahogany table was substantial and impressive. It had been expensive but Terry had picked up thirty chairs to complement it and got them at a bargain price. They were a cheaper wood, but stained to match the table and they were upholstered in rich cream and green paisley brocade. The walls were also dark green and the skirting boards and door were a pristine white. Stephanie had added bowls of flowers, six silver candelabras and some prints of Irish landscapes. The overall effect was of an old-fashioned sophisticated dining-room in a private house.

She closed the door and went back to her office. A good clean and a lick of paint had restored the room to its former state and a new filing cabinet stood in the corner. It was almost as if the fire had never happened. Almost. She sat down at her desk and reviewed her 'To Do' list. There was a Health and Safety official arriving in an hour but she wasn't expecting any problems as the insurance company had already inspected every nook and cranny. When he was gone, she would address the staff. There was a week to go before the official opening but it was likely that some critics would pay a visit before then. Among them, no doubt, would be representatives of the *Michelin Guide*. She must remind the staff to watch out for them.

There was a sharp rap on the door and Liam Dunne stuck his head around it. 'Hi there.'

'Liam! I wasn't expecting you yet.'

He perched on the edge of her desk. 'I wanted to have a look around and settle in before my troops arrived.'

'I hope they're going to work out,' Steph said anxiously.

'Well, all we were short of doing was inspecting their toenails,' he said with a grin. 'Don't worry. They're coming from good restaurants and we've personal references on all of them.'

'True. I want to mention to them the likelihood of visiting critics in the next couple of weeks.'

'I've already warned them but I did say that the service must be outstanding regardless.'

Steph smiled at the earnest young man. What a difference to Sam! 'That's what I like to hear.'

'Right, well, I'll get to work.'

He ran down the stairs whistling and Steph thought how nice it was to have things back to normal again. The phone rang beside her.

'Stephanie West?'

'It's Sean Adams, boss,' Liam's new assistant Brian put the call through.

'Sean?'

'Hiya, Steph. How's it going?'

'Very well but that probably means I've forgotten something.'

Sean laughed. 'Murphy's Law. Listen, will you be in tonight?'

'Well, I've a meeting with Conor and Liam, but I should be home by about eight. I was planning an early night though. Tomorrow's going to be a busy day.'

'Oh, I see. It's just that Karen and Billy are up for a few days and I was going to ask them over.'

Steph groaned inwardly. 'Oh, I don't know, Sean. I'm really knackered—'

'Fine,' he said abruptly. 'I'll take them out. See you.'

'Sean? Sean?' Steph heard the dial tone and hung up. Shit! That's all she needed. God, his timing was incredible. Her phone rang again but this time it was the wine merchant's. She turned her attention back to work and forgot all about Sean and his family.

Stephanie looked around the room. 'Any other questions? No? Conor, have you anything to add?'

Conor smiled at the staff. 'I'd just like to say a word of thanks to everyone for all the hard work. The fire was a terrible business but we can put it behind us now and concentrate on putting Chez Nous firmly back on the map.'

'Hear, hear!' John Quigly said in an uncharacteristic burst of enthusiasm. He flushed as Steph stared at him in surprise.

'I'd also like to wish Stephanie all the very best,' Conor continued. 'And to assure her that I will be working my butt off.'

'You'd better!' Steph retorted to cover her embarrassment and everyone laughed. 'Okay folks, let's call it a night. Go home and get some rest, and we'll see you tomorrow. Oh, by the way, for those of you on the early shift, we'll be having a small celebration tomorrow night after closing. You're welcome to come back in – if you have the energy.'

There was a small cheer and the staff started to gather their belongings.

'Conor? Liam? Can we have a quick word in my office?' Stephanie led the way upstairs. 'Well, Conor. Are we ready?' she asked as she sat down at her desk.

Conor stretched out in a chair. 'I think so. I don't foresee any problems in the kitchen.' He glanced sideways at Liam. 'It's the new waiters I'm worried about.'

Liam reddened. 'There's no need. They know what they have to do and they're all very experienced.'

Steph shot a warning glance at Conor. Why was there always this aggravation between kitchen and front-of-house staff? She sighed. 'I'm sure everything will go smoothly.'

An hour later, she locked up and headed for the car. She was tired but happy that things were back to normal. She wondered guiltily what Sean was doing. She should really have called him back. She looked at her watch. Seven thirty. It wasn't too late. She punched Sean's number in on her mobile, but his phone was switched off. Damn. Oh, well, she'd have to think of some way of making it up to him. Maybe he could bring Karen and Billy into the restaurant for lunch tomorrow. Yes, that would be brilliant! She hummed happily to herself as she turned into the driveway but stopped abruptly when she saw Billy standing on the doorstep, his hand held by a beautiful red-head. Karen. Stephanie got out of the car and smiled nervously. 'Hello, Billy. Karen?'

The girl nodded. 'Yes. Hello, Stephanie, sorry for turning up like this. I'm afraid we missed Sean.'

'Not to worry. Come on inside and we'll try to get in touch with him.' She opened the door and led the way into the hall. 'Where were you supposed to meet?'

'Outside McDonald's in Grafton Street at six, but we got held up.'

'Mummy got lost,' Billy said loudly.

Karen swatted his behind. 'Yes, I got lost. I admit it. I always do when I come to Dublin,' she said ruefully.

Steph laughed. 'I'm the same in Cork – all those one-way streets. Where are you staying? Maybe Sean went there.'

'Yeah, maybe. We're staying in Jury's. Can I use your phone and check?'

Steph waved her towards the phone in the hall and took Billy into the kitchen for Coke and biscuits. 'So, Billy. What do you want to do while you're in Dublin?'

'Go to the zoo,' he said without hesitation.

'It may disappoint you after Fota Park.'

'Naw. They've got snakes and stuff like that. It'll be cool.'

Steph laughed. It was uncanny the resemblance between Billy and his father. He had his mother's fiery mop, but apart from that he was his father's son. The same amazing brown eyes stared back at her and he ruffled his hair in the same impatient way.

Karen walked into the kitchen. 'He was there all right. He left word for me to call his mobile but I tried that and couldn't get through.'

'Me neither. His battery must be flat. Did you leave word in case he called again?'

'Yes. I said we were here. But I don't want to hang around, Stephanie. I know you've a busy day tomorrow.'

Steph flushed guiltily. 'Not at all. Having you here gives me a good excuse to open a bottle of wine. Billy, would you like to watch TV?' Steph led the little boy into the living-room and when he was happily engrossed in *The Simpsons*, she returned to the kitchen and opened the wine.

'Well, it's nice to finally meet you.' Karen took the glass from Stephanie. 'But again, I'm sorry for just landing on you like this. I'm sure it's the last thing that you need tonight of all nights.'

Steph smiled. 'Don't worry about it, I could do with the company. It stops me worrying about what might go wrong tomorrow.'

'You must be thrilled to be back in business again. What with the fire and everything you've had a terrible time. I was so sorry to hear about your miscarriage.'

For some reason the thought of Sean discussing her miscarriage with his former wife made Steph very uncomfortable. 'Thanks,' she said with a forced smile.

'Tomorrow isn't the official opening, is it?'

'No. The decorators were finished earlier than expected so we decided to open for regular business. The official opening is next week. I'll be on Prozac by then!'

Karen laughed. 'I don't know how you do it. I'd never be able to handle that kind of responsibility and pressure. Billy causes me enough stress as it is!'

Steph's expression softened. 'I'm not sure I really believe that. He's a great kid. Sean enjoyed his weekend in Cork and he's really looking forward to spending a lot more time with him.'

'They've become a lot closer and I must say it will make life easier for me if Sean starts to play a more active part in Billy's life.'

'How do you mean?' Steph said.

'Well, my partner, Mike, asked me to marry him but I wasn't sure how it would affect Billy. But if Sean plans to be around a bit more, I think it will be okay.'

'In that case, congratulations.' For some reason the idea of Karen safely married to someone else made Steph feel a lot happier. 'We'll be happy to have Billy here any time. Sean's planning to convert the attic into a special room for him.'

Karen looked at her curiously. Sean obviously hadn't told Stephanie her views on Billy staying in Dublin. 'That's nice,' she murmured.

'So when are you getting married?'

'Oh, as soon as we can get organised, I think. Now that the divorce is through there's no reason to wait.'

Steph stared at her and then looked away quickly. 'That's true. Well, I hope it all works out for you.'

Karen saw the look of surprise on Stephanie's face and realised she'd put her foot in it. Why in God's name hadn't Sean told Stephanie about the divorce? Maybe everything wasn't rosy in the garden after all.

The phone interrupted the awkward silence. Steph picked up the extension in the kitchen. 'Hello? Hi, Sean. Yes, I know, they're here. Okay. Yeah. Okay, see you then. Bye.' Steph hung up. 'He's on his way. Now, tell me. Does Billy still love fried chicken?'

'By the bucketful,' Karen said with a grin.

'Right. Then that's what we'll have for dinner.' She went over to the freezer.

'Oh no, Steph, it's okay, we'll go out—'

'Nonsense,' Steph said firmly. 'It will do me good to keep busy. Anyway I'm starving and I love fried chicken too.'

'You're not really nervous about tomorrow, are you?' Karen was surprised. This beautiful and sophisticated woman looked like very little would rattle her.

'A bit. It's silly, really. I know it will be a total anti-climax. By the way, why don't you and Billy come to lunch tomorrow? I'd love you to see the place and it would give Billy a chance to spend some time with Sean.'

Karen looked surprised. 'Well, I don't know . . .'

'You'd be doing me a favour. I could do with filling another table! And I can promise Billy a kid's special.'

Karen smiled. 'Well, okay, why not? I've never eaten in a restaurant with a Michelin Star before.'

'Well, I'll make sure we live up to your expectations. Let me know what time suits you and I'll set it up.'

By the time Sean arrived the smell of fried chicken filled the house and the two women were working together and chatting comfortably.

'Hi, Sean,' Steph said with forced casualness. 'Grab your son and sit down. Dinner's ready.'

After a fairly relaxed meal, Sean waved Karen and Billy off, having agreed to pick them up for lunch at one the next day.

'Thanks, Steph,' he said as he climbed into bed beside her. He reached for her but she slipped out of his reach.

'No problem. Night, Sean.'

He looked at her back, puzzled. What had he done now?

Chapter Forty-five

'Stephanie? Can I bring in a party of six for lunch, at, say, twelve-thirty?'

'Absolutely, Edward, I'll be happy to fill another table.'

Edward frowned at his end of the phone. 'Is there a problem? You put the advertisement in *The Irish Times*, didn't you?'

'For the full week, but it is only Tuesday.'

'Right, well I'll see you later.'

Steph hung up, but before she lost the nerve she picked up the phone again. 'Hello? Mrs McCann? It's Stephanie West.'

'Oh hello, dear. How are you?'

'Fine thanks. Sorry I didn't call sooner but it's been really busy.'

'That's okay, Stephanie. So when are you coming to see me?'

Right down to business, Steph thought grimly. 'Well, next week is a bit hectic for me so I thought one afternoon the following week.'

'Oh, no, dear. I'm going over to visit my sister in Leeds.'

'Oh, well, it can wait until you get back—'

'No! Oh, no, love. I can't wait until then. What about next Tuesday?'

'Oh, no, you see that's the day—'

'Please, Stephanie. I won't keep you long. I'll meet you in town if it's too much trouble for you to come out here.'

Steph cringed at Joan's reproachful tone. Why, of all days, did she have to pick the day of the official reopening? It was going to be hectic. She couldn't possibly get away.

'Please, Stephanie,' Joan said again.

Steph thought about her last conversation with Ruth. She had begged her to come over but Steph hadn't had time. 'Okay, that's fine. Say about three?'

'I'll have the kettle on. See you then, dear.'

Steph hung up. She didn't know which scared her more. The thought of confronting Joan McCann or breaking the news to Liam and Conor that she had to disappear for a couple of hours on such an important day. The phone rang again, making her jump.

'Hi, Steph. Are you all set?'

'Hi, Liz. Yeah, I think so. Although it's going to be very quiet. We've only filled five tables for lunch and two of them are Edward and Sean.'

'And Annie and me make six. Is one thirty okay?'

'Great! A few more relatives and friends and I might actually fill the place.'

Liz heard the nervousness in Steph's voice. 'Don't worry, Steph. It's only the first day.'

'Yeah, I know.'

'Listen, did you see yesterday's *Independent*?'

'No, why, was there something important?'

'Adam Cullen's piece on me and Chris.'

'Oh, Liz, I completely forgot! Was it okay?'

'It was great, Steph. I'll bring it with me at lunch-time and let you have a look at it.'

'Oh, do! This will really take the pressure off you.'

'Hopefully. Listen, I have to go. I'll see you later.'

As Steph hung up Liam walked in and slumped into a chair. 'It's going to be a very quiet lunch,' he said glumly.

'It won't be too bad, Liam. I've just booked in two more parties. One of six and one of two.'

'Great stuff. And things are looking good for tonight. A couple of Americans just stuck their heads in and made a booking – a party of ten, no less.'

'That's brilliant! Well, I have to go down to talk to Conor. I'll tell him the good news.'

'Good luck,' Liam said darkly.

Steph frowned. 'Problems?'

Liam shrugged. 'Let's say things are a little fraught in the kitchen.'

She grinned. 'I'd be worried if they weren't. Chefs work best when the adrenalin's pumping. Anyway, this is Conor's first big day.'

'But he's been practically running the place for the last year,' Liam pointed out.

'True, but it wasn't his name on the menu. I'll go and have a word. You'd better get back downstairs. It's your first day too, you know!'

'On my way.' Liam shot her a nervous look.

Steph smiled as she watched him take the stairs two at a time in front of her. It was ominously quiet in the kitchen apart from the sound of chopping and stirring. 'Everything okay?' she said brightly.

There were a few mumbles and Conor just looked at her. Oh dear. 'Conor?'

'I'm not happy with the turbot and the avocados aren't ripe enough.'

Steph swallowed hard. Conor was in the driving-seat now and she wasn't going to bail him out. 'You checked the vegetables yourself,' she reminded him.

'I know that,' Conor said through gritted teeth.

'So what are you going to do?' she asked quietly.

He looked surprised.

'It's your kitchen, Conor.'

He nodded and thought for a minute. 'The turbot is too small but if I add some prawns and caviar to the dish it should be okay. And I suppose the avocados aren't too bad. We'll put them in the microwave for a few seconds and see if that helps. If not, I'll puree them with some cream and lemon.'

Steph smiled. 'Good. Well, I'll leave you to it. Good luck everyone.'

There was a more cheerful response this time and she left the kitchen with a grin on her face. In the dining-room a waiter was putting out vases on each table, a single yellow rose in each. Winter sunshine flooded the room making it look warm and welcoming. 'Liam? I think it would be nice if we offered our customers a welcoming apéritif on the house. Just to celebrate our first day. What do you think?'

'Good idea,' Liam agreed.

Steph checked her watch. Thirty minutes to go before opening. She picked up glasses and forks, ignoring Liam's hurt expression. He grinned triumphantly when she found no faults.

'Good luck, everyone,' she said and went upstairs feeling ever so slightly dispensable.

She was back down at the door to greet Edward when he arrived, accompanied by one of his partners and four clients. Stephanie guided them to a circular table towards the back of the room and Liam arrived to offer them drinks.

'Everything okay?' Edward asked quietly, taking in the table for two nearby – the only other occupants.

'Fine,' Steph assured him, trying to look confident. 'There are twenty-five covers booked.'

He frowned. 'Is that good?'

Steph grinned. 'It's all right. Enjoy your lunch.'

Brian moved quietly to her side as she moved in behind the front desk. 'Stephanie? I think that man over there may be a journalist or something.'

'Oh?' Steph took a discreet look.

'Yeah. He looks vaguely familiar, and he asked a lot of detailed questions about the menu.'

'Right, well you know what to do, Brian. Make sure he leaves with a smile on his face. And Brian? Well spotted.'

Brian beamed at her. 'Thanks, boss.'

Karen helped Billy into the back of the car and when she'd shut the door again turned back to Sean. 'Sean, before you get in I just wanted to tell you something.'

Sean smiled in at Billy who was waving at them impatiently to get in. 'What is it, Karen?'

Karen sighed. 'I'm afraid I may have dropped you in it with Stephanie.'

'Oh?'

'Yes. I mentioned that the divorce had come through.'

'Oh,' Sean said again.

Karen looked at her ex-husband in frustration. 'Why didn't you tell her?'

'I don't know,' Sean started. 'No, I do know,' he contradicted himself, suddenly angry. 'I didn't tell her because she wouldn't be interested. Just like I didn't tell her why Billy wasn't coming to stay. She'd think I was trying to pressure her into marriage. Well, I'm not. If she marries me it has to be because she wants to, and I don't think she does.'

'I'm sure you're wrong,' Karen said, looking in at Billy's face staring curiously out at them.

'You hardly know her,' he said curtly. 'Please don't try and sort out my love life on the basis of one evening's conversation, Karen.'

'Sorry I spoke.' Karen went round to the passenger door.

Sean dragged a hand through his hair and got in to the car. 'I'm sorry. It's not your fault. It's just a bit of a sore point,' he murmured.

'I didn't mean to interfere.'

He smiled apologetically at her. 'I know. Right, let's go eat. I'm starving. What about you, champ?'

'Yeah, Dad, but I'd prefer to go to McDonald's.'

'Don't be rude, Billy,' Karen admonished.

'Sorry,' Billy muttered but grinned when Sean winked at him.

'I tell you what, Billy. If you don't like your lunch, we'll go to McDonald's later.'

'Cool!'

Karen gave Sean a dirty look.

'But I know he'll like his lunch,' he assured her. 'Trust me.'

The restaurant was humming by the time Annie and Liz walked in. They paused briefly to say hello to Edward on the way to their table and then settled down to take in the atmosphere.

'It's very busy,' Annie said excitedly.

Liz nodded. 'They must have had some late bookings. They'd only five when I talked to Steph earlier.'

Annie did a quick count. 'Well, I count ten tables now, oh and here comes Sean, that's eleven. Is that Billy with him? Gosh, he's got so big and ... who's that?'

'It must be Karen,' Liz whispered as she returned Sean's wave. 'Oh, she's pretty, isn't she?'

'Mm. They look very good together.'

'Don't worry, Annie. She's got a man.'

Annie smiled in relief. 'Oh, good. Now let's have a look at the menus. I'm starving.'

'Good afternoon, ladies. Can I get you a drink on the house?'

'Steph! How's it going? The place looks great.' Annie squeezed her hand.

'So far, so good. Listen, let me get your drinks organised and then I'll come back and talk to you when things calm down a bit. Wine?'

Lovely. I see Sean's here with his family,' Liz said.

Steph cringed at the word 'family'. 'Yes, I'd better go and say hello. Talk to you later.'

Annie watched her depart. 'Something's up.'

'Why do you say that?'

'Dunno. Just a feeling.'

'Hi folks.' Steph looked down at Sean with his wife – ex-wife – and son. 'Are you being looked after okay? Can I get you a drink?'

'That's okay, Liam's getting them,' Sean told her. 'Everything seems to be going well.'

Steph crossed her fingers. 'So far, so good.'

'The restaurant looks lovely, Stephanie.' Karen looked around in admiration. 'You've created a wonderful atmosphere.'

'Thanks, Karen.'

'It's getting quite busy now,' Sean remarked as another party arrived.

'Yes, thank goodness.' Steph avoided his eyes and turned her attention to his son. 'How are you doing, Billy?'

'Okay. Do they do burgers here, Steph?' He looked around doubtfully.

'Billy! Don't be so rude!' Karen shrugged apologetically. 'Sorry, Steph, you know kids.'

'No problem.' Steph crouched down beside the child. 'You leave it to me, Billy. I'll see what I can do.' She winked at the little boy and went straight into the kitchen.

Conor was moving between his chefs, inspecting dishes and barking orders. 'Marc! That sauce needs more seasoning. Pat! Surely that duck is done by now. Jim! Get a move on with those vegetables, for Christ's sake! My granny moves quicker than you do.'

The young commis blushed profusely as Conor stood over him.

Steph approached her chef nervously. 'Conor?'

'Steph? Yes?' Conor acknowledged absently.

'That very special young customer I was telling you about is here.'

Conor grinned. 'Is he now? Right then, one Conor O'Brien special coming up. Pat? I've got a special order I want you to look after.' He winked at Steph. Now that he was in the middle of the lunch rush, Conor was suddenly relaxed. This was what he was good at. This was what he loved.

Steph left the kitchen shaking her head. It was strange the way different people reacted to pressure. Thankfully Conor seemed to thrive on it – lucky for Billy! There weren't many head chefs who would stoop to cooking burger, fries and baked beans!

Sean was waiting for her in the hallway. 'It seems to be going well.'

'Yes.'

'What's wrong, Steph?'

'Oh, Sean, this is hardly the time for a chat.'

'Fine, then when?'

She sighed. 'We can talk tonight.'

'What time will you be home?' he persisted.

'I should be out by midnight.'

Sean sighed. 'Right. I'll wait up.'

'You don't have to,' she said moodily.

'I want to.'

'Right. Well, I'd better get back to work.' She made her way through the restaurant to the front desk. The man that Brian thought was a journalist was just leaving. 'Was everything all right?' she asked with a polite smile.

'Fine, thank you. I'm glad that you're open again. My compliments to your new chef.'

'Well, thank you very much. I'll pass that on. He isn't new, actually. Conor O'Brien has been with us for nearly three years but he's recently taken over as head chef.'

He nodded. 'Yes, from Chris Connolly. Tell me, isn't that his wife over there?'

Steph looked at him curiously. 'Yes, it is. Liz has actually just started a new business herself. A home catering silver service, associated with Chez Nous.'

'And what's her husband doing now?'

Steph frowned. What was this guy really after? Gossip? 'Chris has moved to pastures new in Galway. You seem very well informed, sir. Are you in the business?'

He smiled. 'No, no, just interested. Well, I'd better be going. See you again.' He collected his companion and left.

'So what do you think?' Liam was immediately at her side.

Steph frowned. 'He has to be from the press. He certainly asked enough questions and he knew Liz. What was his name?'

'Well, the booking was in the name of Jones, and he paid by cash so I'm afraid that's all we've got.'

'Well, make a note of it anyway. Is there anyone else asking questions?'

'The party of four at table 8 all ordered different dishes and they seem to have spent a long time discussing them.'

'Right, well, make sure someone keeps a close eye on them. Don't wait until they ask for service—'

'I know, pre-empt the request.' Liam repeated the mantra that Steph had drummed into them. 'Will do.'

Steph patted him on the back and went over to

join Annie and Liz who were just starting their main courses.

'This is wonderful, Steph,' Liz said through a mouthful of turbot. 'I love the addition of the prawns and the caviar.'

Steph grinned as she thought of Conor's minor crisis. 'Yes, Conor is adding a few of his own touches here and there. How's the venison, Annie?'

'Lovely, Steph. Though I hate to think of the number of calories in the sauce.'

'Then don't,' Liz retorted. 'We're here to enjoy ourselves. I got another booking, Steph, dinner for twelve. You'll never guess who.'

'I give up.' Steph poured herself a glass of water.

'None other than our Minister for Finance.'

Steph chuckled. 'Well, at least he should be able to pay his bill. Sorry, Liz, that's great news,' she added hurriedly. 'You'll get a lot of referral business out of that one.'

'That's what I said,' Annie chipped in.

'So let's have a look at this article, then,' Steph demanded.

Liz rummaged in her bag, produced a piece of paper and handed it reverently to Steph.

Steph read the article in silence and smiled contentedly as she gave it back. 'That's great, Liz. He gives you a great plug, doesn't he?'

Liz grinned. 'Yeah, I don't think Chris was too impressed.'

'He doesn't come out of it too bad,' Annie remarked.

'You don't know Chris,' Liz remarked drily. 'He'll count the words of praise each of us got, and be rightly pissed off if I come out on top.'

'Sod him,' Steph said cheerfully.

Liz laughed. 'Tell me – that guy who just left, who was he? He looked familiar.'

'He knew you too. I don't know who he was. The booking was in the name of Jones. We suspect he's a journalist.'

Liz frowned. 'He's definitely familiar.'

Steph stood up. 'If you remember let me know. Time for me to circulate again. Enjoy your meal.'

Edward's table were rising to leave when Steph approached. 'Was everything all right?' she asked Edward anxiously.

'Wonderful,' he whispered back with a broad smile. 'Tell Conor they said that the food is even better than before.'

'Maybe that's because they were sitting with one of the new owners,' Steph said cynically.

Edward raised an eyebrow. 'You mean you don't agree?'

Steph flushed. 'Touché.'

He grinned. 'I'll call you tomorrow. I hope dinner goes as well as lunch.'

'Thanks, Edward, bye.'

Steph walked him to the door and then went to check on Sean's table. 'So, Billy, how's lunch?'

'Better than McDonald's,' he said through a mouthful of fries.

'High praise indeed,' she said, sitting down beside him. Karen and Sean were just finishing their starters. Liam had brought Billy's main course at the same time so that the child wouldn't get bored. Steph made a mental note to thank him for his thoughtfulness.

'This is all so wonderful, Steph,' Karen said, her

eyes wide. 'The roulade was great and the bread is melt-in-the-mouth.'

'John Quigly, our pastry chef is a very odd man but a genius when it comes to bread and pastries. Wait till you taste dessert.'

'Will you join us for coffee?' Sean said hopefully.

'If I can,' Steph said and walked quickly away. She had no intention of joining them. They looked like a family, a happy family at that and she felt very much the outsider. The wicked stepmother. And every time she saw the tenderness in Sean's eyes when he looked at Billy she felt a knot in her stomach. He was a reminder of what they'd lost. She wondered if Sean was having second thoughts about leaving his family in Cork behind. Maybe that's why he hadn't told her his divorce had come through. Maybe life with her in Dublin – just the two of them – was no longer what he wanted. Maybe he'd finally had enough of her. She sighed miserably and attempted to turn her thoughts back to her work. Her efforts were better employed in the restaurant. At least she seemed to be making a success of this.

Chapter Forty-six

Billy sat in the foyer of Jury's kicking the edge of the table with his trainer. He'd had a great week in Dublin with his dad – even that posh restaurant had been fun – and he didn't want to go home.

'Billy! Stop kicking the table or we'll be thrown out.'

Billy looked up at him with sad eyes. 'When will you come to see me again, Dad?'

Sean squatted down beside him. 'Before Christmas, I promise.'

Billy's eyes lit up. 'Will you take me into town to see the Christmas lights?'

'Sure. And we'd better go and see Santa Claus to make sure he knows where you live.'

Billy looked at him scornfully. 'Of course he does, Dad. He's been coming to our house for years.'

Sean grinned at him. 'So what are you going to ask him for?'

Billy considered the question seriously. 'A mountain bike, I think.'

'Good choice,' Sean said. 'And what would you like me to buy you?'

Billy looked up at his father hopefully. 'A Sony Playstation?'

Sean pretended to look horrified. 'A Playstation? Have you any idea how much those things cost? Your poor dad could never afford one of them.'

Billy's head drooped. 'Sorry,' he mumbled.

Karen thanked the receptionist and walked over to join them. 'Well, we're all set. Go to the toilet before we leave, Billy.'

'Don't want to.'

'Billy,' she said, a warning in her voice.

Billy slouched off towards the gents'.

'Thanks, Sean. It's been great.'

'No problem. I told Billy I'd be down before Christmas. I'll give you a call and let you know when. By the way, we were just talking about Christmas presents.'

'Oh yes?'

'He wants a mountain bike off Santa.'

'Thank God for that. I was afraid he'd changed his mind again.'

'I'll organise it if you like.'

Karen looked a bit uncomfortable. 'Oh, sorry, Sean, I've already bought it. Mike helped me.'

Sean tried to hide his disappointment and his irrational envy of Mike. He'd quite liked the idea of going in search of the best bike for his son. 'No problem. He wants me to get him a Sony Playstation.'

'He asked me too but I told him it was too expensive,' Karen said, shaking her head.

Sean grinned. 'That's what I said, but I'll get it anyway.'

'Are you sure?'

'Yeah. It will save me trying to think of something. I'll take the lazy way out. You don't mind, do you?'

'No, no. I'm sure you can afford it and he will be

chuffed. Why don't you bring Stephanie with you on your next visit?'

Sean studied his shoes. 'We'll see.'

Karen sighed. 'Will you for God's sake talk to the girl, Sean, and straighten things out.'

'Yeah, I will.'

Karen laughed.

He looked up questioningly. 'What?'

'Oh, I was just thinking that I'm probably the last person who should be advising you on your love life.'

Sean laughed too. 'I suppose.'

Billy ran up. 'Ready.'

'Right, let's go.'

Sean carried their bags to the car, kissed Karen and hugged his son. After he'd made sure that Billy was securely strapped into the back seat, he walked around to the driver's door. 'Drive carefully.'

'I will. Bye.'

He stood waving until they disappeared into the afternoon traffic and then made his way to his own car. Talk to Stephanie. It sounded so easy, so straightforward. Easier said than done, though.

He'd planned to talk to her that night that he'd taken Karen and Billy to Chez Nous. But when she finally got home, she said she was too tired to talk. He'd tried again the next morning. Tried to explain about the divorce, but she'd waved away his explanations saying it was none of her business anyway. None of her business? They were living together, for God's sake! Sometimes she seemed like a total stranger to him.

He drummed the steering wheel angrily as he replayed the conversation in his head. He couldn't take much more of this. When Steph had moved back in after the miscarriage things had been a lot better between them. Now the restaurant was open again and things should be looking up for them. So what was going wrong this time? Maybe it was Ruth's mother getting in touch after all this time that had unnerved her. She did seem fairly rattled about it.

He started as the car behind blasted the horn. The light was green. He waved an apology, and on a sudden impulse he indicated, switched lanes and turned in the opposite direction. Talk to Steph? Well, there was no time like the present.

'Steph? Steph, I've just realised where I know that guy from.'

Steph tore her mind away from the invoices in front of her and tried to concentrate on the voice at the other end of the phone. 'Liz? Is that you? Slow down. What are you on about?'

'The mystery guy in the restaurant – Mr Jones?'

'Yes?'

'It was Mr *Godfrey* Jones, no less – affectionately known as God? You must know him, Steph. He's always on the box and he used to write a column for one of the British tabloids.'

'He did have an English accent, now that you mention it. Still, he's not much good to me.' Steph wasn't interested in ex-journalists – especially ones based in a different country.

'No, you don't understand. He moved to Wicklow a few months ago. For tax reasons I think. Anyway, he's been hired to write a food column for one of the Sunday papers.'

Steph's ears pricked up 'One of the Irish papers?'

'Yep. I'm not sure which one.'

'So Chez Nous is going to be his first victim.'

'Don't be so pessimistic. Everything went like clock-work on Tuesday. I'm sure you'll get a great write-up.'

'I hope so.'

'It doesn't really matter what he says,' Liz said matter-of-factly. 'If he raves about you, everyone will come along just to find fault. And if he criticises you, they'll get all patriotic and try to prove him wrong.'

Steph laughed. 'That's true.'

'And any publicity—'

'Is good publicity,' Steph finished. 'You're right.'

'Of course I'm right. Well, I must dash. I've work to do. I'll call you on Sunday. Good luck.'

'Thanks, Liz. Bye.' Steph hung up. She racked her brains for any possible faults the illustrious Mr Jones might have found, but could think of none. She shook her head impatiently. There was no point worrying about it. He'd write what he would write and she was going to have to get used to seeing things in print that upset her. It came with the job. 'Do your worst, Mr Jones. Do your worst.'

Conor cursed and emptied the contents of the pan into the bin. It was his third attempt at that sauce and he still wasn't happy with it. It had to be perfect for the opening. It was his big chance to show off new ideas. He pulled out a cigarette and lit it. Steph wouldn't let him make too many changes to the standard lunch and dinner menus – it was those recipes that had won them the Star. He'd have to introduce his own dishes gradually, establish himself, Steph said. He knew she was right but it was a bit frustrating. He'd hoped that once he was head chef he'd be able to do as he liked. It was a pain having to cook Chris's dishes every day. He ground out the cigarette after a few puffs and started again. He didn't have much time. The rest of the crew would be back soon to start preparing for dinner. He cursed when he heard banging on the front door. He ignored it, but the knock came again. He strode out front, cursing the interruption.

'Hi, Conor. Is Steph here?'

'She might be upstairs,' Conor said gruffly. 'Can you find your own way? I'm in the middle of something.'

Sean looked curiously at the normally good-humoured young chef. 'Sure. Thanks.' He took the stairs two at a time and pushed open the door. He studied Stephanie, who was completely unaware of him. She'd discarded the jacket of her black business suit and opened the top button of the grey silk shirt. Her hair was pushed back behind her ears and she was chewing distractedly on the top of her pen.

'Hi.'

Steph jumped, her blue eyes startled. 'Sean! Hi, what are you doing here? Is everything okay?'

'Fine.' He lowered himself into the chair in front of her. 'I just wanted to talk.'

Steph's stomach turned. 'Can't we do that at home, Sean?' she said, keeping her voice light and friendly, 'I've got so much to do.'

'I'm sorry to interrupt your work but this can't wait.'

Steph looked at the determined look on his face and put down her pen with a sigh. It seems she couldn't avoid a confrontation any longer. Was this it? Was he going to tell her it was over? Was he going to ask her to move out yet again? 'Okay, then,' she said, her voice barely a whisper.

'I'll start, shall I? About my divorce—'

'I told you there's no need to explain—'

'My divorce,' he continued, ignoring her, 'came through a week after you told me you were going to have an abortion. Strangely enough it didn't seem worth mentioning at the time.'

Steph cringed at the sarcasm in his voice.

He sighed. He hadn't meant to get nasty. 'The next time I saw you, you were in a hospital bed. I meant to tell you, of course, but it didn't seem very important any more.'

'That was two months ago,' Steph pointed out shakily.

'Yes it was. But, to be honest, you've been so unpredictable lately that I was afraid to tell you.'

'What do you mean unpredictable?' Steph protested.

'Oh, come on, love! You've been like a cat on a hot tin roof. I thought if I mentioned the divorce you'd think that I was trying to pressurise you into marriage and run a mile.'

Steph flushed. 'I'm sorry.'

'Me too. Now that we've got that out of the way, why don't you tell me what's been bothering you these last few weeks?'

She studied her crimson nails. 'What do you mean?'

'Is it the miscarriage? Is it the call from Joan McCann? You have to talk to me, Steph.'

Steph's expression was closed. 'There's nothing to say.'

'I think there is,' he persisted. 'It was my baby too, Steph. I'd like to talk about him.'

She managed a watery smile. 'It's "him", is it?'

He grinned back. 'Just an expression. I wouldn't mind a little girl.'

'You'd spoil her.'

'Of course.'

She sighed. 'Once I decided to keep the baby, I felt so happy, Sean, and I couldn't wait to tell you. You would have laughed at me. I kept studying myself in the mirror, willing my bump to get bigger! I was so confident, Sean. There was no problem I couldn't solve. I was sure that everything would work out. You and me, the restaurant— And then when I lost the baby . . .' Her eyes filled up.

He leaned over and brushed her hair back out of her eyes.

She took his hand and clutched it tightly. 'I can't believe how much it hurt,' she said shakily. 'Not physically – that might have made it easier. But there was hardly any pain at all. I just woke up and my baby was gone. It was like someone had played a horrible trick on me. I don't think I realised how much I wanted it until that moment. It probably seems silly to you. After all, I was only a few months pregnant.'

Sean looked at her, his eyes bright with tears. 'Don't, Steph. Don't do that to yourself. Don't play down the importance of it. It was our baby. Our baby died. Of course you were devastated, of course you grieved.'

Steph swallowed back the tears. 'I thought it might be a punishment.'

'For what?'

She looked at him, her eyes dark with grief. 'For letting Ruth and her baby die.'

Sean remembered Annie's words and realised just

how accurate she'd been. 'Oh, love, that wasn't your fault.'

Steph sniffed. 'I'm not so sure. I don't know what I believe any more.'

'Do you believe that I love you?' His eyes searched her face.

She touched his cheek, tenderly. 'Yes. Yes, I do. I just forgot for a while.'

'Then that's a start.'

'You were wrong though, Sean.'

He sighed dramatically. 'I should have known I'd be wrong about something.'

'The pills. I'm not hooked on them. I haven't taken any in about two weeks.'

'I'm sorry if I overreacted. I just worry about you.'

She dried her eyes. 'Well, don't. I'm a lot tougher than I look.'

'No, Steph. That's just it. You're not, and don't try to be. No one expects it. You're allowed to be sad. Now what about Joan McCann?'

'I see her next Tuesday.'

Sean's eyes widened. 'The day of the reception?'

Steph gave a wry smile. 'Yes, so don't ever accuse me of putting the job first again.'

'Would you like me to come with you?'

She shook her head. 'I'll be okay.'

'Well, if you change your mind . . .'

'Thanks, but I need to see her on my own.' She smiled tenderly at him, hardly able to believe how much better she felt. 'Was there anything else you wanted to talk about?'

Sean looked blank. 'I don't think so.'

She scowled at him. 'Are you sure?'

He pretended to think for a minute. 'Yep. But if you've something to say to *me* or to *ask* me . . .'

She leaned over and gave him a long lingering kiss. 'Just one thing,' she murmured.

Sean's eyes widened. 'Yes?'

'Well, I was wondering if, if . . .'

'Yes?'

'If you'd like to stay for dinner.'

Sean dropped her hand in disgust. 'Oh, very funny! Well, yes, I will stay to dinner but I warn you, I'm an expensive date!'

'That's okay. I get staff discount!'

His smile faded for a moment and his eyes searched her face. 'Steph? Are we okay?'

She moved around the desk and into his arms. 'I think so.'

'I'm glad,' he said and bent his head to kiss her.

She returned his kiss ardently, and shivered as his hands moved down to her hips, pulling her close against him.

'Oh, don't, I've got work to do,' she protested weakly and pulled away.

'Just one more kiss.' He pulled her back against him. Finally when they came up for air she pushed him towards the door with a groan. 'Please go downstairs before someone walks in and finds the boss in a very compromising position! Liam should be in by now. He'll get you a drink.'

Sean reached down to kiss the nape of her neck. 'I suppose I'll have to settle for that. For now. Don't be long. I want to spend some time with you before the place fills up. Is there any chance of you getting away early this evening?'

'I think that can be arranged,' she murmured, pushing him gently towards the door. 'Now go away and let me make myself presentable.'

Sean grinned and ran down the stairs whistling. Things were definitely looking up.

Chapter Forty-seven

Steph turned off the tap and ran for the phone, wiping her hands in the towel she'd tied around her. 'Hello?'

'Steph? Hi, it's Liz.'

'Hi, Liz.' Steph secured the towel around her and sat down on the bed.

'Well, what do you think?'

'What about?'

'The article, idiot. Haven't you seen it?'

'No. What article?'

'Oh, Steph. Godfrey Jones, remember? It's Sunday, or hadn't you noticed.'

'Oh, right, sorry, Liz. It was a late night last night and I'm not really awake yet. Sean's just gone out for the papers. So tell me, does he slate us or praise us?'

'You sound remarkably calm considering this is your first review.'

'So much has gone wrong already, I've decided that I'll go nuts if I worry about everything. So don't keep me in suspense. What does he say?'

'He's very complimentary.'

'Thank goodness.' Steph sank back against the pillows.

'The only thing he didn't like was the wine list.'

Steph shot back up again. 'Why, what's wrong with it?'

'He says: *The wine list is a little uneven with very little choice under £20.*'

'Bullshit! What else does he say?'

'Well, he's very complimentary about your treatment of younger customers.'

'What?' Steph frowned in confusion.

'He says: *It's nice to see that in a restaurant of this calibre they still look after the little things – or in this case, the little ones! While most of the customers were tucking into quail's eggs, breast of guinea fowl and turbot dressed with caviar – the real thing, folks! – one young man was happily munching his way through a burger and fries!*'

'Oh dear.' Steph sighed.

'What? That's good, isn't it?'

'Not if it means we get an influx of kids all demanding burgers, it isn't. Conor will go berserk!'

Liz laughed. 'I don't think too many people can afford to take their kids to Chez Nous for a burger.'

'I suppose. What does he say about the service?'

'Hang on.' Liz scanned the page. 'Here we are. *Service was unobtrusive and efficient. The staff, while friendly, were happy to stay in the background. This restaurant has changed hands recently, but as it was my first visit to Chez Nous I'm not in a position to tell you whether it has improved or not. Suffice to say I will definitely be coming back.*'

'Well, that's good, I suppose,' Steph said, slightly mollified.

Liz laughed. 'Oh, Steph, if you're not happy with that review, you've got a lot of heartache ahead of you.'

'I know, I know. I suppose I'll get used to it.'

'Really, Steph, this is very positive. Oh, and he does say right at the beginning that it was your first day open after the accident and that the official opening isn't until Tuesday.'

'That's good. I'd better send him an invite.'

'You'd better. Listen, I've got to go. I'll see you on Tuesday.'

'Okay, Liz, thanks, bye.' Steph wandered back into the bathroom to wash her teeth. It was a pretty good review she had to admit. But she was a bit peeved over the criticism of her wine list. She'd taken great pains in making changes to Chris Connolly's selection and had consulted Edward whenever she doubted her own objectivity. If anything, she'd improved the list in the lower price range. But then, she reasoned, Godfrey Jones wasn't familiar with the old list. And he'd admitted that he wasn't in a position to make comparisons.

The hall door banged and Sean ran up the stairs. 'You'll never guess,' he said coming into the bathroom, waving the newspaper.

'There's a review of the restaurant?' Steph said calmly.

'Yes! How did you know?'

'Liz thought she recognised Godfrey Jones in the restaurant the day we reopened but she wasn't sure. She just phoned and read out some of it to me. I believe Billy gets a special mention.'

'He does,' Sean said proudly and handed her the paper.

She read the article slowly, looking for criticisms. 'It's not bad,' she said finally.

'Not bad? God, you're hard to please. It's positively glowing. Especially from Godfrey Jones.'

'You know him?'

'You'd want to be living under a stone not to know him. He's always on the box.'

'Oh. Well, I'd better send him an invite for Tuesday.'

'Are you going in to work today?'

'No. Conor's experimenting today so I think it's better if I keep out of his way. I thought I'd do a bit of work here.'

Sean moved closer and slipped his arms around her waist. 'Why don't you take some time off?' he murmured in her ear and tugged gently on the towel.

Steph smiled. 'Mm, I suppose I could. I tell you what. Give me two hours, and then I'm all yours.'

'Promise?' He kissed the nape of her neck.

'Promise,' she said, resisting the temptation to drag him back to bed there and then. She had to get *some* work done.

He took the paper and headed for the stairs. 'Okay. I'll make some coffee.'

'I won't be long,' Steph called after him. She went into the bedroom humming happily to herself. She took a faded pair of Levis from her wardrobe and a navy check shirt from Sean's. With her hair brushed back into a ponytail, no make-up and the voluminous shirt hanging loosely over her tight jeans, she looked about fourteen.

Sean eyed her appreciatively when she padded into the kitchen ten minutes later in stocking feet. He loved her when she was decked out in one of her dark business suits or in a sexy little evening dress. But he liked it even more when she was like this. She looked so young and vulnerable. And she seemed more relaxed when they were home alone. 'Are you sure you want to work?' He reached for her and pulled her down onto his knee.

Steph planted a kiss on his mouth and stood up. 'Yes, I do. Stop trying to distract me. Why don't you make a start on clearing out the attic?'

Sean buried his head in a newspaper. 'Oh, I don't know.'

Steph frowned. 'You haven't changed your mind about seeing more of Billy, have you?'

'No, of course not.'

Steph shrugged. 'Okay. Well, I'd better get to work. I'll be up in the office if you want me.'

'Joe, take a look at this.' Annie shoved the newspaper under his nose.

Joe opened one eye. 'What?'

Annie poked him in the ribs. 'Wake up. It's an article about Chez Nous.'

Joe grunted and sat up in bed. 'Where are the kids?'

'Playing at Jessica's.'

'Any chance of a cuppa?'

Annie shook her head and went downstairs. She should have brought it up in the first place. It was impossible to talk to him until he'd had his first mug of tea. She carried the large World's Best Dad mug upstairs and handed it to him, before climbing up on the bed beside him. 'So what do you think?'

Joe put down the paper and took a cautious sip of the hot liquid. 'Ah, that's better. He's quite complimentary. A good review from him must count for something, mustn't it?'

'Oh, yes, he's fairly well known. I don't know why he gets at the wine list, though. I think it's fine.'

'I didn't think it had changed,' Joe remarked. He'd

brought a client to dinner there during the week and he'd been very impressed. Joe had told him, with some pride, that the restaurant was now owned and run by his sister. He'd watched with some amusement the man's reaction when he'd introduced them. He'd always enjoyed the effect Steph had on his colleagues. She managed to turn even the most sophisticated of men into drooling teenagers.

'Steph made some changes,' Annie was saying. 'She added more New World wines and, funnily enough, more to the ten-to-twenty pound range.'

'Well, he does say that he's never been there before,' Joe pointed out.

'True,' Annie agreed. 'Are you going to come home before the reception on Tuesday?'

Joe pulled her down beside him. 'What's in it for me?' he murmured.

Annie raised an eyebrow. 'You get to spend more time with your beautiful wife.'

'That sounds okay. Speaking of spending some time together, why don't you come back to bed for a while?'

Annie's eyes widened. 'Joe! What about the children?'

'They're next door, aren't they? They'll be fine for a while.'

Annie slid down beside him. 'I was going to ring Stephanie.'

Joe started to open her shirt. 'You can do that later.'

'I suppose.'

'Catherine, listen to this.' Tom West walked into the kitchen with the newspaper. '*Chez Nous is a bright airy*

restaurant. The large room is spacious and cool, but the atmosphere is warm and inviting. Tables are set with immaculate white cloths and napkins, polished silver cutlery and sparkling good-sized glasses. Tables are large and chairs comfortable, making the idea of going back to work seem ludicrous. The menu makes interesting reading—'

'Let me read it myself,' Catherine said impatiently, wiping her hands on her apron. She took the paper from him and put on her glasses.

'Look at the bit about the service,' her husband prompted. 'Though I'm not sure I like what he says about the wine list.'

Catherine glared at him before turning her attention to the article. 'That's wonderful,' she said happily when she'd finished.

'It is, isn't it? But what about the wine list?'

Catherine brushed that aside. 'What about it? The kind of people who can afford to eat in Chez Nous aren't too worried about the prices now, are they?'

Tom laughed. 'That's true. Let's call Stephanie. Do you think she's seen it?'

'I'm sure she has, but let's phone her anyway and congratulate her.'

'Edward. Hi.' Liz stood back and let him in. She could hardly take her eyes off him. The faded denims, trainers and white shirt took years off him and he looked even more gorgeous than usual.

'Hi, Liz. I hope you don't mind me just dropping in. I'm on my way to Jen's.'

'No problem as long as you ignore the mess. I'm trying to catch up on the ironing.'

'Did you see this?' He held out the newspaper folded over on the page of the review.

'I certainly did. I phoned Steph earlier and would you believe, she hadn't seen it!'

'Pretty good, isn't it? Was she happy? What did you think?' It had seemed like a very good review to him, but then he was only an amateur.

'It was great,' Liz assured him. 'Though Steph wasn't too impressed with the criticism of her wine list.'

Edward grinned. 'She takes her wines very seriously indeed but she actually made very few changes to Chris's original selection. Where's Lucy?' He stretched out in a kitchen chair and watched her iron a pair of miniature dungarees.

'She's at a party – Carol's there too. Is Jen expecting you?'

'No, I just thought I'd drop in on the off chance of cadging a free lunch. Why don't I take you out instead?'

Liz looked at the pile of clothes still to be ironed and thought about the bathroom that needed cleaning. 'I don't think so, Edward. I've so much to do.'

'Oh, leave it,' Edward said carelessly. 'You should get someone in to take care of the housework now that you're working.'

Liz raised an eyebrow. 'Should I? And by the time I've paid a housekeeper and a baby-sitter, what would be left of my wages?'

'If there's nothing left then you're not charging enough,' he said matter-of-factly.

Liz smiled. There was plenty of money left. Sometimes she thought maybe she was charging too much but Conor assured her that she wasn't. She'd been amazed at how much she'd made already, and bookings were flooding in for the Christmas period. She'd refused any bookings for Christmas week itself, determined that Lucy wasn't going to miss out. She'd even invited Chris to dinner on Christmas day. She wasn't thrilled at the idea but she knew it would make Lucy happy. Besides, her parents and Chris's dad would be there too and that would make it easier.

'So what about it?'

Liz started.

'Lunch?' Edward repeated patiently.

Liz threw the blouse she'd picked up back in the basket. 'Yeah, why not? But I have to be back by five to pick up Lucy.'

'Fine, let's go.'

'Not yet.' Liz looked at him in dismay. 'I have to change. Where are we going?'

Edward sat down again with a sigh. 'Well, I'm not exactly dressed for anywhere too formal. How about Morel's Bistro? That way we'll have plenty of time.' The little bistro was less than fifteen minutes' drive.

'Lovely. I'll be five minutes.' Liz hummed happily to herself as she ran upstairs. It was a very cold day, but sunny. Maybe they'd have time for a walk along the pier. She chose a bright red polo neck, black jeans and black ankle boots. She renewed her lipstick – since Edward had taken to calling unexpectedly she always applied some make-up in the mornings – ran a brush through her hair and went back down to join him.

He looked up approvingly. 'Good enough to eat,' he said.

Liz flushed and busied herself with the zip of her jacket.

Edward smiled at her discomfort. She couldn't take a compliment, but it didn't stop him doling them out. He loved the way she blushed. She was so different from Christina. His fiancée had always expected compliments, acknowledging them with a slightly imperious nod. She saw them as her due. It had both amused and irritated Edward.

Liz pushed him out into the hall. 'Let's go. I'm starving.'

'Me too,' Edward said, leaning down and kissing her lightly on the lips.

Liz pushed him away but she was smiling. 'Enough of that. You promised me lunch.'

'So I did.' Edward opened the door and led the way out to the car.

Chapter Forty-eight

'Jesus! Why the hell did I agree to do lunch today? It's going to be a bloody disaster. Isn't table fourteen ready to order yet?'

'No, Chef,' Brian muttered nervously. 'And a man at table five wants to change his main course from monkfish to beef.'

'For Christ's sake!' Conor banged the worktop with his fist, making a nearby trainee jump.

'Chef, the potatoes are burned.' Alan, a young commis, looked at his boss nervously.

'I'll look after that, Chef.' Marc took Alan by the arm and steered him back down the kitchen.

Kevin looked at Conor's flushed face. 'Why don't you concentrate on the food for the reception this evening, Conor, and let me look after lunch?'

Conor nodded gratefully and went out into the yard to have a smoke. Not for the first time, he thanked God that Kevin Nolan had decided to join his kitchen. He checked his watch. Only five hours to go to the opening. How were they going to be ready on time?

'Haven't they even started their meal yet? How are we going to be ready on time?'

Steph looked around the restaurant and cursed herself for staying open for lunch.

'They wanted to take some time before ordering. I can hardly force them now, can I?' Liam said irritably. It was a bloody crazy day. What on earth had possessed Steph to stay open for lunch? They were going to have to work their butts off this afternoon. And Jane had gone home sick, though he thought it was a phobia to hard work that she suffered from. God, they'd got rid of surly Jean and replaced her with sickly Jane!

Things weren't any better in the kitchen. Conor was like an Antichrist. He almost made Chris seem reasonable! The chefs were tiptoeing around him, afraid to speak. Apart from old Quigly, that was. He just carried on in his own little corner, oblivious.

Steph shot Liam a conciliatory smile. 'Sorry, Liam. What time do we need to clear the place if you're to set up on time for tonight?'

'Three at the latest,' he said firmly. Three thirty would probably be time enough but there was no harm in asking for more.

'Okay. I'll drop down later and see how we're doing. Then I have to go out for a couple of hours,' she added lightly, 'but you'll be able to reach me on my mobile.'

Liam stared after her. God, she was going to swan off for the afternoon and leave him to get everything ready *and* deal with Conor. He shook his head. It was about time he asked for a bloody raise.

Steph went back up to the office and sat staring at her checklist without seeing it. She checked her watch nervously. The phone rang, making her jump.

'Hello?'

'Steph?'

'Hi, Sean.'

'Are you okay?'

'Of course.'

'I just rang to wish you good luck.'

'But I'll see you later, won't I?' Steph frowned. Sean had promised to be at the opening.

'I meant good luck with Mrs McCann.'

'Oh. Right.'

'You are going, aren't you, Steph?'

Steph thought for a moment. She could always ring and say she was too busy; after all it was a bit crazy going AWOL today of all days.

'Steph?'

'Yes, of course I'm going.'

'Good girl. Well, I'm sure it will be fine. She probably just wants to chat about old times.'

'Yeah. Listen, I have to go, Sean. Conor's looking for me. See you later.' Steph put down the phone and tucked a lock of hair nervously behind her ear. For the first time in months, she longed for a cigarette. She checked her watch. It was nearly two thirty. She stood up, slipped on her jacket, grabbed her bag and went downstairs.

There were two parties left in the restaurant, one eating dessert and the other on coffees. After a quick word with Liam, she went to each table, introduced herself and explained that they were closing at three to prepare for the opening. She apologised for rushing them and invited them to come back later that evening to join in the celebrations. Both parties were delighted with the invitation and wished her luck. Steph winked at Liam and left the restaurant. If only she could deal with her personal problems as easily, she thought as she climbed into her car. She drove across town and out through Fairview. Traffic was heavy and she checked her watch again. Five to three. She shouldn't be too late. The traffic started to move and she turned up the Howth Road. Not far now. She took a few deep breaths and tried to ignore the butterflies in her stomach. She reached Killester and turned into the small street of terraced houses. She sat in the car for a moment tempted to drive away again, but before she could turn the key in the ignition Joan McCann appeared on the doorstep.

Steph took a deep breath, planted a smile on her face and got out of her car.

'Hello, Stephanie. How are you?'

'Fine, Mrs McCann.' Steph kissed the proffered cheek. She was slightly taken aback at this frail woman. She could only be in her early sixties, but she looked so much older. 'How are you keeping?'

'Can't complain, love. I've just made some tea. I hope it won't be too strong for you.'

'I love it strong,' Steph lied, following her into the room that Ruth had always referred to as the parlour. Steph had only been inside it a couple of times before. It had always been reserved for important visitors and kept locked the rest of the time. Steph looked around the small room full of china ornaments. The red chesterfield suite, now faded, had crocheted covers on the arms and little doilies stood on the small table in front of the sofa, in wait for their teacups. Steph sat down and accepted the tiny china cup and saucer that Mrs McCann handed her. She held it carefully, terrified that the slightest pressure would break it and eventually set it down on the table, not trusting her trembling hands.

'I'm sorry if I bullied you into coming to see me, Stephanie, but I really needed to talk to you.'

Steph was startled by her directness. 'Not at all. I was just a bit surprised to hear from you after all this time.'

'I understand, dear. You were probably terrified to come here.'

Steph gave an embarrassed laugh. 'Just a little,' she admitted.

'I'm not going to interrogate you, Stephanie, or ask you anything awkward. I just wanted to talk to Ruth's friends. I've already talked to Mary, but I can't track Sinead down. Mary thinks she's in Australia.'

Steph frowned. 'Ruth's flatmates? But why? I don't understand.'

'No, of course you don't, dear. I'm sorry. I should start at the beginning. But I'm forgetting my manners. Have a piece of cake.'

'No, thanks.' Steph knew there was little or no chance of her getting the fruitcake down her throat without choking.

Joan put the plate down and took a sip of her tea. 'It all started when Peter died. I put off going through his things for a few weeks. Oh, I let the girls get rid of his clothes and all that, but I wanted to go through his papers myself. There was very little to do as far as his finances were concerned. He'd known for a few months that he was going to die and he used to closet himself in here with the accountant and the lawyer making sure that everything was in order. He transferred everything into my name before he died so we wouldn't have to worry about wills or probate or any of that nonsense. He was a very thoughtful, kind man. And you'll probably find this hard to believe, Steffi, but Peter was also very sentimental. He had this box that he kept at the top of the wardrobe. There were all sorts of mementoes in it. He kept the children's first letters to Santa, every card I ever sent him.' She sighed. 'I didn't want anyone else to go through all of that.'

She stared into the distance, a half smile on her face and tears in her eyes. Steph patted her hand awkwardly.

Joan McCann smiled at her. 'Sorry, dear. Where was I? Oh yes, the box. I put off opening it because I knew it would upset me and bring back a lot of memories. But one day, the day before I called your mother, I felt strong enough to open it.'

Steph looked at her expectantly. She'd obviously found something. Something belonging to Ruth? 'Yes?' she prompted. Joan McCann had that faraway look in her eye again.

'Yes.' Joan pulled herself back to the present. 'Just a moment, dear.' She went to the sideboard and pulled a large, thick envelope out of the top drawer. 'Here we are.' She opened the envelope and carefully extracted the contents. The first was a pale pink envelope, slightly faded and this she put carefully to one side. She riffled through the others and took out two more letters. 'Did you know Des?' she asked suddenly.

Steph put down her cup with a clatter. 'Des Healy? Yes, I knew him.'

'Ruth never told us about him. She was always very secretive about her boyfriends. What was he like?'

Steph swallowed hard. 'Well, we didn't see too much of him. He liked to keep Ruth to himself.'

'But what did you think of him?' Joan said impatiently.

'He was a bit flash for my liking,' Steph replied honestly. 'He seemed to think he was better than the rest of us. He had a job, a fancy car and we were just poor students.'

'Yes, I see. Do you think Ruth loved him?'

Steph had no problem answering this one. 'She was crazy about him. She couldn't see any of his faults. That's real love, isn't it?'

Joan smiled. 'It is when you're very young.'

Steph laughed. 'True. We get less tolerant as we get older.' She thought of how hard she was on Sean sometimes when he'd done nothing to deserve it. In comparison to Des, he was an absolute saint!

'Peter tried to track him down. Des, that is,' Joan said quietly.

'What?' Steph stared at her.

'I didn't know.' She held up the envelope. 'He spent months contacting friends, colleagues anyone he thought might know where Des was.'

'But couldn't Des's family tell him?'

Joan's lips twisted into a bitter smile. 'They were nice enough to him at first but when he kept badgering them they threatened him with the police. They said Ruth's death had nothing to do with Des.'

'But that's terrible? How could they?'

Joan sighed. 'I suppose they were just trying to protect their son. Most parents would do the same.'

'I'm not sure I could be as understanding as you.'

'Peter wasn't,' Joan said sadly. 'He just wouldn't give up. There are letters here dated two years after Ruth's death.'

'It must have been eating him up inside.'

'So you didn't know anything about it? He didn't talk to you?'

'No.' Steph shook her head. 'He called me to find out where Des lived – but that was the night after the funeral. I never heard from him since.'

'And do you know if he talked to the other girls?'

Steph shook her head. 'I hardly knew Ruth's flat-mates. We never kept in touch after . . .'

Joan sighed. 'I see. Then, it seems that I know more than you do.' She handed Steph one of the letters.

Steph looked at her and then down at the letter in her hand. It was dated August 20th. Four months after Ruth died. She started to read.

Savings, Pensions & Invesments Inc.
Dear Mr McCann,

Firstly, please accept my condolences on the death of your daughter.

In normal circumstances I would not reveal personal details about any member of staff. These, however, are not normal circumstances.

Mr Desmond Healy no longer works with this firm. I can give you the address and telephone number of his landlady but I'm afraid he no longer lives there. Perhaps, however, she will have a forwarding address.

I am sorry that I cannot be of more help.

Yours, very sincerely,
Jonathan Lyons
Managing Director

Steph folded the letter and put it back in its envelope. 'It's strange that Des would have left his job so soon.'

'He didn't leave, he was fired,' Joan replied. 'I phoned the landlady – amazingly she still runs the place – and she remembered Des. She heard that he'd got sacked for some shady dealings.'

'Lord, is there no end to this man's talents?' Steph said bitterly. 'Did she have a forwarding address?'

'No, Des was too clever for that. He wouldn't even give her a phone number. He dropped in a couple of times to collect his post.'

'So Mr McCann never caught up with him?'

'Not in person but it looks like his letter did reach Des at some stage.' She handed Steph another letter.

Steph pulled out the single sheet of notepaper. The letter was handwritten and dated July, almost two years later. She frowned. 'I don't understand.'

'You will when you read it.'

> *49 Turtle Grove*
> *London*
> *EC1*

Dear Mr McCann,

You don't know me but I've read the letter you sent to Des Healy some time ago. I'm afraid I can't tell you where he is because I don't know.

He left me and our little girl last month – she is just six months old. I found your letter when I was going through the few things he left behind. I gather from what you said that I'm not the only woman he got into trouble.

But tell your daughter that she had a lucky escape. If .

I'd realised what Des was like I probably would never have had this baby. I have barely enough money to keep myself never mind a child.

If you do ever catch up with him please let me know. I don't want him back but the least he can do is contribute to his child's upbringing.

Please pass on my regards to your daughter – Ruth. Tell her to get on with her life and forget about Des. He's not worth one of her tears.

Yours truly,

Celia Maine.

Steph lowered the letter and stared at Mrs McCann. 'He did it again. I don't believe it.'

Joan nodded. 'She's a lovely woman, I talked to her on the phone a couple of weeks ago. As you'll gather from the letter she didn't know that Ruth had died – Stephanie? Are you all right?'

She nodded mutely. Joan McCann took a bottle of brandy from the sideboard and poured them both a glass. Steph took hers gratefully and took a large gulp of the drink.

Joan reached over and patted her knee. 'I'm sorry, dear. This has all been a bit of a shock for you, hasn't it?'

'It shouldn't be,' Steph said grimly. 'We already knew what he was capable of.'

'But whatever you think about running out on a pregnant girl, how could he walk away from his baby daughter?'

Steph sighed. 'I don't know.' She glanced at her watch and was alarmed to see that it was nearly half past four. 'I'm really sorry, Mrs McCann, I'm going to have to go. Could I come back tomorrow, though?'

'I think you should, Stephanie. We're not finished.'

Steph stared at her. What else was to come? She stood up reluctantly. 'I'm really sorry I can't stay now, I'd love to but—'

'Go and do what you have to do. I'll still be here tomorrow.' Joan McCann smiled serenely and walked her to the door.

'Bye then. See you tomorrow.' Steph gave her a quick hug and stumbled out to her car.

Chapter Forty-nine

It was five fifteen when Steph let herself back into Chez Nous. 'Is everything going okay?' she said timidly, coming up behind Liam.

Liam turned to look at her, with raised brows. 'Very well, thank you.'

'I'm sorry for running out on you, Liam. I didn't expect to be so long. It was important.'

'You're the boss,' Liam said, dismissing her apologies. 'Conor's looking for you.'

'Right.' Steph went back to the kitchen. The noise was deafening. Cold dishes were already laid out on tables near the door and the chefs were working at a frenetic pace. Brendan, one of the kitchen porters, was frantically trying to clear any debris away from the floor around their feet. He was shouted at to work faster or to get out of the bloody way in equal measures. He carried on regardless. Steph saw Conor at the other end of the room, gesticulating wildly at Pat. Pat stood looking at him, nodding occasionally. Steph smiled and wondered if Pat was even listening. She walked up to the two of them.

'Steph, where the hell have you been?'

'Out. Is something wrong?'

'Well, no. It's sorted now.'

Steph smiled at her head chef. 'Well, there you are then. So everything's under control?'

Conor looked almost surprised. 'I suppose it is. The cold dishes are almost finished, four of the hot dishes have been started and we'll do the monkfish and scallop kebabs, the wild mushroom soufflés and the mini steak-and-kidney pies as they're needed.'

'Are we going to stagger the food over two hours?' Steph asked.

'Yes, we'll start with two of the cold dishes, the melon and Parma ham sticks and the chilli tiger prawns and then we'll serve a mixture of the hot and cold dishes, say two at a time.'

Steph nodded in approval. 'Well, if there's nothing else, I'd better go and get ready. You should plan to be out front by about seven, Conor.'

'Will do,' Conor said, with a nervous smile. Cooking was easy. Going out and talking to everyone was a different matter.

After checking with Brian that the white wine and champagne were sufficiently cold and that there was a plentiful supply of ice, Steph ran upstairs to change. While she still planned to wear a suit, she was swapping her usual dark tones for a rich cream brocade Paul Costello creation. Her gold chunky neck chain, bracelet and earrings and very high, beige Bruno Magli court shoes completed the outfit. She'd only time to touch up her make-up, and she noticed that her hand was trembling as she tried to apply mascara. She studied her reflection. She looked strained and upset. She smiled widely, willing herself to look and feel calmer. A cigarette would be very welcome right now. She blended some bronze tones in around her eyelids, added some rich copper lipstick and fluffed up her hair. A spray of perfume and she was ready.

'Steph?'

She jumped as Sean walked up behind her.

'Sorry, I didn't mean to startle you. How did it go?'

Steph returned his kiss. 'There's so much to tell you, Sean, but there's no time now. It will have to wait until later.'

'I'll die of suspense,' Sean complained and then noticed her strained expression. 'Are you okay?' he asked gently.

'Sure.' She smiled wanly.

'You look fantastic,' he said and she did, despite the slight air of sadness.

'Thanks.' Steph looked him up and down, taking in the beautifully cut, charcoal-grey suit, the pale cream shirt and the dark red, paisley silk tie. 'You don't look too bad yourself.'

He held his arm out to link hers. 'Thank you, ma'am. Shall we?'

She took it and they descended together just as Edward put his foot on the first step.

'Oh, there you are. I was just coming to get you. Hi, Sean.'

'How's it going, Edward?'

'Everything seems to be going just fine – no thanks to me.'

Or me, Steph thought ruefully.

'Liam just wants you to have a final look around before he opens the doors, Stephanie.'

When they walked into the dining-room the waiting-staff were lined up along the back wall. They wore snow-white shirts, black trousers and long dark green aprons. Liam stood beside them, impeccable in a black suit, white shirt and dark green bow tie.

Steph smiled at them. 'Is everybody ready?'

Liam stood to attention. 'As ready as we'll ever be.'

'Great. Well, good luck everyone and thanks.' She turned to Edward. 'Have you seen Conor?'

'I put my head around the door but he seemed pretty busy so I didn't interrupt him.'

'Come on then, we've time for a quick chat before we open the doors.'

The kitchen was a lot calmer when they walked in. Some of the staff were out in the yard having a smoke and Conor was going through some last minute details with Pat and Kevin.

'Steph, Edward, is everything ready out front?' He looked worriedly at them.

'It certainly is,' Edward said, 'and it looks like everything's ready in here too.'

Conor grinned. 'Yeah, no major catastrophes so far.'

Steph checked her watch. 'Then I think we'd better open up. Remember Conor, try and be out by seven.'

'Will do. What about the photo call?'

Steph looked at him blankly. God, she'd forgotten all about that! She sprang into action. 'Right. I think we'll do that now. The photographer should be here. How about a couple of shots with some of the fish dishes? They're nice and colourful.'

'Fine.'

'I'll get the photographer.'

When she left them, Edward moved nearer the food. 'Some of your new creations, Conor?'

'They are.'

'Well if they taste as good as they look, you'll be a huge success. Best of luck, Conor.'

Conor took the hand Edward held out to him and shook it firmly. 'Thanks, Edward.'

Steph appeared back with the photographer and the three of them posed in different positions. Steph insisted on a few of Conor on his own and Edward pointed out that there should be some of her on her own too – after all, she was the boss.

Sean put his head around the door. 'Liam's opened up.'

'Right. Good luck everybody,' Steph shouted and followed Edward out to the front door to greet their guests.

The evening flew by in a flurry of activity. A photographer from one of the social pages wandered around snapping anyone who looked vaguely famous. Lavinia Reynolds was holding court in the centre of the room and drinking copious amounts of champagne.

'I can hardly open the bottles fast enough,' Liam told Steph.

'It's worth it if the old biddy gives us a good write-up.'

Adam Cullen and Conor were in deep conversation in a corner. From the look on Conor's face and the way he was gesticulating they had to be talking food. He looked wonderful in his chef's hat and whites and was wearing the dark green silk neckerchief that Steph had bought him to match in with the other staff.

Sean moved quietly around the room, listening in on conversations and watching the reactions to the food. Finally, he came to a stop beside Joe, Annie and Liz. 'What do you think?'

'It's going brilliantly,' Liz said, her eyes sparkling. 'Everyone's raving about the food.'

'I don't see this Godfrey chap.' Joe looked around.

'I'm sure he'll be here,' Annie assured him. 'He probably likes to make an entrance.'

'Well, there won't be much point if the food is all gone,' Joe remarked.

Steph caught the comment as she joined them. 'Don't worry, Conor has a couple of surprises up his sleeve.'

Sean nudged her and nodded towards the door. 'I think the entrance is being made.'

Steph moved towards the man pausing in the doorway. 'Mr Jones? I'm glad you could join us.'

Brian appeared at her elbow with some champagne and she smiled at him gratefully.

'Miss West?' Godfrey Jones asked.

'That's right, but please call me Stephanie.'

'Godfrey,' he replied with a small bow.

'Let me introduce you to my business partner.' She led him over to Edward. 'Edward McDermott, this is Godfrey Jones.'

The two men shook hands. Steph looked around for Conor and saw him slip out of the room. She suppressed a smile and turned her full attention back to Edward, who was explaining the background of the restaurant. Lavinia Reynolds had signalled her photographer and Steph, Edward and Jones posed obediently.

'I see that dreadful woman is here,' Godfrey remarked drily. 'She wouldn't know good food if it jumped up and bit her.'

'That's very harsh,' Steph said reprovingly.

'But true,' Edward said and they all laughed. He watched Godfrey take a small sip of his drink. 'Would you prefer something stronger? I can't stand champagne myself.'

'I'd murder a gin and tonic,' Godfrey admitted.

Edward grinned. 'I'll join you.'

'Leave it to me,' Steph said grimly, and left them and made a beeline for the kitchen. 'Conor? Are you ready to serve the food? Godfrey Jones is about to start in on the G & Ts.'

'Bloody hell! That will kill the flavour of the kebabs! Give me two minutes.'

Steph left him, asked Jane to get the drinks and returned to the two men. They were chatting comfortably now and Godfrey had deliberately turned his back on Lavinia who had been desperately trying to break in on the conversation.

A waiter arrived with the scallop and monkfish kebabs, moments before Jane delivered the drinks.

'I'll hold your drink for you,' Steph offered casually, and carried on chatting while Edward and Godfrey tucked into the food. As she'd expected, Godfrey drank some champagne after eating the fish and she watched in delight as the explosion of flavours hit the gourmet's taste buds. She saw Conor approaching and winked at him. 'Godfrey, let me introduce our head chef, Conor O'Brien.'

Conor smiled shyly. 'Pleased to meet you.'

'I'd shake hands with you, young man, but I'm too busy enjoying your wonderful food!'

He helped himself to another kebab and washed it down immediately with some more champagne. 'Lovely,' he said with his mouth full. 'Truly excellent.'

Conor beamed happily and Edward raised his glass to him in a silent toast. Steph sighed happily. It wouldn't get much better than this.

At twelve midnight, she sat exhausted, listening to her friends dissect the evening.

'Did you see Lavinia's face when Godfrey Jones turned his back on her?' Liz shook her head, laughing.

'She looked as if she'd swallowed a wasp,' Annie agreed.

'The woman was blind drunk,' Joe remarked, trying hard to focus.

'I'm not surprised,' Liam replied. 'Every time I looked, Brian was filling her glass. I think she fancied you, Brian.'

'Oh don't,' Brian groaned in disgust and they all laughed.

'I could have murdered you, Edward, when you offered God a G & T.'

'Well, I wasn't to know, was I?' he protested. 'I'm just a poor ignorant lawyer after all.'

Conor grinned. 'You'll learn. We'll have you helping out in the kitchen before you know it!'

'A toast,' Sean stood up, slightly unsteadily. 'To the new crew of Chez Nous – hey, that rhymes – well done, guys. It was a great night.'

'Hear, hear!' Annie slopped her wine as she raised her glass enthusiastically.

'Cheers,' Liz said.

'Up yours!' Conor grinned happily.

'I've got to go home,' Steph said sleepily.

'We should be going too,' Annie agreed. 'The baby-sitter will go nuts. Shall we share a taxi?'

'Grand. I'll go and phone for one.' Steph went up to the office, rang for a taxi and collected her bag. The day had taken on a slightly surreal quality. Her conversation with Joan McCann seemed days ago. She hadn't allowed herself to dwell on any of it all evening. She'd think it all through tomorrow. She was too tired tonight. She met Conor at the bottom of the stairs. 'Conor, I'm not going to be in tomorrow.'

'Okay boss. We'll manage.'

'And Conor. Well done. You were great.' She reached up to kiss him and he wrapped her in a bear hug, lifting her off the ground.

'Thanks, Steph. Thanks for giving me the chance. You won't be sorry.'

'I know that.'

'Come on, you two, no canoodling in the hallway. I'm a very jealous man.'

Conor clapped him drunkenly on the back. 'That's okay, Sean. She's wonderful but I'm in love with someone else.'

'Hard luck, Steph. It looks like you're stuck with me.'

'Damn and I thought I was finally going to be able to trade you in for a younger model.'

Sean smacked her bottom and pushed her into the dining-room. 'Wait until I get you home.'

'Promises, promises.' Steph giggled and winked at Liz. 'How are you getting home, Liz?'

'Oh, Edward said he'd drop me,' she said casually.

Steph rounded on her partner. 'Did he now? I hope your intentions are honourable.' She wagged her finger under his nose.

'Of course,' he said, his eyes twinkling. 'I'll call you tomorrow, Steph. And congratulations again.'

'Congratulations yourself,' she said, returning his kiss. 'But I won't be here tomorrow. I'm taking a day off.'

Sean staggered backwards, a shocked look on his face. 'A day off? Are you sick?'

'I'll live.'

Through a haze of alcohol, Sean realised that something important was happening tomorrow. He slipped an arm around her and hugged her tight to his side. 'Let's go home.'

Steph stood outside the restaurant kissing Liam, Brian, Pat and John. She told Liam she'd call him in the morning and as the only sober one left, he promised to lock up.

'Check all the ashtrays and bins,' she warned.

'I will,' Liam promised. They were all paranoid now about safety precautions and it wasn't unusual for Liam to walk the restaurant twice checking for fire hazards.

'Good night then, Liam, and thanks for doing such a great job.' She hugged him again and got into the taxi.

Chapter Fifty

Stephanie was still fast asleep when Sean left for work the next morning. He was dying to talk to her about her session with Joan McCann but he didn't have the heart to waken her. He'd got no sense out of her the night before. She'd fallen asleep in the taxi after they'd dropped Joe and Annie and he'd almost had to carry her up to bed. Maybe he'd come home and take her out to lunch. The thought of food made him groan. Still, after some coffee he'd probably feel a bit more human.

Steph heard the front door close and hopped out of bed. After a quick shower, she dried her hair, put on a pair of jeans, a heavy cotton shirt and leather ankle boots. She applied her make-up quickly and ran downstairs. After dumping her mobile phone into her large brown leather shoulder bag, she grabbed her suede jacket and ran out the door.

Joan McCann lived only five minutes away but Steph headed in the opposite direction. She made two stops. The first to collect scones and soda bread, still warm from the baker's oven, and the second, to pick up a bouquet of pink roses. She checked her watch. It was only ten o'clock but Joan would probably be up. Fifteen minutes later she stood on the small doorstep and rang the doorbell.

'Stephanie!'

'I'm sorry, Mrs McCann. Is it too early?'

'Not at all, love, I've been up for hours. I've no reason to any more but I can't seem to get out of the habit. Come along in.'

Steph smiled as she followed her into the small kitchen. This was much more familiar territory. She'd sat here many times drinking milky coffee, moaning about teachers and homework, or wondering what to wear to the dance on Saturday night. 'I brought you these.' She put the scones and bread on the table and handed the flowers to the older woman.

'Oh, thank you, dear. I do love roses.' She looked in the bag. 'And scones! Lovely! I haven't baked in ages. I suppose it's because I had to do so much of it over the years. I'll make a cup of tea and we'll have some.'

A few minutes later, Steph, biting hungrily into a thick slice of bread smothered in butter, looked up to see Joan McCann smiling at her.

'This takes me back. In that outfit you look like a schoolgirl.'

Steph rolled her eyes. 'I don't feel like one, but sitting in this kitchen does bring back a lot of good memories.'

'Was Ruth happy then?'

Steph was surprised by the question. 'Yes, of course she was. She was so sure of what she wanted to do, where she was going. She had so many plans.'

'She couldn't wait to move out,' Joan said sadly.

'Only because she needed some privacy from the other kids and she wanted somewhere quiet to study,' Steph assured her. 'It was nothing to do with you. She loved you. She loved you all.'

'She was a good girl and I know that I didn't give her enough time, but it was so hard.'

'And she knew that.' Steph squeezed her hand. 'She was so grateful that you were prepared to put her through university. She knew how difficult that was for you both and it meant an awful lot to her. She was always talking about the things she'd buy you when she got her first pay cheque.' She thought for a moment. 'I think it was going to be a fur coat for you and a remote-control colour television for her dad.'

'I don't think she'd have been able to afford all that on one salary cheque!' Joan McCann laughed, but her eyes were bright with tears.

'With the job she was planning to get it would have been no problem. She'd have done it too,' Steph added quietly.

'Yes, I do believe she would. How long had she been seeing Des?'

Steph considered the question. She'd met Sean just before Des arrived on the scene. 'They would have been going out for about eight months.'

Joan shook her head. Even after all this time, it was hard for her to accept that her daughter had been sleeping with her boyfriend. They'd hardly known each other. Eight months! It was nothing! Ruth had never told them she was in a serious relationship. The first they'd heard of Des Healy was after Ruth died. 'I wish I'd met him,' she said with a heavy sigh.

'Really?' Steph was surprised. She'd only seen Des once since Ruth died and she could hardly bear to look at him.

'Yes. I'd like to have known what it was about him that attracted Ruth. But I don't agree with what Peter did.

Spending all of that time trying to track the lad down – what was the point?'

'I suppose he wanted answers.'

'He should have told me what he was doing.'

'I'm sure he was just trying to protect you.'

'He couldn't protect me from lying awake at night wondering where I'd gone wrong,' Joan said sadly. 'Why my brilliant, beautiful daughter couldn't face the thought of living. Why she couldn't turn to me, her own mother.'

'Don't think like that, Mrs McCann, please.' Steph looked at the distraught woman, her own eyes filling up. 'If anyone should feel guilty it should be me. I'm the one that let her down.'

Joan wiped her eyes and looked at Stephanie curiously. 'What do you mean?'

Steph took a deep breath. Finally the moment had arrived. There was no going back now. She looked Joan squarely in the eye. 'Ruth called me that day. The day she died. She wanted me to come over.'

'And you didn't?'

Steph hung her head in shame. 'I had a date. I told her that I'd meet her for lunch the next day.' Her voice broke.

'Oh, you poor girl. Has that been bothering you all of these years?' Joan's eyes were full of sympathy.

Steph gulped back her tears. 'I let her down. I knew how depressed she was. If I'd gone around to the flat she'd be alive today.'

'Now you're just being silly,' Joan said briskly. 'You might have stopped her doing it that night, but she would have done it eventually.'

Steph gaped at her. 'That's what Mam said,' she said faintly.

'She's a sensible woman, your mother. I've talked to the professionals about this, Steph. The hospital sent a counsellor out to see me. She was a very kind lady. And she explained that Ruth had probably been planning the suicide for a while. It's very unusual for someone to do it on impulse and succeed. And Mary told me that she'd been very calm and controlled on the Saturday. Apparently that's the way people are after they've decided—'

'But I'm telling you she was really depressed on the phone that evening. And instead of going over there and trying to cheer her up I went out with Sean.' Stephanie knew that she shouldn't be offloading her guilt onto Joan McCann's narrow shoulders. She should be trying to comfort the woman.

'What I'm saying, Stephanie,' Joan explained patiently, 'is that while she may not have intended to do it that actual night, it would definitely have been on her mind.'

'I still should have been there,' Steph said stubbornly.

'It's only natural that you feel that way, love. You two were such close friends. But how do you think I feel? It makes me very sad that she didn't feel she could come and tell me what was going on. I wish we'd been closer. But we can't change the past, Stephanie. I've got the rest of my children and my grandchildren to think of and you've got your whole life ahead of you. Ruth would want us both to get on with it.'

'But I was so stupid,' Steph said as she realised the mistake she'd made. 'Ruth told me she was going to have an abortion. She was quite cool about it. How could I have ever swallowed that? Ruth was dead against abortion.'

'That's nice to know,' Joan said, wiping absently at the silent tears rolling down her cheeks.

'Why didn't I see that? She had never any intention of getting rid of the baby. That's why she was calm. She'd already decided what she was going to do. Oh God!' Steph couldn't believe her own stupidity. Ruth had known that night as they talked on the phone what she was going to do. Like Mrs McCann said, she probably just hadn't decided when.

Steph felt all her control slip away and great racking sobs engulfed her.

Joan shoved a tissue into her hand. 'I'll leave you alone for a minute,' she said hurrying from the room, dabbing at her own eyes as she went.

Steph gave in to the tears and it was several minutes before she got her feelings under control. She was dabbing uselessly at her face with the sodden tissue when Joan McCann returned.

Joan produced a box of tissues with a sad smile. 'I thought we might need these. You'll be all right now, love. You've got a lot off your chest and it will help you put the past behind you. Now I hope this won't upset you even more but I thought you should see it.'

She put a pale pink envelope on the table in front of Stephanie.

Steph looked nervously at the envelope. 'What is it?'

'Just read it, love.'

Steph picked up the envelope and slipped out the single sheet of pale pink notepaper. She gasped as she unfolded it, immediately recognising the distinctive slant of Ruth's handwriting.

Dear Mum, Dad,

    Please forgive me for doing this. It seems the only answer – I can't explain why. I'm pregnant and life as an unmarried mother is not the future I'd planned for myself. I can't do what he wants me to do. I know now that he doesn't really love me. It's not his fault. It's not really anyone's fault. It's just the way it is.

    I'm sorry I've disappointed you and I'm sorry the money you invested in me has been wasted – I wish there was another way.

    I love you both. You're the best parents in the world – please forgive me. Tell everyone I'm sorry.

    All my love,

    Ruth

Steph put it back down on the table and felt the tears start to well up again. 'Poor Ruth.'

'Do you see what I mean, though, Steph? She'd made up her mind about what she wanted to do. If you'd come over that night she probably would have listened to all your good advice and still gone ahead and done it some other time.'

'It's such a waste.'

'Yes. Yes it is.'

Steph looked at her. 'You've been so kind to me. I was so sure you would blame me. That you'd hate me for being such a bad friend.'

'No, love. You were a kid yourself at the time. I'm sure it never crossed your mind that Ruth would do such a thing.'

'No. No it didn't. Did Mr McCann ever catch up with Des?'

Joan shook her head. 'No. And poor Celia didn't either. But I think it's better that way. I don't think I'd want to see him now.'

Steph shuddered. 'I don't think I'd be able to stand in the same room as him.'

'It wouldn't be easy,' Joan agreed. 'No, I don't care about him now. It's Ruth I'm interested in. I want a full picture of what her life was like after she left home. I want to know as much as possible. Somehow, the more I learn, the closer I feel to her. That's really why I wanted to talk to you. You seemed to know her better than anyone. I want you to talk to me about her, Steph. Tell me everything. Does that sound silly?'

Steph shook her head with a sad smile. 'No, not at all. I've spent the last fifteen years trying to push her out of my mind. I didn't want to talk about her or think about her, and when I did, I just felt guilty for letting her down and I hated Des Healy for letting her down too.' Steph put her head in her hands and started to cry again.

Joan moved closer and put an arm around her shoulders. Steph cried harder. She cried for Ruth, for Des, for Joan and for herself. And then she thought of her baby and Ruth's and cried even harder. Joan rocked her gently, smoothed her hair and made comforting noises, and Steph cried on. When the sobs finally abated, to be replaced by hiccups and sniffs, Joan left her and returned a moment later with a bottle of brandy and two glasses.

'It's a bit early,' Steph protested half-heartedly.

'Nonsense. It will do us both good.' Joan poured two

large measures and put one glass into Steph's hands. 'Let's drink to Ruth.'

'To Ruth,' Steph agreed solemnly and took a gulp of the fiery liquid.

'Good girl,' Joan said and tossed down half of her drink. 'Now I think you should tell me about you. No offence, love, but I don't think all of those tears were for Ruth.'

Steph sighed and told her about the fire, the baby and her original plan to have an abortion.

'You poor pet,' Joan said when she'd finished. 'You're too young to have such heartache. But you will be a mother some day. And you'll be a good one.'

Steph stiffened. 'I don't think so.'

'Of course you will,' Joan said firmly. 'It sounds like you have a good man. Make the most of your time together. It goes so quickly.'

It was Steph's turn to give Joan a comforting hug. 'Do you miss him very much?'

'Oh yes. But I'm happy too. It's terrible to watch someone you love in pain. It makes it easier to let them go.' She blew her nose and drained her glass. 'So is Sean the one and only for you, love?'

Steph nodded. 'Though I know I don't deserve him. I've been really horrible to him recently.'

'Then you must make up for lost time. Don't waste a moment, Steph.'

'I won't—' She was interrupted by the shrill of her mobile phone. 'Sorry,' she said, rooting in her bag for the offending instrument. 'Hello? Oh, Sean.'

Joan beamed at her.

'Lunch? Oh, I don't know . . .'

Joan rolled her eyes. 'Will you listen to her? Go,' she commanded.

Steph laughed. 'Okay. I'll see you at home. Bye, love. He must be psychic,' she said after he'd rung off.

'You go and meet him and tell him what we've talked about.'

'But I thought you wanted to hear all about Ruth . . .' Steph started to protest.

'I think we've done enough talking for the moment. I can wait. We have all the time in the world.'

'Well, is it okay if I come back tomorrow?'

'Drop in anytime. But only on one condition. Call me Joan.'

Steph laughed. 'Okay. Joan.' On impulse she leaned over and hugged her. 'Thank you.'

'For what?'

'Listening, understanding. I feel better than I have done in a very long time.'

'I'm glad to hear it. Now go and meet your man. And bring him to meet me sometime.'

'I will. You'll like him.'

'I'm sure I will.' Joan waved as Steph pulled away from the kerb and disappeared out of view. She went back inside and took up the pink envelope, stroked it gently and kissed it. 'Rest in peace, my love. Rest in peace.'

Chapter Fifty-one

Liz put down the phone after calling both Chez Nous and the house and wondered where Steph had got too. Her mobile was off or out of range, so God only knew where she was. Liz looked at the papers in front of her, frustrated that she couldn't reach her friend and congratulate her. There were two write-ups and a wonderful photograph of Conor, Steph and Edward and they hadn't been expecting anything until the Sunday supplements. She picked up the phone again and dialled Edward's office. She'd never called him there before, but today was different, she decided. She just had to talk to him! She felt herself blushing as his secretary asked her name. Dammit, this was ridiculous!

'Hello, Liz. How are you this morning?'

'A little fragile,' Liz admitted. 'How about you?'

'Once I'd had four Alka-Seltzer and three cups of coffee, not bad. Have you seen the papers?'

'Yes. That's why I called. Isn't it wonderful?'

'It seems to have gone well.'

Liz laughed. 'God, you're the master of understatement, do you know that?'

'I'm a lawyer,' Edward pointed out. 'Listen, I was

456

going to try and get hold of Stephanie and arrange a small celebration. Will you come?'

'I've been trying to get hold of her, but she seems to have vanished off the face of the earth. When and where did you want to meet?'

'I thought between five and six at the Merrion. Don't worry about Steph. I'll track her down.'

'Fair enough. You can count me in.'

'When's Lucy coming home?' The little girl had been spending her mid-term break with her dad. In a rare moment of consideration, Chris had offered to take her so that Liz could enjoy the opening.

'She'll be back on Saturday.'

'Mm. And have you any jobs on between now and then?' Edward asked thoughtfully.

'No, as it happens, I don't.'

'Then why don't you put on your glad rags this evening and we'll have dinner in Guilbaud's?'

'You're pushing the boat out, aren't you?'

'We're celebrating, remember?'

'Okay you've talked me into it. I'll see you in the Merrion.'

'Great, bye, Liz.' Edward put down the phone and buzzed his secretary. 'Louise? See if you can pull a few strings and get me a table in Guilbaud's for two people at eight, will you?'

Sean filled Steph's cup.

'Don't,' she protested. 'I'm half drunk as it is.' Having lunch in the Japanese restaurant had been Sean's idea. And it seemed quite a good one at the time – except for the number of flasks of sake they'd managed to get through!

He topped up his own cup. 'So what? We've a lot to celebrate.'

'We're meeting Edward and Liz to celebrate,' Steph reminded him. 'But at this rate, I'll be ready for bed by seven.'

Sean grinned wickedly. 'Well, if you insist! We could always go for a walk to sober up.'

'But it's freezing!'

'Don't be such a wimp.'

Steph looked down at her casual clothes. 'And I have to go home and change. I can't possibly turn up at the Merrion looking like this.'

'You look fine.'

'You're just saying that.'

Sean rolled his eyes. 'Okay, why don't we go into the Blackrock shopping centre and I'll buy you something more suitable.'

Steph raised an eyebrow. 'Now that's very generous of you. What are you after?'

'I've already told you that.'

She laughed. 'Well, thanks, but I'd really prefer to go home and grab a shower.'

'In that case, my dear, you'd better drink up.'

'Okay, but first, a toast.'

'To Ruth?' he asked gently.

'No, not this time. This time I'd like to drink to us and to our future.'

'I can think of nothing I'd rather drink to. To us and the future.'

'Our future,' Steph corrected and drained her cup.

Three hours later, looking very chic in a black wool dress

with a high neck and a short skirt, Steph walked into the bar of the Merrion. Edward and Liz were already there.

Liz jumped up to hug her. 'Steph! Congratulations! Isn't it wonderful?'

Steph smiled and returned the hug. 'It's great,' she agreed. 'Oh, champagne, lovely. How are you, Edward?' She kissed his cheek before sitting down next to Liz.

'I'm feeling a lot better than I was this morning. But then that wouldn't be hard.'

Sean grinned. 'We did push the boat out a bit.'

Edward poured them some champagne and lifted his glass. 'And we're not finished yet. To Chez Nous.'

'To Chez Nous,' they chorused.

'You look wonderful, Steph.' Liz studied her friend closely. Steph always looked great, but tonight she was almost glowing.

'Thanks very much. You don't look too bad yourself. I thought we were only meeting for a drink?'

Steph was studying her friend. She looked stunning in a red velvet dress that was quite simple in style but had a daringly low neckline.

'We're going on to dinner in Guilbaud's,' Edward said casually.

'Great idea. We'll come too,' Sean said enthusiastically.

Steph kicked him. 'Maybe they don't want company, Sean.'

Liz flushed. 'Of course we do. Edward?'

'Certainly.' He stood up. 'I'll go and see if I can arrange it.'

'You've spoiled everything, Sean!' Steph hissed as he walked away. 'I'm sure Edward wanted to have Liz all to himself.'

'Stephanie,' Liz said warningly.

Steph flashed her a bright smile. 'Sorry.'

'Have you just found out you've won the lottery or something?' Liz hadn't seen her friend this relaxed and happy in quite a while.

Steph glanced at Sean. 'I went to see Ruth's mother today,' she explained.

'Oh.' Liz gaped at her, at a loss for words.

'It helped me a lot. We talked about Ruth, about what happened. She made me feel better than I have since . . .'

Liz squeezed her hand. 'I'm so glad for you, Steph. Still, it must have been upsetting.'

'I've cried bucketfuls,' Steph said with a tremulous smile.

'And how is the poor woman doing?'

'She's amazing. Her husband died of cancer a few months ago.'

'That's terrible.'

'It's what made her contact me,' Steph explained. 'You see she found out that Peter – that's her husband – had spent years trying to catch up with Des.'

'And did he?'

'No. But he found another girl whose life Des had ruined. She had a baby.'

'The bastard!'

'We always thought he was a low-life, didn't we, Steph?' Sean said grimly.

Edward arrived back to a brooding silence. 'Did I miss something?' he asked lightly, sitting down.

'We were just talking about old times,' Steph explained.

'Not very happy ones from the looks on your faces. Come on, folks, this is a celebration.'

Sean held out his glass to be topped up. 'You're right. So did you manage to squeeze us in for dinner?'

'I certainly did.'

'I haven't stopped eating and drinking all day,' Steph complained. 'If we continue like this my liver will be shot by Christmas.'

'Actually champagne has healing properties. It's really rather good for you.'

'I'd like to believe that, Edward, but I'd say that's a rumour started by Krug's PR man.'

'Well, it's certainly making me feel a lot better,' Liz said happily.

'Until tomorrow,' Steph said darkly.

'Oh, I don't care. I don't have to get up and get Lucy off to school and I don't have another job for a week.'

'That's the spirit,' Edward said and ordered another bottle of champagne.

After a wonderful dinner and several more drinks, Steph and Sean fell into a taxi and headed for home.

'You all right, love?'

Steph struggled to keep her eyes open. 'Wonderful.'

'You're a different person tonight, do you know that?'

'Am I?'

'Yes, you are. You're very relaxed. I think that chat with Ruth's mam has done you the world of good. I know it made you sad, but even so.'

'I do feel better. I'm not sure why. I suppose it's because Joan made me realise that I wouldn't have been able to change Ruth's mind even if I'd had the chance.'

Sean hugged her close to him and kissed her fore-head. 'No, love. You wouldn't.'

She looked up at him. 'I really love you, do you know that?'

'I know that,' he said softly. 'And I love you too.'

Steph woke at six the following morning. She lay quietly for a moment, listening to Sean's breathing before slipping out of bed as quietly as possible. She grabbed her dressing-gown, picked up her handbag and padded down to the kitchen in her bare feet.

After putting on a large pot of coffee – they were both going to need it – she inspected the contents of the fridge. Excellent, eggs, bacon and some white pudding. That would do. She switched on the radio and the grill and hummed along to Boyzone as she worked. While the food sizzled on the grill, she made a pile of toast and broke two eggs into the frying pan. She served up the food and set a tray. Then she took the small box out of her handbag. It had been there for quite a while now. It was about time that it saw the light of day. Steph opened the box and smiled down at the contents. Yes, this was definitely the right time. She'd never been so sure of anything in her life.

She carried the heavily laden tray upstairs, set it down on the dressing-table and opened the curtains.

Sean groaned. 'Oh, God, what time is it?'

'Seven.'

'Bloody hell. Ring the teacher and tell him that Sean is too sick to go to school today, will you?'

Steph laughed. 'I certainly will not. There'll be no skiving off in this house. What a bad example to set for your son. Now sit up. Breakfast will soon sort you out.'

Sean sat up and sniffed appreciatively as Steph put the tray down in front of him. 'What did I do to deserve this?'

Steph sat up on the bed beside him. 'Well, quite simply you're the most wonderful man in the world and I love you.'

Sean stared at her. Steph wasn't usually so vocal. 'I am?'

'You are. Now, there's something I have to ask you.'

'Yes?'

She handed him the box.

Sean looked at it and then back at her face.

Steph looked nervous. 'Well, open it,' she urged.

Sean opened the box and stared down at the platinum signet ring.

Steph took a deep breath and looked him straight in the eye. 'Sean? Will you marry me?'

Sean stared silently at the ring.

'Oh please say something,' she whispered desperately.

He dragged his eyes away from the ring and looked up into her face. 'Yes.'

'What?'

'I said yes. Yes, I'll marry you. Yes, I love you. Yes, I want to spend the rest of my life with you.'

He reached for her, almost toppling the tray and all its contents.

Steph saved it, laughing shakily. 'Careful.'

Sean moved the tray on to the bedside table and took her in his arms. 'Are you sure, Steph?' His eyes searched her face, and he smoothed back her tousled blonde hair.

She looked into his eyes with a confident smile. 'I'm very sure. Now, don't waste all my hard work. Eat your breakfast.'

'It seems a bit unromantic to eat after a proposal.'

Steph gave him a lingering kiss. 'Rubbish. You're going to need your strength. Why do you think I woke you so early?'

Sean slid the ring onto the third finger of his right hand. 'Ah, I see.' He piled bacon and egg on to a slice of toast.

Steph watched in dismay. 'Aren't you going to wear it on your left hand?'

'No. That's where my wedding ring will go.'

Steph gaped at him. 'Oh. Will you wear one?'

'Of course I will. I have to make it clear to the legions of women who chase me that I am no longer available.'

Steph raised an eyebrow. 'Legions, eh?'

'Certainly. This will break a lot of hearts.'

'Tragic,' Steph said drily. 'How do you think Billy will take it?'

'I think he'll be delighted. At least now he'll be able to come and visit.'

'What?'

'Oh, shit, you weren't meant to find out about that. Bloody hangover.'

'Tell me,' Steph ordered.

Sean sighed. 'Karen said she wouldn't let Billy visit while we were just living together. She said it would be contradicting everything that she'd taught him.'

'That's a bit narrow-minded in this day and age,' Steph retorted.

'Well, to be fair she's never let Mike stay over either.'

Steph smiled up into his worried face. 'We'd better get married soon then, hadn't we? And you'd better get started on the attic.'

Sean pulled her into his arms and kissed her soundly. 'You are the most amazing woman, do you know that?'

'No. But I do know I am a very lucky woman. Thanks for not giving up on me.'

'I didn't have a choice,' he said simply. 'There's no other woman for me, Stephanie. You're my life.'

Her eyes filled up and she hugged him fiercely. They cuddled and talked for a while until Steph caught sight of the time. 'We'd better get a move on or we'll be late.'

'What do I care?' Sean stretched lazily. 'I'm the boss.'

'The boss with a lot of responsibilities. A fiancée and one son – so far.'

Sean's eyes softened. 'I'd love us to have a family, Steph.'

'So would I,' she admitted.

'I wasn't sure you'd want to after . . .'

'The miscarriage? I didn't. I'll never forget my baby but I'm ready to move on, now.'

He kissed her, a long, warm, sweet kiss and then he pulled her down in the bed with a grin. 'Let's start trying now.'

'Sean, don't!'

'Don't what? Do this?' He kissed her neck. 'And this,' he kissed her throat. 'And this.' His head moved down to her breast and she gave a small groan.

'Well, maybe . . .'

Epilogue

'She'll murder us,' Liz said for the umpteenth time as she surveyed the buffet with a critical eye. She stood in the kitchen doorway, where she could keep an eye on her little sister, Cathy, who was acting as lookout.

'Of course she won't,' Annie said cheerfully. 'Every bride secretly wants a hen party.'

'Not Steph!'

'Rubbish. As soon as we get a couple of glasses of champers down her throat, she'll be fine. Is everyone here?'

Liz glanced into the other room. 'Think so.' She'd opened the doors between her living-room and dining-room and the doors to the garden so that there was plenty of room for the guests to move around. It was a beautiful balmy June evening and several women were sitting outside enjoying the evening sunshine.

Annie helped herself to a smoked salmon sandwich. 'I never thought this day would come.'

Liz grinned. 'Yeah, hard to believe she's finally taking the plunge, isn't it? I'd almost given up on her.'

'I think Sean had too. These sandwiches are lovely, Liz. My God, it's great having a mate in the catering business.'

'Thanks – I think. It was so funny yesterday. Steph dropped in and I was right in the middle of getting everything ready. I had to pretend that I was catering for a party last night. But you know Steph. She wanted to know who, where, when. I was sure she was going to twig what we were up to.'

'She's here!' Cathy squealed excitedly.

'Okay, everyone,' Liz roared down the room. 'As quiet as little mice please.' She closed the door and was standing in the hall when the doorbell rang. She waited a moment and then opened the door. 'Hi, Steph.'

'Hiya, Liz. How are you?' Steph hugged her friend and stood back to look at her. 'You look very flushed. I hope you haven't gone to any trouble.'

'No, no. Annie's inside. You go on in and I'll just check on things in the kitchen.'

Steph eyed her suspiciously. 'Okay.' She pushed open the living-room door and then took a step back in surprise at the throng of women standing smiling at her.

'Surprise!'

'Oh my God,' she muttered, but no one heard her as they broke into a chorus of 'I'm Getting Married In The Morning'.

Annie kissed her and shoved a glass of champagne into her hand. 'Try and look like you're pleased, there's a good girl.'

Steph pasted a smile on her face. 'I suppose this was all your idea.'

'Me?' Annie's green eyes twinkled.

Steph was about to say more but she was dragged away and immediately surrounded by well wishers.

'Hello, Stephanie. Congratulations.'

'Joan!' Steph's eyes widened when she saw Ruth's mother standing in front of her.

'I hope you're going to be very happy. I'm sure you will. Sean's a lovely man.'

Steph and Sean had visited her a few times and attended a memorial service for Ruth. Steph had cried her heart out but felt remarkably better after it. 'You're coming to the wedding?'

'I wouldn't miss it, love. And Celine thinks all of her birthdays have come together. She says it's going to be the wedding of the year. She has me driven mad talking about hats.'

Steph laughed. She'd told Joan to take a partner and Joan had decided to give her daughter a break from her two boisterous babies.

'I don't think she's too impressed.' Liz watched Steph nervously.

'She's having a ball,' Annie said serenely. 'You take care of the food and I'll take care of her glass. She'll have the night of her life.'

Steph moved from one group to another, glad that at least Liz had only invited family and close friends. 'Hi, Mam.' She plonked down on the sofa beside her mother. 'You could have warned me.'

Her mother smiled mischievously. 'And spoil the lovely surprise?'

Steph glared at her. 'Are you sure you're not Annie's mother?' She took a sip of champagne. 'Well, at least I know things won't get out of hand if you're here.'

'Oh dear and I only came because I wanted to see the stripper.' She burst out laughing at the expression on her daughter's face. 'Enjoy yourself, love,' she added gently. 'You deserve it. You're going to be so happy.'

Steph hugged her. 'Yes. I think I am.'

It had been a wonderful few months. She'd gone to Cork with Sean for a few days before Christmas and they'd spoiled Billy rotten while they were there. They'd even had a meal out with Karen and Mike, which had been surprisingly enjoyable.

'Disgustingly civilised,' Liz had said.

Chez Nous had got two more reviews, and both were complimentary. And the icing on the cake had been the publication of the *Michelin Guide* in February. Not only had they held on to their star, but their general rating had gone up a notch too. Conor had been over the moon. The only sad point had been when Marc had decided to go home to France. He'd been offered a position as sous-chef in an excellent restaurant in Lyons and Steph and Conor just had to be pleased for him and wish him well. She knew that she'd hear his name in the future. He was going to be a fine chef.

The party was in full swing when Steph slipped upstairs with Liz for a natter. Steph sat, trying to focus on her reflection in the mirror while Liz stretched out on the bed.

'You're not annoyed with us, Steph, are you?'

'I bloody well am. But I'm enjoying myself anyway,' she added with a grin.

'Oh, good.' Liz was relieved. 'Edward said you'd hate it. He even thought you might walk out.'

Steph looked horrified. 'I'd never do that on you, Liz! Don't mind him. He was just winding you up.'

'Probably. It won't be the first time.'

'You two are getting on really well, aren't you?'

COLETTE CADDLE

'We're doing okay,' Liz said loftily.

Annie put her head around the door. 'What are you both doing up here? You're supposed to be circulating.'

'I'm not supposed to do anything I don't want to,' Steph said, picking up a bottle and topping up her glass. 'It's my party.'

'And you'll cry if you want to,' Annie sang. 'Fair enough.' She hoisted herself up onto the bed beside Liz. 'So any second thoughts yet?'

Liz looked shocked. 'Annie!'

Steph smiled. 'None.'

'That's not natural,' Annie insisted. 'I had second, third and fourth thoughts.'

'My poor brother.'

'He's done all right.' Annie grinned smugly.

Steph took the bottle of wine, climbed up between the two of them and filled their glasses. 'Well, I've no doubts. Mind you, we've known each other thirteen years. If I don't know what I'm getting into by now, I never will.'

Liz put an arm around her and gave her a sloppy kiss. 'I think it's brilliant. Sean's always been nuts about you.' She lifted her glass. 'To a wonderful day and a wonderful life.'

'Hear, hear,' Annie said, downing her champagne and hiccuping.

Steph giggled. 'You're drunk.'

'I am not! I'm just happy.'

'I've seen you happy before,' Liz remarked. 'It's usually just before you pass out.'

'Rubbish.'

'Listen, you two. Seriously,' Steph wagged a finger at

them. 'I just want to say thanks for everything. You're very good friends.'

Annie waved her hand magnanimously. 'No problem. We love you, don't we, Liz?'

'We do, we do.' Liz smiled vaguely at them, wondering why her two friends had suddenly become four.

'Thas nice,' Steph said sleepily.

'We should really go back downstairs.' Annie curled up more comfortably on the bed.

'Umm.' Steph slid down beside her, slopping some champagne on her skirt. 'We'll go down in a minute.'

'Right.'

'After I tell you my joke. Is a great joke. A man and a giraffe walk into a bar . . .'

Liz shoved her head under a pillow and Annie groaned.

'And he said to the barman. A pint for me and a pint for the giraffe . . .'

COLETTE CADDLE

SHAKEN AND STIRRED

In the marketing offices of CML, life for the team is about to get shaken – and stirred.

PAMELA LLOYD-HAMILTON. Elegant, feminine but professional. The ambitious single-minded partner in her husband's successful business seems to have it all.

Except the heady days of champagne and cocktails are now just a distant memory.

DOUGLAS HAMILTON. Struggling to maintain the immaculate façade of their marriage as he comes face to face with his own mortality.

GINA BARRETT. On the verge of the promotion she's been longing for and her first major presentation in dreamy Marrakech. Life would be perfect if only she had a man. Getting them, that's easy. Keeping them ... now that's another story.

SUSIE CLARKE. A bright young designer who gets a lucky break in the company. Except she's Catholic, pregnant and God help her when her father finds out ...

Shaken and Stirred – can their lives ever settle again?

HODDER AND STOUGHTON PAPERBACKS

COLETTE CADDLE

A CUT ABOVE

Don't miss Colette Caddle's new novel, A CUT ABOVE, coming from Hodder paperbacks in Spring 2002.

Toni was incredibly flattered when razor-sharp surgeon Theodore French showed more than a professional interest in her. But after several years of marriage, she realises that his cold disciplinarian stance is more than skin deep.

As fellow directors of a clinic which needs an injection of cash to survive, they are now in dispute over the ethics of cosmetic surgery.

Stitched into a family by a stepdaughter she has grown to love as her own, Toni begins to regret throwing over her ex, an attractive anaesthetist. Particularly as he has just met someone new.

But just as she comes to a decision about her future, Theo disappears, cutting off all her options.

HODDER AND STOUGHTON PAPERBACKS